"Sharissa! You are dropping your defensive spells!"

"I know! Trust me!" She hoped the elf Faunon would not press her, for her own resolve was wavering. What if she were playing into the talons of the Seeker?

The last barrier fell... and the Vraad sorceress was deluged with vivid images of what had been and what might be.

Sharissa saw a vision of fur, teeth, and huge claws digging through earth but received no name for the monstrosities...

The image blurred and she was back in the cavern, but her view kept shifting, as if she were traveling through the system of passages leading deep into the earth.

Faunon was shouting in her ear, trying to stir her, but his words were so long and drawn out that they sounded like moans. Everything around her had slowed.

Pain and then total emptiness rocked her. The sorceress screamed, knowing that what she *had* felt was *death*...

ALSO BY RICHARD A. KNAAK

Firedrake
Ice Dragon
Wolfhelm
The Shrouded Realm
Shadow Steed

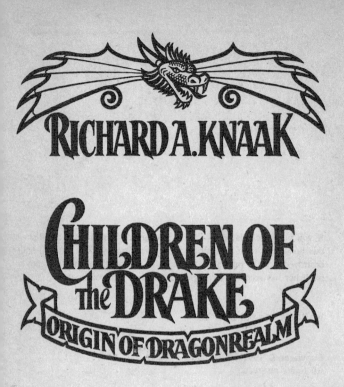

RICHARD A. KNAAK

CHILDREN OF THE DRAKE
ORIGIN OF DRAGONREALM

WARNER BOOKS

A Time Warner Company

WARNER BOOKS EDITION

Copyright © 1991 by Richard A. Knaak
All rights reserved.

Questar® is a registered trademark of Warner Books, Inc.

Cover illustration by Larry Elmore
Cover design by Don Puckey

Warner Books, Inc.
666 Fifth Avenue
New York, NY 10103

W A Time Warner Company

Printed in the United States of America

First Printing: December, 1991

10 9 8 7 6 5 4 3 2 1

I

"What do you think?" Rayke asked, prodding at the feathered corpse at their feet. The body, nearly petrified, was that of one of the Sheekas, the lords of the land. It was manlike in form, had walked upright and had the usual limbs. It was winged as well and covered from head to clawed foot with feathers. The face was very avian, even down to the eye structure that forced a Sheeka to cock the head to the side so as to focus on a target, and the beak was designed for rending the toughest of flesh. Besides these natural weapons, the Sheekas had cunning minds, too, a formidable combination that had allowed them to rule for several thousand years.

Rayke seemed disappointed, as if someone had deprived him of some dark pleasure.

Seen together, the two elves who stood over the sprawled form might have appeared to be brothers. They were of a similar height and both were clad in the same forest-green outfit that consisted of a shirt, pants, shin-length boots, and hooded cloak. Both had light-brown hair that only barely covered their curved ears, and eyes that were the color of spring.

Physical appearance was where the similarity ended. Faunon, younger than Rayke by a hundred years though each looked as if he had seen no more than thirty summers, often thought that his companion was, by far, more bloodthirsty than even the old ones who clung so tightly to the ways of pomp and circumstance that they were always challenging one another to duels. It was fortunate, then, that he and not Rayke had been put in charge of this expedition into the lands of the avians . . . or what had *once* been their lands. So far, they had only found those hapless victims like this one, Sheekas who had fallen prey to some spell they had unleashed in an attempt to rid themselves of their rivals, the more ancient, armadillolike Quel.

Unfortunately, it seemed that the spell had proven more detrimental to the spellcasters than to the intended targets. The Quel lived in the southwestern portion of the continent, so there was no telling for the time being what damage they had actually suffered. A party of elves was headed that way and, if they returned, their information would be pooled with that of this band.

"I think," Faunon finally replied, recalling Rayke's question at last. "I think that they must have made a terrible mess of trying to reverse their spell, whatever it was. This can't be the result they wanted," he concluded, stating the obvious because one had to do that sometimes with Rayke.

Faunon turned around and gazed at the massive peaks to the north. Somewhere in there was an aerie, that much they knew. It was still occupied . . . the elves had seen one or two Sheekas fluttering among the mountains . . . but by only a token flock, not the massive horde that had lived there only a decade before. The inhabitants there had suffered not one calamity but two in the past ten or so years. There was evidence of a third group that had come and gone like the wind . . . yet who had seemed to clean up after themselves so as to leave little trace for the elves. All that he had discovered was that this other race had fought the Sheekas, held their own against the large flock here, and then abandoned the place for somewhere else.

But where?

"Let's go back to the others," Rayke muttered. He looped his bow around his head and his left arm. The question of the third group meant nothing to him. The council had ordered them to discover the extent of the damage to the empire of the Sheekas, not an easy task since the birds did not have an empire as elves understood it but rather vast communities that controlled great regions of the continent. As far as Rayke and most of the others were concerned, their duties ended there.

That was one problem with his people, Faunon thought as he stepped back from the rock-hard corpse. They either had no inclination toward curiosity whatsoever or they were obsessed with finding out about everything under the sun. No moderation save in a few individuals such as himself.

"Just a minute more, Rayke," he returned, putting just enough emphasis in his voice to remind the other elf who was in charge here.

His companion said nothing, but the flat line of his mouth spoke volumes enough. Rayke had angular features that reminded Faunon of a starving man, and the look on his face only added to that effect. Angular features were not uncommon among the elves, but Rayke's were more severe than most. Faunon's own visage was a bit rounder, more pleasant, so some of the females of his tribe were apt to tell him time and time again until their lilting voices got too much on his nerves and he had to excuse himself from their company somehow. There was another problem with his people: when they saw something they wanted—or someone—they became very, very persistent. He sometimes wondered if he was really one of them.

"Well?"

Faunon started, realizing he had lost track of things. Doing so in front of Rayke made it doubly annoying. He pretended instead that his daydreaming was actually a collecting of his thoughts. "Notice anything wrong with this?"

"With what?"

"The bodies and the land."

"Only that there are a lot of the former scattered around the latter." Rayke smiled, pleased with his clever response.

Faunon kept his own face neutral, trying to hold back his anger. "And the land seems relatively untouched, doesn't it?"

The two of them scanned the area, though each had done so several times already. There were inclines where it was obvious that there had been none before, for trees and bushes jutted at angles no self-respecting plant would have chosen, almost as if something had dug up the ground and then only halfheartedly tried to repair the devastation. A few trees appeared to have withered and petrified much the way the avian dead had, but most of the wooded region seemed fairly healthy overall. Still, Faunon found it astonishing that he was the only one who had paid any note to the peculiarity of the landscape.

The other elf lost hold of his smile. "It *does*. We've come across some areas where the land was overturned, but, even there, the plants and smaller animals were thriving."

"As if they had been bypassed, protected . . . or perhaps

healed,'' he added, suddenly feeling that the last was closer to the truth.

"Protected by what? Certainly not the Sheekas. They would have protected themselves first, I think."

"Perhaps by whoever fought the bird people and then vanished," Faunon suggested. Likely, they would never know. This land, which his own people could not claim as their birthplace, having fled to here, as legend put it, from the horrors of another world countless millennia ago, had an air of mystery about it that defied the efforts of the elves. Faunon himself knew that the Sheekas and the Quel had not been the first masters here; that, in fact, several other races had preceded them. This was an old world despite its vitality.

Rayke sighed. "Are you going to begin *that* again, Faunon?"

"If need be! It isn't enough to know that the Sheekas have suffered a calamity that may speak the end of their reign; we have to know if their disaster has the potential to reoccur! If we—"

Something huge went crashing through the trees, sounding as if it had fallen from the sky at a remarkable speed. Faunon, whirling, caught sight of a huge black shape moving in and out of the trees that finally registered in his mind as a horse . . . but *what* a horse! A stallion, to be sure. He stood taller than any that the elf had ever seen and ran with a swiftness that the wind would have been unable to match. If the steed was responsible for the din they had heard, he had changed his ways in swift fashion, for now the animal ran as silent as the shadows he so resembled.

"What *is* that?" Rayke whispered. He had turned pale. Faunon knew that his own visage matched in shading.

"Let's follow it!"

"*Follow* it? Do you see how fast it runs? We will never catch it!" The other elf sounded almost relieved at the last.

"I don't intend to catch it! I just want to see what it is! Follow me!" Faunon raced after the black beast, darting around and over obstacles as only one of his kind could. He did not hear Rayke, but he knew his companion had too much pride to stay behind. Not that it would have mattered to Faunon if he had. Catching a glimpse of this swift phantom was paramount in his mind, and he knew that it would require his best efforts to do that. Against many another creature, an elf's speed would have proven a match; not so, this animal. He had known that from the start. What he also knew, however, was that the mighty steed raced toward an open field. There, his quarry would be quite visible, though distant. Faunon was not too concerned with the distance. Elves had excellent vision. Besides, like Rayke, he did not want to get *too* close to anything as massive and powerful as the black horse. He only wanted to ascertain its existence and the path it was taking. By no means had he ever thought of trying to do anything more.

The horse, however, had apparently had other ideas.

He almost ran into it and wondered how he could have ever missed seeing so terrifying a figure. It loomed over him, having somehow managed to turn back and come upon them without making a sound. Faunon did a very unelflike thing and slipped, collapsing to the earth less than an arm's length from the demonic stallion.

"I have come back, but this is not the place!" the fearsome figure bellowed down at him. It had long, narrow eyes of the coldest blue, eyes without pupils.

Faunon wished he had an answer that would please the ebony monster, but only air escaped his mouth. He could not even utter so much as a single sound.

"This is the place but it is *not* the place!" One hoof gouged a track in the ground. The elf was all too aware of what that hoof could do to his head if the steed decided to remove him.

The unnerving animal stared at him for a short time. Faunon held his breath throughout the study, wondering what the beast found so interesting. Then he felt the probe. It was surprisingly tentative for so powerful a creature, almost as if the ebony stallion were shamed by his own actions.

Mere moments later, the head of the beast snapped back. He scanned his surroundings in renewed fascination. "So that is it! Astonishing! So many things to learn!"

With an abruptness that left the elf's mouth hanging, the darksome steed backed up, turned, and raced back in the direction it had been heading earlier. Faunon's acute senses noted that there was no trail of any sort on the physical plane, though he did smell power of an unidentifiable sort. It was as if a ghost had come and gone, though that made no sense considering that he and Rayke had, in their initial encounter with the demon, heard the animal before they saw him.

"Are you all right?" Rayke asked from somewhere behind him.

"I'm . . . fine." He was actually surprised that he was. The shadowy steed had owned his life for the duration of their brief meeting. Faunon could think of a dozen different ways he could have been killed. He had been thinking of them throughout his trial despite his best efforts not to. Had the demonic stallion noted those fears at all during his probe?

The other elf's hands were around his torso as Rayke helped him to his feet. A quiver still ran through the former's voice. "What *is* that thing? No horse! Not even one of ours! Was it a shapeshifter?"

"Yes, no, and maybe. I was too at a loss to think much about it while he was here. I doubt that was one of us, though. The sorcery needed for that sort of change would kill most of us! No, there was something wrong with that horror, as if he came from some place other than this world. Somewhere very different."

The two stood staring at the spot the ghostly horse had abandoned. Finally, Rayke asked, "What did he want, Faunon? The way he spoke, he was looking for something. Do you know what?"

Rayke knew of the probe, perhaps had even been probed himself. Faunon shook his head. "I don't know, but he found something in my mind that satisfied him...he was *gentle* about it, Rayke! He could have plundered my mind; I could feel he had the will to do so, but he didn't!"

That part seemed not to concern his partner. Rayke continued to stare after their departed intruder. "Where do you suppose he went?"

"East. Straight east."

Rayke grimaced. "There's nothing that way."

"Maybe he plans to go on straight to the sea...or *beyond* it."

"Maybe." The other elf's eyes widened. "Do you suppose he had something to do with the death of these Sheekas?"

It was a thought that had not occurred to Faunon, and he had to credit Rayke for the concept. "I don't know. We may never know."

"I'd be happy with that. Let's get back to the others, Faunon. Let's get away from here before it decides to come back!"

There was no argument over that. They had discovered all that there was to discover—unless something *else* ran past them—and it would be dark before long. Faunon generally had no fear of the dark, but, after this encounter, he had a growing desire to be back among his fellows where there was the comfort of numbers.

As they hurried through the woods, moving nearly as silently as the shadow steed had, a nagging feeling grew in Faunon's head. He was not one for signs and omens, being one of the newer generation of more *practical* elves, but he could not shake the sensation that the creature he had faced was yet one more hint of something vast to come, a change in the land as he and his people knew it. If the Sheekas were truly nearing the end of their reign, as the Quel had before them, then someone would come to displace them. The land had seen such change time and again, though the elves had never been part of that cycle, merely onlookers.

Ducking under a low branch, Faunon grew more troubled as his thoughts progressed. The Sheekas and even the Quel had been predictable creatures; the elves knew where they stood with those two races. Who was to say that the same would hold with their successors? Who *would* their successors be? There were no other races that could claim dominance.

There was little to justify his fears, but he believed in them nonetheless. As they neared the spot where the others were to meet them, Faunon discovered that he was, for the first time, hoping for the continued survival of the arrogant avians. The elves knew how to coexist with them, if no more than that. The next masters might feel that there was no need for his race to continue on.

They had escaped such a fate once before, when, legend had it, they had discovered the path that freed them of the horrors of the twisted world of Nimth and its lords, the sorcerous race called the Vraad. At least that was one threat that the elves no longer had to fear, Faunon decided, drawing what little comfort he could from that.

Nothing the future held could ever match the cruelty of the Vraad.

II

The colony had lasted for fifteen years now. This world did not bow to their will as the last had and, far more important, they no longer had the strength to back their arrogant desires. Now they were often forced to do things by hand that they once would have scoffed at performing so. It was a long, frustrating fall from godhood for the Vraad, for they had, back in dying Nimth, been born to their roles. They had escaped to this world from the one they had ruined with little more than their skins and had discovered too late that, for many, Vraad sorcery would not work here the way it had before... at least not without terrible effort and more than a little chance of the results being other than what they had sought.

Yet, for all they had succeeded in accomplishing during those fifteen long years, there were many who still could not accept that the godlike days of yesteryear were at an end. They had once moved mountains, quite *literally*, and some were determined that they would do so again—whatever the cost. Thus, those that had some success with their spells ignored the side effects and consequences.

Lord Barakas, patriarch of the Tezerenee, the clan of the dragon, was one. He had come to this world with the intention to rule it, not be ruled *by* it. Even now, as he and two of his sons sat in silent contemplation of the sight before them, the dreams of what might have been and what might still be filled his thoughts nigh on to overflowing.

He stared west, utilizing the tallest hill in the region so as to get a glimpse of not just the lands but the seas farther on as well. The riding drakes, great green creatures that more resembled massive but unprepossessing lizards rather than the dragons they were, had begun to grow restive. The patriarch's sons, Reegan the Heir and ever-obedient Lochivan, were also growing restive. Lochivan was the slightest of the three, which by no means meant that he was small. It was just that Reegan and Barakas were two of a kind, huge bears with majestic beards; two giants who looked ready to bite off the head of any who dared so much as cough in their direction. All three riders bore the same coarse features that were dominant throughout the clan, though Lochivan's were tempered a bit by some additions passed down to him by his mother, the Lady Alcia. He also had a mix of brown and gray in his hair. Barakas and his heir had darker locks, though a streak of silver had spread across the patriarch's head over the last few years. Other than that, Reegan was a fairly good physical copy of the dragonlord. Beyond the physical, however, the resemblance ceased. The heir lacked much in terms of the patriarch's vision.

The sun, directly above, continued to bathe them in heat. Lochivan shifted, trying to keep cool in the cloth padding and dark-green, dragon-scale armor that clan members fairly lived their lives out in these days. Long ago, when they had been lords of Nimth, it would have been less than nothing for him to utilize his skills to make the body-encompassing armor both cool and weightless. Here, in what he considered a damnable land at best, such effort meant wasted energy and nothing more. The magic of this world still refused to obey him with regularity. Only a few had any true power, and even fewer had abilities comparable to the Vraad race of old.

None of the three were among them, though the patriarch came near. Near but not enough for what he desired.

That was why neither Reegan nor Lochivan dared to disturb their father. This period of contemplation was all that kept him from striking out at random at his own people.

"How far do you think it is?" Barakas suddenly asked. His voice was flat, nearly emotionless. That hardly meant he was in a quiet mood. Of late, the patriarch had become mercurial, going from indifference to rage at the blink of an eye. Many Tezerenee wore marks of his anger.

Lochivan answered the question, as he always did. Reegan might be heir apparent, but he lacked subtlety, something needed for times like this. Besides, Lochivan knew the answer that would suffice; it was the same one he had given his father for the past three weeks. "Not far enough to escape our grasp forever. Not by far."

"True." The Lord Tezerenee's eyes did not focus on the lush lands below, but at the glittering sea near the horizon. His prize lay not on this continent but across the stunning expanse of water in another land. He had even given it its name, one that had spread to this place though he himself could not think of it as anything but "the other continent." Across the seas lay his destiny, his *Dragonrealm*.

"Father." Reegan spoke quietly, but his unpredicted interruption could only mean that he had some news of importance to convey. Reegan would never dare speak to his father without a very good reason for doing so.

Barakas looked at his eldest son, who indicated with a curt nod that the others should turn their attention to their left. The dragonlord shifted so as to see what had caught Reegan's eye and gritted his teeth when he saw the reason.

One of the Faceless Ones. It was a parody of a man, having no features whatsoever, not even hair or ears. It was as tall as a normal man and wore a simple, cowled robe. It was also facing—if one could use the term—the three riders, watching them with its nonexistent eyes and unperturbed by the fact that the trio was now staring back.

"Let me cut it down, Father!" Reegan's voice pretended at disdain, but a barely noticeable quiver revealed the fear that the creature stirred within his breast. Lochivan, too, was discomforted by the sight of the harmless-looking being.

"It is forbidden to do so," Barakas reminded his son, his own voice taking on a steely edge. He, like his sons, would have desired nothing more than to crush the interfering horror beneath his mount's clawed feet or cut it to ribbons with his sword. Anything to wipe its existence from this world.

"But—"

"It was forbidden by the *Dragon of the Depths*!" the patriarch snapped, referring to a being he had, over the past decade, come to think of as the Tezerenee dragon totem come to life. When the Tezerenee had faced annihilation at the hands—talons—of the bird creatures in that other land, the god had burst forth from the ground wearing a body of stone and molten earth. It had scattered the Sheekas, or Seekers, as the Vraad preferred to call them, with only words. It had taken the surviving clan members and sent them to this continent to join their fellow Vraad, utilizing only the least of its power in the process.

Two things that the Dragon of the Depths—the Lord Tezerenee's own name for the entity—had commanded had remained with Barakas. One was that there might come a time when the

Tezerenee would return to the Dragonrealm in triumph. Lord Barakas yearned for that day. The other thing touched him in the opposite manner. His god had ordered that the Faceless Ones be left unharmed. They were to be allowed to do what they desired or else.

For the Tezerenee, that was almost unthinkable. They shared more than a legacy with the unholy creatures; they shared a common origin, at least in the physical sense. It was one that kept them from ever truly feeling comfortable among their own people, even though most of the other animosities had died over time.

Barakas took up the reins of his mount. "Let us be gone from here! This place no longer soothes!"

Reegan and Lochivan acquiesced with great eagerness.

Steering their drakes around, the three urged their animals back in the direction of the city. They had some slight difficulty at first, for these animals were not mindbroke as had once been the way. Mindbreaking back in Nimth had been a simple process by which the Vraad had taken the will of their mounts and shattered it, leaving an emptiness that the master could fill as he deemed necessary. It had always made for very obedient steeds. Unfortunately, mindbreaking now had a high casualty rate and the Tezerenee could ill afford to lose many drakes. Unlike the western continent, where the Tezerenee had *intended* to go, drakes were fairly scarce on this continent.

Another fault among many that this place had, as far as Barakas was concerned.

The mounts finally gave in to their riders and, building up speed, raced up and over the winding landscape. The crimson cloaks that Barakas and Reegan wore, designating them as clan master and heir apparent, respectively, fluttered madly behind, looking almost like bloodred dragon wings. The refugees' city lay in a valley and so much of their trek was downhill, though smaller hills forced them to take a route that twisted back and forth often. Here, the drakes held an advantage over their equine counterparts. Their claws dug into the slope, preventing them from stumbling forward and throwing their riders to their death. Horses had their own advantages, true, and more than the reptilian mounts, but a riding drake was more than just a beast that carried a Tezerenee from one point to another. It was a killing machine. Few things could stand up to the onslaught of a dragon, even as simpleminded a one as the mount below the patriarch. The claws would slice a man to segments; the jaws could snap a victim in two without strain.

Most important, they were the symbol of the Tezerenee.

The city soon rose before them, from the distance looking like little more than one massive wall. The new inhabitants had rebuilt the encircling wall first, making it almost twice the height of its first incarnation because their overall loss of power had made them fear everything. The city itself had been a vast ruin when the Vraad had first come, an ageless relic of the race from whom they—and countless others, it appeared—had sprung. Those ancients had been far more godlike than the Vraad could have ever hoped to be, easily manipulating their descendants into a variety of forms. They had sought successors to their tired, dying race. In what could best be described as irony, their final hope lay in one of their earliest failures—the Vraad. The Lord Tezerenee's kind had been abandoned to their world, a *construct* of the ancients, where it was supposed they would kill themselves off. Instead, the Vraad had outlasted nearly everyone else. Only the Seekers still held on, but they were already in their decline, so the Dragon of the Depths had said.

To Lord Barakas, the rebuilding of the city was a waste of effort that he had only condoned while he bided his time.

"Dragon's blood!" Lochivan swore, pointing at the path ahead. "Another!"

Near the very gates of the city there stood a figure identical to the one that they had left behind no more than moments before. For all Barakas knew, it *was* the same being. *They* had the power to flaunt. The Faceless Ones were, after all, all that remained of the minds of the very ancients who had built the city. They still sought, in their own mysterious way, to manipulate the future of their world—meaning the Vraad. The Lord Tezerenee gritted his teeth; it was by his doing that they had been given physical forms through which to interfere further.

Of their own accord, the gates swung open in time for the returning Vraad. The Faceless One, like his predecessor, remained passive as they neared. Barakas could not help touching his own face as they rode past the still figure. The skin Barakas touched felt like the skin he had always known, but it was of the same origin as the body that those ghosts now wore. Every Tezerenee, save one, wore a shell created by the now-lost combined magical might of the clan. Even a few non-clan members, outsiders whose loyalties had extended to the patriarch, had such bodies. It had seemed like the perfect solution when no way had been found to cross from Nimth to the Dragonrealm in a physical manner. Through the aid of one Dru Zeree, the only outsider Barakas respected, the Vraad had rediscovered the secret of ka, or spirit travel. The ka, guided by others, could cross the barrier that the bodies could not. There was only one major stumbling block: the spirits needed a suitable host.

It was Barakas himself who had come up with that solution. Though they could not cross, the Vraad could influence their future world through sorcerous means. It meant a dozen or more individuals acting in concert for even the slightest of spells. For the arrogant Vraad, that was an impossibility that only the Tezerenee, who were used to working with one another, could overcome. Under the patriarch's masterful guidance, they had created an army of golems whose ancestry could be traced to the larger, more majestic cousins of the very mounts he and his sons now rode. Those soulless husks were to have waited for the tide of Vraad immigrants, but things had gone wrong after only a few hundred had been molded. First, those to whom the task of manipulating the spell of formation had fallen vanished without a trace; Barakas suspected that the ancients had been at fault there, also. Then the damned ghosts had stolen most of the bodies for themselves.

The creature was lost from sight as the riders moved farther on into the confines of the city. The patriarch drew no comfort from that. As far as he knew, there were probably half a dozen more of the horrors observing him and his sons from less conspicuous posts. It was their way.

Dru Zeree had once explained to him that the last of the ancients had released their spirits into their world, giving the lands themselves a mind of sorts. The golem forms provided by the patriarch's plan had offered an opportunity for that mind to provide itself with hands to further its work, an apparent oversight the founders had not thought of until it was too late. Barakas had never known how much of that explanation to believe and did not really think it mattered. What mattered was that an army of ghosts had stolen not only his creations, but the empire he would have had if the rest of the Vraad had been forced to swear fealty to him in return for access to their new world. Worse yet, each of the walking monstrosities reminded him that a part of him lay rotting back in foul Nimth . . . unless some scavenger still living had already devoured him.

The gates closed behind them, the magic of Dru Zeree flaunting itself once more. As hard as he had strived, he could not match Zeree's abilities. Even his counterpart's daughter, Sharissa, was more capable. Yet another bitter pill he had been forced to swallow each day of each year.

A few Vraad wandered about, looking much more scruffy than they had back in Nimth. Without nearly limitless power to see to their every whim, they were being forced to maintain their appearances through more mundane means. Some were not proving adept at the process. They wore robes or shirts and pants, all fairly simplistic in design considering the extravagant and shocking garments most of them had once worn. Several Vraad were clearing rubble from another crumbling dwelling. They were sorting out the good pieces for use in either building the structure that would replace this one or for some other project, perhaps another useless tower. To Barakas the working Vraad looked more pathetic than industrious.

The gods have fallen, he thought. *I have fallen.*

Still, the city had regained bits of its ancient glory. Someday, it might be completely whole again. Children were becoming more numerous than they had back in Nimth, though that was not quite so impressive as it sounded when one considered there had rarely been more than a few dozen young at any time during the old days. Near-immortals with no taste for familial relationships did not tend to make ideal parents. Those few who chose to do so generally ended up fighting their offspring at some point. Barakas, in creating his clan, had turned that energy outside rather than inside. His people, the only true clan in Vraad society, now numbered over one hundred again, not including additional outsiders who had sworn loyalty to him during the past decade and a half. Children were rampant in the section of the city that he had taken over.

Some of the locals turned away at sight of the three Tezerenee. The patriarch ignored them, their anger being both misdirected and petty in his eyes. Faced with the loss of the majority of the golems, Barakas had sent his own people through, effectively abandoning his former allies for the most part. If they wanted to blame anyone, he had argued in the beginning, it should be the Faceless Ones themselves. He had acted as any of them would have acted. The clan came first.

At least they were no longer clamoring for the deaths of every Tezerenee. It had been the dragonlord's people who had helped them cope with their new, mundane lives, for the Tezerenee were adept at surviving with only their physical abilities. Barakas felt justified in thinking that this colony would have been dead if not for his folk. Even Dru Zeree and Silesti, the third member of their triumvirate, could not argue with that. There were not enough adept sorcerers to guarantee everything.

His thoughts were disturbed by the appearance of a tall, well-formed woman with flowing silver-blue hair that nearly fell to her waist. The white dress she wore clung to her form, marking its perfection. Her gait indicated a confidence she had never had before her arrival in this world. She was possibly one of the most accomplished spellcasters they had now, though, being less than four decades old, the newcomer was little more than a child by Vraad standards.

She was Sharissa, daughter of Dru Zeree.

Barakas pulled back on the reins, slowing his mount in gradual fashion so as not to appear overanxious. He glanced quickly at Reegan, whose eyes were wide as he followed every movement of the young woman. The patriarch had been encouraging his eldest to pursue the lone offspring of his rival for quite some time, and Reegan had been only too eager to do just that. While Barakas prized her for her status and sorcerous abilities, he knew that his son saw her in more coarse terms . . . not that the patriarch could deny her beauty. Sharissa had changed somewhat in the time since their coming. Her face was rounder, though the cheekbones were in evidence. Like other Vraad, she had crystalline eyes, aquamarine gemstones that grew brighter when they widened. Her brows were arched, giving her an inquisitive look. The expression on her face seemed to be one of mild amusement, but Barakas knew that it was actually because her mouth curled upward naturally.

"Lady Sharissa," he called out, nodding his head.

Her thin yet elegant lips parted in what he knew was a forced pleasantness. She did not care for many of the Tezerenee—save self-exiled Gerrod, came the unbidden thought. Barakas quickly smothered any further notions concerning that son. Gerrod had chosen his own way, and it had meant a hermetic life that defied everything Barakas had taught his people. As far as the patriarch was concerned, the relationship had ended there.

"Lord Barakas. Lochivan." She smiled at them, nodding in return, then finally added, "*Reegan.* How do you fare today?"

"Always well when I see you," Reegan blurted.

Barakas was almost as surprised as Sharissa at his eldest's words. The young Zeree colored a bit; she had not expected such complimentary bluntness from the hulking figure. The patriarch held back a smile. She could hardly claim that he had engineered that comment. It was too obvious that Reegan's stumbling words had been his own. For once, his son had taken the initiative. If there was one thing that Sharissa had no defense against, it was honesty.

"How is your father?" he asked, filling the silence that had started to grow too long for his tastes.

"He is well," Sharissa returned, looking a bit relieved. For all her skill and knowledge, she was still naive in the ways of relationships. Her father had kept her away from most of the other Vraad for the first twenty years of her life—and she was less than twenty years older now. A short time to the long-lived Vraad race.

"And his mate?"

"Mother is also well."

Barakas took note of her use of the term. The Lady Ariela Zeree was not Sharissa's mother; she was not even a Vraad, but an elf from this world. Dru's daughter had never really known her birth mother, though, and she had come to care for the elf so much that it seemed only natural to call her father's mate *mother*. Barakas hid the distaste he felt. The elf was a lesser creature, wife of Zeree or not. She did not belong among the Vraad.

He realized that Sharissa was waiting for him to say something more. It disturbed him that he found himself drifting off so much more of late. Had it something to do with the white hair he had discovered of late . . . or the wrinkles at the corners of his eyes?

"Lady Sharissa, you know a little about those *creatures*, don't you?" Lochivan suddenly asked. He did not have to elaborate as to what creatures he referred to. Everyone knew he meant the Faceless Ones.

The Lord Tezerenee glanced at his younger son, but held his peace.

"I know a bit." She was cautious. Like most of the Vraad, she was ever wary of their desire for domination. Barakas wanted very much to assure her that she need not have worried; there was already a place for her among them. Such vitality and power could not be wasted.

```
         EDWARDS BOOKS

05/01/92   06:04   E      O    10058
   1 @   4.95  1560763191 $       4.95
              FR DRUIDHOME TRI
   1 @   4.99  044636153A $       4.99
              CHILDREN OF DRAK

SUBTOTAL                     $     9.94
TAX    @  5.00%              $     0.50
TOTAL                        $    10.44
TENDERED  Cash               $    11.00
CHANGE                       $     0.56

            THANK YOU
     BEST IN PAPERBACKS AND HARDCOVERS
```

"Have they shown any purpose? Do their actions mean anything at all? All they do is stare . . . if you can call it that, since they have nothing with which to stare! I keep thinking they know something. Fifteen years of staring must have *some* purpose! It's gotten worse during this past year, too!"

She was interested; the patriarch could see that. Sharissa was interested in anything that had to do with her new world. "You noticed that? They seem more attentive of late; I thought that, too. I can't think it means us any harm, however. They want us to thrive."

Do they? Barakas wanted to ask. Again, as with so many other things, he held his tongue.

"What about your father? Dru works with them in their citadel. Surely, he knows more."

Sharissa shook her head, sending fine hair cascading back and forth. Reegan was having trouble keeping his interest in her from growing too obtrusive. He had always had that trouble.

"Father always says it's like working with a jigsaw puzzle with more than half the pieces missing. Somehow, they teach him things, but he never realizes it until afterward." She smiled at Lochivan, seeming to forget for the moment that he was a Tezerenee. "It frustrates him no end."

"I can imagine."

The two of them talked to each other with an ease that stirred Barakas. The patriarch was truly the father of his people, having cultivated no less than fifteen sons and several daughters over the centuries . . . likely many more that he had forgotten about, too. Of those he recognized, the two most intelligent had proven bitter failures to him. Rendel had betrayed the clan, seeking his own way in the Dragonrealm. He had died, thanks to his own foolishness. His shadow, younger Gerrod, was no better. It occurred to him now that here was one who could fill the gap of knowledge the other two had left. He had only thought of Lochivan as superbly obedient, never intelligent. Yet . . .

Sharissa was glancing his way, and he wondered when she had turned her attention to him. She was now all artificial politeness again. He had slipped and allowed his thoughts to show, something he would have never forgiven any of his people for doing.

"If you will excuse me, I must prepare for an excursion. Someone came across one of the founders' earlier settlements."

"Oh?" Lochivan leaned forward. "Where?"

"Northeast. I must be going now. Good day to you all." She nodded to the trio and departed at a pace that emphasized her sudden desire to be away from them.

Reegan's pained expression reminded Barakas of a sick drake. Lochivan turned to his father the moment Sharissa was a fair distance away, and the two of them exchanged glances. Northeast was where Gerrod had, of late, made his home. It might be coincidence, but, then again, it might not be.

"Shake yourself out of that stupor, Reegan," the Lord Tezerenee ordered at last. He then returned his attention to his other offspring. "Lochivan, I give you leave to depart. I know you, too, have things that you must attend to. Yes?"

It took only a moment for Lochivan, who had not had *any* duties to attend to, to understand what his progenitor was saying. He nodded. "I do. My thanks."

The younger Tezerenee twisted the reins and urged his mount away from the other two. Barakas turned one last time to his eldest, his heir.

"Dragon's blood, idiot! Snap out of it and come along! You can't very well sit there mooning all day!" He had miscalculated Reegan's desire for Sharissa. The last thing he needed was a lovesick hulk. When desire ruled, the mind became worthless— and with his eldest that was doubly so.

Reegan managed to stir himself, urging his mount to follow that of his father. Barakas hid his disgust under a mask of blandness. He should have known that Reegan's words to Sharissa had not been born of any cunning but of true infatuation for the young Zeree.

His mind awhirl with thoughts concerning the future of his clan and the potential that Sharissa Zeree promised that future— if the patriarch had his way—Lord Barakas could not be faulted for not noticing yet a third of the featureless entities he so loathed. It watched the backs of the two Tezerenee grow smaller and smaller as they rode away, then, evidently losing interest, it turned and started off in the direction that Sharissa— then Lochivan—had gone.

III

Sharissa had not wanted to confront the Tezerenee, especially Barakas and Reegan. It was, she knew, impossible *not* to confront one or another member of the dragon clan. During the past five years they had become especially noticeable in this part of the city. The anger that many Vraad felt for them had faded with time and the knowledge that the Tezerenee had proven invaluable over and over almost since the beginning of the colony. The clan now held greater influence with their race than they ever had back in Nimth, although she doubted that the patriarch saw it that way. Though he had always pushed for physical prowess, the dwindling of their sorcery to near nothing meant that their lack of numbers would now hurt them in battle. Still, more than a few of those outside the clan now looked to Barakas for leadership. Emboldened, the Tezerenee were once more walking among their fellows, daring their rivals to do something.

So far, things were still in balance. Silesti still held the majority of the folk in his hand, and her father influenced both sides to work with one another and ignore gibes and covert glances. It was Dru Zeree more than anyone else who kept the triumvirate successful. Left to their own devices, Silesti and Barakas would have begun the final war among the Vraad the same day the refugees had arrived in this world.

Barakas hoped to swing the balance to his side, and one method involved Sharissa's marriage to Reegan.

"Not if I have anything to say about it," she muttered. Sharissa did not particularly hate Reegan, and his words had touched the romantic part of her, but he was not what she sought. She was uncertain what it was she *did* seek, but it could never be this younger, more coarse version of the patriarch himself. Reegan would become his father in all save cunning. The heir was a creature of strength and skill, but not knowledge. He needed Lochivan to guide him in subtle matters.

Lochivan. Sharissa wondered if the Lord Tezerenee knew that his other son was one of her closest friends. Never a lover, but more like the brother she did not have.

As she walked, her eyes absently marked the progress that had been made of late. The western and eastern portions of the city, which was actually more of a giant citadel, were almost completely rebuilt. Most of the ancient buildings had been found to be too untrustworthy and had been torn down as needs arose. Thanks partly to the powers of the few who had the necessary aptitude for sorcery here and the physical work of the many who did not, there were now several towers and flat-roofed buildings. They were a bit too utilitarian for her tastes, but she hoped that would change. Most of the structures were empty, optimistic thoughts of a growth trend in the Vraad population making the people continue working after they had re-created enough of a home for the present inhabitants. It was a good way to keep them busy, too. That was one thing all members of the triumvirate had agreed on from the first.

There were a few traces of Vraad taste that she did see. Some of the arches were a bit more extravagant than they should have been, even to the point of being decorated with fanciful creatures. A wolf's head over one doorway gave her pause, reminding her too much of memories of Nimth. She knew, however, that the carving was actually a symbol designating they who lived there as among Silesti's favorites. Unconsciously following in the footsteps of his enemy, the third member of the triumvirate had chosen to make the wolf one of the marks by which his authority was known.

Something stepped out of a shadowy alley, startling her. She kept from losing face by stifling the gasp before any of it escaped her lips.

A smooth, featureless visage stared back at her. She, like Barakas, referred to them as the Faceless Ones, but most Vraad called them the *not-people*, likely because they did not want to have to accept them as anything remotely akin to their own kind. There were traits the beings had that touched too close to those of her kind.

The Faceless One confronted her for only a moment. With an impatient movement, it shifted around her and kept going. Sharissa followed its departure until it was out of sight, then exhaled the breath she had forgotten to release in the shock of the encounter.

A stray yet disturbing thought edged its way to the forefront—

had the Faceless One seemed nervous? Generally, they did not go darting around those they ran across, but either changed direction completely or circled around their victim with a slow, almost casual pace. They did not go scurrying along as this one had. It was almost as if something else were occupying the creature's thoughts.

What could so demand the attention of one of the beings that it would lose the reserve that its kind had become noted for over the years?

Then Sharissa felt the first stirrings of another presence—one so powerful and so *different* that it might as well have been purposely announcing its coming. Perhaps it was; she could not say for certain. All she knew so far was that this was no Vraad... save perhaps Gerrod, who was capable of many extraordinary changes.

A pall of silence wrapped itself over the area, as if others were sensing the same as she. Reaching out, she touched upon the strength of this world. Of the few who had adapted almost completely to their new home's ways, some now claimed they saw a spectrum when they sought the power. Others claimed that their vision was that of a field of crisscrossing lines going on into infinity, lines of force. Sharissa knew that neither group lied; she was the only one, evidently, who saw both, depending on the whims of her subconscious. It was the most probable reason why she had become, without exception, the most adept of the Vraad. Even her father, who had learned from both his bride and the Faceless Ones, could not match her. What did confuse Sharissa was that Ariela, who had been conceived and raised on the other continent, also could not match her adopted daughter. The elf claimed to know of no one among her people who touched upon the powers with the ease that the young Zeree did.

There were times when Sharissa felt proud of her unique position... and times when it became a heavy burden and a threat. Among the Vraad were those like Barakas who saw her as a tool or were merely jealous of her abilities. Everyone tried to manipulate her, but she had learned to handle most of them. In the final days of Nimth, one of her father's former lovers, an enchantress named Melenea, had used Sharissa's innocence in a ploy that had almost meant the death of both Zerees and Gerrod Tezerenee. It *had* meant the death of her father's familiar, Sharissa's childhood companion. Sirvak had died defending his master and mistress from Melenea's horrible pet,

Cabal. That incident had steeled Sharissa's heart. No one would ever use her again, not if it endangered those she cared for.

The presence was growing stronger, as if whoever it was raced toward the city . . . from the *west*, she now saw. The nearer to the city it came, the more astonishing its power was . . . and the more inhuman it seemed to be. No Vraad could possibly claim such ability, such *otherness*.

Father, she recalled with a start. *I have to tell Father!* It might be that he knew already, but one could never tell. Sharissa reached out to him with her mind, trying to establish a link. Linking minds was more chancy than it had once been, possibly because few now had the ability to maintain it long. In the case of her father and her, the trouble was compounded by the fact that Dru Zeree was not quite in this world, but in a compact dimension where the founders had built their last citadel before they had chosen to give their souls to the land. While those within could observe or contact the outside, breaking through the barrier from the true world was something only their blank-visaged avatars could do with any consistency, or so she thought. There were only theories as to how they communicated among themselves.

Father? She held her breath for a time, awaiting his response. When the familiar touch of the elder Zeree's mind failed to manifest itself, Sharissa tried again. All the while, she felt the ever-closing presence of the outsider, the . . . *creature*. It made her wonder how the Tezerenee could have failed to notice such a being; Barakas might be a shadow of his former self, but he was still one to be reckoned with. How could he have failed to sense the coming intruder?

There was, as yet, no answer from her father. If he had noted her summons at all, he would have contacted Sharissa by now. That meant the only recourse was to go to him herself. Her expedition all but forgotten, she turned and headed in the general direction of the city square. It was there, in a bit of the city that by Dru's own command had been left untouched, where she would find the tiny, hidden rift that was the entrance to the pocket universe of the founders, the place where her parents now spent most of their time. The path would be open to her, she hoped. There had been occasions when Sharissa had been forced to wait until her father departed his private domain in order to talk to him.

A few Vraad, making their own way to whatever projects held their attention, stepped aside as she rushed past them without so much as a glance. Whether they felt anything, she neither knew nor cared. If anyone else was disturbed by the newcomer, then they could follow her or come on their own.

One body did *not* move aside for her, and she almost ran directly into it. Sharissa *would* have collided with the other figure, save that a pair of strong hands caught her and held her still.

"What is it? Something must be amiss for you to go running blindly into folk!"

"Lochivan! I can't talk! I have to find my father!"

The Tezerenee released her. "Then I will walk with you. You can tell me why you're so upset that you have not teleported instead of wasting so much time *walking*."

Sharissa colored. She stepped past Lochivan and resumed her journey. The Tezerenee fell in beside her, easily matching the pace. He had grown up on quick marches.

"I thought it would be best not to attempt such a spell," she finally replied. Sharissa had never told anyone, not even Dru, why she so rarely employed such timesaving spells. Teleportation had been a dangerous, foolhardy thing in the last days of the old world, and it had nearly cost her father his life. The younger Zeree knew she was being ridiculous, but she had never gotten over her fear that one day a teleport spell would send her into some place from which she would never return. It was impossible to explain the feeling to anyone who could no longer perform the spell. They would have hardly felt sympathy for her plight.

"Why? What is it?" Lochivan asked, his brow furrowed. He was uneasy about something, perhaps several somethings. Sharissa wondered if he felt the oncoming stranger's presence.

"Something...someone...of a different...I can't explain it, but don't you feel the approach of a presence in the west?"

"Is that what that is?" He glanced in the direction of the gate through which he and the others had entered earlier. "But anything that close...we should have seen it during our ride...."

"That's what I thought, too." A suspicion formed. "Did you, Lochivan? You are probably one of only two of your folk that I might expect a true, unmasked answer from. Did you see anything? Sense anything?"

"Nothing!" The vehemence with which he answered revealed his deepening worry. "There's nothing west but forest and plains...and the seas, of course. Dragon's blood! *Seekers?*"

He had come to the same conclusion she had. The magical guardians of the city, the founders' ancient servants, had been her only other choice. Formless save when they chose to dress themselves in the very earth and rock, as the one the Tezerenee called the Dragon of the Depths had, the guardians felt of this world, this ancient place. Not so the newcomer. There was only the slightest trace of this world on the intruder, as if it had briefly been a part of this place but had, as Sharissa noted again, come from somewhere beyond. Since Nimth was closed off, that left only the other continent and its masters. It *had* to be the Seekers, yet were they not part of this world, too?

Lochivan paused and removed one of his gauntlets. "Sword and shield! What a time for this!"

Despite the urgency of the situation, she paused. Her companion's presence was comforting, which soothed her enough to keep her thoughts from running too amok. It would be worth the time to wait for him, providing it was only for a few seconds. Besides, the frustration in his voice made her curious as to his difficulties. "What's wrong?"

He reached in between his dragonhelm and his armor and started scratching with such a fury she thought he would draw blood. "A damn rash! Nothing deadly, but it's spread around the clan quite a bit! The skin gets dry and stays that way! Sometimes it itches so badly that I'm forced to stop everything and scratch until . . . until it becomes tolerable again."

Lochivan pulled his hand away and replaced the gauntlet. He sighed. "As it finally has, thank the dragon. It's over. Get moving!"

A bit surprised that a warrior like Lochivan would succumb to a rash during a moment of crisis, Sharissa nonetheless said nothing to him and did her best to keep from revealing any of her thoughts. She would have to mention this plague of irritation to her father when there was time. It might only be a rash now, but who was to say what it might become in the future?

They had barely progressed more than a dozen steps before the sorceress nearly came to a halt herself.

Something was in the square they were trying to reach. Something that was the same presence she had noted outside only a few minutes ago! Now it was *inside* and *ahead* of them! Yet, it had just been *outside*—

"Serkadion Manee!" she uttered, stunned. The name of the

ancient Vraad scholar was a favorite oath of her father, and she had picked it up over the years.

Lochivan did not have to ask what was wrong. As she turned and looked at him she could see that the Tezerenee felt what she did. . . . Who could not? Sharissa scanned those Vraad standing or walking nearby. They were all pausing in their present interests and twisting about to stare in the direction of the square. A silence had fallen upon everyone in sight. One or two had enough presence of mind to make note of the duo moving toward the source of the disruption. To the young Zeree, they looked almost frightened. In their hearts, many Vraad feared that, now mostly bereft of their fabulous abilities, they would become easy prey for some outside threat.

That might very well be the truth, Sharissa realized.

"I have to teleport," she announced, her words more to steel herself for the task at hand than to alert Lochivan.

"I'm coming with you."

"Hold on to my arm, then."

He did, holding her a bit tighter than he likely thought. The clan of the dragon, meaning the patriarch, frowned on any show of fear, regardless of the reasons. There were times when she felt pity for the sort of life that Gerrod and Lochivan had endured.

Grimacing, Sharissa transported them to the square.

Her first thought was that it had grown as dark as night even though there were still a few hours of sun left. Then she noted, with much chagrin, that her eyes were squeezed shut.

"Gods! Look at him, Sharissa! Have you ever seen something as grand and startling as that?"

She opened her eyes with care. There were other people around already and all of them were just as entranced by the great beast in the square.

"A horse!" she whispered. A glorious ebony steed! She had always loved her father's horses, magnificent mounts that he had bred without any use of magic—almost as a challenge to himself. Yet, no horse she had seen could measure up to this creature. . . .

It was this steed that her senses had noticed. It was this animal that emanated the unbelievable power that so disturbed the minds of nearly every Vraad, whatever their sorcerous abilities.

"Where is he? I will not be denied him! I will not again be

thrust back into the cursed nothingness I was forced to endure for so long! Where is my friend, Dru Zeree?''

Sharissa knew then what and who this was. He was called Darkhorse and he had, for a time, aided and traveled with her father after the sorcerer had been lost in the ghost lands where Nimth and Barakas's Dragonrealm had intertwined like two cursed lovers, together yet unable to touch one another. The guardians, in obedience to the millennia-old instructions of their lost masters, had seen the shadow steed as an aberration that could not be allowed to exist here.

In deference to Dru, they had not destroyed him, but rather exiled him . . . supposedly forever.

They had underestimated the creature.

People shuffled nervously around the square, uncertain as to what the ebony stallion might do. Many of them had abandoned something or another. A few folk were even half-dressed. Even though most of them had not heard of Darkhorse, they recognized sorcery of a kind that was in some ways even greater than what they themselves had once wielded.

"You look like Dru Zeree!" the thundering voice accused the crowd. He pondered this for a moment, then asked, "You are Vraad?" An icy, blue eye focused on one unnerved person after another, finally fixing on the only Vraad there who did not turn away: Sharissa. "*Where* is my friend?"

"Sharissa!" Lochivan hissed, grabbing hold of her from the side.

She blinked, realizing she had been about to fall forward and wondering what it was about Darkhorse that brought on such a reaction. She had almost thought she was going to fall *into* him . . . but that was ridiculous, wasn't it? Yet the sensation had been strong, even demanding, until Lochivan had stepped in to rescue her.

The demonic stallion tossed his head, such an animallike action that it destroyed some of the uncertainty Sharissa felt. She took a deep breath and stepped up.

"I am Sharissa Zeree, Dru's daughter. I—"

"Aahh! Little Sharissa!" Darkhorse bellowed with pleasure. His change of manner was so abrupt that Sharissa forgot herself and stood there with her mouth open.

Darkhorse trotted toward her. "Friend Dru spoke of you during our travels! How delightful to see you! How wonderful to find you after an eternity of cursed searching for this place!"

"Careful, Sharissa!" Lochivan whispered. He had one hand on his sword, though she was uncertain as to what he imagined he could do with it. From what little the sorceress knew and what little she had seen, it would take more than a blade to stop this creature.

"Careful, *indeed*!" Darkhorse snorted in response. His hearing was remarkable. "I would not harm the appendage of my friend Dru!"

"Appendage?" Sharissa was not certain she had heard right.

"Shoot? You were part of him and are now separate, yes? What is that called for your kind?"

"Offspring. Child. Only I was not part of him, but actually the . . ." She trailed off, thinking how long it might take to explain the process of birth to an entity that did not understand the concept in even the most remote terms.

Several of the onlookers had turned to her, not because of her inability to explain something to Darkhorse, but because she was on speaking terms with the invader. Relief was spreading among them, however. The great sorceress was once more dealing with their problem. This incident would only add to her prestige, a good thing since it was already assumed that she would take her father's place on the triumvirate should something happen to him.

Darkhorse surveyed his surroundings. "You have altered much in the shape of this place, albeit not where I stand! I feared I might have come to the wrong place, but then I recalled this one area and opened a quicker path to it! There have been so many worlds, so many universes I have searched through!"

He had made no comment concerning the protective spells that the Vraad had enshrouded their city with over time, spells that would have given *her* pause but did not, it appeared, even deserve acknowledgment on his part.

The intruder sighed, a very human sound that he must have learned from his former companion. Sharissa sensed the longing and the weariness. "Fifteen years is a long time, I imagine," she said, trying to soothe him. "It can be an eternity."

He gave her a strange look. "Through your father I have some understanding of the term *years*, little Shari! Know that when I say I have spent an eternity searching for this place, I am not being facetious or exaggerating! In your fifteen years, I have crossed a thousand thousand lands in as many worlds! Time, I have discovered, does not move the same everywhere and moves not at all in the cursed place friend Dru so aptly called the Void!" Darkhorse twisted his head so that he stared at the heavens. "The sky is more cluttered than the Void could ever be, even if this place were thrown into it! How could I have ever survived such an existence before Dru came?"

The question was not one he expected an answer for. Sharissa waited until the huge creature had calmed before saying, "My father will be happy to see you again. I can take you to him if you want."

"Little one, that is exactly what I was attempting! Last I knew, friend Dru was in danger and I had been thrust back into a place I hoped never to see—or perhaps *not* see is closer, I cannot say—again! I thought he might be in the room of worlds in the castle of the old ones, but I could not find the opening to that small universe! I feared those beings who guarded it when last I was here had sealed it, but there is no trace of them . . . and I could hardly forget the smell of those cursed horrors!"

Lochivan joined Sharissa and leaned close. "Should you not do something about all these people? They look like little children asked to solve a complex thaumaturgical question that has baffled masters! Assure them that all is well."

She saw the sense of that. Raising her arms, the sorceress called out. "There is no need to worry! There's no danger, no threat! This one is a friend of my father, and I will vouch for his actions!"

It was a pathetic speech as far as Sharissa was concerned, for it went nowhere toward answering the many questions that must be flowing through the minds of the Vraad who had assembled here. She added, "You will hear more from my father when he has had time to speak with our guest. I promise you that."

That was still not satisfactory in her mind, but the others seemed willing to live with what she had told them, understanding, perhaps, that they were lucky to know what little they did. The other two members of the triumvirate would be more vocal. Sharissa glanced at Lochivan; Barakas would know soon enough. Whatever friendship she shared with this Tezerenee, he was loyal to his father.

"You'd best go, too. I don't think I am in any danger, not from everything my father told me about Darkhorse."

"I should say not!" bellowed the beast.

Looking very, very uncomfortable, Lochivan bowed to both

of them. To the young Zeree, he said, "Best I be the one to tell my father. I'm truly sorry, Sharissa, but he *should* know about this." He stopped, his words sounding as pathetic to him, no doubt, as Sharissa's had to her. "Be prepared for him. Darkhorse changes the balance if he stays around. You and I both know that."

The Tezerenee turned and joined the many others who were slowly splintering away from the crowd. Sharissa mulled over his warning even as she smiled at the darksome steed. If he chose to stay for any length of time, he *would* change the balance. Those whose loyalty teetered even a little would flock to the support of her father. Darkhorse was a potent ally. If the members of the triumvirate ever came to blows with one another, the demonic stallion might easily prove the deciding factor. Dru Zeree had no ambitions other than keeping his people together, but the same could not be said of Barakas and Silesti. The latter was one of those who had more than one legitimate reason for despising the patriarch of the Tezerenee. Several years of working side by side had not lessened the tension between them.

Darkhorse was scuffing the rubble-strewn soil with the impatience of one who is at last within striking distance of his goal after an epic odyssey but cannot find the front gate. Sharissa quickly joined him. "It's this way. The Faceless Ones moved it."

"Faceless Ones?"

"'Not-people'?" she added, wondering if he knew them by that title.

"I know not these others. Are they Vraad, also?"

"No, they're—" The young Zeree broke off. Better to show him one than try to describe the living legacies of the founders. She scanned the square, looking for the inevitable form watching them. Her eyes narrowed as her search progressed. Darkhorse waited in silence, his chilling gaze following hers.

The area was devoid of the featureless beings. Sharissa, thinking back, could not recall seeing one since her encounter in the alley. That particular creature had rushed off, as if unsettled. None of its fellows had been among the crowd that had gathered at the coming of Darkhorse. That alone made her nervous. Why would the Faceless Ones, who studied most everything else around the Vraad, avoid the startling return of the Void dweller?

Was there something they feared about Darkhorse? Vengeance? Surely not! The guardians had dealt with the ebony stallion as they might have a tiny insect. Their masters, even though only reflections of what they once had been, were not without their skills.

"Well? What is it you want to show me? Come! I wish to see little Dru again!"

"Let me show you the way, then." Still at a loss concerning the absence of the not-people, Sharissa led the shadow steed to an area to his right. Several Vraad still looked on. It did not matter if they saw where the entrance to her parents' home was. Only those the sorcerer desired to allow in would be able to cross the rift. She had no idea if Darkhorse would be allowed to make the journey unimpeded or whether she would have to find her father first. They would discover that in a moment.

A ripple in the air was her first sighting of the hole. As she neared it, Darkhorse close behind, it seemed to widen for her. Within its boundaries, the sorceress could make out a huge wooded meadow. Flowers dotted the field, sentinels in a sea of high grass.

Sharissa put one foot into the tear in reality, then stepped through. The square, the entire city, had vanished. She turned around and saw the rip. A huge, jet-black form filled its dimensions.

"At *last*!" Darkhorse trotted through the magical entranceway unimpeded. "At last I am here!"

She could not help smiling. "Not yet, but soon. We still have a short distance to go."

His disturbing eyes followed the lay of the land. He laughed. "Only this? After the journey I have suffered, this is scarcely more than a single step!"

"Then let's take that step." Sharissa could hardly wait to see the look on her father's face when he saw the surprise she was bringing.

From the edge of the square, Lochivan observed the departure of Sharissa and the monster. He had hoped that it would be unable to cross, but that hope was shattered a second later when it vanished behind Zeree's daughter. Yet another piece of news that would interest the patriarch.

Abandoning his watchpost for where he had left his mount, the Tezerenee pondered the significance of the demon's arrival. Though he was not one to whom prescience had been gifted,

Lochivan knew that this was a moment of destiny in the lives of the Vraad. The creature called Darkhorse altered everything, and he knew that the Lord Tezerenee would work to make the future one to his liking.

Lochivan wished there were someone else who could relay the tale to his father. There was not, however, and he was, after all, his sire's son. Even if it might someday mean the death of Sharissa's father, his duty was ever to the clan.

The last thought disturbed him most, but, as with so many in the past, he merely buried it in a secret place in his mind and hurried to perform his duties as a good son always did.

IV

In the eastern quarter of the city, behind a wall of belief that divided those who followed the dragonlord from those who did not, Lord Barakas held court. Sleek red dragon banners hung from the walls. Torches created a legion of flickering specters from those folk assembled. A young wyvern, hooded, stood perched on a ledge to one side of the dais that made up the far end of the chamber. The hall was, to be sure, a mere shadow of the grand, looming citadel that the Tezerenee had once occupied before the migration, but any lack of presence upon this structure's part was more than made up for by the numbers now kneeling in respect to the patriarch. Outsiders, meaning those not born to the clan, outnumbered the armored figures by a margin that made Barakas smile. He had dreamed of such a kingdom, though he now knew it to be tiny in comparison to the vast numbers the Seekers boasted. Still, it was progress. With so many now obedient to his will, his prestige had grown . . . and that, in turn, meant even more followers. One day, not too distant, he would be undisputed master of all.

Then he recalled the gray that was spreading in his hair and the wrinkles forming on his face and the smile died. He could not be growing old. Vraad did not grow old unless they chose to do so.

Guards clad in the dark-green dragon-scale armor and fierce dragonhelms of the clan lined the walls. Most of them were nephews, nieces, cousins, and offspring. There were both men and women, each of them skilled with the weapons they held. They were doubly deadly now; the near-disaster against the Seekers had given most of them a true taste of battle. In the eyes of their fellow Vraad, who had never more than dabbled with weapons, it made them ominous, fearsome sights to behold.

"Is something amiss, my loved one?" a throaty voice whispered in his ear.

Was she growing older, too? Lord Barakas turned to his bride, the Lady Alcia. She was still the warrior goddess, even in regal repose upon her throne, striking and commanding. Like her husband, she was clad in armor, though of a lighter, more form-fitting type. The patriarch took a moment to admire her lithe body. Tezerenee armor was designed with appearance as well as safety in mind... and the patriarch had always enjoyed the female body. This was not to say he did not respect his wife's abilities. When the Lord Tezerenee was away, it was the Lady Tezerenee who maintained control of the clan, who organized all major activities. She was, he would gladly admit, his other half.

"Barakas?"

The patriarch started, knowing that he had drifted off again. In any other person, it would have meant nothing; most people were prone to daydreaming. Not so Barakas. There had never been time for daydreaming. The formation and then growth of the clan had always demanded his total attention. "I'm fine," he finally muttered under his breath so that only she could hear him. "Only thinking."

She smiled, something that tended to eliminate the severe cast of her otherwise aristocratic features. The Lady Alcia was always most beautiful at these times.

Barakas straightened in his throne, gazing out at his people. "All may rise!"

The crowd stood as if his words had caused someone to pull up the strings of several hundred marionettes. Even most of the outsiders, who had not been raised from birth in the martial traditions the dragonlord had created and, therefore, could not have reacted to his command with the same precision, moved in fair form to their feet. They were learning. Soon, everyone would learn.

Reegan, standing by the right of his mother, stepped forward. "Is there anyone with a boon to ask of the lord of the clan?"

Two outsiders, already rehearsed by others for this moment, stepped forward into the empty area between the dais upon which the thrones stood and the main part of the great hall where the crowds waited. One was a man who had been stout at one time but had lost much weight now that he was forced to do physical work to survive. The other was a woman of rather plain face and form who wore a gown that had seen better days. She had tried her best to recapture the beauty that had once, no doubt, been hers in Nimth, but makeup could not perform sufficient magic for her sake. Both supplicants were nervous and wary.

"Your names," the heir asked without emotion.

The man started to open his mouth, but a form in the back of the chamber caught the patriarch's attention and he signaled for silence. Esad, another of his sons—by his bride, that is—indicated that there was a matter needing the patriarch's personal attention. Esad, like most of the Tezerenee, knew better than to interrupt court with anything trivial. The dragonlord's interest was piqued. He turned to his lady.

"Would you hold court for me, Alcia?"

"As you wish, husband." She was not surprised by his request. Over the centuries, the Lady Alcia had performed this function time and again. Her decisions were as final as his own. A supplicant who failed to gain her support would lose more if he tried to convince the patriarch to alter the decision. That supplicant might also lose his head.

"Kneel as the Lord Tezerenee departs the court!" Reegan cried out in the same emotionless voice.

The throngs obeyed without hesitation, though a few newcomers were openly curious at this sudden breach of form. Barakas ignored them; his eyes were still on Esad. Now he saw that Lochivan was with him. So much the better. Lochivan would not be back so soon unless he had something terribly important to report.

The two younger Tezerenee stepped back out of the main hall as their father met them. Both went down on one knee, as did several guards on duty in the corridor.

"Stand up, all of you! Lochivan. Is he your reason for summoning me, Esad, or do you have another matter?"

"None, father," the helmed figure replied, a bit of a quiver in his response. He had never been quite the same since the clan's crossover and the near-destruction of the Tezerenee by the Seekers had only added to the damage within his mind. Something inside had been broken. Esad had become a disappointment to the patriarch.

"You are dismissed, then."

Esad bowed and walked away in silence. Barakas put an arm around Lochivan's shoulders and led him down the corridor in the opposite direction. "What matter brings you back so soon? Something concerning the younger Zeree?"

"In a sense. Father, what mention has Dru Zeree made of a huge pitch-black stallion called Darkhorse?"

"Not a horse at all, but a creature from beyond. . . . One of our demons of legend, perhaps. Master Zeree is tight-lipped when it comes to his first journey here before we crossed." The patriarch paused in midstep, then backed up to look into his son's eyes. "Why do you want to know?"

Lochivan looked as if he was not certain his father would believe what he was about to say. "It . . . he's *here*. Today, mere minutes after we separated, he materialized in the city . . . in the square. Surely you *felt* his power!"

"I felt something as I dismounted. Your brothers Logan and Dagos have been ordered to discover what it was."

"They are on a wasted mission, then. I have seen all that anyone could see of this . . . this leviathan. He crossed all of our barriers and entered the city untouched, materializing, in all audacity, in our very midst."

"Seeking, no doubt, the rift to Zeree's private world, Sirvak Dragoth, as he calls it." The Lord Tezerenee's tone spoke volumes concerning his envy. To have a kingdom all your own . . . and to waste it on only two or three Vraad and a hundred or so cursed not-people. It had been a point of contention among the triumvirate. Dru Zeree passed on only whatever secrets he felt obliged to pass on. The rest remained to him and his family alone.

"Sharissa spoke to him—"

"He listened to her?"

"As if she were his tried-and-true friend! She is the daughter of his companion . . . his teacher, too, I suspect. For all his bluster . . ." Here Lochivan shifted a bit, uneasy about voicing his opinion on so unpredictable a subject. "For all his bluster and power, this Darkhorse sounds more like a child than an ageless demon."

Barakas considered that for a moment. "What finally happened?"

"She led him through the rift and into her father's domain."

"He was not *barred* from entering it?" More than once, Tezerenee, at their lord's command, had covertly tested the doorway to Zeree's pocket universe. In most cases, they had not even been able to locate it, much less try to enter. Those that *had* managed to discover the tear in reality walked through it as if the rift were only air and not a gate at all.

"He walked through with ease."

"Interesting." Barakas stalked down the hall, each element of information being turned over and over in his mind. Lochivan scurried along, knowing he had not been dismissed yet. As he had expected, his father's interest was piqued.

Sentries in the corridor snapped to attention as their lord walked past, unmindful of their presence. Lochivan, trailing, nodded to each and scanned them for any slack behavior. That many were related to him did not matter; if he failed to report or reprimand someone who was not performing their duties to their best, it would be he who suffered, son or not. After all, Barakas had offspring to spare; one son more or less would not touch the patriarch's heart.

"He will have to depart Zeree's bottled world at some point," Barakas announced.

"Yes, my lord."

"He is a creature of vast power. Not as vast as the Dragon of the Depths, of course, but still a creature to be wary of, I suppose."

"It would seem that way." Lochivan's visage, what could be seen of it behind the helm, had grown perturbed.

"And we have some little power to work with, especially if we work in concert." *To a point!* Barakas added to himself. It was becoming more and more difficult to do even that much, almost as if the land was seeking to wipe all vestiges of Vraad sorcery, which demanded and took rather than worked *with* the world, from existence.

Lochivan chose to remain silent, trying to decipher what it was his father intended.

The Lord Tezerenee turned down a side corridor. His eyes wandered briefly to a nearby window that overlooked the jagged, decaying courtyard of some ancient noble—so he imagined it to be, that is. Whether this had been the home of some noble was a matter of conjecture; the truth was lost to time. Barakas liked to think of it as such, however, just as he liked to think of the debris-covered yard as his personal training ground. Each day, Tezerenee fought on the treacherous surface, testing their skills against one another or some outsider seeking to learn from them. The ground was left purposely ruined; no true battle took place on a clear, flat surface. If they fell, they learned the hard way what could happen to a careless fool in combat.

Tearing his gaze from the window, Barakas made a decision. He smiled and continued down the corridor at a more brisk pace.

"Lochivan," he summoned.

"Father?" Lochivan stepped up his pace and managed to catch up to Barakas, though it was hard to maintain a place at his father's side. Barakas moved with a swiftness most of the younger Tezerenee could not match at their best.

"You are dismissed."

"Yes, sire." It was to his credit that the younger warrior did not question his abrupt dismissal. During the course of his life, he had come to know when his father was formulating some plan and needed to be alone. Lochivan turned around and returned the way he had come. Barakas took no note of his departure. Only the thoughts melding together within his mind interested him.

A patrol, making its rounds, quickly made a path for him. There were three warriors, one a female, and two drakes about the size of large dogs. The warriors, their faces obscured, stiffened like the newly dead. Barakas started past them, then paused when one of the drakes hissed at him, its darting, forked tongue seeming to have a life of its own.

Barakas reached down and petted the beast on the head. Reptilian eyes closed and the tail swept back and forth, slapping against the legs of its human partner. The Vraad tugged on the leash he held, pulling the drake's collar a bit tighter in the process. Studying beast and handler, the patriarch's smile widened.

To Sharissa, it was as if her father had become a small boy. He had greeted Darkhorse with an enthusiasm second only to that which he displayed for his own family. She understood his excitement. Friendship was rare among her kind. Only the circumstances of their escape from Nimth had forced the Vraad to treat one another in a civil manner. Many still held their neighbors in some suspicion, although that had lessened since the first turbulent year.

Watching him now, standing among the sculpted bushes of the courtyard and talking in animated fashion with the huge, soot-skinned Darkhorse, Sharissa realized how much her father himself had changed over the last few years. She had always marveled at the differences he made in this little world and the one outside, but never at the changes those endless tasks had performed on him. His hair was a dying brown, more white now save for the impressive silver streak running down the middle. He was still narrow and nearly seven feet tall, which somehow was short in comparison to the shadow steed, but his back was slightly stooped and he had lines in his hawkish visage. The trimmed beard he wore had thinned out, too.

Fifteen years had altered him, but, for a short time, he was again the majestic master sorcerer that she had grown up loving and adoring.

"He had always hoped the dweller from the Void would find his way back," a strong yet almost musical voice to Sharissa's side informed her.

Ariela was shorter than Sharissa, which made her *much* shorter than her husband, Dru. Her hair, like the younger Zeree's, was very pale and very long, though in a braid. Her arched brows and her tapered ears marked her as an elf, as did her emerald, almond-shaped eyes. She wore a robe akin to the dark-blue one worn by her mate, but this one somehow found the curves of her body with no trouble whatsoever. Ariela was trim, athletic in form, and skilled with a number of weapons, especially the knife. Her aid had proven as invaluable as that of the Tezerenee had in keeping the refugees alive until they could fend for themselves.

"I can't blame him. Darkhorse is unbelievable! What is he? I still don't understand!"

"Dru calls him a living hole, and I am inclined to believe that."

"He has flesh, though." It *looked* like flesh upon first glance. Sharissa had even touched it. She could not deny, however, that she had felt a pull, as if the ebony creature had been about to swallow her . . . body and soul.

Ariela laughed lightly. "Do not ask me to explain any further! Even your father admits that he only hazards guesses."

Nodding, Sharissa looked around. Other than the four of them, there was no one in sight. During every other visit she had made to Sirvak Dragoth, the Faceless Ones had been visible in abundance. Now, as it had been in the square, they had vanished. "Why are we alone?"

The elf frowned. "I have no idea, and Dru was too excited to notice. They were here until just before you announced yourselves." She studied her stepdaughter's eyes and whispered, "Is there something amiss?"

In a similar tone, Sharissa replied, "You know how they seem to be everywhere. Before Darkhorse materialized in the city, I came across one that I can only describe as agitated. It hurried away, and when I looked for it I couldn't find it. Then, when I reached the square, I found hundreds of Vraad but not one of them!"

"That is not normal . . . if I may use the term in regard to them." The not-people were watchful to the point of obsession. Any event of the least significance was liable to attract their unwanted attention. An event of such magnitude as Darkhorse's return should have attracted more than a score. Though only living memories of the founding race, the entities had continued to perform their ancient tasks without fail. That they would cease now was beyond comprehension.

"You *chose* to return to this place? Remarkable!" the fearsome steed roared. Both women turned and listened.

"My curiosity overcame my fear," Dru responded. He indicated the tall structure that was the bulk of the citadel. "So much our ancestors knew! So much that was lost when they passed beyond!"

"Not far enough for my tastes! I still desire another confrontation with their servants! They had no right!"

Dru had no answer for that. Sharissa had heard him say the same thing more than once. He had feared that his unearthly companion would be forever lost in the Void or some place even worse . . . if any place could be worse than a true *no*place like that.

Darkness was beginning to descend, and the shadows began to shroud the sorcerer. Neither Dru nor his daughter had ever found a plausible explanation for the heavens and the differences in time among the various realms created by the founders. How could there be suns and moons for each? Dru had explained once that the ancients had succeeded in separating slices of reality, so to speak, from the true world. Each realm was a reflection of the original, but altered drastically by both the founders and time. The spellcasting necessary for this was all but forgotten.

It was disturbing to understand that Nimth, too, had been but one more reflection, a terrarium where the Vraad had been raised up and then abandoned.

"I understand your feelings, Darkhorse," Dru was saying, "but Ariela and I have come to care for Sirvak Dragoth as much as anyone could care for their home."

"Sirvak Dragoth? Is that what this place is called?"

"I named it thus." The elder Zeree glanced at his daughter. Sharissa felt her eyes grow moist as he explained the origin of the name. "I had a familiar, a gold and black creature crafted with careful attention to its personality. Sirvak was loyal and as good a companion as any. It helped me raise Sharissa after her mother died. Sirvak perished saving her life just prior to our leaving Nimth. For what deeds it performed for both my daughter and myself, I saw no more fitting memorial than to give its name to this citadel." He paused, clearing his throat. "I'd rather have Sirvak back . . . but a new familiar could never be the same creature."

Darkhorse shook his mane in obvious discomfort. "I understand friendship, little Dru, but love is beyond me! That he was a good memory to you is all I can comprehend!"

The shadow steed laughed then, an abrupt thing that jolted all three of his companions. One eye twinkled at Sharissa. "But come! Let us speak of joy! Darkhorse has found his friend at last! This is a good thing! I have missed your guidance, friend Dru, your knowledge of the countless things abiding in this cluttered multiverse!"

"And I welcome the chance to talk with you, but I have other tasks that require my attention. My kind depend on me, Darkhorse. A decade and a half is not enough to ensure the future of the Vraad, especially as weak as we have become."

"Then what of your offspring . . . an interesting word. Did she truly leap from you?"

Sharissa chuckled and was joined by her parents. Darkhorse's random lapses in the understanding of language was one of the many things she recalled about the creature from her father's tales. The leviathan was, in many senses, the child that Dru had described. It only proved how different his mind-set was from those of humans and elves. So knowing and powerful, yet so naive and defenseless in other ways.

"I would be happy to spend time with you, Darkhorse, as long as you understand that I, too, have duties to perform."

"Duties! Tasks! How you must enjoy them, so important do they sound!"

No one tried to correct him. Besides, Sharissa realized, she *did* enjoy much of her work. There was still so much to learn about their new home. The deep maze of catacombs and chambers beneath the city had barely even been touched. Gerrod's discoveries, which she had completely forgotten about in all the excitement, now beckoned once again. It was still a welcome change, considering her first twenty years of life had been confined mainly to her father's domain.

"It's settled, then." Dru stifled a yawn. He and Ariela were early risers, often already active well before dawn. The couple always ceased what they were doing, however, when it came time to watch the sun rise over the horizon. Sharissa joined them now and again, but always kept to one side. Her parents lived in yet another world of their own when they watched the arrival of day together.

"You are weary," Darkhorse pointed out, ever ready to state the obvious. "I recall that you enter into the nothingness you call sleep when this happens. Is that not so?"

"Yes, but not immediately." The elder Zeree rose. "I know you don't sleep, Darkhorse, and you rest only on occasion, so is there some distraction I can offer you?"

The ebony stallion glanced at Sharissa. "Will you also be entering sleep?"

"Not for a while."

"Then I will join you for a time, if you do not mind?"

She looked from Darkhorse to her parents. "I was planning to return to my own chambers back in the city. Will that be all right?"

"The other Vraad are likely still leery of him, but if you stay together, there should be no problem." Dru smiled at his former companion. "Try not to frighten too many people . . . and keep your lone wanderings to a minimum until I've spoken to my counterparts in the triumvirate."

"I will be the image of discretion and insignificance! No one will take notice of me!"

"I doubt that." The master mage chuckled. "A few of those fine folk might even benefit from a jolt or two, now that I think about it!"

"Do not encourage him, Dru," Ariela warned, though she, too, laughed at the vision of still-arrogant Tezerenee running across the shadow steed in the dark of the moons.

Sharissa kissed both her father and her stepmother on the cheek. In Dru's ear, she whispered, "How are things progressing?"

"I pick up something here and there. I've expanded the dimensions of this little dreamland of mine . . . and I think the changes are making some sense at last. Have you talked to Gerrod?"

"He refuses to leave his dwelling and he's grown more distant, almost like a shadow." Sharissa paused. "Gerrod still insists the lands are trying to make us over again, that we'll become monsters like the Seekers or those earth diggers you mentioned, the Quel."

A bitter smile replaced the pleasant one Dru had maintained up to this point. "We were monsters before we ever crossed to this world. We only wore more attractive masks then."

"The people are changing. . . . I mean . . . not like Gerrod said, but becoming—"

"Will you two be whispering to one another all evening? If so, perhaps *I* might as well accompany Darkhorse back to the city." Ariela's arms were crossed, and she wore an expression of mock annoyance.

"I'm leaving," the sorceress said, dressing her words in a more pleasant tone. To Darkhorse, she asked, "Will you follow me?"

"Would you like to ride, instead?"

"Ride?" She had not thought of that. They had walked the entire way from the rift to the courtyard because she had not thought of Darkhorse as a mount, but rather a being much like herself. *Ride* a sentient creature such as this, one that her father termed a living *hole*?

"You need have no fear! Little Dru rode me quite often! I am stronger, more swift, than the fastest steed! I do not tire, and no terrain is my equal!"

His boasting eased her concerns. "How could I resist such superiority?"

"I only speak the truth!" The demonic horse somehow achieved a semblance of hurt.

"I believe you." She went to his side and, once he had knelt, mounted. There was no saddle, but the fantastic creature's back moved beneath her, shifting into a more comfortable form. If only all horses could make their own saddles!

"Take hold of my mane."

She did, noting that it felt like hair despite knowing that it was not.

"Take care, both of you," Dru said, waving.

"We're not going on any great journey, Father!"

"Take care, anyway."

Darkhorse roared with laughter, though Sharissa was not certain as to why, and reared.

They were racing through the gates of the citadel and down the grassy meadow below before she had time to realize it.

It may have been that Darkhorse felt her stiffen, for he shouted, "Have no fear, I said! I will not lose you!"

She wondered about that. When Darkhorse had mentioned he was swift, she had still pictured his speed in terms of an actual mount, not the creature who had raced toward the city from the western shore in a matter of minutes. Now, Sharissa flew. Literally flew. The ebony stallion's hooves did not touch the ground; she was certain of that. Her hair fluttered straight back, a pennon of silver-blue reflecting in the light of a moon that was not one of those existing outside of this domain.

They were through the rift and once more in the ruined square before Sharissa even thought to ask if Darkhorse knew where the tear was located. Now she understood her father's vivid yet unsatisfying telling of his rides with the black steed. One had to experience it to understand.

The days ahead, Sharissa decided, would be interesting indeed.

In the citadel that was and was not his, the sorcerer and his elfin bride walked arm in arm to their chambers, not even bothering to watch Sharissa and her fearsome companion depart, for Dru knew the Void dweller's ungodly speed well. Thus it was that neither noticed the return of the Faceless Ones, the not-people, at the exact moment that Darkhorse and his rider returned to the true world. They stood without the walls, all those who had chosen to return to flesh and blood, and stared with sightless gazes after the vanishing duo. If Sharissa could have seen them now, she would have noted a different emotion than the uneasiness she had observed in the one in the city.

— **V** —

Three days had passed. One day he might have understood, but not three. Sharissa Zeree did not ignore her promises. She had said she would come, and he had prepared for her—three days ago. Now he could sense her nearing presence, at *last*, but there was another with her, one who fit nothing in his experience. Sharissa had brought someone with her, but who it was defied his abilities. He knew only that the two of them would be within sight of his hut in little more than a minute.

Hardly enough time to prepare himself. The glamour cast three days past had faded.

What goes on here? Gerrod Tezerenee wondered as he pulled the hood of his cloak about his head, carefully assuring that his features would be shadowed. With so little time available, it was possible he might blunder and cast a spell of insufficient strength. It would not do for her to see what had become of him . . . though eventually *all* Vraad might suffer the same fate. How ironic that he should be one of the first.

His eyes on the window facing the southwest—and the city he avoided with a passion—the warlock tried to concentrate. He had to finish before she was too close, lest she notice his conjuring and wonder. Dru Zeree's daughter was far more knowing than she had been when they had first met. Then, she had been a woman in form but a child in mind. Now, Sharissa walked among the Vraad as one to whom those thousands of years her senior paid homage. She was *the* sorceress.

A tiny figure on horseback materialized at the horizon. Gerrod frowned and lost his concentration. A single rider. Sharissa. What she rode upon, however, was like no steed he had ever known. Even from here he could see it was taller than the tallest horse and stronger, the warlock suspected, than any drake.

It dawned on him then that what he felt was the ebony mount. *It* was the source of great power that he had sensed.

The pace the creature set ate swiftly at the distance separating Sharissa from the hut that Gerrod presently called his home. Cursing silently, he forced himself to concentrate again on the glamour. It would be a hurried, confused thing, but it would have to do.

A light wind tickled his face. Gerrod allowed himself a sigh of relief. It was no true wind that had touched him, but rather one that indicated his spell had held. He wore his mask once more.

"Gerrod?" Sharissa was still far away, but she knew that, at this distance, the Tezerenee could hear her with ease.

There was no time to locate a looking glass and inspect his work. He would just have to hope that he had not given himself some horrible disfigurement. That would be bitter irony, indeed.

It was late afternoon, which meant that the sun was more or less behind the newcomers. Gerrod knew he would have to work things so that it was Sharissa and her—*what?*—that had to suffer the sun. He dared not let the light shine too bright upon his visage.

"Gerrod?" The slim figure leaned forward and whispered something to the tall stallion, who *laughed* loud and merrily. Sharissa shook her head and whispered something else.

It was time for him to make his entrance . . . or exit, since he was presently within his hut.

Black cloak billowing around his somber, gray and blue clothing, Gerrod stepped out into the sun, his head bent downward to maximize the shadows he desired. His heavy boots on the rocky soil alerted Sharissa of his presence.

"Gerrod!" Her smile—a *true* smile, not the one formed by the natural curve of her mouth—caused a twinge within him that he pretended to ignore.

"You are late, Mistress Zeree." He had meant to say it as if her tardiness had hardly mattered, but instead it had come out as if he had felt betrayed. Gerrod was pleased that she could not see his face now, for it was surely crimson.

"I'm sorry about that." She dismounted with ease. "I brought you a visitor I think you'll be interested in meeting."

He studied the equine form before him, noting how it was somewhat disproportionate to a normal horse. After that, he nearly stumbled, for the longer he gazed at the beast the more Gerrod felt as if he were being drawn into it. In an effort to escape the sensation, the warlock looked into the creature's eyes—only to find he had made a mistake. The pupilless, ice-blue eyes snared him like a noose, nearly drawing him further to the brink of . . . of a nameless fate he had no desire to explore further.

Blinking, he withdrew deeper into his cloak. There was always safety there. A cloak had spared him the anger of his father more than once while he had still lived among his clan. It would protect him now.

"What is it?" he asked.

"*It?* I am no it! I am Darkhorse, of course!" The stallion pawed at the earth, digging gullies in the hard, rock-filled ground. "Talk to me, not *around* me!"

"Shhh!" Sharissa pleaded to the menacing form. "He was not being insulting, Darkhorse! You should know that by now! He can't be blamed for not understanding what you are, can he?"

"I suppose not." Mollified, the beast ceased his excavation. He trotted a few steps closer to the warlock, who dared to be defiant and not back away, though he desperately wanted to. What *was* this monstrosity?

"Easy," the sorceress suggested to her companion.

"I merely wanted to see him better!" Darkhorse studied Gerrod's darkened visage so thoroughly that the Tezerenee knew the stallion saw through his glamour. "Why do you hide in such shadow?"

"Darkhorse!"

"My own desire, nothing more," Gerrod returned, speaking a bit more sharply than he had wanted. This was not going the way he wanted it to; he had no control over the situation. Between Sharissa's belated appearance and her unbelievable companion, the warlock could not think quickly enough.

"Darkhorse!" The slim woman came between them, guiding her companion back to a more decent distance as she spoke. "What Gerrod chooses to do is up to him; I've warned you about how we Vraad are. We are very much individuals; I thought three days would have shown you that already."

This beast is responsible for her not coming sooner, Gerrod noted. He had assumed as much, but it was a part of his nature that he liked to have things verified for him. It also made Sharissa's absence more forgivable in his mind. What was he compared to the mighty Darkhorse?

As he wondered that, memories concerning the unsettling creature returned to the warlock. Master Zeree had spoken of his unusual companion during his temporary exile from Nimth, an accidental exile due to too much curiosity upon the sorcerer's part. Gerrod had taken some of the elder Zeree's tale as pure embellishment, finding that the concept of a being such as Darkhorse was beyond him at the time.

Not so now. The hooded Tezerenee knew now that, if anything, Dru's story had failed to fully emphasize the astonishing nature of the ebony stallion. Small wonder. He doubted that tale could do justice to what stood before him.

"You apologize to Gerrod," Sharissa was telling Darkhorse. The warlock found that amusing; she treated the leviathan as if he were no more than a child. Yet Darkhorse *did* look contrite.

This creature . . . a child? Gerrod could not believe his own notion.

"I apologize, one called Gerrod!"

"Accepted." It was fortunate that the hood and the glamour hid his expression; the smile on his face would have likely angered both newcomers. *A child!*

"I'd wondered what became of you, Sharissa," the warlock said, seizing control of the conversation now that he had a better idea of what it was he faced. According to Dru Zeree, Darkhorse was an eternal creature, but one that had, it seemed, a very limited experience with things. Gerrod knew how to handle such personalities. "I can see now why you might have forgotten."

She colored, a simple act that somehow pleased him. It was a becoming sight . . . not that *he* cared about such things. His work was all that mattered.

"I'm sorry, Gerrod. I had to make certain that people grew used to Darkhorse as soon as possible, since he intends to remain for some time. The best way was to let him be seen in my company as I moved about the city. Whenever I needed to talk to somebody, I would introduce him to them."

Excuse me, have you met Darkhorse yet? Gerrod found the scene in his mind almost too much for him to handle without laughing. "And how successful were you?"

Sharissa looked less pleased. "Too many of them are distrusting. They think my father will use him as a tool to reorganize the balance of power in our triumvirate."

Her last words darkened the Tezerenee's mood. "My father being one of the chief proponents of that fear?"

"Actually, he has not come to confront Darkhorse yet. Silesti has, however."

What Silesti did was of no concern to Gerrod, but what the warlock's father did was. *You've remained in the background, have you, Father? What, I wonder, are you up to?* The patriarch was not one to sit back during a potentially volatile situation.

"I find that interesting," he finally responded. "Have *any* of my clan made the acquaintance of your friend here?"

"Only Lochivan. The rest of the Tezerenee don't seem interested."

What Lochivan knows, Father knows, Gerrod wanted to say. He knew that Sharissa enjoyed his brother's company, but he also knew that Lochivan was an appendage of Lord Barakas. It would have been impossible to convince the younger Zeree of this fact, however. She saw Lochivan much as she saw Gerrod—Tezerenee by birth but with minds of their own. Not like Reegan or Logan or Esad or any of the others.

"If the rest of the clan shows no interest, it's because my dear sire is *very* interested." He shifted around them, forcing the two to turn in order to face him. Better and better. He nearly had the sun behind him now. Gerrod found himself able to relax a bit more. "Never trust a sleeping drake."

His meaning was clear, but he saw that Sharissa did not take it to heart. "Lord Barakas can scheme all he wants. What could he possibly do to Darkhorse?"

Many things, Gerrod wanted to say, but the ebony stallion cut him off.

"Who is this Lord Barakas? Why should he wish me trouble?"

"Lord Barakas Tezerenee is my father," the warlock explained, his eyes seeing memories. "He is cruel, ambitious, and as deadly as the monster that graces the clan banner."

"This is your parent?" Darkhorse shook his head, sending his pitch-black mane flying back and forth. It *looked* like real hair... "You speak of him with disgust, possibly even *hate*! I do not understand!"

"Gerrod and his father have had differences," Sharissa offered in a diplomatic manner. "Lord Barakas is ambitious, Darkhorse. It would be wise to be careful when you do meet him. I doubt that he can cause any true problem, however. Not one of his people has the skill to match you—or even come close, for that matter—in power."

"I *am* amazing, am I not?"

"I would rather not speak of my father anymore, if you do not mind." The subject had stirred the warlock's insides. He could taste the bile. To Sharissa, he said, "I assume you have finally come to see my discovery. It's hardly as magnificent as I first thought, but there are a few fascinating items you might be interested in studying. It is late to be starting, but we can still—"

The guilty look she flashed at him made Gerrod stop.

"I'm sorry, Gerrod. Actually, I mostly rode out to explain to you why I was gone and how I won't be able to come here for a while."

Anger and a sudden, unreasonable feeling of having been betrayed stirred the hooded Tezerenee's baser instincts. He came within a breath of reaching out with his mind to a source of power she could not know he controlled, one that would allow him to strike out at random with sufficient results to assuage his bitterness.

"Too much is happening right now," Sharissa went on, oblivious to his warring thoughts. "If Darkhorse is to stay among us, he has to be made a familiar sight to the others. There's talk among many of Silesti's faction that my father will use him to put an end to the triumvirate. They think he plans to rule from Sirvak Dragoth as some sort of despot, if you can believe that!"

"*Your* father?" The anger dissipated. How could anyone who knew Dru Zeree believe the sorcerer would ever desire to rule the Vraad? The elder Zeree was nearly as much a hermit as *he* was. He had only agreed to be part of the triumvirate in order to keep Silesti and Barakas from killing one another and the rest of the Vraad in the process.

"Would that be so bad?" the demonic steed asked, his voice booming. "Friend Dru is a remarkable creature! He would only do good for your kind!"

"It was toilsome enough to get them to live with one another, let alone follow another Vraad's commands. Master

Zeree is admired by many, but, in the eyes of our folk, the triumvirate guarantees that no one Vraad's will can be law. We are a very suspicious, individualistic race.''

Darkhorse shook his head again, a habit, Gerrod realized, that signaled the beast's confusion.

''I'll try to explain later,'' Sharissa said. She gave the warlock an apologetic smile. ''I *will* be back . . . and you *could* come to see me once in a while.''

''Perhaps,'' was all he said in reply. They both knew that he would never voluntarily return to the city. That would mean contact with his clan, possibly with his father.

Sighing, Sharissa stepped to the side of her inhuman companion. Darkhorse bent his legs in a manner that would have crippled a true steed and lowered himself so that she could mount. Gerrod saw the creature's back ripple and shape itself to conform to the rider.

''It won't be too long,'' the sorceress added, trying to make the best of things. ''Father can only do so much. He needs my help in all this.''

He said nothing, knowing that any words escaping his lips now would do nothing but weaken their friendship. That might make her decide *never* to return. Then he would be completely isolated from his kind.

''Good-bye, Gerrod.'' Her smile was a bit feeble, possibly because she could not read his shadowed face and, therefore, did not know if he was angry or merely hurt. Sharissa knew how much he looked forward to her visits, and the warlock had assumed that she also looked forward to them. At the moment, he was not so certain anymore.

''Watch yourself,'' the Tezerenee blurted. ''Never trust a sleeping drake, remember?''

''She has nothing to fear while I am near!'' roared Darkhorse. He laughed at his own unintentional rhyme.

''As you say.''

The ebony stallion turned toward the direction of the city, reared, and was already off before Gerrod could even raise a hand in farewell. Sharissa waved back at him for a brief time, but the lightning speed with which the astonishing creature ran forced her to soon abandon that act in favor of further securing her grip on his mane. Within moments, the duo were dwindling dots in the distance. Gerrod had wondered why she had ridden all the way out to him merely to tell him she would not be able to stay, but now he saw that, to Darkhorse, the distance separating the city from his habitat was little more than a short jaunt. Their much slower arrival had been planned; a speeding Darkhorse might have been mistaken for some dire threat.

"So understanding about some things, yet still so naive about others." He hoped she was correct about his father. Barakas was hardly the type to sit calmly while a potential threat such as the ebony terror represented was allowed to roam among the Vraad at will.

Knowing he was now safe, Gerrod removed both the hood encompassing his head and the glamour masking his features. It was good that Sharissa was, to a point, predictable. She had the skill and power to teleport from the city to here, but she would not make use of that ability. Her uneasiness when it came to the spell was what kept his secrets safe from her. As long as Sharissa gave him the time, he could hide what he was becoming and what he had discovered.

She would have been shocked if she had seen his unprotected visage. Even his erstwhile parents would have likely felt some sympathy for his plight, especially as they would soon follow him . . . as *all* Vraad would.

His hair was turning gray, and there were lines gouged into his skin that only age could have wrought. The others had never thought about how their sorcery was what so extended their life spans, but he had found out the truth the hard way. His own experiments, which had taxed his lifeforce further, had turned him into a creature older in appearance than either Dru Zeree or the patriarch. He could have been his own grandfather, the warlock thought in sour humor.

Sharissa would have sought to aid him, but he wanted nothing of her sorcery. He would not give in to this world, become one of its creatures. Gerrod was certain that the Vraad faced either death from old age or, if they surrendered themselves completely to their new home, a worse fate. Dru had told him of how the Seekers and others like them had once had the same ancestors as he. The founders' experiment had altered them, made them monsters. He was no more willing to fall to that fate than he was willing to let the decay of his body take him. Somehow, someway, he would save himself.

Whatever or whoever the cost, he reminded himself as he stared at the empty horizon over which Sharissa and Darkhorse had disappeared.

* * *

"What is the purpose of this?" Rayke wanted to know. He was tired, and when Rayke was tired he grew incredibly irritable. The other elves kept silent, knowing that this was between him and Faunon. It was yet another tiny stab at the latter's authority, which had grown a bit strained of late, what with Faunon's insistence on exploring every hole in the ground, no matter how small.

Faunon, contrary to their belief, would have welcomed interference. Rayke was making *him* irritable. Had they not been told to be thorough? With the bird people in disarray, this was the perfect opportunity to make a better study of the outlying cave systems dotting the southern edges of the mountain range. The one they now stood before had all the marks of once having been used on a regular basis by either the avians or someone else.

"Try to hold your voice down to a mild eruption," he whispered at Rayke. "Unless you are so eager for a fight you are purposely shouting loud enough for every Sheeka in the world to hear."

"At least that would be something more worthy than this poking around holes," the second elf muttered, nevertheless speaking in much quieter tones.

"This will not take long. If this one does not extend into the mountain deep enough, then the others will not, either. If they *do* go farther, then the council will want to know, just in case they decide the time has come to claim the cavern aerie."

Rayke grimaced. "The council would not sanction anything as energetic as a footrace, let alone an assault on even a near-abandoned aerie."

For once, they found common ground. "They would be fools not to take advantage of this. Think of what the birds must have stored in there. Look at what we found just lying scattered about the countryside!"

One of the other elves shook a sack he carried. It was about the size of his head and quite full. The sack represented the party's greatest treasures, the enchanted medallions that the avians generally carried or wore around their throats. The precision and power of such artifacts was legend even among the elves, but there had been few for the race to study, for the bird people guarded them jealously and most were designed to destroy themselves if their wearer perished. These had not. If

Faunon was correct, they had simply been abandoned. Why, he did not know. That was for the council to decide; they enjoyed endless theoretical debate, especially when it meant they could ignore more pressing matters.

Let them play with these while others take up the gauntlet, Faunon thought. *We'll make this world something more than merely a place we ended up. We'll make a future for ourselves!* Deep inside, he knew that he was dreaming. The elves as a race would never organize themselves sufficiently to make a difference in the world they had found. Too many believed that simply existing alongside the animals and plants was all the meaning there was to life. It was simple and it was safe.

"Well? Are we going in, then?" Rayke, now that he had given in to Faunon again, was eager to get things over with.

"Not all of us have to go in. Two or three should be sufficient."

"The two of us, then." It was always Faunon and Rayke. Faunon went because, as leader, he felt he was responsible for everything they did. If he was leading his party into danger, it was only right that he act as the spearhead, so to speak. Rayke, of course, preferred to do anything but sit around and wait. The others, less inclined to act unless they were commanded to, were more than willing to let the duo take the risks. Traveling and exploring were fine for them, but they were now more than willing to head home.

"The two of us," Faunon agreed. Despite their constant arguing, both elves knew they were safest with one another. Each could depend on the other to be at his back if it came to a fight. The rest of the party tended to fight as elves always fought, as a collection of individuals, not a team.

"Give us an hour," he told the others. "If we are not back by then . . ." *If we are not back by then, we will be dead or, worse yet, prisoners of the birds,* he finished in his head. There was no need to tell the others what they already knew.

Rayke had already pulled out a small glow-crystal from one of the pouches on his belt. The tiny crystal worked better than a torch when it came to producing light. Each member of the party had one. Faunon retrieved his own, and the two elves started forward. Rayke already had his sword handy, and Faunon followed suit as they stepped into the cave.

It had definitely been hollowed out by other than natural means, he saw. The walls were too smooth, the floor too flat.

That was both encouraging and worrisome. It meant the tunnel system probably did go where he believed it did, but it also meant that they were more likely to run into trouble if anyone or anything was still using the cave.

There were a few tracks on the ground, mostly those of animals. The spoors were all old, so he did not fear that they would surprise a bear or young drake at some point. If they had, it would have informed him of one fact, that searching the cave was of no use. The avians would never let a wild animal take up residence in one of their active passages.

"We are heading earthward," Rayke commented. The mouth of the cave was already an uncomfortable distance behind them.

Faunon held the glow-crystal before him and verified his companion's words. They *were* heading into the earth. He suspected he had been wrong after all. The birds tended to dig upward, toward the sky they loved so, rather than down. Why would . . . ? He smiled at his own stupidity. "This might not be the birds' work."

"Quel?" Rayke had evidently picked up on the notion at the same time as he had.

"They did control this domain at one time."

"Quel, then."

Both elves grew more relaxed. If this was indeed a Quel-made tunnel, they had little to fear from its builders. The only Quel still active were those existing in the region of the southwestern peninsula . . . *if* they had not suffered the same disaster as the birds had. For all Faunon knew, the Quel had finally passed the way of the previous masters of this world.

Again, he wondered who the new masters of the realm would be. Why could it *not* be the elves? Why did his people sit back and let others rule?

He knew he must have said something out loud, for Rayke turned to him and asked, "What was that?"

"Nothing."

"We are going to be out of sight of the entrance in a moment if we keep heading down and to the left like we are doing."

Faunon saw that it was true. He was tempted to turn back, but decided that they might as well go a little farther. A tiny feeling nagged at his mind, as if he were just sensing the fringe of something. When the elf tried to concentrate on it, however, it almost seemed to pull away to a place just beyond his ability to reach.

The tunnel, he decided, though the explanation did not suit him. *It is all this earth around us.* Tunnels were for dwarves, assuming any still existed, not elves. Elves enjoyed sunshine, trees, and—

"Water!" Rayke snarled, turning the word into an epithet. He had good reason to do so, Faunon thought as he, too, gazed at the sight before them.

The passage dipped farther down...but the rest of it was submerged beneath a vast pool of water as inky as a moonless, starless night. It almost looked as if someone had purposely filled the tunnel up at this point.

"That ends it, Faunon." The other elf started to turn.

"Wait." Faunon was all for departing as well, but he wanted to get a closer look at the pool. With the crystal before him, he stalked over to the edge and knelt. His face and form were reflected back at him, ghoulish parodies of the original. Even this close, he could see nothing beneath the surface. Faunon was tempted to drop the glow-crystal into the pool and watch its descent, but the unreasonable fear that he would disturb something best left not disturbed made him pause.

"You will not see anything! I can tell that from here. Why do you not just—"

Sleek, leathery hands rose from the pool and clawed at Faunon's throat.

"Get back!" Rayke rushed forward, his blade extended toward the water.

Faunon lost his grip on the glow-crystal and it plummeted through the water, momentarily illuminating the world beneath. He saw, for an instant, his attacker, a broad-jawed, amphibious creature built along the lines of an elf. It had round, almost froglike eyes and webbed hands and feet. Without thinking, he thrust with his sword at the water dweller and had some slight satisfaction when the blade bit into one of the creature's arms.

A second blade passed by Faunon's right. The point of Rayke's sword skewered the monstrosity through the neck. It let out a bubbling gasp and shuddered. By now, the crystal was far below. Faunon's attacker became little more than a stirring in the black depths of the pool. Occasionally, the ever-receding speck that was the gem was briefly covered by some part of the thrashing creature's limbs.

At last, the surface of the pool grew still. The body of the would-be attacker did not float to the top, yet another odd thing. The glow-crystal had sunk out of sight, revealing the incredible depth of the tunnel.

"Quel tunnel, definitely," Faunon said, rubbing his neck and thinking about the claws that had almost torn his throat. "But that was a Draka. They serve the birds."

Rayke cleaned the tip of his blade off. "Draka are not generally so bloodthirsty . . . and they are usually cowards more often than not. That one wanted to tear you apart."

Again, Faunon felt as if something was nearby. He knew better than to try to concentrate on identifying it. Better to leave now, before it grew too interested in them. The other elf apparently did not feel whatever it was he did, so perhaps, Faunon hoped, it was just a touch of paranoia or exhaustion.

"Can we go now?"

He nodded to Rayke and stood. A quick wipe cleaned his own blade well enough for now; he would do a more thorough job on it when they were away from here.

"Where to next?" his companion asked as they abandoned the submerged passage.

"South."

"South?" Rayke looked at him wide-eyed.

"That *is* the direction you want to go, is it not?"

"South. Yes, but I thought you . . ."

Faunon took the one last glance back at the pool just before their trek took them around the curve and blocked his view. He thought he saw bubbling at the surface, but he had no desire to go back and investigate further.

"I changed my mind. I think I would like to go home."

The other elf did not press further, which, to Faunon, was a good thing indeed. It meant he would not have to try to explain a growing fear that had no basis other than a simple, nagging sensation in the back of his mind . . . a sensation that he somehow sensed was, like the fearsome stallion, only a precursor for things to come.

VI

As much as she disliked having to tear herself away from Darkhorse, there finally came a point when Sharissa had to return to some of her other duties. She had come to realize that the very night after her unsatisfying visit to Gerrod when, returning to her domicile, the sorceress found petitioners. Their grievances were petty, as far as she could recall, but it had been her idea to take on some of her father's lesser roles in order that he might deal with more important projects. In time, Sharissa hoped to convince him that it would be good if he took on subordinates. Unlike his counterparts, Dru tried to do everything for fear that, if he did not, the balance of power would shift too far to one side. It had almost been impossible to make him give her this much. Not that she had not had enough to do without taking some of *his* work in addition to her own roles.

Like father like daughter? she thought wryly.

The petitioners were dealt with accordingly, but Sharissa soon rediscovered her other projects. One of the few Vraad who worked with her brought up the subject of the system of subterranean chambers existing beneath the city. In some places, the surface level was proving treacherous, for time had weakened the earth here and there and one person had already died when the floor beneath him gave way and he fell to his death. At some point, Sharissa had started organizing a mapping campaign that would seek out the weak areas. It now became evident that those involved had no idea what they were doing when she was not there to supervise them. How, she wondered, had her kind ever survived the crossover? Sometimes the sorceress was amazed that they could even feed themselves.

Darkhorse was gone when she looked for him. The next day, she found he had returned to Sirvak Dragoth, but not before shocking several inhabitants by racing about the city perimeter in the dead of night.

"You can't do that," Sharissa scolded, pacing the length of the chamber where she did her research. It was part of an oval building that had once contained a library, although all the books had crumbled with time. The young Zeree was starting to fill the shelves with notebooks of her own, however, and, with the aid of others, hoped to one day gather a collection as vast as the multitude of mantels indicated the collection of the founders had been. She had once feared that Darkhorse would not be able to maneuver himself through the narrow, winding halls, but Sharissa had forgotten that he only *resembled* a horse. Watching him shift and shape himself accordingly had been a novel if stomach-wrenching experience. "Do you want to undermine what we've accomplished? If you go scaring folk needlessly, they'll fear you all the more! Have you any idea of the image you project?"

The massive, pitch-black steed laughed. His chilling orbs were all aglitter as he voiced his amusement. "A fearsome one, indeed! One fellow dropped to his knees and pledged his loyalty to friend Dru...and all I did was *wink* at him as I passed! Nothing more!"

"Do you want them to fear my father?"

He sobered. "It is not Dru that they fear; it is me!"

"And you represent him."

"I—" The sight of so menacing a creature suddenly struck still by understanding almost made the sorceress forget her annoyance with him. The feeling did not last long, however.

"You have much to learn about the pettiness and suspicious nature of the Vraad, Darkhorse."

He was slow in replying, but what he said surprised her at that moment, though, in retrospect, she would realize that she had seen it coming. "I do not care for the ways of the Vraad very much. They are not like Dru or you. They curse me behind my back, thinking I have ears as weak and foolish as theirs, and call me monster! They do not *try* to understand me, while I have willingly struggled to comprehend all things around me! Nothing I do lessens their fear and distrust! I have acted in all ways I can think of, yet they care no more for me than when I first appeared in the square!"

Darkhorse did something then that Sharissa had never seen him do. He turned his head to the left and blinked. In all the time the sorceress had spent with him, she had never seen the ebony stallion blink. That, however, was nothing compared with what occurred immediately after, for a brilliant glow materialized before the eternal, a glow that expanded in rapid order.

A portal! Darkhorse had not made use of this skill since his stunning arrival, and so it had taken Sharissa a moment to comprehend what it was the eternal was doing. His every movement reminiscent of a frustrated child—the young Zeree recalled herself—Darkhorse gave her no time to react. He was through the magical gateway and away within seconds. She had barely time to call his name before the portal shrank into nothing, leaving her standing alone in the middle of the chamber without a notion as to where he had gone or what he planned to do.

"Serkadion Manee!" Sharissa wanted to throw something against one of the walls, but forced herself to stay where she was until the desire died. Why was nothing easy? Why did everyone have to fight her, no matter how minuscule the reason?

Sharissa waited, but after several minutes passed and the shadow steed did not reappear, she knew it was futile to sit and worry any longer. Darkhorse was predictable in some ways. He would return to the square and then to Sirvak Dragoth. Either that or spend a few hours running wild through the woods and plains—hopefully without spooking anyone else. He had done this once before. Of one thing she was certain: the eternal would not abandon the city, not while his companion of old remained there. He had no one else to turn to and, unless she had misread him, which was possible but not likely, the dweller from the Void desperately craved friendship. It was as if Darkhorse had tasted a fruit long forbidden to him. Had he not, after all, searched world after world for her father after the guardians of the city had exiled him from this place?

Realizing that Darkhorse would return only when Darkhorse chose to, Sharissa returned to her work. There was always so much to do, so much to organize. Ever the first to admit she was very much a reflection of her elder, the sorceress knew that, before long, she would become so engrossed in what she was doing that the day—and, she hoped, the shadow steed's *tantrum*—would pass without her even realizing it.

First on her agenda was the mapping situation, something long overdue and growing even more so each week. That led her to a reconstruction phase recommended by one of the Vraad who assisted her. It had something to do with an expected need to increase food production through farming, she recalled. . . .

* * *

"Lady Sharissa?"

She looked up, blinked several times in rapid succession when it occurred to her that it was getting dark in her chamber, and then frowned when the unsightly figure standing near the hall entrance moved closer. He carried an oil lamp that served more to add an appearance of ghoulishness to his features than it did to illuminate the room. That he had gotten this far meant he had bribed one of her aides. She would have to speak to them in the morning.

"Bethken, isn't it?"

He bowed, somehow keeping the lamp balanced at the same time. "It is, yes, lady. I know it grows late, great lady, but I wondered if I might—"

Trying to hide her disgust, Sharissa waved the robed figure forward. Bethken had once been a stout man—by choice—but fifteen years had taken their toll on his girth. For some reason, though, his skin had never taken a fancy to his new slimness and had, therefore, merely gathered in layer after layer of loose flesh about his person. Bethken looked very much like an old waterskin just emptied. As for his loyalties, he had none. Like many Vraad, he was technically under her father's banner, but that was mostly because the others had never had anything of sufficient value to sway him. No doubt, he had come in the hopes of gaining something of value from her. "What is it you want?"

"First, allow me to offer you light." He put the oil lamp down on one of Sharissa's note sheets, staining it in the process with oil.

The sorceress wanted to scream, but she knew that was bad form. For many Vraad, Bethken's way was as close as they could come to being congenial. It was not supposed to matter to Sharissa that what he seemed more like was a serpent sizing up a tasty field mouse.

In an effort to avoid further damage to her work, either from stains or, worse yet, a flash fire, she took the lamp, placed it on a stand nearby, and said, "My thanks to you, Bethken, but I can provide my own light."

The petitioner stumbled back as the chamber became brilliantly lit by a soft, glowing spot near the ceiling.

"Gods!" The other Vraad looked up, an envious expression blossoming as he admired her handiwork. "If only I could . . ."

"You came to see me for a reason?" She did not care for the

way his eyes grew covetous when he turned his attention back to her. He could see her much better in this light, true, but it was not merely lust for her that she read. Bethken was one of those to whom a loss of power was like stealing the food from his mouth. He hungered for it, and the wonders it could give him. In Sharissa he saw much of what he hungered for.

"It is always glorious to see such skill in these dark times, lady." The man fairly fawned upon her. Any success he might have had, however, was countered by the constant shifting of his loose skin as he talked and moved. "Would that we could return to the days of our greatness."

"I doubt even you would want to return to Nimth now."

"Hardly!" He looked shocked, as if she were mad to even make mention of such a thing.

"Good." Sharissa nodded. "Now, what is it you *want*? I have many things to do."

"The demon; he is not about?"

"Darkhorse is no demon, Bethken, and, as far as your question . . . do you see him here?"

His laughter was forced. "Forgive me, Lady Sharissa. I meant him no insult. It's just that it would be better if he were not here; he might grow heated at some of what I wish to convey to you."

If you ever succeed in conveying it, the sorceress thought wryly. "Go on, please."

Bethken bowed again, sending his folds of skin into renewed jiggling. "You know that Silesti's faction has been vocal concerning their fear of the dem—your companion?"

"Of course."

"I have heard that Silesti thinks to go beyond mere words, that he desires to *remove* the creature."

He was obviously hoping for some sort of dramatic reaction, but Sharissa had no intention of satisfying him. She had heard the rumor already and knew it to be false. Silesti had admitted to Dru that the thought had crossed his mind, but he had decided that it would be a breach of faith to Sharissa's father, whom he respected and, though neither man would admit it, even liked. Silesti trusted Dru, and the elder Zeree trusted the somber, black-suited figure.

"Your news is hardly news to me."

The man looked crestfallen. It was interesting how so many people came to her with what they imagined was important information. Like Bethken, they wanted compensation, of course. To be owed a favor by any of the members of the triumvirate or even someone close to them was a coup indeed.

"He seeks to call a meeting of the triumvirate, at which point he will—" the unsightly man babbled.

"Strike. He'll kill my father and the Lord Tezerenee and chain Darkhorse." *As if chains could hold an entity such as the shadow steed.*

"I thought—"

"You do have my thanks for trying, Bethken. I'm sorry that you went to the trouble of coming all the way here for this. I hope you don't have far to walk."

Her less-than-subtle hint that he had overstayed his welcome mortified the wrinkled figure. He hemmed and hawed for a moment, then bowed once more.

"Perhaps another time, Lady Sharissa. It was no trouble, and I have the satisfaction of retaining a memory of your beauty. That is reward enough. Good night!"

Bethken remained bent over as he backed out of the chamber. It was not until he had vanished from sight that Sharissa recalled his oil lamp. She started to call after him, then decided that he knew by this time that he had forgotten it. Certainly walking about in the dark should have informed him of the fact. If Bethken returned for the lamp, Sharissa would give it back to the horrid man and turn him out again. If he did not, she would have someone return it in the morning.

Her research soon enveloped her in a cocoon of forgetfulness. More than once she had followed in her father's footsteps, sometimes finding the morning sun creeping across the table where she worked. Each time that happened, Sharissa swore she would not do it again.

She finished writing notes about another of her pet projects, a study of the effects on the various individuals who made up the population of the city. Of late, many Vraad had grown more weathered in appearance. She could not bring herself to think of them as old, because then she would have to think of her father dying at some point. Still, it was highly probable that, in abandoning Nimth, the Vraad had lost part of what made them near immortal. Something in the sorcery of Nimth that was missing in this world . . . unless this was some trick of the lands themselves.

Looking up, Sharissa thought, *Could what Gerrod said once*

be true? Could this world be changing us to suit its, the founders', desires? Is that what the Faceless Ones are doing among us?

Almost as if conjured by her thoughts, a shape seemed to move across the entranceway. Sharissa squinted, but the figure, if it *had* been there, was now gone. Thinking of Bethken, she rose and walked carefully toward the outside corridor. At her command, the ball of light floated down from the ceiling and preceded her into the hall. Sharissa glanced left and right, but the corridor was empty.

She had no idea what the hour was, but knew it had to be very late. Returning to her notes, Sharissa started to straighten things away, fully intent on returning to them after a good sleep. Her task had barely begun, however, before her attention was caught by a flickering motion to her side.

It was the oil lamp. The sorceress smiled at the apprehension she had briefly felt touch her. Reaching over, she doused the flame.

Her hands succeeded in preventing her fall to the floor, but only just so.

If someone had asked Sharissa to describe the sensation she had just experienced, the young Zeree might have best put it as the lifting of a veil from her eyes. The night was the same, but it was now part of her existence, not merely a thing in the background.

. . . sa!

"Darkhorse?" She shook her head in order to clear her thoughts further. Had there been a voice in her head, one that reminded the sorceress of the ebony stallion? Sharissa waited, hoping to catch something more. The Vraad had some ability in mindtalk, but this had been no Vraad. She was not even certain there *had* been a voice. Perhaps it had been a stray thought of her overworked mind, but then, what had it concerned? *Sa* was no word she recalled, but it was the last syllable of her own name, and Sharissa had, at that instant, felt an urgency.

The nearest window gave her a view of the center of the city. She strode over to it and peered outside. One of the moons was visible—Hestia, if she recalled—but nothing out of the ordinary was revealed in the dim illumination the harsh mistress of the night offered.

"I'm a tired fool," she muttered, smiling at her own silliness. If Darkhorse had called to her, he would certainly have tried again after having failed to reach her the first time.

The eternal was nothing if not persistent. In fact, it was more likely that he would have materialized before her rather than call to her using the less-than-trustworthy method of mindtalk. For one with the stallion's abilities, it was a simple thing. For the weakened Vraad, it was much, much more difficult. No, Darkhorse had not called her; she could not sense his presence anywhere—

Anywhere? Her mind snapped to full alertness at last.

Sharissa could not sense Darkhorse anywhere. He was in neither the city nor the surrounding countryside. When he had first come to the western shores of this continent, the sorceress had felt him almost at once. She had been the only one, as far as she recalled. If *she* could not find him, then it was certain that no one else could either.

Sirvak Dragoth! He has to be there! Though there was no reason to believe the eternal was in danger, Sharissa had a feeling of foreboding. She knew that he was *not* in Sirvak Dragoth. Even from there, Sharissa had always been able to vaguely detect his odd magical emanations, an apparently natural and ongoing process of the stallion's nebulous "body."

Nothing. It was as if Darkhorse had left the continent. While it was very possible he had, she could not see him leaving in so abrupt a manner, even after his petulant attitude earlier. He would have come to speak to her, to say good-bye. In many ways, the leviathan was very predictable. Sharissa knew him very well after only these past few days. His habits were ingrained to a degree that even the most predictable human could not match.

Her work completely abandoned now, Sharissa pondered what to do next. If her fears were without merit, then she was thrusting herself into a mad, futile chase. If there *was* merit, then what *had* happened to her father's old comrade . . . and did her father know?

The desire for sleep was beginning to nag at her, but it was still only an infant in strength. The longer she delayed, however, the more dominant the demand would become. Sharissa began plotting her move, knowing that her time limit was short; the sorceress had already taxed herself the night before.

It was a shame, Sharissa thought, that she had no hound to follow his trail—providing Darkhorse had even left one. He moved more like the wind, and the only way she had ever been able to keep track of him was by reports from fearful and angry colonists and her own higher senses. Gathering information would take too long, and she had already tried to detect his present position.

The whimsical notion of the hound intruded upon her thoughts again, but it took Sharissa time to understand what it was her subconscious was trying to tell her. What use was a hound when she had no trail, and what did it have to do with her now useless ability to sense where Darkhorse was at this moment?

A hound followed a trail left by its prey, but there was no trail . . . was there?

"Not *physical*, but maybe magical!" she hissed, frustrated at herself for not seeing it sooner. Darkhorse was unique, being a creature whose very substance was akin to pure power given sentience. Yet, both Vraad sorcery and that of this world left a residue of sorts.

Did Darkhorse leave such a trail wherever he went?

She searched with her mind, seeing first the prismatic view of the world, then the lines of force that crisscrossed through everything. That the others who held some degree of power saw only one or the other when they sought to use their abilities always bothered her, for she wondered why she had been singled out. In fifteen years, the sorceress had never been able to train anyone to see the lifeforce of the world as she did.

To her surprise, the trail was clear. So foreign a magic was Darkhorse that he was a blight upon the otherwise colorful and organized landscape Sharissa perceived. Even after nearly a day had passed since his frustrated retreat from her scolding, the memory was still strong.

I didn't see this? It was not so surprising, in retrospect. Did she study her shadow every day? What about the footprints she left in the soil when she went walking in the fields beyond the city? When one was astride so overwhelming a being as Darkhorse, even the world itself faded into the background.

"Sharissa?"

The voice startled her so, coming as it did after so many hours of solitude. Sharissa turned, already knowing who it was who had invaded her chambers. "Lochivan? What do you do here at *this* hour?"

The Tezerenee chuckled and stepped into the light. He carried his helm in the crook of one arm, allowing Sharissa to see the clan features he tended to hide more often than not. In truth, between Gerrod and his brother there was no comparison; Lochivan favored his father's ursine features far too much to be considered

handsome. "I drew a late watch. The patriarch plays no favorites, especially where his own children are concerned. When my
watch was over, I could not sleep. I thought the solitude of the
city would help, so I walked." He shrugged. "I've known of
your habit of staying up till all hours for years now, Sharissa. I
thought you might be awake when you *should* be sleeping. When
I saw the light and your figure outlined in the window at one
point, I knew I was all too correct in my assumption."

She was chagrined; it was true that this was not the first time
he had stopped by. It was only that his timing could not have
been worse... and his presence reminded her of who in the
city would most profit by Darkhorse's disappearance, though
she found it hard to believe that the entire clan could muster the
strength to threaten him.

"Is something wrong?" He had taken her silence to be, in
part, an acceptance of his presence. Lochivan gazed around the
vast room as he joined her, his eyes resting on Bethken's
unwanted gift. His mouth crooked upward at the ends as he put
his helm on the table and examined it.

"A present from someone trying to worm his way into my
favor," she explained, then, realizing she had never answered
his first question, added, "Nothing. Nothing's wrong. I was
just about to retire for the evening."

"What's left of it." Lochivan put the lamp down. "I
probably shouldn't bother you, then. I can come back during
the day."

Despite herself, Sharissa could not help feeling that there
was something amiss with the conversation. She knew what she
was *not* telling Lochivan, but was there something else that he
was not telling her?

"Lochivan, what do you know about Darkhorse?"

His eyes told her she had guessed correctly the reason for his
being here. It had been too coincidental, even recalling his
previous visits.

He said nothing, but there was now a tiny flame, a match or
some minor use of power, at the tip of his index finger. The oil
lamp flickered to life....

Sharissa reread the notes she had taken on the subterranean
mapping project. *Should take care of any worries, she thought.
Now if they'd just do it the way I've described it and let me get
on to something else!*

Looking up from the table, the sorceress had the oddest feeling that something had passed her by, some event she should recall. Considering the many duties she had usurped from her overworked parent, not to mention her own research, Sharissa was not surprised that she might have forgotten something. Her eyes wandered the room in a distracted manner while she tried to think of what it was.

Her gaze came to rest on the oil lamp, which blazed high even after hours of use. The slim sorceress studied it further, finding some doubt in the image before her but at a loss as to explain just exactly what was out of place.

Should she douse it? A part of her saw the needless waste of oil, yet it seemed so unimportant a task, hardly worth rising for. She could always douse it when her work for the night was finished. That was not that long, was it?

Still, when she turned back to her work, her mind refused to leave the lamp to its function. It was as if the simple object was becoming the focal point of her existence.

I'll just douse the flame and put it out of sight. It had to be getting very late if she was so concerned about a simple object. Sharissa started to rise, but then her attention wandered to a page of notes concerning a reconstruction phase that somehow involved future food production. The sorceress sat down and started to read. The plan had merit, but had she not read something similar to it? The more she perused the notes, the more the sorceress wondered at the familiarity of the recommendation.

The parchment fell from her hand. At the bottom of the recommendation was an analysis of the plan—in *her* handwriting and dated this *very* evening!

"Serkadion Manee!" she swore. Small wonder it sounded familiar to her; she recalled now reading it and making the suggestions at the bottom. How could she have forgotten it? Had the night drained her so much?

A shadow on the table flickered, as though living.

Sharissa turned and stared at the lamp—which she knew she had planned to dispose of at some point.

The sorceress rose from her chair with such fury that the glow she had cast to light the chamber grew momentarily into a miniature sunburst and the chair itself went tumbling backward as if seeking to escape her. Sharissa resisted an impulse to return to her work, to begin anew her research that she had abandoned earlier.

The closer she moved to the lamp, the stronger the flame became. The young sorceress found herself slowing more and more. She renewed her efforts instantly, knowing that if she continued to slow at the rate she had been, she would never even come within arm's reach of her goal.

She all but closed her eyes as her fingers neared the flame, for it not only blazed as bright as her own magical light had, but the movements of the fire had a hypnotic effect.

"You've fooled me before! Not again!" she snarled at the innocent-looking lamp.

The flame rose high, almost causing Sharissa to pull her fingers back lest they be burned. Instead, she remembered herself and reached forward to end the battle between the devious trap and herself. "Not good enough!"

Tongues of hungry flame washed over her hand, seeking to blacken and curl her slim fingers before finally reducing them to ash. So it would have been if Sharissa had been any other person. Reflex had made her pull back the first time, but thought had reminded her that she was, after all, one of the most powerful spellcasters among her people. This pathetic thing before her was a clever but not so potent toy whose greatest strength had been its anonymity. Now that she knew the enemy's choice of weapons, there was no difficulty. It had only been the lamp's hypnotic gleam that had stayed her so far.

Her hand came down on the source of the flame and she cupped the mouth, holding her hand over the opening until she was certain she had ended the threat. A simple probe verified that the lamp was once more just a lamp. As long as she did not light it, it could not assault her mind. That was how she had evaded its trickery last time, only to fall victim to it again when—

"Lochivan!"

She knew her anger and her growing exhaustion were making her reckless at a time she should be thinking clearly, but that did not seem to matter the more she thought of the betrayal. Lochivan had always been her good friend, almost as much as Gerrod . . . who *had* warned her that his brother's good company meant nothing when the patriarch gave a command.

"Lochivan, damn you!"

The Tezerenee *did* have Darkhorse. She remembered everything now, including the brief contact between the ebony stallion and herself. True, Sharissa could no longer sense the eternal, but she knew the trail would point to the drakes and their masters. "Lochivan, you and Barakas better pray to your Dragon of the Depths that Darkhorse escapes and gets you first!"

It would mean a spell of teleportation. She had cast such a spell only a few times over the years, her irrational fear that she would end up in some limbo similar to the Void keeping her from performing the spell on a regular basis. Darkhorse needed her aid, however. She could not know if her father had sensed his former companion's danger, and Sharissa did not have the time to seek him out—not in her distraught mind, that is. Each moment that passed, and too many had passed already while she hesitated, made rescuing the shadow steed more and more unlikely.

She raised her arms and took a deep breath. A moment to collect her thoughts and she would be gone.

A disturbing sensation brushed her mind. Something flashed around her neck, making it all but impossible to breathe.

Behind her, a voice, Lochivan's voice, calmly said to another unseen intruder, "Just in time. I told you not to doubt me."

Sharissa's world became a buzzing blur . . . then a shroud of silence and darkness.

VII

"Gerrod."

He looked up at his sudden guest, the enveloping hood masking any surprise he felt at the newcomer's intrusion.

"Master Dru."

In the light that did succeed in invading the hut, Dru Zeree was a fearful sight. Gerrod's eyes narrowed. The sorcerer's hair was going gray, and there were lines across his visage. He was worn out from something, yes, but Gerrod recognized something else, something that those who saw the elder Zeree every day would not pay so much attention to because they themselves were probably suffering a similar fate.

The sorcerer was aging. Not at so great a pace as the Tezerenee was, but aging nonetheless. Gerrod shivered. It was yet another confirmation of his fears about this land. *Still*, the warlock could not help thinking selfishly, *Master Zeree has at least had the luxury of enjoying a healthy life span of a few thousand years or so. Why is it I who is cheated?*

"I need your help, Tezerenee. You know him better than I, and I think you have the ingenuity that will enable you to follow him wherever he has taken her."

The warlock shifted, knowing he looked more like a bundle of cloth than a man. He did not care. The cloak and hood allowed him to withdraw from the world for a time. His few visitors also tended to believe that his appearance was designed to unsettle them. "You might explain a little what that statement is supposed to mean to me."

Dru sighed, trying to remain calm. "Barakas has Sharissa. I'm sure of it."

Despite his best efforts, Gerrod could not prevent himself from jerking to attention. "What do you mean? Does he think he can hold her in his private little kingdom? My sire has always been mad, but not stupid! What's happened? Is it civil war at last?"

His visitor waved him to silence. "Let me . . . let me explain better." Dru visibly collected his thoughts. "At some point probably three days ago, Sharissa and Darkhorse vanished. . . ." He shook his head. "You don't know of Darkhorse, do you? I suppose I have to explain him—"

"I know him. Continue on."

A puzzled look flashed across Dru's visage, vanishing the instant he resumed his tale. "They disappeared. No one noticed until the next day. I should have, but Sharissa often lost herself in projects lasting through the night. As for Darkhorse, the pocket universe supporting Sirvak Dragoth seems to dull my perceptions of his presence. It wasn't until I left the citadel and returned to this world that I noticed his absence. Soon after, people began asking about Sharissa. I found she had ridden out of the city in this direction—"

"She visited me. That was how I knew of your Darkhorse." Gerrod mouthed the words with care, not wanting Sharissa's father to know just how upset he was becoming. The sorcerer might then wonder why this Tezerenee would be so torn over his daughter's disappearance. They were known to be friends, of course, but still . . .

"She returned from that visit. I found that out later on. After questioning a few more trustworthy souls, I learned she was last known to be at work in her chambers. Someone said I should look for a man named Bethken, who had evidently sought Sharissa out for some reason, but I couldn't find him. His quarters were empty. Anything he could have carried was gone."

"You think he's under my father's protection."

Dru took a deep breath. Gerrod knew that the worst was yet to come, and he had to admire the elder Zeree's ability to remain coherent throughout what must surely be an ordeal of the greatest magnitude for him. "I journeyed to the eastern sector of the city, not wanting to believe the patriarch would do something so foolish, but rumors, substantial ones, kept insisting otherwise." The sorcerer shook his head. "I'll not go over what I discovered concerning Darkhorse, save that I think he fell to your clan also. His disappearance . . . *total* disappearance . . ."

He touched his temple, indicating that Darkhorse was beyond even his higher senses. Gerrod had already suspected that. He, too, had noted the absence of the creature upon waking that morning. Not knowing any better, he had merely assumed that Darkhorse had departed on some exploration with Sharissa. It would not have been at all surprising. She hated teleportation, and the phantom steed gave her a way of crossing distances in little time.

Gerrod looked up and saw Dru anxiously waiting for him to digest what had already been told. "And what did my father say about all this? I assume he gave you some imperious speech."

"The sector was empty. They were all gone."

"*What?*" In his shock, the warlock knocked over a sheaf of notes, spilling them on the stone floor he had so carefully constructed for this, his latest abode. He ignored the scattered sheets. "What do you mean? Gone? Preposterous!" Yet, despite his words, Gerrod recalled his own past and how swift the clan could be when it desired to move from one location to another. It was one of many aspects of his father's constant war games, the need to move while the enemy was distracted.

Move over a thousand people during the dead of night? The patriarch would hardly leave his followers behind, not if he was planning a new empire. "Where did they go? East seems likely."

"I can't say for certain. Darkhorse's presence could very well be shielded from me, I suppose." The elder Zeree was tired, so very tired. Gerrod could sympathize, being just as driven in his own way. If anyone knew of his research and the hope and fear some of it stirred inside him, they might be tempted to put an end to the warlock . . . or praise him as a hero to his folk. Gerrod had no desire for either destiny. He was not even comfortable with his great discoveries. They promised death as much as they promised life.

"They must have left *some* trail!" There was something amiss. Something more that the master mage had not yet revealed to him.

He was given the answer almost immediately. "There is a trail, a vague and possibly false one, but I lack the ability to follow it to its conclusion. I told you about my time in the Void and how I finally escaped, didn't I?"

"You are surely not suggesting . . ."

"Darkhorse can open . . . paths . . . into other realms. He did so for me that once." Dru's features relaxed for a moment as his memories surfaced, then, recalling his daughter's predicament, the sorcerer continued. "I may be crazy, but it explains why I can find no trace. I've searched east as far as I dare, but I've known from the start that they didn't head that way. No, I think that perhaps because they held Sharissa, Barakas was able to force Darkhorse to create a path for the Tezerenee to march through—a path I believe must extend, not to anywhere on this continent, but to a domain the patriarch hasn't been able to forget despite the last fifteen years."

"*The Dragonrealm.*" Gerrod said the name his companion could not, the cold tone in his voice much like the tone he might have used greeting his father, the clan master. It was almost too much to accept, but it was so very like the elder Tezerenee to plot such madness and make it work. Paths beyond this world that led to the Dragonrealm. His father, after years of bitter loss, at last having the means by which to build himself a grand empire. The magic of the creature called

Darkhorse doing so easily what, to the warlock, was a feat even the Vraad at their most powerful would have had difficulty in performing.

Sharissa stolen.

"Will you help me?" Dru asked in expectation.

"What is it you want of me?"

"A way to follow them. I know you, of anybody, must have some theory. Silesti and I have more than enough volunteers. This time, the drake and his children will be made to pay!" The sorcerer's hands crackled with power.

Gerrod marveled at the power before him even as he was revolted by it. Each time Sharissa had come to visit him, he could not help thinking how this same power had, under the control of the founders, made creatures like the Seekers from men who had once resembled the Vraad.

"You seem far more capable than I in this matter," he pointed out. "If anyone has the ability, it's you."

The glow faded with an abruptness that made Gerrod blink. Dru put his face in his hands. "I *can't*! Nothing I know is sufficient!"

"Your blank-faced allies—"

"Walk about as if all is right in the world! If I had less faith, I might believe they were, in part, responsible for no one finding out until after it was too late! A thousand souls and who knows how many drakes and other animals . . . and they vanished *overnight*!"

Recalling how their sorcerous servants had acted toward the creature from the Void, in the end exiling him for what was supposed to be forever, the warlock did not doubt that, from the first, the not-people had seen Darkhorse as an agent of chance disturbing their carefully crafted experiment. It was not beyond his imagination to visualize their pleasure at the shadow steed's sudden departure. That Sharissa had also been taken was merely incidental.

Gerrod knew his belief in this was built on his own distaste for the featureless beings, but he cared not a whit. They were, in his eyes, the enemy. It was one of the few opinions he shared with his former clan.

He stared for a time at the one Vraad other than Sharissa he had truly come to admire. Dru ran his hands through his graying hair, the silver streak somehow remaining unmussed throughout the motion. Gerrod realized that Dru had probably not slept since discovering that Sharissa's disappearance coincided with the departure of the Tezerenee. There was even enough worry left over for the monster the mage called friend, although Gerrod was only mildly interested in the ebony stallion's fate. It was Sharissa who mattered.

The warlock came to a decision. It was not one Gerrod liked, but, he admitted, it was the *only* choice he could have ever made. "I may be able to do something. I need five days."

"Five days." There was no life in the master mage's voice when he spoke. Dru Zeree was no doubt thinking what could happen in five days. His daughter might be dead or, as far as Gerrod was secretly concerned, suffering a fate worse than death.

Becoming a Tezerenee through marriage to one of his siblings, likely Reegan.

It was no secret that the patriarch coveted her abilities. He was likely convinced that she would pass her powers down through her children—a possibility to be considered, the warlock admitted to himself. Dru saw Sharissa as only a hostage for Darkhorse's cooperation, which was just as likely. Given time to recover his reason, he would recall the second choice, too. By then, however, Gerrod hoped circumstances would change.

"Five days, yes. I want you to do something for me during that time."

"What?"

Gerrod leaned forward, whispering as if the two of them were being watched . . . and who could say for certain that they were not? "Keep a careful eye on the not-people. Note what they do and do not do. Observe what they observe."

"What is it you expect me to find?" Given a task, Dru Zeree was restored to life. His love for his daughter was a weakness, but Gerrod knew that it could also be strength. Yet, where he himself was concerned, the warlock thought love was fine, but not when it went so deep that it prevented one from thinking straight. He considered himself fortunate that he had never reached such an extreme. Those who cared too much, be it for one of their own blood or even a lover, tended to allow themselves to be drawn into foolhardy predicaments.

"It is too soon to say," he said, finally responding to the other's question. The warlock was sincerely thankful that his visage was more or less obscured from the other Vraad. It would not do for Dru to see his expression at this moment. "Trust me that it's necessary."

"All right."

"There is no more to say, then. Good day to you, Master Zeree." Gerrod turned away and pretended to reorganize his notes. He heard Dru shift for a moment, as if the latter was uncertain how to handle the curt dismissal. Gerrod continued to play with the sheets until the silence had stretched more than a minute. At last, with a casual air, he turned back to where Dru had stood. The sorcerer was nowhere to be seen. The warlock shook his head. For all his ability, Dru Zeree was helpless without Gerrod's aid. Under other circumstances, it might even have been comical.

Rising, he began to search among his few belongings for a box he had stolen, unbeknownst to either Zeree, from their citadel back in Nimth. Master Zeree might realize that the request for five days was a ploy, although the warlock doubted that. It was best to begin now, however, on the off chance that the sorcerer *might* return early for another reason. If so, Dru would find that Gerrod had exaggerated a bit about the time he needed for preparations. Not five days, but rather five *minutes*. Five minutes or not at all . . . if he succeeded in finding the box he sought.

Gerrod pulled aside a ragged bit of cloth that had once been a bag and stared down at his prize. He picked up the box gently and carried it over to the floor, opening it even as he knelt.

The warlock mouthed a few nonsensical syllables as he surveyed the contents, the sounds acting as a memory trigger that slowly began awakening the power that slumbered within him. From the box, he picked out a single perfect crystal, a prize from Dru Zeree's lost collection. *You will do for a focus, I think.* What, he wondered, would the other Vraad do if they knew that he had recaptured some of what they had lost in crossing over? What would they offer him for a return to at least a shadow of their glory days, their days of godhood?

What would they offer him for the chance to truly call upon Vraad sorcery without draining their own lifeforce?

Nothing he *wanted*.

His nose began to itch. Gerrod sniffed the air. If he closed his eyes, he could almost imagine he had returned to Nimth. The same sweet, decaying smell permeated everything. It was always so when he dared to awaken the link he had wrought.

The seemingly impenetrable barrier that the founders' sorcerous servants had placed around Nimth had finally given in to his onslaught, albeit at great cost. Gerrod could now draw strength from the world of his birth and use it in this one rather than burn away his own lifeforce as his brethren did. However, there were limits. Even though he had breached the barrier, the warlock could not widen it. He had tried more than once, risking the contamination that Vraad sorcery spread in small doses over his new homeland . . . and himself. Perhaps it was even some subconscious hesitation on his own part that made him fail to open the breach further; he could not say.

Still, it was not enough. With time, he suspected he could extend his life span, but not truly give himself the immortality he had come to desire. There had to be another way.

What if one could bind the sorceries of the two realms together . . . ? Gerrod found himself abruptly wondering. He swore at himself and forced such dangerous notions from his mind. He would save Sharissa and the creature Darkhorse and that would be the end of it. His other goals, his dreams, would have to wait for a different solution. To touch upon the lifeforce of this domain would be tantamount to surrendering to it the way the others were, one by one. It would also open him to a fate worse than dying—becoming a monster like the Seekers.

The Tezerenee knew he was stalling, that he was, deep inside, afraid to take the final steps.

"Sharissa." His own blood held her prisoner. The lord drake and his children. His father. His father had Sharissa.

Gerrod slammed the crystal onto the floor, knowing it would take harsher treatment than that to crack the artifact. Afraid he might be, but he would hold back no longer. If nothing else, the warlock would go through with the rescue, not just for the sake of the woman, but to shatter the arrogant dreams of his former people . . . and especially his not-so-dear father.

He smiled as he thought the last.

"That was not there when we came this way," Rayke commented.

"Yes, I think I would have noticed it," Faunon retorted. He reprimanded himself immediately after, knowing that Rayke's statement was born of uncertainty, possibly even a little fear. Faunon could not blame him or any of the others for that fear; his own rash reply had sprung from the same emotion.

"Where did it come from?" one of the others asked. The elfin leader was certain each and every member of the party had asked the same question over the last hour.

Well? he asked himself. *Where did it come from?*

They peered through the woods at the huge stone citadel, a masterful yet oppressive piece of building. It looked massive enough to house a few thousand folk, and its principal tower rose so high into the air that Faunon almost wondered if it overlooked some of the lesser mountain peaks. He knew the last was only a trick of the eye, but still . . .

"No elf ever built something like that! No Seeker, either!" Rayke's hand squeezed the grip of his sword.

"Not in only a few days' time."

"Look there!" whispered a younger elf to Faunon's right.

A drake rose into the sky. The elves shunned the creatures out of principle; they were ill-tempered monsters who tended to try to take bites out of anything that moved. Drake meat was not all that tasty, either. It was not the beast that caught their attention, however, but what journeyed *with* the draconian horror.

"Someone *rides* it!" Rayke blurted. His eyes grew large. Faunon stared in wonder at the rider. It was roughly the size of an elf, though much more massive. The dark green armor it wore blended with the skin of the drake, making the two almost seem like one. A ferocious helm that mirrored the toothy visage of the mount obscured the rider's features. Faunon was not even certain the newcomer resembled anything approaching elf. While it appeared to be shaped akin to the members of the expedition, the same could have been said of the avians or the Quel.

"There is another one!" someone else whispered.

"More than one," Faunon corrected. Behind the second duo came a third and a fourth. "It is a patrol."

"We should leave here, Faunon!"

"They might find us any moment—"

"Be silent!" Rayke hissed. "Lest you help them find us all the sooner!" Faunon's second turned to him. "What do you say? Do we leave or do we risk it longer? This must certainly be of interest to the elders!"

"But not at the cost of our own lives. We should move farther back and to the west. We will find thicker cover there, but a much better view."

The party took heart from his rapid decision. Faunon hoped they felt calmer than he did. This was hardly what he had expected. When he had asked himself who would be the future rulers of this domain, he had hardly expected the answer so soon. It was very obvious that these newcomers had arrived with the intention of conquering themselves an empire. Sooner or later, they would cross paths with the elves. It behooved the party to discover what they could of these potential—*potential? . . . certain!*—adversaries.

Moving with a silence that would have done them proud even among their own kind, the elves abandoned their position. A good thing, too, Faunon saw. The route the flyers were taking would soon bring them too near the elves' former location. Had the group stayed where they were, the patrol would have seen them from the sky.

Against aerial combatants, Faunon knew his men had no chance. It would take more than a few arrows to pierce the hides of the drakes and, judging by the skill with which the armored figures controlled their beasts, trying for an eye or mouth would be nearly impossible. The newcomers did not wear their armor purely for show; they moved like warriors born.

Time passed far more quickly than the elfin leader would have preferred. He glanced back and saw that the drakes had not yet reached the abandoned position. That struck him as a little odd. Their pattern of flight should have brought them over the wooded area by this time. It was that danger that had made moving quickly so critical.

Rayke came up beside him, trying to make out whatever it was that disturbed his companion. "What is it? Have they seen us?"

"It could be nothing. . . ."

They heard a faint crackling in the woods to the east. To Faunon, it sounded like a death knell . . . for all of them.

"Ready yourselves!" he whispered. "They are coming for us!"

More than a dozen toothy monstrosities, each carrying one of the armored figures, burst through the woods not more than a breath or two after his warning. That was time enough for the elves, however. Arrows flew from those who had carried bows, striking at the forerunners. Each struck a vital part of some rider's body, but, unfortunately, the armor proved too strong.

Even tinged with elfin magic, the shafts only bounced off, save one lucky strike that went through one of the eye holes of the nearest rider. The figure fell backward, dead in that same instant, but his stirrups would not allow him to fall off and so he bobbed up and down like some macabre puppet while his mount kept pace with its brethren.

"Archers! Mounts first!" Faunon knew the riding drakes could not be maneuvered so well this close. The trees and bushes worked to his advantage for the moment, but soon the drakes would be close enough to make use of their talons and teeth. He wanted them dead before that.

Though the results were, for the moment, unseen and unfelt, a second battle had also progressed. Elfin magic met a sorcery that felt so vile, so self-destructive, that Faunon wondered what sort of creatures they fought. He had hoped his men would have an advantage there, but such was not to be. At the moment, the two warring magics were at a stalemate, though how long that would last was anybody's guess. Faunon suspected the tide would *not* be turning in the elves' favor. Already he could feel the strain on his mind, and he was only shielding, not attacking, with his somewhat lesser sorcerous ability.

The riders were being forced to spread their line because of the trees. An arrow burst the eye of one drake, causing the draconian horror to halt in its charge and seek in vain to remove the cause of its pain. The rider struggled for control.

We have a chance! Faunon thought as he readied himself for the first attacker.

He heard the beating of wings above him and knew they did not belong to the Sheekas.

The aerial patrol had known their position all the time. "We have been tricked!" With a sinking feeling, Faunon watched the drakes descend even as those on the ground continued to surge forward. Of the dozen who had burst through the trees, two were dead. Nine riders still lived, but four of them were on foot. Perhaps if his men broke for the thicker foliage, they might be able to regroup and make a better stand there—

"Faunon! Watch your back!"

The voice was Rayke's. Faunon rolled to one side and heard a *whoosh!* as one of the flying drakes soared upward again, its wicked claws thankfully empty.

Another elf was not so lucky. One of the archers, paying too much attention to the armored figures darting in and out of the trees, did not notice the diving horror until he was plucked from the ground. The hapless victim had only time for a short scream before the drake took his head in its massive maw and *bit* down.

Faunon turned away, wanting then to heave the contents of his stomach out. He fought the nauseating feeling, but only because he knew others might suffer while he was giving in to his lesser emotions. Better to turn those emotions to energy.

Watching the sky for any other threats, he moved into the trees to his right. The battle on the ground had been joined, with three of the attackers taking on their elfin counterparts in hand-to-hand. Riders on drakes rushed back and forth, chasing after elusive prey. Faunon's men knew what he also knew but could not acknowledge. They would *die* here. Outnumbered and outflanked, they would perish to a man, but not before taking out as many of the newcomers as possible. That was what the elfin leader planned, also.

The drake riders above had forgotten him in the chaos, his one attacker perhaps thinking his mount had slashed the elf to death even though it had not succeeded in grasping him. Whatever the case, Faunon was going to use his anonymity to his best advantage. If he could get behind the armored foes, he could come up on them one at a time and take them down until someone finally noticed him. It was not the most admirable way to fight, but Faunon had always been a pragmatist.

A drake came bounding toward his hiding place, but its rider was nowhere to be seen. Faunon held his sword ready, hoping he would not have to waste himself on the leviathan. Providing it did not kill him, the noise would certainly alert the enemy.

Fortunately, the wind was Faunon's ally and the creature itself seemed more interested in flight than battle. Faunon saw why: one of its eyes was closed and bloody, and it was bleeding profusely from a neck wound. Part of the elfin blade that had performed what would be, in a matter of minutes, the killing stroke, still remained lodged in the wound. That meant its owner was probably dead. He hoped the unknown elf had at least killed the monster's master.

He followed the bleeding drake's path until it was safely away, started to turn his attention back to the task at hand, and then returned his gaze quickly to where the beast had vanished.

Barely visible among the trees was a trio of riders clad akin to the attacking force. These, however, sat and watched with a confidence that marked them as the leaders. One, as massive as any bear the elf had ever come across, even wore a crimson cloak. He and the others seemed to be watching the pitched battle with mild interest, nothing more.

Faunon decided to change his choice of targets.

The sounds of battle were beginning to die behind him as he made his way to the threesome. That meant the others were either dead or captured. Faunon was ashamed with himself for leaving them, even if it had been to try to inflict worse damage on their adversaries. Still, there was little he could have done once the airdrakes had joined the battle, and now he had a clear opportunity to deprive the invaders of hopefully one or more leaders. It was possible that these riders meant little in the hierarchy of their people, but it would make some of their kind a bit more wary of simply going out and slaughtering elves if they knew that they, too, were at risk.

"Get out of there!" someone barked.

Faunon jerked to a halt, thinking he had been discovered. A second later, a warrior on foot appeared, the sword in his left hand being used to prod the wounded drake ahead of him. They were moving in the same general direction as the elf. He held his breath and waited. Neither seemed particularly inclined to attentiveness, which was his only hope. It did lessen his chances of success, however. He wondered if there were more warriors lurking in the woods around him and if he could avoid them long enough to at least take one of the patrol leaders down.

The drake had stopped and was sniffing the air. The armored figure poked at it with his weapon. "Move or you'll rot right here! Dragon's blood, you're a stupid one!"

A chill ran down Faunon's spine as the drake turned and began to sniff the air in the elf's direction.

The wind had started to change.

Unmindful of its cursing warden, the wounded animal started back. The elf readied his sword and, as an afterthought, tried to prepare a spell. While his higher senses were acute, his practical abilities were less than most of his kind. It was why he could only shield himself with sorcery during a battle. Some, like Rayke, could do battle on both the magical and physical planes, and at the same time.

Slowing, the drake sniffed again. It was only a few yards

away now. The armored guide joined it and tapped the beast's side with the sword one more time. "Turn around!"

The drake swayed, its injuries draining more and more of its energy, but it would not turn. It hissed at the trees shielding Faunon from the sight of the warrior.

"Is there . . ." The armored figure grew silent, then studied the area that so interested the drake. Faunon knew his luck had run out.

"Lord Reegan! There's one of them he—" The warning was cut off as the elf burst from his hiding place and jumped his discoverer. Raising his sword, the warrior tried to defend himself, but, not apparently expecting the reflexes of an elf, moved too slowly. Faunon pushed the blade aside and thrust at the place where the helm and the breastplate met. Unlike Rayke's successful strike at the Draka, the elfin leader was unable to put the point of his weapon through his opponent's throat. The blade cut a crimson trail across the one side of the warrior's neck.

"Kill!" the armored figure shouted, his breath coming in gasps. He backed away, hands clutching at the wound and his helm, which had been shoved upward and was obscuring his vision.

Faunon had no time to finish him, for the drake, though dying, was still a deadly foe. It snapped at him, trying to avoid its handler as it shifted for better position. The elf jumped away, trying to keep close to the wounded warrior, who had, to the former's surprise, fallen to his knees.

Somewhere, he knew, the three riders were converging on him, but he dared not take his eyes from his present predicament. The drake clawed at him, but weakness made it come up just short. Faunon tried to impale its one good eye, but the drake, perhaps having learned from the loss of the other eye, shied.

No longer needing to fear discovery, the elf unleashed a spell. It was a haphazard one, his first having been lost at some point in the battle, but he thought it might give him the precious seconds he needed.

A voice, coming from an invisible source behind the drake, commanded, "Back! Away from him! Now!"

The reptilian menace halted and sniffed the air. It was puzzled and uncertain.

"Back, I said!" The voice was that of the warrior whom

Faunon had wounded. The warrior himself lay sprawled on the ground, blood over half his armor. Confused, the drake hissed at the world in general and remained where it was. Its limited mind could not comprehend that the tiny creature before it was playing it for a fool. The mimic spell that Faunon had cast was one he had used on occasion in the past to success. He carefully raised his sword, ready to try one last strike should the drake disobey the voice, as it had before, and charge the elf.

Panting, the wounded beast started to turn. Faunon began to slip back into the woods, hoping he still had a moment or two before the others came for him.

He screamed as a mind-numbing pain shot through his right side. Looking down, he saw an arrow protruding from his thigh.

"Well?" asked a gruff, disappointed voice. "Why don't you finish it off?"

"The drake or the elf?" countered another. There was a convivial tone to this one's voice, as if he might be as willing to offer Faunon a drink as he might be to kill him.

"What do we need the elf for?"

"Father will want him. You know he said he wanted a captive."

Faunon's entire body throbbed. He heard the sound of drakes trotting and looked up at his captors. It was, of course, the trio that he had been trying for before the wounded beast had given him away. The massive figure with the crimson cape was looking at a thinner warrior to his right who carried in one hand a bow. Behind both of them came the third. He evidently had a lesser place in the hierarchy, for his posture was that of one who is among his betters only by sufferance. All three still wore their helms. With all that had happened, Faunon still did not know what they looked like.

"We have that other one," rumbled the bear.

"He will be dead before long, Reegan. I only wounded this one so he could not run. He should satisfy Father."

The one called Reegan turned to the third member of their party and pointed at the limp, armored form by the weary drake. "See to him."

Faunon was beginning to feel neglected. Had they forgotten he still had a sword? He held it before him, daring the one who had dismounted to come closer.

The calm rider shook his head. "Put that down. It will not do you any good."

"Come to me and see!"

"I think . . . *damn!*" Reaching up, the armored figure took hold of his dragoncrested helm and removed it. Faunon saw a pale visage that, if it struggled, might be called handsome in a poorly lit chamber. He studied the ears. Unlike an elf's, they were rounded.

The eyes were the most disturbing feature. They were crystalline. He had never heard of such a thing. Beautiful but cold. Round where the elfin orbs were almond-shaped.

Could they be . . .

"Bothering you again, Lochivan?" the ursine rider asked. For the first time, Faunon noticed how that one's helm had been designed so as to allow the heavy beard to flow free.

Lochivan was scratching at his neck. "I must be allergic to something here! It's been worse since we crossed!"

The third rider, who had been inspecting the warrior sprawled in the grass, called out, "He's dead. Blade severed the artery in his neck."

"A good strike," Reegan complimented. "Let me see your weapon."

"You don't think—" A force that nearly tore his fingers off yanked the long, narrow sword from his grasp. It went spiraling through the air, at last landing perfectly in the left hand of the massive warrior. Reegan turned and nodded to his companion, as if proud of what he had just accomplished.

"I told you. The power has returned to us. I don't know how or why, but it has." Lochivan had ceased his scratching. A vivid red mark covered his neck. He smiled slightly at the wounded elf, who was starting to sink to the ground from a combination of exhaustion, pain, and simple frustration. "Reegan is very fond of weapons," he explained companionably. "More so than most Tezerenee."

"Is that what you are . . . Tezerenee?" It was not a name familiar to Faunon, yet it filled him with relief. Their bearing, their arrogance, had reminded him of something else, some fearsome demon from stories that his mother had told him.

"We were born to the Tezerenee, the clan of the dragon," Lochivan offered. He replaced his helm, and Faunon, studying it, could not help but be drawn by the eyes of the dragon. They matched those of the man who wore the helm. Lochivan indicated Reegan. "My brother and I. These others, they are Tezerenee by adoption; that is why they fight with less skill. All of us, however, are known together as the *Vraad*." The warrior cocked his head in what might have been actual curiosity. "Being an elf, I thought you might have heard of us."

Faunon pressed himself against the tree that was still, at least in theory, supporting him. He stared without hope at the two mounted riders.

"I think we can take that for a positive response," Lochivan finally said. He glanced at the warrior standing ready by the corpse of his fellow.

"Bind him and drag him back to the citadel."

VIII

"You see, demon? I keep my promises. You've done what I've asked and I've woken her. I hardly need to have done that, you know."

Sharissa's soul swam in a sea of emptiness. The voices were all she had to latch on to, and they had, until now, seemed so very, very far away. Now, however, she found herself moving toward them with ease.

"I see that you like to give freely what is not yours to give, what actually belongs to the one you claim to give it to! That is what I see!"

They were familiar voices and, though she did not care for one of them, they promised light where she could only recall darkness.

"Do not bestir yourself, demon. The bonds that hold you have not weakened in the slightest. I would rather have your willing cooperation than this need for pain."

Closer. Sharissa knew she had almost found the light.

One of the voices shrieked in unbridled agony. Her flight slowed as she sought some way to give solace to the one in pain. There was nothing Sharissa could do, however. She knew she would have to wait until she was back in the light.

The shriek died down into silence. Then, just as she feared she would become lost again, the first voice spoke. Its tone was smooth and, despite the sympathetic words, mocking. "You force me to do things I would rather not do, demon. *You* are the one causing yourself pain."

"Darkhorse?" Sharissa could not yet see, could not even sense her very body, but memory, at least, was returning. At the moment, it seemed the most precious thing she possessed.

"That should be enough to satisfy you. Now, back where you belong."

"The Void swallow you, Lord Bara—"

"Darkhorse?" Sharissa struggled to open her eyes. Memories of the attack returned. She had been a fool. Something in the spell of the lamp had alerted the Tezerenee to the fact that she had freed herself a second time. It was a simple spell, one well within the ability of many Vraad, and she had not thought of it.

Why the lamp, though? Why cloud her perceptions if they planned to take her?

"Are you feeling ill at all?" Barakas Tezerenee asked from the darkness.

A dim crack of light sliced its way through the endless black void. As the sorceress struggled, it grew into a band of murky shapes and movements. "Darkhorse, where—"

"Shh! Take it slow, Lady Sharissa. You've been asleep for over three days. That deep a slumber turns the body numb. It takes time for the blood to regain momentum."

"Barakas." She turned the name into a curse. "What have you done to Darkhorse? To me?" Sharissa regained a vague sense of her body. She tried to move her hands, but was unable to tell if there were any positive results.

"You will come to understand, my lady. Before long, you will even stand in the forefront of our destiny."

"The Faceless Ones take your speechmaking!" she shouted, putting all her renewed energy into her response. To her dismay, she almost found herself sinking back into the darkness because of her anger.

"I *warned* you to take it slow. You'll likely have a rampaging headache because of your tirade."

Sharissa tried to draw upon the lifeforce of the world, only to find a wall within herself that would not permit even the least of spells. It was a mental block, as if each time she sought to do something, her concentration slipped just enough to make her attempt fail.

Something wrapping around her throat . . .

"What did you do to me, Barakas?"

His form—it could only be *his* form—grew larger, nearly filling her limited field of vision. He could be no more than a yard away, yet the patriarch would still not come into focus. "Merely something to keep you from reacting without thought. This is something that should be talked out after you've had an opportunity to see what we've accomplished, what we intend."

"My father won't stand for this, Barakas! Neither will Silesti! Between the two of them, they have the numbers to overwhelm your pathetic little army."

Her body was nearly her own again, though, at the moment, that seemed no great victory. Every muscle screamed agony, not surprising since she had not moved in three days. With an effort, the sorceress reached for her throat.

"It won't come off unless I wish it."

"You expect me to follow you in anything when you treat me like this? What have you done to Darkhorse? I thought I heard—"

"He will recover. He left me no choice. Perhaps *you* will be able to convince him of the correct way of things once you've had a chance to taste our harvest."

The huge armored figure was slowly coalescing into something with distinct features. Sharissa, struggling, was able to raise herself enough so that she could rest on her elbows. It allowed her to focus her gaze better on the patriarch's own crystalline eyes. "You are waxing poetic, Lord Tezerenee, but all the pretty words and familiar speech won't convince me of anything other than the fact that you are not to be trusted." She gritted her teeth, knowing how her next words would probably affect him. "You, patriarch, have no concept of honor whatsoever. I'd rather believe that the smile of a drake has nothing to do with its hunger than believe one promise of yours."

The back of his hand caught her squarely on the right side of her face. Sharissa rolled onto her side, panting and bleeding, but also satisfied with the reaction. She was also thankful the patriarch had not been wearing his gauntlets.

Turning back to her "host," she displayed the marks of his anger. "As I said, no concept of honor."

Barakas was gazing at his hand, as if it had betrayed him. He looked up, studied her damaged face, and frowned.

"My deepest apologies, Lady Zeree. I have not slept since you forced yourself upon us. I will have someone take care of your injury and, at the same time, bring you something to eat. Tomorrow, after we have both rested, I will show you my world." With no more farewell than that, the patriarch turned quickly and stalked toward a doorway that was only now visible to the recovering sorceress.

"Barakas! If you think I plan on merely waiting here..." Sharissa rose, her legs unsteady, and took a step after the dragonlord, who was already in the outer corridor.

One hand on the door, Barakas took one last look at the young Zeree...and slammed the thick wooden door shut. Sharissa heard the sound of a key turning in a lock and swore under her breath. "Barakas!"

She put a tentative hand on the door and pushed. It would not give. Sharissa had known it would not, but had felt compelled to try anyway.

"Damn you, Tezerenee!" Her legs began to buckle. Utilizing what strength she had left to her, the sorceress stumbled back over to the simple bed that was, she now saw, the only piece of furniture in the chamber aside from a single chair in one corner. Her legs gave out just as she crawled onto the bed.

Sharissa rolled onto her back and scanned her surroundings. A narrow slit near the ceiling allowed only minimal sunlight in. One torch provided the rest of the illumination, not that the gray, spartan chamber offered any visual attractions.

Three days! Where was her father? Where were the other Vraad? Barakas had at last broken the tenuous peace that had existed since the creation of the triumvirate. Was there an army even now surrounding the eastern sector of the Vraad city? If so, why could she not hear anything?

Memories of the impassioned voice of the dark eternal returned to her. Barakas Tezerenee had forced him to aid the clan's cause. In what way? Her heart beat faster. Had Darkhorse turned the others away? Was her father dead? Did Barakas rule now?

Her questions, her very thoughts, began to fragment as the beating of her heart was echoed in her head. Sharissa put a hand to her temple and tried in vain to ease the pounding. Nothing helped. The sorceress did not even have power enough to rid herself of the headache. For that, too, she cursed the Lord Barakas Tezerenee.

When sleep at last claimed her again, she welcomed it with open arms.

"Sharissa?"

It was a female voice that tore her from the bliss of true, unforced slumber, and at first she thought it was someone else. "Mother?"

"No, Sharissa, only Lady Alcia."

Her eyes snapped open. The striking warrior queen sat beside her, a bowl of food in one hand. Behind the matriarch stood two female Tezerenee in full battle readiness. Whether they were daughters of the lady or merely clan sisters, Sharissa neither knew nor cared. Only one woman truly held importance in the clan of the dragon, and that was the patriarch's bride. "He fears to face me again?"

Alcia smiled, a surprisingly soft expression for so commanding a visage. "He still sleeps. I thought it would be better if I spent some time with you first and tried to answer some of your questions."

"Good! Where is my father? Where is this place? What do you think—"

Her visitor held up a warning hand. "Not yet. I will answer questions, but only after you have eaten, young one. And do not try to ask me questions while you eat, either. You will get nothing more from me until this bowl is empty. Do you understand?"

Mention of food and the relentless smell rising from the bowl forced Sharissa into surrender. She gratefully took the bowl and spoon from the Lady Tezerenee and started in on the contents. It was a stew of some sort, filled with meat and vegetables and seasoned to perfection.

Watching her eat, Lady Alcia looked almost like a doting mother. "I am so *very* glad you enjoy it. I made it myself, but I've rarely had someone from outside who could tell me if I've succeeded with it. Tezerenee make terrible critics. They will eat anything, even if only to prove they could live off moss, if necessary."

The last brought a brief smile from Sharissa. She often

forgot that the ruling mistress of the clan had been born an outsider and that much of the blood of the clan could be traced to her. "It is good. Thank you."

"Not at all. Please keep eating. You will find it will strengthen you."

It was true. Though this was not enough to satiate her, Sharissa at least felt well enough to move. Her headache had also receded, though enough of it remained to remind her of what she had experienced earlier.

"How long did I sleep this time?" she dared to ask after swallowing her latest mouthful.

"Only a few hours. It was just after dawn when you were disturbed the first time. The sun is now directly overhead. No more questions until you finish. I mean that."

The remaining contents of the bowl vanished in quick fashion. Though she had gulped much of it down in order to ask some of the many questions that burned within her, Sharissa could not help feeling disappointed, too. She wanted more—at least another bowl.

"That is all." Alcia took the bowl and spoon from her and put it aside. "You have to ease your hunger gradually, or else you are liable to make yourself sick. You can eat in a little while, after your stomach has settled again."

Now that the time had come, Sharissa's anger rekindled itself. She recalled again the patriarch's temper and the voice of Darkhorse. The voice and the *pain*. "Where's Darkhorse?"

"He's been put away for now." Lady Alcia's tone reminded Sharissa of Lochivan's friendly manner of speech. The young sorceress was suddenly reminded of the fact that, while it was true the woman before her had been born an outsider, she had spent countless centuries as the bride of the dragonlord and the mother of most of his arrogant children. Sharissa could no more trust her visitor than she could Lochivan.

"What does that mean?"

Rising, the Lady Tezerenee took hold of Sharissa's arm and guided her up. Rest and food were already working their wonders. The sorceress found she could walk with only the slightest difficulty. *Something else in the food besides meat and vegetables,* she decided.

Sharissa had not forgotten her question. She repeated it the moment she was certain her legs would not collapse.

The matriarch sighed. "That is something Barakas or Lochivan could explain better—"

"Lochivan!" Sharissa spat on the floor. "If he comes within sight of me—"

"He lives to serve his father," Alcia said, taking her charge by the shoulders and massaging some of the muscles. "Would *you* do any different?"

"My father is a good man!"

"By your standards. Tezerenee have different standards. Most Vraad have different standards. You look fit enough for a walk, I think." As she said the last, the Lady Tezerenee snapped her fingers. One of her shadows stepped to the door and opened it. The other moved until she stood behind her mistress and the outsider. Sharissa was reminded of lithe hunting wyverns as she observed their movements. These were women born to the clan, not adopted like many newer Tezerenee. Barakas had allowed newcomers to swell his ranks over the last decade and a half, but evidently still reserved the most vital roles for those of his blood. Guarding his mate was likely a position open only to the most skilled.

"What about my questions? You said you'd answer them."

"Some of them will answer themselves when we get outside. At the very least, showing you what my husband has achieved will aid any explanation. You *should* get some walking in, too. Judging by your back, I would have to say that every muscle in your body needs to be loosened. Come along."

With Lady Alcia guiding her, Sharissa made her way to the corridor. Each step seemed easier than the last. "You seem to have a *magical* touch when it comes to cooking, my lady."

Her regal companion smiled politely. "It is a wonder what one can do with the proper ingredients and skills."

They spoke no more for quite some time, Sharissa, knowing she would receive no useful answers from her host, being satisfied with inspecting the domicile of the clan. She found the endless gray corridors and windowless chambers disturbing, their appearance more reminiscent of the unsightly citadel the Tezerenee had abandoned back in Nimth. Yet, these had to be some of the deeper levels in the eastern sector, didn't they? Where else could Barakas bring her? Had he spent the last fifteen years so greatly redesigning his tiny domain into a miniature version of the one he had lost? It seemed a futile and outrageous project even for the patriarch.

More and more she felt as if she were back in mad Nimth. The dragon banner hung on every wall. Armored warriors, male and female, stood guard everywhere. A drake patrol, the two beasts straining at their leashes, passed them just before they reached a staircase leading *downward*. Sharissa lost all interest in the toothy hunters as she paused to stare at the steps. The sorceress had come to assume that she was in some lower level, possibly beneath the surface, but this staircase spiraled down at what first appeared to be forever.

"We have five levels to descend to the surface. Is that too much for you? Do you feel weak?" Alcia put a hand on her shoulder, but Sharissa was not taken in by the concern. If the matriarch had thought it would serve her people's interests, she would have been just as willing to *push* her down the steps.

"I can make it." There was no attempt to hide the edge in her voice. It was best to remind the Tezerenee that she did not consider herself the guest they wanted her to believe she was.

"Do not let your defiance make you foolish. You could hardly plot any escapes if you collapsed on the staircase and fell to your death, could you?"

Sharissa looked up at the Lady Tezerenee, but the latter's visage was unreadable. Unfortunate as it was, Sharissa saw much in what Lady Alcia had said. While the food had aided greatly in restoring her strength, her control over her body was still a bit tenuous. Who was to say that she might not miss a step?

"Perhaps it would be best if you held my arm."

"Of course."

As they started down, Sharissa's legs quivering a bit, the sorceress remembered the collar around her throat. *Very odd that I could forget this*, she decided. Subtle magic? If she grew complacent about the collar, it might not be long before she *did* find herself listening to the words of Barakas. More than ever, Sharissa knew she had to struggle to keep her concentration on her predicament. She could not be sidetracked by anything that did not directly deal with the situation.

Tezerenee sentries saluted smartly as her royal guide passed them. After a moment, it occurred to her that they were also saluting *her*, as if she were a visiting dignitary and not a prisoner.

"This honor isn't necessary." She made no attempt to hide the sarcasm.

"You are the daughter of Dru Zeree and a capable sorceress in your own right. Your status is high among our folk. It may be that, before long, your status will be even higher."

"If you mean will I marry Reegan and add my power to your people, you've—"

"Here we are," Alcia interrupted, acting as if she had not even noted her charge's retort. They had reached the bottom of the staircase.

To each side, massive corridors extended into eternity. Turning around, Sharissa saw yet another corridor, this one even greater than the others.

The great hall, she decided. The Tezerenee would reveal it to her before long; Barakas loved to hold court. Considering the high marble columns and the polished stone floors that made up what was basically a walkway, she suspected the great hall itself would be more sumptuous than past Tezerenee courts.

Where is this place? Nothing in the eastern sector matched this place. There were places more splendid, but they were in the styles favored by the founders, not the more deliberate tastes of the dragon men.

"Sharissa?" Lady Alcia stood with one arm extended toward two huge, iron doors, each with the symbol of the clan worked into the very metal. Only two guards stood at the doors, but they were possibly the largest Tezerenee she had ever seen other than the patriarch and his heir. If they were not Alcia's sons, then they were the products of the Lord Tezerenee's occasional outside liaison. Love his bride he might, but Barakas saw part of his duty as clan leader to include the relentless task of increasing their numbers in whatever way necessary.

Thinking of the differences between Gerrod and Reegan, the young Zeree wondered if the Lady Alcia had secretly formed a few liaisons of her own. They might be Tezerenee, but they were also Vraad.

She rejoined her guide. As they and their bodyguards approached the doors, the two sentries opened the way for them, visibly straining as they pulled the doors open.

Sunlight flooded into the corridor, blinding an unsuspecting Sharissa. She gasped and put her hands over her eyes. Her companion took hold of her.

"I'm so sorry! I should have realized that your eyes would be sensitive after three days of darkness or dim light. You had no trouble with the torchlight in the halls and on the stairs, so I merely assumed—''

''I'll be fine.'' The sorceress removed herself from the matriarch's grip. ''I can see well enough already to continue.'' She blinked in rapid succession. A myriad pattern of spots made it impossible to focus on anything, but she could make out general shapes enough to walk without stumbling. ''Lead on.''

''Very well.''

A cool breeze, very welcome after the stifling air of her cell, caressed her cheeks. The air smelled of life unspoiled by human intrusion. It smelled . . . *different*.

Even before her eyesight had cleared, she knew she was no longer in the city.

The Tezerenee led her out into the world. Like a blind person newly granted sight, the sorceress tried to see everything. The tall, menacing tower of the citadel, the utilitarian buildings that flanked it on each side and held, she knew, the riding drakes. A massive protective wall that surrounded the patriarch's private domain. Sentries walked the wall, each warrior ready for the worst. Airdrakes carried patrols over the walls. Following the route of one such patrol, her eyes were suddenly attracted by a chain of mountains in the distance. They were unfamiliar to her, yet she felt she should know them.

In what could only have been three days, the Tezerenee had evidently built themselves a stronghold. It was as ugly in its own way as their own, with their typical jagged towers and harsh lines. The clear blue sky, the light breeze, and the birds singing in the distance seemed, when forced to endure alongside the citadel, mere parodies of their once-glorious selves. Nothing remained beautiful around the Tezerenee.

Sharissa turned on the Lady Tezerenee. Her bodyguards readied their blades, but the warrior queen waved the two back. ''How did you do all this? Where did you get such power? The effort to create all of this—''

''Was beyond us, yes. Even now, though our power now is greater than it was these last years, this still would have required months of effort. Fortunately, there was one who *did* have the strength.''

The young Zeree's eyes narrowed dangerously. ''You made Darkhorse do this! You made him do this with my life as the key to his cooperation!''

"We never threatened your life." Lady Alcia scratched her neck as she spoke. Like Lochivan's, it was red and dry. Sharissa recalled his mentioning some rash or minor disease spreading through the Tezerenee and wondered if she would suffer that along with everything else.

"Why don't you quit acting as if I'm a guest?" The sorceress tugged at her collar. It grew surprisingly tight, making her choke. The Matriarch reached forward and pulled Sharissa's hands away from her throat.

The collar became bearable again.

"Perhaps we should go back inside."

Sharissa slapped her hand away, which made the bodyguards bristle again. "Why don't you—What is that?"

Two Tezerenee were dragging a limp figure between them. He was slighter than either and his clothing reminded her of her stepmother's clothing.

"It would really be best if you . . . Sharissa! Stop!"

Too late. Sharissa darted past one of her companion's watchdogs and raced toward the two warriors dragging the still form. "You there! Stop! Now!"

Still holding their captive, the Tezerenee turned to see who was shouting. They looked at the ungraceful figure in white and then at one another. One reached for a blade, but the second shook his head and said something that she could not make out.

Lady Alcia's people were no doubt right behind her, but Sharissa did not care. She had to see who it was they had and whether the poor soul was still alive. Most of all, she had to see if he was what she thought he was.

As she neared them, the guards looked past her and nodded. When she sought to lift their prize's head so that she could see his features, no one stopped her. The sound of heavy footfalls grew louder behind her.

There was no denying the visage. There were differences, of course, but his race was not in question. He was an elf.

Judging by the blood and bruises, he had resisted their questioning. Sharissa glanced up at the two guards, but they were untouched by her smoldering eyes.

The elf began to cough. His eyes opened, handsome almond-shaped tears. It took him a moment to focus and, when he did, he seemed surprised.

"Eve—even among the living death there—there is beauty. Impossible to—to believe you have such a heart of stone."

He had taken her for one of them. "I'm not—"

"You must come back with us now, Lady Sharissa," a cold female voice said. The Lady Alcia's bodyguards stood directly on each side of her. Coughing once more, the elf forced his gaze upward, despite the fact that it obviously hurt him to move so much. He eyed the two with interest, then returned his gaze to Sharissa.

"My lady," the bodyguard urged. "This is not something to concern yourself with."

As if on cue, the two warriors holding the elf turned their prize away and once more began to drag him away. Sharissa started after them, but the bodyguards held her back.

"He was part of a force of elves that sought to come upon us through stealth and kill us. With the demon's aid, we detected them and caught *them* by surprise."

"You made Darkhorse aid you in killing them?" The sorceress doubted that the story was as Lady Tezerenee had told it. More than likely, the elves had been scouting the citadel, wondering what it was. Still, what was a party of elves doing on the eastern continent when—

"I see by your eyes that you've finally come to the realization. I wondered for a time whether or not your mind was functioning well." Lady Alcia nodded, the smile on her face much akin to the one the patriarch wore when he was pleased with results. "Yes, this is indeed the Dragonrealm, Sharissa."

"How could you...Darkhorse again! Everything you've accomplished is because of him! You still haven't brought me to him! Is he dead? Injured?"

At a signal from the matriarch, the bodyguards politely but firmly began to guide a struggling Sharissa back toward the citadel. Lady Alcia walked before them, still acting as if she and Sharissa were amiable companions. "How do you kill a thing that does not, by any standards we know, live? He's been disciplined, but no more than any other disobedient subject has. When he performs well, he is rewarded as well."

"*Rewarded?*" Other than freedom, the Tezerenee could have nothing the shadow steed wanted.

"We want him to be a part of the clan's destiny as much as we want you to be."

"You want him to save you from the Seekers! Even Darkhorse

won't be enough to hold them back! He'll probably laugh while the bird people tear your empire down around you!''

''The avians no longer represent a threat . . . at least, not one that we cannot deal with ourselves.''

Sharissa stretched forward, trying to come alongside the Lady Tezerenee. ''What do you mean?''

Alcia considered the question for a time before finally replying, ''It might be better to show you.''

''Show me?''

''We brought a few of them in for study. So far, we have not found a cause for their fate.'' The matriarch had altered direction. The two bodyguards steered the helpless Sharissa after her. She did not struggle, for once truly wanting to follow. If what Lady Alcia had said was true, then there remained no force capable of withstanding the Tezerenee, especially if Darkhorse was their tool.

''You know,'' her host remarked, stopping and turning around so that the two faced one another. ''I think this would be an excellent opportunity to show you the true depth of our strength!''

''What do you . . .'' Sharissa began, but Lady Alcia merely snapped her fingers . . .

. . . and they were standing in another chamber, a dark, dank place lit by torches. A Tezerenee leaning over a table looked up. Sharissa, still in shock from the unexpected teleport, did not immediately recognize his shadowed visage.

''You did that as if it were nothing! All four of us! But I thought that you—''

''The old ways are returning. It is as if Nimth is part of us again.'' A smile, a Tezerenee smile, slowly spread across the striking face. ''We are not the near gods of our past, but we are again a sorcerous power to be respected.''

''It's as if our destiny is being drawn for us by the hands of the founders themselves,'' added the figure by the table. ''The day promised to us by the Dragon of the Depths has come.''

Sharissa struggled with her captors. ''Lochivan!''

''I hope you will find it in your heart to forgive me, Sharissa.'' Lochivan wore no helm; he seemed actually sad, though she was not so willing to believe him after his betrayal. ''I truly think it would have been best if—''

''That will be all, my son.''

''Forgive you, Lochivan? I wouldn't—''

He vanished before she could finish. Sharissa ended with a scream of frustration instead.

"When you are more willing, the two of you should talk," the Lady Tezerenee said in a calm voice. She pointed at the table. "For now, this is what should concern you. This is what you wanted to see."

Sharissa blinked and glanced without care at the thing on the table. An artifact. A statue carved to resemble a Seeker. Of what interest . . .

"She does not understand. Bring her closer."

In silent obedience, the two bodyguards brought Sharissa within an arm's length of the table and its contents.

She gave it another glance . . . and could not pull herself away from the thing's contorted form. The careful detail of horror, the avian eyes staring at death. The mouth open in futile rejection of fate. The awkward sprawl of the body.

It appeared the consistency of marble, this thing before her, but Sharissa knew that if she touched the long, sleek wing or the muscular torso, she would not feel stone, but rather feather and flesh.

"The Dragonrealm is ours, and without even a fight," Lady Alcia said with satisfaction. Sharissa looked up, unable to think of anything sufficient to say. The matriarch added, "My husband is disappointed. He so much looked forward to a good battle . . . with us winning, of course."

As she spoke the last, one hand absently scratched at the reddish area on her neck.

IX

From the tower in which his private chambers lay, Barakas Tezerenee watched the vanishing of his wife and the others. Sharissa Zeree would be suitably impressed with the way of things by the time Alcia was finished. Her encounter with the elfin prisoner had been perfectly orchestrated, as he had expected. There lay potential in that meeting; unless he missed his guess, she would try her best to speak to the prisoner in private . . . although it would not be so private as she believed.

All things come together, the patriarch thought in satisfaction. He patted a square container upon which the mark of the Tezerenee had been emblazoned.

"Father?"

Barakas turned and faced Lochivan, who had materialized, as was proper, on one knee with his head bent downward. "All goes well, my son?"

"Yes, my lord. Sharissa is in the chamber even now. By this time, she is aware of the nature of the corpse."

"Perhaps she can tell us what happened. That would be an added prize."

"Does it matter so?"

"We must strive to further ourselves. If the legacy of the avians can aid us, so be it." The patriarch looked down at his son. "You are a few minutes early."

Lochivan did not look up. "I deemed it more beneficial to our goals that I depart the chamber. Sharissa is not comfortable in my presence."

"She will have to learn if she is to marry your brother."

This time, the younger Tezerenee *did* look up. His helm hid much of his visage from his parent, but Barakas knew his son's mind. "Is that necessary, Father?"

Barakas started to scratch his wrist, but fought down the urge. "I listened to you. I allowed you to use that sycophant to drop off your little gimmick. You had raised good points. Now, I see that we no longer have to worry about Dru Zeree following us . . . not, at least, for quite some time."

The kneeling figure did not speak, knowing there was more to come.

"Your toy failed. She fought it, proving she has a will worthy of the Tezerenee. The crossover had not yet commenced, and her interference might have brought the rest of the Vraad down on us, something I did not wish at the time." Something caught the corner of his eye. He turned, but all he saw was the box sitting on a table. A simple magical test of the barriers proved they still held, so he knew that it was not an escape attempt he had noted.

Lochivan made the mistake of looking up. Barakas returned his attention to his son. "I find I am more than satisfied that taking her was the correct maneuver after all. Reegan needs a strong hand to guide him. She will be that guiding hand once I have molded her properly.'' He folded his arms. ''Now, do you still have qualms?''

''No, sire.''

It was a lie and they both knew it, but the Lord Tezerenee also knew that he could rely on Lochivan to obey him in all things. ''Very well. You are dismissed. . . . Wait.''

''Sire?''

''Tomorrow, I want a force ready to ride to the mountains, ground and air forces.''

''Yes, Father.''

''Go.''

Lochivan vanished without even rising. It was an act that attested to the rejuvenation of the Tezerenees' power. They were not yet the masters they had once been in Nimth, but that day could not help but be drawing near, the patriarch believed.

He started to turn back to the window once more, when, for the second time, something caught his eye. It was gone before he could do any more than register its existence, but the Lord Tezerenee froze where he was, for there was something familiar about the shape, a shrouded, possibly human shape.

Quickly moving to the box, he touched the seal. There had been no trickery; the box was, indeed, still protected against assault from both without and within. He felt the presence trapped inside stir to renewed fury.

''Struggle all you like, demon,'' Barakas whispered to the one imprisoned within. ''You *will* bow to my control, or else I'll leave you in there and lose you somewhere in the deepest cavern I can find.''

The struggling subsided. Fear was gaining ground. Barakas had introduced Dru Zeree's deadly companion to a place even worse than the emptiness of the Void. It had not been difficult to uncover the shadow steed's principal weakness. He feared to be alone.

In the box, there was not even the nothingness of the Void to share Darkhorse's fate, only the ebony creature himself.

''That's better. If you behave yourself, I will even let you see Lady Sharissa again.'' It would serve as a lesson to both. He would see that she was helpless despite being free to move about, and she would note that even a might as great as he was little challenge to the Tezerenee.

It was the next step in breaking their will.

Removing his hand from the box, Darkhorse's ungodly prison, Barakas scratched at his throat. He still wondered about the image. Was it a trick of his eyes, eyes that had, of late, not seen as well as they should have? Was it just his imagination? If so, why pick *that* one image to conjure to life?

Why would he imagine the startled vision of his traitorous son, *Gerrod*?

Something had gone wrong terribly wrong and he didn't know what to do and he didn't know where he was and how he had ended up here but the last thing he remembered was *almost* reaching his goal but his father had been there, *hadn't* he?

"*Stop it!*" Gerrod screamed at himself, not caring a whit at the moment how mad he must look. He put his hands to his ears as if by doing so he could silence his own inner voice. Yet, the insane thoughts rambled on for several breaths before the warlock was finally able to bring himself under control.

In perverse fashion, it was his *father's* words that provided the willpower.

We are the Tezerenee. The name Tezerenee is power. Nothing is greater than our will.

Until this moment, those words had always struck him as contradictory and simplistic. For all his father's speeches, only *one* will really mattered among the clan of the dragon—the patriarch's, of course. Now the words reminded Gerrod that his father would not allow madness to rule him so easily. The Lord Tezerenee would fight it with as much strength as he would a physical foe. It all depended on how you focused that strength.

Gerrod would not allow himself to fail where he knew his father would succeed.

Through silent contemplation, he brought order to his thoughts and quelled, if not cast out, the fear. It occurred to him then that he had closed his eyes upon losing his hold on his destination and had not opened them again.

From the darkness of his inner self, Gerrod found himself thrust in the light of . . . *nothing?*

For lack of a better term, he was willing to call his surroundings white, though white implied something, if only light and color, and this was neither. It was simply a vast nothingness.

"Dragon's blood!" he hissed, momentarily slipping to a favorite Tezerenee oath.

He was floating helplessly in what could only be the emptiness that Dru Zeree had tried so desperately to describe, but always in so very inadequate terms. Gerrod could see why. Nothing, no words, could match the truth. There was no description that could do justice to the Void.

Calm. He had to remain calm. Master Zeree had escaped this place, and so would he.

What had happened? Gerrod recalled his brief intrusion into the real world and the sudden vagueness of his destination, as if the teleport spell no longer had a certain path to fix upon. His father had been there, a risk the warlock had been willing to face, but not the dweller from the Void. Why? The spell should have brought Gerrod to Darkhorse, unless there was some unforeseen barrier. . . .

A box. He recalled a box. There was something about it that had drawn him, something—

"You are not other I."

"What?" Gerrod looked around, trying to find the source of the voice.

"Other I was becoming boring. Maybe you will be entertaining."

"Who is that? Where are you?" the warlock shouted. He tried to turn around, but in the Void it was impossible to say whether he had achieved any result or not. Certainly, nothing but emptiness spanned his field of vision. It might have been a different nothing than the moment before, but how would he know?

"I am here."

A vast hole opened up before the floating Vraad. Gerrod's stomach began to turn. This was sounding too familiar to him. The hole quivered. Gerrod wondered how one could have a hole in the middle of emptiness. This was a part of the Void's tendencies that he had never come to terms with even after mulling over the story for years. The natural laws that he was accustomed to had no meaning here. If the Void felt a hole could exist in the midst of what was basically a *bigger* hole, then so be it.

"You're real!" Gerrod's blurted remark was superfluous at best, but staring at this creature, even after having faced Darkhorse, he could not help but want to deny the sight before him.

"You have a funny inside voice. It makes all sorts of funny noises."

It was reading his thoughts, the surface ones, at least. Dru Zeree had mentioned that Darkhorse had done the same—

"Darkhorse? What is a Darkhorse?" The black, bottomless hole grew larger, its borders coming within a few yards of the nervous Tezerenee.

The warlock kept a careful rein on his thoughts. Any loose notion would be easy prey for the creature . . . and there was no promise that it was as friendly as Darkhorse had been.

"Darkhorse is like you."

"There is nothing like me." The blot was proud of that fact. "There was other I, but other I is gone."

"Darkhorse is other I. It . . . he has a new name."

"A name?"

What sort of mind did this creature have, Gerrod wondered, that it could read his thoughts well enough to learn his speech but not understand various terms and ideas? Master Zeree had described a similar situation with Darkhorse, but not how irritating it could be. There were already too many emotions vying for mastery over the warlock without one more addition.

"What . . . is . . . a . . . name?" With each word, the hole grew larger. Gerrod now found himself truly having to worry that he would be devoured, swallowed, or whatever the case might be if the creature continued its growth.

"A name is what you call something. I am Gerrod. If you talk to me, you might mention my name so that I will know that you are speaking to me."

"Gerrod, you are amusing, Gerrod. Gerrod, what else do you know, Gerrod? Gerrod, come and Gerrod entertain me further, Gerrod!"

"That's not what I meant." He wondered if it mattered that his visage was still covered by his hood. Would his annoyance and fear register to this bizarre horror?

The hole chose that moment to swell further. Gerrod tried to wave himself away.

"Why do you do that? Why do you wiggle your appendages so?"

"You . . . your *body* would swallow me! If you get any closer, I'll die—" It could hardly understand that term. Gerrod hurriedly sought another. "I'll be no more. I won't be able to entertain you again!"

The blot paused, but its tone did not encourage the young Tezerenee. "You . . . fear . . . me."

He could not deny it. "I do."

"I like its taste." The dweller from the Void seemed to consider things. At the very least, it was both still and silent for several breaths. "You are more entertaining than the other things I have met!"

"Others?"

"I absorbed them! It was fun, but this is more fun! I think I shall play with you!"

"*Play?*" Try as he might, Gerrod could not keep the quiver from his voice. Could it be that the spell, unable to fix upon one creature, had brought him instead to one akin to what he sought? How else to explain his meeting this brother of Darkhorse's so soon after his debacle?

Was it that soon? Had not Dru Zeree said that time was not a consideration in the Void? How long had he actually been there?

I will not allow panic to rule me! he thought, teeth gritted. *I have to get away from this thing before it loses interest in me and decides to . . . to . . .* The warlock found he could not bring himself to complete his thought.

"Do something else for me!" the hole demanded.

What did he know about Darkhorse that he could use to divert the creature's attention? "Can you make yourself take up less area?" He indicated with his hands what he meant. "Can you make yourself this big, for instance?"

The blot was suddenly the very size he had indicated. Gerrod blinked in astonishment at the speed with which the dweller reacted to his suggestion. He had known that the shadow steed was swift to react to things; Zeree had made that clear. What had not been clear was *how* swift those reactions were. He would have to be careful about what he did. Gerrod could not allow the monstrosity to know what was happening.

"Now what?" bellowed the blot, its voice still reverberating with harsh consistency in the human's ears.

Now what? indeed! Have it become a horse like its brother? No, that would likely rely on the dweller's searching through the warlock's thoughts for an image of a horse. Gerrod had no desire to allow this entity to go rooting around his mind. It might not leave him the same.

A shock tore through his system, so abrupt that Gerrod had

no time to brace himself for it. He screamed loud and full and could not say when he at last was able to stop.

"*Entertain me, I said.*" The cold tone left no doubt as to where the agony had originated.

"You—"

"The other little things like yourself, they were entertaining for a time! I found they did interesting things when I touched them like that! I learned much from them! I learn much from you! I even have a *name* now!" It giggled, a disquieting sound. "I fooled you I did! A good game, wasn't it? Here you explain to me what a name is and I *had* one all the time!"

Mad . . . inhuman, utter madness! It babbles like an idiot, but an idiot who could easily erase my existence whenever it chooses, the Tezerenee thought, his panic, despite his efforts, gaining too great a foothold. How could he divert the insane creature long enough to find a way out of this emptiness? There had to be something in what Dru Zeree had told him about Darkhorse!

"You were very clever," he finally told the hole. "You had me tricked completely. You were almost as clever as Dark—the other I you mentioned. He was very, very clever."

The blot stirred, swelling in size again. Gerrod wondered if he had gone too far. A notion had formed, but Gerrod was not certain whether it had any merit yet. Much of his success would lie in the dweller's arrogant yet childlike ignorance.

"I *formed* other I! Was that not most clever of all? How could other I, this Darkhorse creature, be more clever?"

The warlock's ears pounded. He clapped his hands over them and shouted back, "There are many ways to be clever! Some are more wondrous than others! Let me tell you the story!"

As if understanding his pain, the eternal's voice grew soft, almost subdued in tone. More and more, Gerrod was coming to respect Darkhorse for what he had become. *This* horror, on the other hand . . . "What is a 'story'?"

Gerrod hesitated. "Are you playing with me again? If you are, I won't bother telling you what a story is!"

"I am not playing with you! What is a story? Is it fun? I want fun! I understand fun!"

"It can be very fun." He would have liked to debate its concept of fun, but, being Vraad, Gerrod knew that his own folk, when ruling Nimth, had often acted just as sadistic, just as mad, while "enjoying" themselves. "A story is a . . . Suppose I told you about other I's clever trick and how I know of it. That would be a story of sorts." It would also be the opening he needed. There *was* something in Master Zeree's tale that could help him . . . and he had nearly let it pass!

"Your other voice hides! Why?"

He stiffened. The creature had almost caught his thoughts, his "other voice." "It has to hide before I can tell you a story. That . . . that is the way I am!"

The blot shrank again, evidently satisfied with the explanation. Gerrod felt as if he teetered on the edge of the proverbial precipice; his adversary was an unpredictable quantity. Any move, any wrong word, could spell the warlock's end.

"Do you want to hear my story?"

"It might prove amusing! I like to be amused, you know! How does a story begin?"

Gerrod breathed a sigh of relief. "Sometimes they begin with words like 'Once there was . . .' or 'Long ago . . .'. This one begins 'There was a man named Dru Zeree . . .'."

He went into the story, editing, as best he could under the circumstances, any mention of how the outsider Zeree had found himself here or how the sorcerer and his newfound companion had left this place. While he told the tale, Gerrod tried to mull over his own manner of escape. Vraad sorcery had not worked for Zeree. Might—he hesitated to even consider it—might the magic of the founders' world work here? He was capable of it, Gerrod knew that much, but to finally give in to it. . . .

His unnerving companion remained quiet throughout the story. The hooded Vraad put aside his other worries and concentrated again on the creature, for the tale was nearly complete. It was being entertained, that much was obvious. Would it follow through on his suggestion? Did it suspect what he had in mind and was simply playing with him?

". . . and when the other I burst forth, he was a new creature, a wonderful, huge beast who called himself Darkhorse!" What would his father think of him, floating in limbo telling stories in order to preserve his life?

"*I* have a name! Do you want to know what it is?" The blot sounded so much like an anxious child that Gerrod almost laughed despite the danger to him.

"What is it?"

"I am *Yereel!*" The hole swelled to mammoth proportions. Gerrod waved his arms and legs back and forth, but he felt himself being drawn into the gaping mouth that was his unwanted companion.

"Y-Yereel! Stop! Please!"

Yereel shrank down to a tiny blot litle bigger than the warlock's hand. It—*he* seemed more appropriate now—giggled again. "I frightened you! Good! The taste stirs me as nothing else does!"

A decidedly different path of development than Zeree's creature took, the Tezerenee thought again. *How very unfortunate for me.* He decided to make no comment about the creature's— Yereel's— choice of names. If the dweller was happy, it was to Gerrod's advantage. In the meantime, the warlock had to press on. "Did you enjoy the tale?"

"Very much! Can I make one?"

"If you like. I have something better to entertain you with . . . and a way to prove yourself more clever than Darkhorse."

Though it was impossible to read any emotion in a hole, Gerrod was certain Yereel was intrigued.

"What is this way?" the blot finally asked.

"Change yourself as he did."

Hesitation . . . then, "I have never done such before."

"Neither had Darkhorse."

"I do not have this 'horse' to shape myself like."

The Tezerenee allowed himself a quick smile, hoping such a facial movement was beyond the dweller's comprehension. "That would only prove yourself *as* clever as him. If you want to prove yourself *most* clever, then you need a new form, one that Darkhorse did not do."

Yereel almost whimpered. "I *have* no other form to copy! There is only you and I!"

Gerrod pretended to consider that problem. "Well, then you could shape yourself into something like me! Darkhorse never did *that*! That would prove you more clever!"

"Wonderful!"

"It might be too difficult for you, though. . . ."

"Not so! Watch!"

Still the same tiny hole in the midst of nothing, Yereel began to turn in on himself. He continued to turn in on himself, never seeming to lose any more self. The warlock thought upon Dru Zeree's description of the metamorphosis. There were similarities and differences in what Yereel attempted now, but all that mattered to Gerrod were the final results.

The change in the dweller's appearance became more noticeable. Now, instead of a hole, he began to resemble a shell. Gerrod was not inclined to touch him and see if what he observed was true. During the course of their trek, Darkhorse had more than once absorbed adversaries like the Seekers, even though he had sported a more substantial form.

The shell toughened. Now was the time to test his theory. The hooded warlock leaned forward and asked, "How are you succeeding?"

From Yereel there was no response.

"Can you answer me? Can you hear me?"

Still nothing.

Darkhorse had entered what Master Zeree had believed was the equivalent of a pupa stage in insects. He had literally readjusted his essence in order to exist more comfortably in the real world. That transformation had lasted a day or more, if Gerrod recalled. He had no idea how long Yereel's would last, especially since time was not a known quantity in the Void, but he hoped it would prove sufficient for his purposes.

Gerrod exhaled. As simple as his triumph seemed now, it had taken a great deal out of him. Yereel was unpredictable; victory still might only prove to be a false dream if the dweller chose to burst free of his cocoon before the warlock was away.

"My spell brought me to this point. Vraad sorcery *must* work in this place!" Zeree had claimed it did *not* or, at the very least, did to no worthwhile effect. Despite those pessimistic thoughts, Gerrod was determined to attempt Vraad sorcery first.

He tried to pinpoint his destination. As it had been just prior to his accident, Darkhorse's presence could be felt somewhere beyond the emptiness of the Void, but not strong enough that he could latch on to it. Worse yet, Yereel's nearby form distracted him to the point where he finally gave up in disgust. Whether or not Vraad sorcery would work for him—and considering the link he had forged, he still believed it might—his current location made it impossible to be effective.

He could not return home. The shadow steed's position had been his sole point of concentration. The founders' world was lost to him—unless he attempted Sharissa's way.

"You're a fool, Gerrod!" Every breath he wasted meant that

much more chance of still being here when the spherical shell floating before him hatched. He would have to give in, but only this once.

How had Sharissa described it? Relax and give himself over to the magic? There was supposed to be a spectrum or lines of force.

He saw neither, but he did feel a strange tingling in his body, as if some living force had permeated his entire form. A new wave of panic threatened to drown him, but he fought it off. This outworld magic would not twist him to its own interests! It was he who commanded!

Something briefly shimmered before his eyes. Not a spectrum. Not a field of lines crisscrossing into infinity. More like a path floating in the nothingness.

A path? Mention had been made of paths utilized by Darkhorse when he and the sorcerer had made their escape from the infernal nonplace. Reacting out of habit, he tried to snare it as he might a rabbit for food. Only when it proved impossible to find again did he think about what he was doing. Vraad methods did work with the sorcery of the founders' world, but not without great effort and a high level of chance.

"All right, damn you! Take me! Only this once!"

He relaxed his body, if not his mind, and let the power flow into him. It was more than a tingle now; he itched, but from *within*.

Paths, the warlock thought. *There are paths. I just have to open my will to them.*

It reappeared, a long, winding path running through the emptiness into a distant glow far beyond. Gerrod smiled. With the same presence of mind, he made himself drift toward the inviting trail. There was probably a better way to do what he had succeeded in doing so far, but he would leave that, as he had left so many things already, to more contemplative times. All that the warlock cared about now was reaching the path that would lead him to the Dragonrealm.

Another gleaming path crisscrossed the first.

His eyes narrowed. Even as the second brightened into view, a third and a fourth, one unconnected to the others, materialized. Gerrod swore under his breath, then openly as a horde of trails shooting this way and that formed before his eyes.

The Void was not so empty. In fact, it was cluttered beyond

imagination, but by things so insubstantial that even a creature like Yereel had apparently never noted them.

Which one was the correct path?

He tentatively reached out with his mind, working as best he could *with* his newfound might, not against it. As a Vraad sorcerer, he would have been able to sense some of the differences between the paths. Hopefully, it would be the same now.

The first trail he stared at vanished a breath later. It was not one he wanted, that much he knew. Encouraged, Gerrod touched others and watched them fade away as his mind discarded them as possible choices. Most simply felt wrong, as if he knew without actually knowing that they went to a place the warlock was not interested in visiting. A few disturbed him greatly... and one was so chilling, so disquieting, that he abandoned it in near panic. Yet, wiping his brow, he was encouraged. Only a few dozen paths remained where there had been an endless array. Many had disappeared without his even studying them; it was possible his subconscious was now aiding his efforts.

Several more dwindled away to nothing, but then Gerrod recalled his companion. He felt an intense need to turn and reassure himself. It was more than merely sudden worry; he was absolutely *certain* that he had to turn around.

He did.

The cocoon was pulsating.

Yereel would soon emerge... and then what would Gerrod do?

He whirled around and scanned the paths remaining to him. Still too many to be certain.

"You're a fool!" he muttered.

All paths but one vanished as he made his choice. He knew it would take him to the land of the Dragonrealm, but no more. That, at this point, was all that mattered.

As if discouraged by final decision, his body was suddenly standing on the very trail. Gerrod took an anxious step forward. As thin as it appeared, it held him quite readily. It was narrower than he had thought, and Gerrod tried not to imagine what might happen if he took a misstep.

The same inner alarm that had warned him to look back now fairly shook his body with its intensity.

The Tezerenee needed no more encouragement. He raced

down the glimmering, ethereal path and did not hesitate in the least, not even when the expanding glow before him suddenly flared and swallowed him up.

Blue sky and rocky hills welcomed him. Gerrod, caught up in the welcome change of scenery around him, ran blindly for several steps before stumbling and falling.

Every oath learned under the tutelage of his father came back to him as he struck the hard soil and tumbled over and over again. Soft and comforting plant life was unheard of here. At the very least, none of it existed to ease his collisions. Only when he found a rock too large to roll over did the unfortunate warlock come to a halt.

How long he lay there Gerrod could not say. The outside world was only a blurred image when the Tezerenee forced his eyes open for a moment. He tasted blood and was surprised he was not drowning in the stuff. His body was bruised from top to bottom. Gerrod did not even want to know if he had broken anything, so he merely continued to lie where he was, hoping the pain would go away or that unconsciousness would claim him.

Someone prodded him with a heavy, blunt object, stirring him. Gerrod was aware that he had dozed, but not how long. The pain had lessened, though it was by no means insignificant. The prodding began again, this time at some of the more sensitive points of his body. Yelping, Gerrod scurried back as best he could and forced his eyes to open. At first, the same blurriness affected his vision. Gradually, however, things began to come back into focus.

Gerrod found sight did not improve his situation any.

The creature was taller than he would be if he could stand. It was also about twice as wide and none of that was soft. It was dull brown in color, although there were hints of orange. Parts of it glittered, as if someone had sprinkled it with diamonds. The blunt object turned out to be the top of a massive battle-ax.

He saw that there were at least five of the beasts, all of whom chose that moment to start hooting at one another as if discussing his fate. Gazing around at them, Gerrod could not help feeling he had been captured by some overgrown but quite vicious armadillos who had learned to walk on their hind legs just for this very purpose.

They were Quel.

X

The weeks that passed were tense and dismal for Sharissa. She could find no way of removing the collar; twice she had almost suffocated, although no one else was aware of that fact. Barakas Tezerenee, who had spoken to her only thrice in that time, had promised to let her speak to Darkhorse . . . but the promises proved insubstantial. Most of her waking hours were spent with Lady Alcia or one of the other women of the clan. Sharissa found the patriarch's daughters as alike as most of his sons. She could not recall any of their names, and most of them even seemed to look alike. At least among the sons there was a little disparity.

Only Reegan and Lochivan seemed to matter now. Esad was also around, but his purpose in life was to carry information to his father and then scurry from sight. The rest were as identical as their sisters, cousins, and even those outsiders who had lived among the Tezerenee for a time.

He makes them all in his own image, she decided wryly when observing the Lord Tezerenee giving orders to the military expedition to the mountains. *Reegan most of all is his reflection.*

Three times she had been subjected to the advances of Reegan. He was pathetic in some ways, actually adoring her while he also lusted after her. His confusion kept him harmless for the most part, although he had tried to take more than her hand the second encounter.

Lochivan, whom she had wanted never to see again, had been the one to interrupt what might have proven to be something worse. As if standing in the shadows and waiting for just such an occasion, he had come stalking toward them, two guards flanking him, and informed his brother that they were wanted. It was only after they had departed, leaving the two sentries to lead her away, that she had recalled her bitterness toward the amiable but treacherous Tezerenee.

She presently sat in her chambers, far more attractive ones than she had first received. Something was going on outside, something that had the Tezerenee stirred up. Her new chambers were on the uppermost floor of the citadel, barring the tower. This allowed her to view the courtyard and grounds and the mountains in the distance, a splendid view if not for the dragon men.

Rising and moving to the window, Sharissa peered outside. The gates were opening, and several riders were coming through. Those riding the airdrakes flew over the walls to join their brethren. To her disappointment, the expedition seemed fairly intact; the sorceress had hoped they might be decimated by some hitherto unsuspected force of Seekers.

Her eyes began to wander across the courtyard . . . until they focused on a figure she had been trying to see again. The elf, as usual, was accompanied by unwanted companions who dragged more than led the prisoner to a small, rather insignificant building to the left of her window. This was the first time he had been removed from the lower-level cell that had been his home since being captured. Did that mean he had finally told them what they wanted, or were the Tezerenee merely bored with him?

Suddenly she wanted out of her room. She had that much say, if little else. Sharissa departed the window, heading now for the door. It was not locked, but she had no intention of trying it. There were certain ways things were done around here, and she had come to accept them.

"Guard!"

A moment passed, a moment that seemed an eternity, before someone opened the door. One of her nameless female bodyguards stepped in, weapon ready. Sharissa had not even attempted to remember her bodyguards' names; the guard changed so often that it was impossible to keep one name or another straight.

"You wished something, Lady Sharissa?"

"I *wish* to go outside and get a little air."

"You do not need my permission to do that. I am here for your safety and to see to your needs."

The tall, slim sorceress put her hands on her hips, her only rebuttal to the claim that the Tezerenee had just made. "I know the courtyard is open to me, but I also know that you will be watching me . . . for my own good. I merely thought I would inform you first.''

The guard stood there as if not sure she understood the mind of this outsider. That was as Sharissa wanted it. A touch of arrogance with a touch of confusion. Act both cooperative and defiant. She found, with few exceptions, that the clan had trouble coping with her.

Her only true threats lay in Lochivan, Lady Alcia, and, of course, Barakas himself.

The courtyard was abuzz with Tezerenee crowding around the returning force. Sharissa, wandering on the outskirts of the assembled throng, noted the positive aura of the Tezerenee. The news the expedition brought was favorable. That could only mean that they had faced no true opposition and that the aerie of the Seekers was either abandoned or so pitifully defended that nothing stood in the clan's way of claiming it.

She caught a glimpse of Lochivan, who had, at the last moment, not led the expeditionary force. That honor had instead gone to his younger sibling, Dagos, whom she knew little about and, therefore, did not want to risk making suspicious by asking too many questions just yet. Dagos was almost a nonentity, automatically obedient to his lord and sire and having little personality to call his own. Why he had been chosen to lead was a decision she questioned, but trying to second-guess the patriarch was impossible.

As she surveyed the crowd, she kept an eye on her guard. The woman was caught between her duties and her interest. That was as Sharissa wanted it. She moved nearer the crowd, always walking away from her shadow. The guard also moved nearer, which only made her curiosity grow. The Tezerenee's eyes lingered on Lochivan and Dagos, who were discussing something animatedly.

Sharissa, the chaos shielding her, slipped away toward the elfin prisoner.

She felt no great victory for outfoxing the sentry; the woman would find her. What the sorceress wanted, however, was a few moments of private conversation so that she might take the measure of her fellow captive. If he still had any will left, there was a chance he could aid her in truly escaping. If not, he might still be able to give her some idea about the surrounding territory and where she might go.

Another reason, and one she would not admit to herself, was that, like her father and Gerrod Tezerenee, she had an overactive curiosity about new things . . . or people.

She entered the building where he was held. There were no guards. They had joined the others, an indication of how important the purpose of the expedition had been to the clan. Sharissa made her way down a short corridor and peered through the first cell door she found. Being the sole prisoner incarcerated there, Sharissa was not surprised to find him on the first attempt.

It was doubtful that the elf even needed guards; after more than one thorough questioning and little food or water, he was more of a shell than a living creature. His wrists and ankles were chained, and the chains resembled her collar, which explained why he had tried no magic. His head hung forward, as if he slept, but the moment she put a hand to the bars of the cell, he looked up.

The fire was still in his eyes. They had beaten his body, but not his will.

"I remember you." Though a bit hoarse, his voice was smooth and correct. "You look so innocent compared to the others. I suppose it works to your advantage."

"I am not one of them."

"You . . . you look like one of them, although you dress more like a woodland spirit than living death. You also walk around freely."

She leaned forward, inspecting him with a different perspective now. "You don't sound as beaten as you appear."

He laughed, but it turned into more of a croak. "I am very well beaten, mistress!"

"No, I think you're holding out better than you pretend."

"You think I *want* this to go on and on? You think I enjoy this pain?"

His lips were chapped, and it was clear he was suffering from dehydration.

Sharissa searched the area, but she could not find any water. Nor did there seem to be a key to his cell. She would have to talk to him from here.

"Listen to me! I'm not one of them! We're part of the same people—"

"Which makes you a *Vraad*." He took no pains to hide his distaste.

"We are *not* all the same! Look at this!" She nearly put her hands on the collar, but restrained herself at the last moment. Sharissa hoped he would recognize her predicament, else she would be forced to prove herself to him in a more painful manner.

He stared at her neck, but said nothing. She waited, always fearing that someone would, in the next breath, enter the building and deprive her of a chance for private conversation. After a time, the elf closed his eyes. The sorceress tried to ready herself for a demonstration that would, she hoped, convince him before it killed her.

"You *could* be a trickster," he commented without opening his eyes. "The collar could be nothing more than display for my benefit."

"I can prove it to you easily enough." Sharissa began to tremble. It would not be an easy thing. She was brave, but no one liked the thought of accidentally choking themselves to death.

The elf's almond-tear eyes opened, burning into her own. He shook his head as best his bonds would allow him to do. "That will not be necessary. I think . . . I think I will trust you on this."

A sigh of relief escaped her. "Thank you. I was willing to prove myself, but this is hardly an experience I've come to enjoy."

"I know the feeling." He rattled his chains and pointed at his own collar. "My name, mistress—the one I give you, that is—is Faunon."

"I am Sharissa Zeree. Definitely a prisoner like yourself."

"I've seen how they treat you, mistress, and I wish they would treat all their prisoners so!"

She reddened. "I didn't mean to downgrade what they've done to you! It's true I've been pampered, but only because they think I will become one of them."

His smile unnerved her. "Perish such a horrible notion! That would be like turning a flower into a weed!"

Time had to be running out. "Listen, I only came to see if you still have the will to escape. I know only tales about this region, and I'll need your help!"

"How fortunate for me."

"I would help you regardless of whether I needed you or not!" Ariela had never been this difficult to talk to! Still, she could not blame the elf for his rather cynical attitude. "Are you interested?"

He managed to give her a dry chuckle. "Do you think I would prefer to stay here?"

"I don't know when I'll be back yet. There's...there's another who has to come with us, but I have to find where they've hidden him."

The elf gave her a quizzical look, but she had no time to explain about Darkhorse. "Never mind! I promise I'll be back soon!"

"I am in your hands. Thank you for giving me something to think about."

For some reason, his last statement, coupled with his expression then, made her redden. The sorceress rushed to the door leading out of the building and quickly listened for any sound of movement. It had long ago occurred to her that she had been extremely fortunate so far. Was it possible that they had *wanted* her to meet with Faunon? It was the sort of devious plot that Barakas appreciated.

So much the better. If they were willing to give her the opportunity, she would find a way to make them regret it.

There were a few Tezerenee in sight, but none of them was facing her direction. Sharissa slipped out the door and hurried away, trying to put as much distance between her and the elf as possible. They might be watching her at this very moment, but she could play the game. If it turned out that she was incorrect and that no one knew where she was, then her precautions were appropriate.

Sharissa had a sudden desire to return to the days of her childhood, when things had been much, much more simple and straightforward.

Lord Barakas summoned her later that day. It was a formal audience, meaning she would stand and listen, speaking only when required. Her bodyguard informed her of this latter part as they walked to the audience. Sharissa hardly paid her any attention. She would not change. The patriarch expected her to be defiant, and she had no plans to disappoint him.

They were nearly there when a tall, dragonhelmed warrior stepped out of a side corridor and blocked their path. "I will escort the Lady Sharissa from this point on. You may retire for a time."

"Yes, my Lord Lochivan."

Neither said anything until the other Tezerenee had departed. Then, before the sorceress could build her bitterness up for a sufficient verbal volley, Lochivan removed his helm and said, "I apologize for bringing you to this place. I tried my best to leave you out of all of this, but you were too willful."

"You mean I saw through your treachery!"

"Too late, if you recall. It was not treachery, either. You know my first loyalty is to the clan. I did succeed in convincing my father that, if you were left behind, there would be less support for Master Zeree if he chose to follow us. For you, the other Vraad would rally; for Darkhorse, they would be less inclined. You and your father were the only danger to the success of our plan."

His manner was companionable, as usual, but Sharissa had no faith in appearances. "Whether you tried to help me or not hardly excuses what you helped to do to Darkhorse! Where is he? Again and again, I've asked the patriarch about him! He promised to let me see Darkhorse, then *refused* later!"

Lochivan scratched his throat with his free hand. The young Zeree saw that the rash had spread; the Tezerenee's skin was red and dry, almost scaly. She almost felt a compulsion to touch her own throat, but she knew that it was not a rash that afflicted her. Only a collar.

"Matters came up." The warrior would not elaborate on the subject, but continued, "Tonight is intended to make up for that. You will see Darkhorse at the audience."

"Will I be able to talk to him?"

"*That* I cannot say." Replacing his helm, Lochivan reached for her arm. She gave it to him with great reluctance and only because she now desired the audience. He smiled through his helm, but Sharissa turned away, choosing instead to look forward. Her companion grunted and began to escort her to the Lord Tezerenee's court.

The two of them had barely started when another warrior came down the hall. Lochivan stiffened, and Sharissa instinctively clutched his arm tighter. The Tezerenee coming toward them weaved about as if either drunk or wounded. No blood decorated his breastplate or his dragon-scale armor, but neither did he appear to be inebriated.

Lochivan was furious. He released Sharissa and stopped before the newcomer. "What is the *matter* with you?"

"Painnnn..." the Tezerenee rasped. He refused to look up. One arm wrapped across his torso, while the other helped him guide himself along the corridor. Sharissa's fear turned to sympathy. Now that he was closer, she could see that he was wracked by pain. Tezerenee or not, he needed help. The concerned sorceress reached for him, but Lochivan barred her with one arm.

"Leave him be." To the bent-over figure he commanded, "Stand up! Remember that you are Tezerenee! Pain is *not* a consideration!"

Sharissa glanced at her companion, who had, while he talked, almost become his father.

"Yesss... yes, my lord!" The warrior straightened, but his body quivered. He did not look at the two, however, and Lochivan did not seem inclined to press the suffering warrior for any more.

"That is better! Have someone look at you! You may go!" Lochivan turned away with an imperious air about him, as if the warrior no longer existed in his eyes.

"By your leave," the trembling figure managed to get out. He marched away, stumbling now and then.

Sharissa watched him vanish down another hall. She whirled on Lochivan.

"That man was practically dying! He could have found someone to look at him by now if you had not insisted on appearances!"

"I held him for only a short time. He is a Tezerenee; he is trained to live with pain." He took her arm. "Now, come! The Lord Barakas Tezerenee awaits you!"

She allowed him to take her arm, but made it clear with her tentative touch that she loathed his very existence. Since his treachery, the sorceress had seen Lochivan in a new light. Many of his mannerisms now appeared forced, as if the true Lochivan was some creature hidden within the body that walked beside her, a creature that only played at humanity. He might as well have been a drake instead of a man.

They had walked little farther when they arrived at their destination. Two iron doors, again flaunting the dragon or drake that was the symbol of the Tezerenee, stood before them. Even as they neared the doors, guards reached out and opened the way for them. Within the chamber, someone who evidently had remained alert announced their coming.

"Lady Sharissa Zeree! Lord Lochivan!"

Sharissa was just wondering whether all the Tezerenee went by "Lord" or "Lady"—all of the patriarch's *children* did—when the sheer immensity of the grand court finally struck her.

The chamber almost seemed designed to hold the entire clan, plus every outsider loyal to the patriarch. The ceiling floated so high above her head that, had it been colored the same as the sky, she would have been willing to believe that they were outside. Banners hung everywhere, almost as many as there were Tezerenee. Fully armed guards lined the walls from the entrance to the marble dais on the far end. Wary handlers kept leashed young drakes under control. On the shoulders of several of the assembled figures, both armored and not, were perched hunting wyverns.

"Come along," Lochivan whispered. She had been so over awed by the assembled throng and the massive dimensions of the chamber that she had paused.

Ahead of them, seated on tall thrones that were, in turn, located on the uppermost level of the dais, were the lord and lady of the Tezerenee. Lady Alcia sat in regal splendor, calmly observing the two newcomers. Lord Barakas, on the other hand, leaned on an elbow and brooded over some thought. From his expression, it was clear he barely noticed Sharissa or his son.

Between and a step behind the thrones stood Reegan. His hands were behind his back, and he stood as if inspecting his legions . . . which, in a sense, he was doing. For the first time, she saw him as the power he would become should Barakas die. He only needed more tempering, something the patriarch wanted her to take a part in.

I might as well marry a drake!

Lochivan continued to walk her down the long, carpeted path that led to the clan master and his bride. When they were nearly halfway there, Barakas finally looked up. By the time they had reached the end of their journey, an open area just before and below the dais, his eyes had become fixed on her.

"Lady Sharissa," Lochivan announced, at the same time falling to one knee in deference to his parents. Sharissa made no move to follow his example; she was no Tezerenee, and kneeling would be seen only as a weakening of her will. Instead, the captive sorceress nodded to her hosts, beginning with Lady Alcia.

Barakas gave her a patient smile. "My Lady Sharissa Zeree. Welcome."

She said nothing. Beside her, Lochivan rose.

"Your reluctance to be here is understandable, and your will is admirable. You have been very patient—"

"I've had no choice!" the sorceress snapped.

"—and I hope that soon you will be able to dispense with that uncomfortable collar." The patriarch went on without pause. He straightened, and turned to the rest of those assembled. "Loyalty is utmost. Obedience is rewarded and defiance is punished."

On an unspoken signal, a Tezerenee brought forth a large box. It was elaborate in design and, although Sharissa's senses were dulled, very likely magical in some respect. The warrior knelt before Barakas and presented it to him. Nodding, the patriarch took the object and dismissed the newcomer. Barakas turned back to Sharissa and her unwanted companion.

"Please be so kind as to step back."

Lochivan took her arm and pulled her gently but firmly to the front row of the assembled followers. As he did, he whispered, "Say nothing! Watch first!"

Sharissa, who *had* been on the verge of speaking, clamped her mouth shut. She had wanted to ask again where Darkhorse was and when she would be able to see him. She had even planned on mentioning how the patriarch had *promised* her and then apparently broken his promise. Despite the absolute power he wielded among his clan, Barakas was a slave to his pride.

"We have come into our own once again!" the Lord Tezerenee uttered. His hand ran along the side of the box, as if he were caressing it. The young Zeree realized he was performing some sort of spell as he spoke. "Our powers are still far from their glory, but they *have* increased, almost as if we are linked to Nimth once more!"

The last statement made Sharissa frown. There was something in it she felt she should know about, but what that was she could not say. What concerned her more at the moment was the box and its purpose in all of this.

"I now demonstrate for our guest some of the extent of our might!"

He opened the box.

"Freeeee! By the Void! Freeee!" The near-mad voice bellowed in relief. Sharissa felt the floor vibrate as the prisoner of the box burst forth, still screaming its happiness at being released.

A thick black substance poured from the box to the floor below the dais. As it flowed, it took on shape, becoming more and more one distinct form. Sharissa needed no one to tell her who it was; his voice alone had sufficed.

"The emptiness! All alone! Curse you, Barakas Tezerenee! Only you could make a place more horrifying than the Void!"

Darkhorse stood before the patriarch and his mate, pupilless, ice-blue orbs glittering in swelling anger. His hooves tore at the stone floor, gouging valley after valley.

The sorceress could hold back no longer. She pulled free of Lochivan, who was somewhat dazed by the shadow steed's remarkable entrance. "Darkhorse!"

"Who calls?" The ebony stallion swung around and glared her way, not immediately recognizing her. When he finally did, he was so overjoyed he laughed. Most of those in the chamber put their hands to their ears. Barakas remained unmoving. "Sharissa Zeree! At last!"

He started toward her running figure. They were almost within reach when Sharissa felt the familiar but frightening touch of her collar. She could no longer breathe. Darkhorse halted at the same time she did, but not, it appeared, because of her predicament. Rather, he was trembling, as if he, too, suffered from pain.

On her knees, she tried to imagine what to do. Her collar was choking her, but she had made no attempt to touch it. Strong hands took her under the arms. As the slim woman fought for breath, she was dragged back from her one friend.

The collar grew loose.

"You . . . you call *me* demon, Lord of the Tezerenee! You are the monster!" Darkhorse trotted a few steps farther away from the sorceress. "I might have survived, but you would have *killed* her!"

"She will be fine," the patriarch responded. He remained calm, almost uninterested in events.

Leaning against Lochivan, who was the one who had pulled her away, Sharissa realized that Barakas had once more planned well. He had allowed both of them to learn in the most deadly way that they could not come within a certain range of one another, lest one or both suffer. More than likely it would be her, although the patriarch had evidently discovered many of the eternal's weaknesses.

"Can you stand?" Lochivan asked quietly. He sounded both unnerved and ashamed. "I had no idea what he planned. I would have warned you about your friend if I had."

She did not reply, choosing instead to break free of his grip and rise on her own. Once certain her legs were sturdy enough, she looked first at Darkhorse, who still looked to be in pain, and finally at the patriarch.

"I must apologize, Lady Sharissa. A necessary measure. The demon has been of great value, doing by himself what we cannot—as yet—do en masse."

"I always—" She coughed, her lungs still not fully satiated. "I always thought you believed in as little sorcery as possible. Was it not you who preached of the true strength being that of the body?"

"A good warrior utilizes the best of weapons for each situation. Your demon friend gave us access to our rightful empire. While we experimented with the powers we found reemerging within us, he built this citadel with his own skills. Through his efforts, we were able to secure ourselves while we developed."

"And this is how you reward him!" She indicated the box. "What sort of horrible trap is *that*?"

"This? This is merely a box." He held it up for her to see. Across from her, Darkhorse cringed like one whipped again and again who must now stare at the very tool that had done the evil work. "There are a few minor additions, spells that make it impossible to hear all but my voice and prevent something within from speaking to any but myself. It is proof against his sorcerous being and only I can open it, but it is, in the end, still only a box. It inflicts no pain upon him."

"It is *agony incarnate*!" roared Darkhorse. "I cannot move! I cannot speak! He becomes my only contact! I have been so *alone*!"

Careful to avoid stepping too near Darkhorse, Sharissa moved toward the patriarch's throne. Sentries instantly appeared before their lord, their weapons ready for the sorceress.

"Away!" Barakas rose and pushed them aside with his free hand. He put the open box in the crook of his arm and surveyed the defiant Zeree. "You had something to say?"

What *could* she say that would not be empty bitterness? Barakas held the upper hand. He had given her this audience just to humiliate her, to show how hopeless her cause was. "Would anything I say make a difference to you, dragonlord?"

"Very much, in fact," he said, reseating himself. Though he now wore an apologetic expression, as if he regretted his earlier actions, Sharissa knew better. "The collar is a great travesty that you should not have to endure. Your place should be beside us!" At those words, Reegan, who had been standing quietly behind his parents, suddenly grew attentive. Feeling his eyes upon her, Sharissa forced herself to keep her own attention focused on the patriarch. She would not acknowledge the heir, her intended mate if Barakas had his way.

"I have no desire to even stand *near* you, Lord Tezerenee. I never will."

The assembly broke into a fearful murmur. Others had likely died for saying less to the very face of Barakas Tezerenee. Yet, despite the implications, the patriarch seemed unconcerned about the remark. Instead, he stroked the lid of the box once, then gently closed it. Darkhorse shuffled back a few steps out of what could only be fear. Energy crackled around the subdued stallion, and he seemed to freeze. Some bond tied him to the box.

"Remove the collar."

Renewed whispers spread through the clan. Lochivan marched up to Sharissa, who stood as lifeless as stone. What could the patriarch be planning? Did he think she would simply stand there once her abilities were hers to utilize again? She could—

As Lochivan reached up to her neck and touched the collar, Sharissa realized she could do *nothing*. Fight? Even if she were the greatest power among these Vraad, she could hardly expect to take them all on and win. Barakas would be the most well-protected target of all. Flee? Where would she go? What would happen to Darkhorse . . . or even Faunon, whom she had made a pact with? She could hardly escape without them, especially with both so helpless. Who was to say how much Darkhorse in particular would suffer?

Lochivan slipped the magical collar from her throat, but Sharissa felt no eagerness. Another collar now threatened to suffocate her. It was a collar forged from her fear for the others, notably Darkhorse. She saw now why Barakas had not taken her insult to heart; he knew she would follow him, if only because she could not abandon a friend. He might not even know about her visit to Faunon, but he certainly knew how much the ebony eternal had come to mean to the sorceress.

"Sharissa . . ." Darkhorse muttered, his tone indicating he also knew why she did nothing now that her powers had been restored.

She was once more alone before the clan master, Lochivan having stepped back with the deadly manacle. One hand slowly went to her throat, where she absently rubbed the skin. The act unexpectedly recalled to her the constant scratching many of the Tezerenee did during the course of the day. Sharissa let her hand drop.

"Good," Barakas said, nodding at the same time. "You see? Your welfare means much to us, Sharissa Zeree. I want you to work *with* us."

Cooperation? Work *with* the Tezerenee? Was there something more to this audience besides her humiliation? Had the patriarch found himself in need of her abilities?

Barakas leaned forward, as if speaking to the sorceress as a fellow conspirator in some plot. His voice, however, was loud enough for all to hear.

"There is to be a second expedition, a larger one, to the mountain aerie abandoned by the bird people. It will be led by myself and leaves in the morning." He shot a glance at Darkhorse. Though the shadow steed moved his head and glared back, it was evident that he could still do little else. Whatever spell bound him to the box made his ability to move subject to the will of the patriarch. He might as well have been a puppet on strings.

Pretending to forget the eternal, Barakas looked at the cautious spellcaster before him and continued, "Your knowledge and skills would be invaluable to our effort, Lady Sharissa. We would like you to join us."

Or Darkhorse will suffer? she wondered. Had the patriarch passed on to her a silent, veiled threat or had he so turned her that she now saw imaginary plots in each movement, each *breath* he took?

"Of what use would I be to you? Even now, shorn of your trinket and in full use of my powers, there's nothing I can do that you cannot do." Now it was her turn to glance at Darkhorse. "Through fair means or foul."

Again there was stirring among the Tezerenee. A normal

court under the patriarch no doubt consisted of Barakas preaching and his followers nodding in silent obedience. Even Sharissa's rebuffs, as futile as they probably were, were jarring to the Tezerenee and their loyal outsiders.

Barakas leaned back in his throne. The time had come for the fatal thrust. She steadied herself, wondering what he could throw at her that would bring about her willing cooperation in a Tezerenee effort.

"Are not the founders a particular interest of yours?"

She said nothing, afraid what might come out.

He read her expression and nodded. "The avians are merely the latest of a continuing chain of squatters. The first and true lords, if the word brought back is true, were the *founders*—our *accursed* godlike ancestors!"

"The founders..." she whispered. Her strength began to abandon her as she realized he knew exactly how to play on her desires.

"It is one of their places of power."

Sharissa could not, would not face Darkhorse as she bent her head earthward and replied in a quieter, resigned voice, "I'll go with you."

The Lord Barakas Tezerenee nodded imperiously and, looking up at his people, announced, "This audience is at an end."

A legion of silent specters, the throng began departing the court. A hand fell softly onto the young Zeree's shoulder. She looked up at Lochivan, but did not really see him. Her mind was back to a time, fifteen years before, when she had been manipulated time and again, mostly because of her lack of experience in dealing with her kind. Now, it appeared as if a decade and a half had never been. Once more, she was being turned this way and that like a small child. Frustration and anger smoldered within her as it never had before.

Her expression must have altered, because Lochivan quickly took his hand from her shoulder.

I will not *be manipulated again!* Last time it resulted in the death of a friend.

The sorceress whirled and followed the other out, not even bowing to the lord and lady of the Tezerenee as was probably proper. Lochivan, reacting late, was forced to follow behind her. She *would* journey with the Tezerenee to the cavern. She *would* do her best to unravel whatever legacies the founders and their successors had left there. She *would* find a way to free Darkhorse . . . and Faunon, too.

Most of all, she would ensure, in some way, that the Tezerenee, *especially* their master, would never make use of those legacies.

——— XI ———

Two days among the Quel had answered no questions for Gerrod. He still had no idea how long he had been adrift in the Void. To his own way of thinking, it had been a mere handful of hours, but he knew from his talks with Dru that time played tricks where the domain of nothingness was concerned. What might seem hours might prove to be months. For all he knew, his people were dead or, worse yet, Sharissa was a valued member of the clan, bride to the heir and mother of his children.

A heavy thump against his back sent him flailing to the ground. Around him, the Quel unleashed a chorus of hooting. From earlier confrontations, he had come to the conclusion that this was the bulky creatures' equivalent of laughter.

Rising with as much dignity as he could muster, the Vraad scanned his surroundings once more. They were traveling southwest and, while Gerrod was not yet certain, he suspected he was far from where he wanted to be. In the distance, there appeared to be a vast body of water, possibly a great sea, but trying to focus on it was impossible. For the last day, he had been forced to shield his eyes from everything, even his inhuman companions.

The problem lay in the fact that *everything* around him *glittered* like so much perfect crystal. The Quel themselves were not excluded; being so close, they were sometimes blinding. Looking down helped a bit, but even the rocky ground beneath his feet sparkled.

He knew the cause. This region was laden with crystalline fragments of all shapes and sizes, scattered about as if at some point there had been a great upheaval, perhaps the shaping of this land by the world itself.

The glitter of the Quel was not natural but camouflage. Their shells consisted of a series of folds that, at birth, must have been much more open. In each fold were countless gems that the shell had eventually grown over, albeit not completely. Any Seeker in the sky would be half blinded by the landscape already, and the crystals on the Quel would make them blend into all that glitter.

How well that protection worked outside of this region was debatable.

The crystals had one more use that was no doubt planned by their users. They had a dizzying effect on those unused to them. Somehow, the Quel had identified him as a spellcaster; it might be that they had even spotted him coming into the Dragonrealm. Upon deciding to let him live, which had turned out to be the point of an unintelligible argument that had lasted more than a quarter hour, one of the armadillolike creatures had dragged him forward and thrust a particularly bright gem before his eyes. The blindness caused by the bright sunlight reflecting off of the gem had been temporary, but it had been accompanied by what he had taken at the time to be simple heat reflection. It had given him a headache, which he had thought of as a minor nuisance until he tried to clear his head. The concentration he needed was not there. Had he tried any serious escape attempt utilizing his abilities, it was just as likely he would have included himself in any attack on his captors.

The headache had vanished, but only so that the dizziness could replace it.

Another hour passed. The sun was on its downward arc, which, unfortunately, put it before the travelers. *Am I to go permanently blind?* he wondered. His companions were indifferent to his situation; they appeared to have a series of eyelids, all but the outermost one transparent to a certain point. The brighter it became, the darker their eyes appeared to grow as another lid slid into place. He wondered whether it was a natural ability or whether they had altered themselves much the way the Vraad had once.

A heavy hand—*paw*, as far as the disheveled Tezerenee was concerned—took hold of Gerrod's arm and dragged him to a halt.

"What is it?" he snarled, both frightened and angry. He

wanted to teach these overgrown beasts their place, but, to his misfortune, they already knew it. To them, *he* was the animal.

The one who had stopped him raised its battle-ax and pointed to one of the minor hills that had just cropped up to their right. Gerrod spent more time staring at the weapon than at yet another of the land's unremarkable features. He had felt its weight more than once, usually when he was swatted with the flat of it, and knew that no human could have lifted it from the ground, much less used it in so casual a manner.

The Quel beside him hooted and pointed at the hill again. The Vraad started toward it, but was pulled back as if he weighed less than nothing. The Quel hooted again.

Gerrod shook his head, hoping that they understood by now that this was his way of saying he did not understand. The warlock had been shaking his head quite a bit in the past two days.

Frustrated, the massive creature prodded the earth and made his prisoner look down.

Something was burrowing through the ground toward them.

He tried to back away, but the Quel held him. The burrowing form moved closer. Gerrod tried to formulate a spell, but the dizziness prevented him. His captors had brought him here to be sacrificed to some horror they worshiped. It had to be. Whether it killed him or not, he would have to try a spell... *any* spell!

A swat on the head put an end to that thought. His head pounded and his ears rang, all in addition to his ever-present impediment.

It burst forth, claws ready... and proved to be nothing more than another Quel, only larger than the others.

The warlock found himself falling before the newcomer, propelled there by the one who had taken his arm.

A snouted visage looked down upon him, contempt for his pathetic little form more than apparent. One head-sized paw reached toward him, claws bared, and Gerrod was almost certain he was about to breathe his last. Instead of crushing the warlock's skull, an act that would certainly have required little exertion on the Quel's part, the earth-digger took him by the collar and dragged him closer.

"Dragon's blood!" he gasped. His shirt and cloak collars were pulled so tight that it was nearly impossible to draw air.

His new captor hooted several times to the other, who

returned his noises with some of their own and then turned away. They were departing.

What now? the bedraggled Vraad wanted to know. Only one thing came to mind, but surely the armored monstrosity would not—

Gerrod in one hand, the Quel effortlessly began to burrow in the ground.

"No! I can't! Stop!" He struggled to free himself, but his horrific keeper took no notice of his weak efforts. Visions of being buried alive shook Gerrod's very being. The earth grew nearer and nearer; he might have been sinking in quicksand. Already, most of the Quel's unsightly form was covered with dirt. Only the wrist and hand that held his captive were still visible.

The warlock took a deep breath and barely had time to hold it before his face met the ground. He shut his eyes and prayed that death would be quick.

Loose dirt tried to enter his nostrils. Gerrod could not move his hands forward and was forced to exhale through his nose in order to clear it. He began struggling for more air.

The Quel and he broke into a vast tunnel.

Light of a limited source allowed him some inspection of his surroundings. The dim glow came from several crystals lined along the tunnel wall. Those nearest were brightest. Gerrod tested the air—having no other choice by this time—and found it dry but breathable.

He was aware that this could hardly be the same tunnel that his present guardian had come from. Most likely, it stood some distance beneath or to the side of the one the Quel itself had burrowed. Why it had chosen to make a path of its own rather than take this one in the first place was a question Gerrod doubted the Quel would answer even if the two of them could understand one another's language. Like Zeree's Seekers, the earth dwellers had mind-sets much different than those of the Vraad. Perhaps this tunnel was specifically reserved for the transportation of surface creatures like himself.

Satisfied that his charge was in fair shape, the Quel pulled the Tezerenee to his feet. From somewhere a long, needlelike spear materialized. Gerrod could not recall seeing it before, but there had been no time for such unimportant observations until now.

The Quel pushed him ahead and leveled the spear. Gerrod understood his meaning and hastened to comply.

He had walked only a few yards when he began to sense the intense aura of sorcery all about him. Some feature about this place seemed to draw from the natural forces of the land. Gerrod was near a place of power, a well of magic of sorts. It was not merely the crystals in the walls; their only purpose seemed to be to light the portion of the tunnel where travelers happened to be. Still, Gerrod had enough knowledge of crystal sorcery to realize that the Quel might have other gemstones that gathered the raw energy of the world for their later manipulation. There were many things that could be achieved through that particular magic that normal Vraad sorcery—and possibly even Dragonrealm sorcery—could only struggle in vain to achieve.

If I can find those gemstones . . . There might yet be a way out of all of this, Gerrod decided.

It occurred to him than that he had not felt any dizziness since being brought to the tunnel.

He turned on the Quel, who froze and readied the spear, and cast a crude but deadly missile of fire at the creature.

The armadillolike horror hooted in derision.

Gerrod's mouth hung open as he desperately tried another gambit. He could *sense* the power around him; why could he not cast even the simplest of spells?

Sufficiently amused, the Quel ceased hooting and jabbed at him with the spear, clearly desiring that the tiny, weak thing before it stop playing and keep walking. Gerrod did so, his resistance all but dead. Whatever caused power to gather here was drawing what he attempted to summon even before he could make use of it. The warlock was as helpless as ever. His only consolation lay in the fact that he no longer suffered from any dizziness.

It did nothing to soothe his weary mind.

The Quel proceeded to steer him down tunnel after tunnel after tunnel. It was not long before Gerrod gave up trying to memorize his path; the tunnel system consisted almost entirely of one winding trail crossing another. There were at least two points where he was almost certain they had backtracked. His guard, however, continued to steer him along with purpose.

Claustrophobia began to set in. They were on a downward route—at least *that* much Gerrod had been able to tell, little good it did him. The tunnels were growing narrower. He pictured the many tons of earth above him and what would happen to the tunnel should a slight tremor occur. It was with great relief that he finally noticed the brilliant illumination far down the opposite end of the latest tunnel. So certain was the tired warlock that they had somehow reached the surface again that he almost started running. Only a reminding hoot from the Quel behind him kept him from doing so. For the rest of the trek Gerrod struggled to maintain his composure. A spear in his back—*through* his entire torso, more likely—would make his return to the outside world a short one, indeed.

It was not until he was mere yards from the mouth of the tunnel that it became clear that this was *not* the sun that glowed so bright.

Gerrod stepped out into the last domain of the Quel.

To call it a city was perhaps to use a misnomer. There were no streets, no buildings as a Vraad would know them, and the Quel he saw moving around were not going about the mundane daily activities that made up city life. Gerrod had spent a few days in the Vraad colony during its first years, mostly at the request of Dru Zeree or his daughter when they needed his assistance with some project, and he recalled some of the things he had seen his people doing in order to get through yet another day. The creatures before him, some so distant they were little more than shapes, moved with purpose. Whether they climbed the walls of the massive cavern, burrowed from one tunnel to another, or simply walked across the smooth floor, they traveled as if their existence depended on it.

He looked up and found what he had taken for the sun. The ceiling of the cavern was dotted with thousands of crystals, but, unlike the gems in the tunnels, they were not the actual source of the light. Instead, he saw that the light came from elsewhere, perhaps even the surface, and was reflected again and again by the array spread throughout the ceiling. It was a masterful manipulation of the crystals' natural abilities and required no sorcery—something that would have been impossible under present circumstances anyway.

The Quel who guarded him had come to his side and was also staring out at the city, but not for the same reason. It located another of its kind, who looked more or less exactly like every other Quel that Gerrod had seen, and signaled to it.

The other monster hooted a short reply and climbed along the wall toward the duo.

Both fascinated and horrified, the warlock could only watch. That such huge beasts could move about so nimbly down here and climb from one precarious position to another was astounding. He hoped they did not plan on having him attempt to mimic their skill; if so, it would be a short climb—and a fatal fall.

"Sharissa Zeree," he whispered. "What have you gotten me into?"

Gerrod soon found that he had once more been turned over to another guard. The newcomer looked him over, reached out with a speed remarkable for its size, and wrapped the helpless Tezerenee in a one-armed bear hug. While Gerrod struggled to keep from being cracked into small pieces, the massive, armadillolike creature managed a handhold on the wall and pulled itself out of the tunnel and into the huge cavern. One-armed, the Quel somehow scurried across the wall for some distance before diving into yet another tunnel. Even as it landed on its feet, it released its prisoner. The warlock fell to the floor an ungainly sight.

More tunnels followed. Gerrod was convinced that this *was* to be the rest of his life. He pictured himself going from tunnel to tunnel—with occasional panic-filled rides in the arms of leaping Quel—until he came out of the other side of the world. Would that be the other continent? he wondered. Likely not. With his luck it would be the bottom of the middle of the sea.

He tried another spell at one point, a spell whose results would be for his eyes only if it did succeed, but the strange power that the Quel race controlled still held sway. Sorcery would not save him here; he would have to rely upon his mind and body.

When they came at last to yet another lit cavern, the warlock gave it only a cursory glance at first. It held only a few Quel, who darted this way and that or stood conversing near the center, and not much else. A few tunnels dotted the sides of this chamber.

There was a pause that dragged out much too long for Gerrod. He turned to his captor and, though he knew the creature understood him as well as the warlock understood a drake, asked, "Well? Which way?"

He nearly lost his composure when the guard looked down at

him as if listening and then abruptly pointed toward the group clustered around the center of the chamber. It was pure coincidence, the Tezerenee told himself. The Quel could not possibly understand him; that had already been proven . . . hadn't it?

A deep grunt from his companion warned him that he had a very short time limit within which to respond to its command. The needle spear that this one also carried emphasized more than that particular point.

As Gerrod stepped into the cavern chamber, the Quel within looked up from whatever they were doing and stared at him. Unlike those he had met so far, these eyed him more with an open curiosity than with contempt or hatred. Gerrod met the studious gaze of one and noted an intelligence there that was far above those who had brought him here.

The Quel conversed for several seconds, the sounds emitted by the sentry indicating the respect in which it held the others. When that was done, the one who had matched gazes with Gerrod stepped forward. It waved a paw at the warlock, who walked in cautious fashion toward it, his eyes constantly returning to the guard. Quite suddenly, Gerrod wanted to leave this place and return to the monotony of the tunnels or even the blood-coursing fear of a cavern crossing. He knew now that he had at last reached his destination.

As ever, the Quel seemed to take his responses with a touch of amusement. Dru Zeree's short experience with the monsters had told the warlock little; most of the Quel the sorcerer had encountered had died shortly after in combat with a party of Seekers.

Would that I could trade places with you now, Master Zeree, Gerrod thought sourly.

Behind him, he heard the guard depart.

A host of Quel descended upon him before he was halfway to the one who had summoned him forward. The hooded Tezerenee buried himself in the confines of his cloak and cursed his inability to defend himself. Even a sword or ax would have been nice. It would have at least given him some comfort in his final moments.

They hovered about him, gesturing and hooting to one another like a parliament of owls. Several of them spoke to him, their unintelligible comments often ending on a questioning note.

One outshouted the rest, possibly the same one who had first waved to him. It indicated he should follow it. Glad of anything that would free him of the imposing circle of figures, Gerrod obeyed.

There was a platform in the center of the room, a low one, which was why he had not seen it behind the Quel when he had first arrived. On it were arrayed several rows of crystals, some in patterns and some not. Many individual stones had been purposely cut to create new shapes. The Quel leader—Gerrod was willing to *assume* that this was the leader—picked one up and held it out to the Vraad.

Fascination momentarily overwhelming caution, he took the crystal from the outstretched paw.

Understanding—cooperation—question?

Caught unaware by the immediate influx of images and impressions, the Vraad dropped the gem. The chaos in his mind evaporated like so much early-morning dew. "Manee's madness!" he swore, eyeing the jewel as if it were alive.

"What was that you . . . did you . . ."

The Quel who had given him the crystal pointed to it again. With so many fearsome faces around him, Gerrod could do nothing but obey, yet he moved with as much caution as he felt they would allow him. He had a fair idea of what purpose the crystal served, but the sensations that had invaded his thoughts had frightened him.

His hand snared the gem . . . and the impressions returned to torment his mind.

Weak . . . elf . . . question? . . . Quel . . . enemy . . . question?

"Not so fast!" The images became jumbled. The warlock saw distended versions of himself and the Quel. There was also what must have been an elf.

The crystal served as a way of communication, but it was limited when dealing with two such diverse minds. A Quel obviously did not think in the same terms as a Vraad. Still, it was better than no communication at all. Gerrod simply had to puzzle out the images.

He wondered why his captors needed no such gems, but then recalled all of the crystals embedded in their armored hides. Why not include one of these among the rest? They would never be without a means of understanding an outsider. The guards *had* understood him after all; it was just that *he* had been without a means of translating *their* words and thoughts.

Elf . . . question?

Did they think he was an elf? "No, not an elf. I'm a Vraad. Vraad."

Vraad . . . question? . . . nest . . . question?

What did they mean . . . "Do you want to know where I come from?"

He felt an impression of approval. The Quel, long experienced in this method of communication, were having an easier time understanding him.

Though he did not have to speak, Gerrod felt more comfortable doing so. "I come from—" Should he tell them about Nimth? The colony? "I come from across the seas to the east."

No other land . . . statement! . . . arrival here . . . question?

They refused to believe in the other continent. Could this be the work of the guardians, the founders' magical servants? "I came from across the seas. I didn't mean to come here. It was an accident."

Land is dying . . . statement! . . . Sheekas . . . Seekers . . . same . . . question? . . . loosen living death . . . horror . . . statement! . . . Lost . . . statement! . . . winged ones triumphant . . . statement!

"Wait! Please wait!" Too much at once! "The land is dying? Which land?"

He saw the very terrain he had walked through for the last two days. For the first time, he felt the despair of the armadillolike race. Why had he not noticed the bleakness of the landscape the first time? There was some plant life, but it was widely scattered and barely able to sustain itself. "This land? This land is dying?"

The Seekers—his host had picked up the Vraad name for the avians—had unleashed some living death upon their foes. Gerrod felt a chill when the Quel thought about what had happened. Whatever the avians had loosed had sucked the life from this domain.

"I understand . . . I think."

He was buffeted by more. Now that he had been told of the disaster that had befallen them, the Quel showed him the dead, petrified corpses that were cold to the touch. Gerrod watched wave after wave of Seekers dive from the sky to finish the task, not an actual event, he discovered, but simply the way the Quel visualized their slaughter by their avian foes. They had not actually seen any of the bird people since the last desperate gamble that had saved a portion of their race. It was a certainty among the Quel that the Seekers would soon be on their way.

Their mortal foes would find this domain bereft of survivors. The earth dwellers had planned for this eventuality.

Cities abandoned . . . statement! . . . the dead left behind, a trick on the birds . . . statement! . . . survivors gathered in this cavern, a place unknown to the Seekers . . . statement!

It was becoming a little easier to understand them. Each time the Quel told him of something, the crystal indicated whether it was a query or a comment. He admired the skill with which the artifact had been crafted, but wondered how the gems could work so close to whatever it was that made sorcery impossible here.

It occurred to him that he had not tested his powers in the last few minutes. Perhaps he was no longer bereft of his abilities. It might be interesting to—

The same images and impressions struck him again, only with more force. This time, he paid more attention to them; realizing that there must be a reason they were telling him all of this. What he had taken for a city, for instance, had not been such, at least not compared to what the images revealed to him. Though underground, what the Quel passed on to him was more like what he would have recognized as normal. There were buildings and roads, yet all of it was still deep beneath the earth. The huge cavern that he had passed through had been dug out as a precaution, a place for the Quel to flee should their cities be assaulted.

And so they had been.

More and more was impressed upon him until Gerrod had finally had enough. He put up a halting hand—hoping the Quel understood its meaning—and said, "You want something of me. What is it?"

You elf/not elf . . . statement!/question?

He nodded slowly. "Yes, I am not an elf, but there are similarities." Had he gotten the meaning correct? Should he tell them that they and the elves shared with him a common heritage? Should he mention to them that the Seekers as well were related? Gerrod covertly scanned his companions and decided that it would not be an intelligent move to introduce such radical notions to creatures who could tear him apart without exerting themselves. "You had your patrols searching for elves, didn't you? One of them just lucked onto me instead.''

Several Quel broke into muted conversations. The warlock knew he had guessed correctly; they had sought out an elf, and the patrol, not familiar with the Vraad race, had taken him for one of the woodland dwellers. In their eyes, the physical differences between elf and Vraad were fairly nonexistent.

Short path of travel . . . statement! The Quel leader took Gerrod by the arm, its grip surprisingly gentle. The ravaging claws were carefully turned so as to not rip into his arm. He marveled at the difference between this group and the various guards that had dragged him across half this region. Here he had been treated with a grudging sort of respect, as if these Quel understood that, while he was different, he was capable in his own right.

Could they aid him in his own quest? If he assisted them in whatever their endeavor was, they might be willing to do the same. He chuckled at the thought of legions of the creatures bursting forth from the ground beneath his father's feet. So concerned with the sky and the surface, the Tezerenee would never expect an invasion from under the earth. The patriarch knew of the Quel, but, to him, they were only a story retold by his respected rival, Zeree. The Tezerenee had actually faced the Seekers; they were a recognized threat.

The Quel who held him glanced his way when the warlock started chuckling, perhaps trying to understand what the sounds meant. The crystals might translate the sense of amusement, but Gerrod had no idea of their limitations. He had picked up emotions here and there during their peculiar conversation, but they were always associated with impressions directly transmitted to him. Nothing that did not matter to the situation at hand had been conveyed to him. He hoped his mastery of the astonishing crystals was sufficient to prevent his own random thoughts from being sent out. Until he became more proficient, the Tezerenee decided again to continue speaking out loud in order to keep his thoughts focused.

More proficient? How long, he wondered for the first time, would he be here? Despite their politeness, the hulking creatures had not once indicated that the Tezerenee would be allowed to leave even if he *did* perform whatever task they needed him for. Like many Vraad, the Quel might be capable of smiling, or however they expressed themselves, while at the same time burying their spears or axes in one's back.

To Gerrod, the tunnel he was led into suddenly grew very oppressive, reminding him of the path to a crypt. His, perhaps.

It grew cold, the first time Gerrod had felt cold since coming here. Even the Quel seemed touched by it, for they slowed their pace and a few looked around in what a Vraad would have been growing anxiety touching upon fear. Only the leader seemed nearly the same; its peculiar eyes blinked constantly, but it alone kept the steady pace. The warlock was not reassured, however. He had met enough madmen and fools. For all he knew, the worst of them now dragged him by the arm toward chaos incarnate.

They came to the mouth of yet another cavern, but unlike the others, this one was as black as Darkhorse. Gerrod could see nothing within even after allowing his eyes to adjust. As he turned to his guide, the warlock saw the rest of the band back away a few steps.

The leader's eyes surveyed him from head to toe. Was he being measured? Had the Quel begun to wonder about Gerrod's ability to survive whatever lurked within?

"What is in there?" he asked.

You/we . . . yourself/ourselves . . . statement!/question?

What could *that* mean? He asked the question again, but received only the same response. It made no sense no matter how he turned it. The impressions were jumbled, uncertain. Gerrod came to the conclusion that the Quel could not explain, might not even know. Maybe that was why they needed an outsider like an elf. Whatever lay waiting within the darkness could very well be beyond their comprehension. Once more, he was reminded of how different their minds were from those of his people. It might be that there was nothing for him to worry about.

Gerrod did not believe that for a moment.

As it turned out, his choice was made for him. The Quel leader gripped his arm tight enough to make the Vraad gasp . . . and dragged him inside. The others hung back and waited.

Somehow Gerrod found himself in front of the Quel leader, though he could only tell that by touch. The creature's grip was now the only thing he could be certain about; his eyes could make out nothing in the darkness, and all sound appeared to have ceased the moment they entered.

The Quel released its grip and vanished into the darkness.

"Wait! Where are you?" The warlock turned around, but he could not find the path back even though it should have been visible. "Dragon's blood! Don't leave me in here! I cannot see a thing!" He feared to move, uncertain as to whether his next step would take him over some unseen brink or into the waiting arms of . . . of what?

When, however, it became apparent that no one would be coming to retrieve him, the warlock finally dared a tentative step forward.

A thousand blinding suns brilliantly illuminated the chamber. Gerrod put an arm before his eyes and drew the hood of his cloak over his face. After such complete darkness, the light was doubly harsh. He would have stayed as he was, wrapped tight in his cloak, but for the whispering. He could not make out what they said, but there was a familiarity to their voices, almost as if they were all the same voice, but speaking of different things. None of them heeded the others in the slightest.

They have thrown me to a legion of madmen or demons! he decided. *Monsters who, no doubt, I will soon join in madness!*

What *was* it about the voices that sounded so familiar to him? There were differences, to be sure, but the tones and inflections were the same regardless of that. He knew those voices, knew them to be only *one* voice.

One voice . . .

"Cursed Nimth," the Tezerenee whispered. "What sort of mockery is this?"

He slid the hood back a little and found the light more tolerable now. The discovery disappointed him, for Gerrod had hoped for an excuse to keep from looking. Now, the only thing holding him back was his own cowardice.

The mocking laughter of his father assailed his ears, but Gerrod understood that out of all the voices he heard, his sire's was the only one solely of his imagination. The rest were very real.

He looked up and saw them—the faces in crystal.

They were everywhere, the faces, because, unlike the other chambers, there was nothing here *but* crystal. The floor, the ceiling, the walls—from tiny, indistinct specks to huge, horrifying demons, the faces were all about. They babbled on in a frantic manner, as if their very lives depended on his understanding them. Try as he might, Gerrod could not make out one true word. He strained to hear the whisperings of an ancient, balding seer and the harsh mutterings of a hooded fiend whose face refused to focus for him. Another, a young, amiable figure with a shock of silver hair amidst a field of brown, talked to him as if they were close friends. Even still, the warlock could not make out what the other was trying to convey, despite desperately wanting to understand *one, any one,* of the phantoms trapped in the crystals. He knew them now, knew them as well as he knew himself.

That was who they were. No matter how changed—and some were very, very changed—they were *all* Gerrod.

——— XII ———

Sharissa hated the riding drakes. She hated their appearance, their attitude, and their smell. They could not compare to a horse. Yet, she had been forced to ride one these past two days. The beast was stupid, and it often grew sidetracked. Once it had even snapped at her for no reason whatsoever.

The patriarch listened to her complaints with the air of one tolerating a whining child. It made no difference whether or not she was having trouble with her mount; Tezerenee used drakes for riding, especially when it was always possible that they might be engaged in combat at any moment.

The force that journeyed to the mountains moved with caution. Teleportation was still a spell beyond most of the Tezerenee, and so they were forced to travel in a more mundane manner. The patriarch also distrusted the absence of the Seekers. Barakas might claim that the aerie was abandoned, but he apparently believed that there was risk enough that rushing into things might result in chaos. He had even brought along a very submissive Darkhorse, who turned his head every time Sharissa attempted to speak with the eternal. Darkhorse was ashamed of his actions, despite the fact that much of what he had done had been for her sake. The captive sorceress did not blame him for anything, but trying to tell him that was proving impossible.

Evening came at last. Barakas gave Reegan permission to give the signal to halt. The heir did so in a sullen mood; he still burned over his father's decision to leave his mother in control of the burgeoning empire. Reegan had assumed that the patriarch's being absent would allow him to exercise his long-overdue desire to rule. The heir had even argued with Barakas at some length, but the end had been inevitable. All that Reegan could do was sulk afterward, and he had done so with a determination almost admirable.

Sharissa was just descending from her troublesome steed when a familiar and unwanted voice rose behind her.

"Allow me to help you, Sharissa."

"I can do without your help *or* your friendship, Lochivan!" she retorted, dismounting as she spoke.

He aided her nonetheless. "I understand your bitterness and I know that nothing I can do will make up for the wrongs you believe of me, but we will be together for quite some time—all our lives, in fact."

"I thought is was Reegan the patriarch wanted me to marry, not you."

A brief chuckle escaped him. "I might admit to having had some thoughts on the subject; I like to think that you might find me a bit more entertaining than my bullish brother. That was not what I meant, however. I merely refer to a fact that you must come to face before very long—that you are now and shall ever be a part of us. There is no going back."

She tried to take her pack from the drake's back, but Lochivan moved around her and took it before she could even touch it. "Only a body of water separates me from my father and the other Vraad. Either they will come for me or I will go to them."

Lochivan signaled to another Tezerenee, who rushed over and took charge of the riding drake. That detail taken care of, the patriarch's son started walking, Sharissa's pack still under one arm. The slim woman followed, if only because she knew that he would keep walking regardless of whether she followed. As long as he had her pack, Sharissa knew she would have to listen to him.

"The crossing is deadly; the elf your father took as a mate must have told you that."

"She survived, didn't she?"

"Others perished. Besides, do you think you can sail there all by yourself?"

"I have the use of my abilities back—no thanks to you and yours, Tezerenee."

He paused before a clear, smooth location that would leave her near the very middle of the camp. Coincidentally, several Tezerenee stood patrol nearby. "The elves, I understand, are not without their own measure of power. We may be mighty, but the elements must always be respected."

Reaching out, she tore the pack from his hands. "When have the Vraad ever respected the elements? Have you so easily forgotten Nimth?"

"Hardly. I have learned more than you think, Sharissa. I respect this world. That will *not* keep me from doing my duty to the clan, though. The Dragonrealm must be brought under control. This idiocy of one race after another passing beyond must end. Already it seems to have claimed the Seekers. We are, if you recall, the founders' last hope for a successor. We cannot disappoint their memory."

While he had been talking, Sharissa had knelt down and opened the pack. Each of the food items she removed could have been conjured instead of carried, but Barakas wanted sorcery kept to a minimum. Unlike the millennia of excess that Nimth had suffered under the Vraad, this world was more grudging. The Tezerenee might be able to use the old world's sorcery, but it still drained them physically. Even Sharissa had bodily limitations. Barakas claimed he wanted everyone at their best should an attack occur. It was also possible that the Seekers might not yet know that they were coming. An excessive use of magic might alert the avians and destroy any advantage of surprise the expedition had.

Sharissa doubted that these were the foremost reasons. She suspected that the patriarch wanted his men to take the aerie without the aid of sorcery; it would serve to bolster morale and add credence to the belief that an empire in this land *was* their true destiny.

"Listen to me!" Lochivan hissed as he came down on one knee next to Sharissa. His voice was very low and very anxious. "I *am* your friend whether you believe me or not. I am thinking of you!"

"As long as it doesn't interfere with your noble thoughts

concerning your clan. I'm tired, Lochivan. Go talk to one of your brothers or sisters or cousins or anyone, but stop talking to *me*.''

He rose, a dark shadow outlined by the last dim rays of the sunken sun. "You and that elf . . . two of a kind!"

"What about the elf?" Sharissa tried her best not to look too interested.

Lochivan took her interest as an opening. "I have to spend another fruitless evening trying to convince him of the futility of holding back any longer. With his companions dead and his people far away, he should be reasonable. Instead, he merely grits his teeth and stares into space."

She barely heard most of what he said. "What have you done to him *this* time?"

The edge in her voice did not go unnoticed. "Only what must be done. We have been careful; damaged, he is no good to anyone. He knows this land better than we. His knowledge must be added to our own."

Could she possibly—? The thought was so outrageous that she nearly discarded it immediately. Sharissa looked up at the dark figure of Lochivan. "*I* could speak to him if you would only let me."

"Why would you want to do that?"

His disbelief was expected. Why would she help the Tezerenee? The sorceress hoped her answer would soothe his suspicions. "I want to save him from any more of the hospitality of Barakas—him *and* Darkhorse. Let me see what I can do. If I succeed, I expect to be able to spend a bit of time with Darkhorse, too."

"You *expect*—"

She raised a hand. "Does not the patriarch say that those who serve shall be rewarded? Have I asked that much?"

Lochivan was silent for so long that Sharissa feared he had rejected her suggestion out of hand and was merely marveling at her gall. Then he laughed.

"I will ask for permission. It may amuse him as much as it does me." He began to depart, then turned back and, in a quiet voice, added, "It may come as no surprise to you that you are being watched."

"I hardly thought Lord Barakas *wouldn't* safeguard against my good intentions. I think I know what might happen should I desire to test my abilities."

That produced another good-natured laugh. "You would be wasted on Reegan, Sharissa."

She busied herself with her blanket and did not reply.

"I am dismissed, I see. Should I gain permission for you to speak to the elf, I will send word. Until then, good evening to you." His heavy boots crushed fallen twigs and leaves as he moved off. Sharissa waited until the sounds grew faint before turning around to watch his departure.

"I would rather marry Reegan," she whispered. "At least *he* I can trust to be consistent."

"Lady Sharissa?"

The sorceress blinked sleep from her eyes. Night still shrouded the land, but that did not tell her anything of import. "Is it near morning?"

"No, my lady." A female warrior was bent over her, helm in one arm. Dressed in something finer than armor, she probably would have been attractive. Tezerenee had in general done without magical alterations to their face and form, preferring to live with what nature had chosen for them. For many Tezerenee, that meant less-than-pleasant features. A few of the patriarch's offspring, such as Gerrod or his late brother Rendel, had been fortunate enough to gain more from their mother than their father.

"What hour is it?"

"We are barely past midnight, Lady Sharissa."

The warrior was scratching her cheek. In the light of the partial moons the sorceress could see that the same dryness that many Tezerenee suffered had spread to this one's cheek, ruining what beauty she did have.

Sleep made the sorceress slow. There was a reason why a Tezerenee might have come to her now, but she could not think of what it was. "Then why have I been disturbed?"

"The Lord Barakas Tezerenee has given you permission to speak with the elf."

"Alone, of course."

"Of course, my lady."

They both knew this was far from the truth, but arguing about it would avail Sharissa naught. She would merely have to be careful how she spoke with Faunon. He would understand why. The elf was no one's fool.

Sharissa rose. "Give me a moment." She picked up some of

the food, including some of the Tezerenee wine Reegan had given her. That the clan of the dragon could make such excellent wine was their only saving grace in her eyes.

When she was ready, the Tezerenee led her to the wagon where Faunon was kept. Two sentries stood ready to receive them. Sharissa expected to see Lochivan nearby, but could not find him. It did not break her heart.

Her guide spoke to the others and indicated Sharissa. One of the guards nodded and both stepped aside. Nodding as if their obedience was to be expected, the sorceress strode past them and over to the wagon door. The Tezerenee preferred a wagon that was more of a room on wheels, including windows and a door. There was no real need for such an elaborate structure where a simple cloth-covered wagon would have sufficed; the wagon was merely a result of the clan's tastes. In some ways, it resembled a tiny citadel. Sharissa knew that it was even protected to some extent by defensive spells.

A light from within blinded her when she opened the door. Her eyes, accustomed to the darkness, took a moment to recuperate. Sharissa saw that a lamp illuminated the interior and wondered if it had been left specifically for her use. The lamp hung on a hook in the ceiling. Beyond it were several mysterious sacks from which emanated a slight magical aura, but nothing that made her worry. Supplies of some sort; she had seen their like often.

Other than the sacks and the lamp, only one other item decorated the wagon's interior.

Faunon.

He was chained so that he could sit on the floor with his legs outstretched, but there were other chains above those, an indication that sometimes he was forced to stand, probably during questioning. Physically, Faunon looked no worse than he had the last time the tall sorceress had spoken to him. Vraad torture, however, did not necessarily leave its marks on the skin.

She closed the door behind her, even though that did not mean that they could not hear her. It would give them a sense of privacy at least. "Faunon?"

The worn figure did not respond.

"Faunon?" Sharissa's voice quivered. Had they killed him and left the corpse there for her to see? Was this Lochivan's mad jest on her?

His chest rose and fell. Sharissa breathed a sigh of relief, more horrified at the thought of his death than she would have believed. The elf was the only being other than Darkhorse that she could think of as a friend.

He looked up. His handsome features were marred by dark circles under his eyes and very, very pale skin. Despite the excessive anguish he had gone through since last they met, the fire was still alive in his eyes. As they focused on her, the flames burned brighter, as if her presence heartened him.

"Lady Sharissa." He coughed. "I was told you would be coming. I thought their words just another torture. I thought I would never see you again."

"I couldn't get to you." It would do no harm to speak a little about their last encounter. She knew by now that they *had* at least known of it, if not what the two had actually said during that encounter. "Then, I found you had been moved."

"These Tezerenee like to play games. One . . . one of those games is to move me from one place to another, with each . . . each progressive accommodation worse than the last."

Sharissa moved close enough to touch him. "I'm sorry. I should have tried harder . . . for both you and Darkhorse."

"And what could you have done? There is a saying among us elves,"—he gave her a weak smile, "—one of our *many* sayings, that more . . . more or less means one should wait for the proper time, for eagerness and overconfidence have brought down many an empire. In this land, we have seen much truth to that."

His ability to still find strength despite the situation encouraged her.

"I asked them to let me talk to you, Faunon. I told them I might be able to gain your cooperation."

"You will always have my cooperation. It is only these Tezerenee who will not."

"There must be something you can tell me, something that will save you from further questioning for the time being. Something about the land or about the caverns in the mountains." She was almost to the point of pleading. If she failed, the Tezerenee would only redouble their efforts in regard to the elf. Sharissa's heart beat madly when she thought of that.

Faunon shook his head. "I told them about the caverns. What little I know. I warned them to stay away, that even the Seekers no longer trusted the place."

"Why is that?"

He laughed, but it was a bitter sound. "I told them that something *evil* lives in the lower depths. They, of course, thought I was trying to pass on some ancient legend, but this thing is a recent horror. My people have spied upon the aeries before, including the caverns, and no one has ever spoken of any monster."

"Are you certain?" Unlike Lochivan or Barakas, Sharissa was willing to believe what the captive elf was saying. She could see the truth of what he said in his eyes. She could see many things in his eyes.

"As certain as I am of anything," he replied, but his voice was distant, as if his mind were elsewhere. Sharissa blinked and turned away until she was certain she could face him without reddening.

"Is there anything else you could tell them? Are there many Seekers left here? Have you seen the upper caverns?"

"I saw a huge, unearthly stallion race to the east. It was weeks ago, but they might—"

She shook her head. "That was Darkhorse."

"Darkhorse?" He gave her an appraising look. "I thought the name only fanciful. There are many such names among us elves. When you used this Darkhorse's name, I did not think it was meant to be so literal. For a Vraad, you make interesting friends. First an ebony demon and then myself. I thought your race rather arrogant toward outsiders."

"Are all elves the same? You hardly seem as formal I was always told."

"I take your point." Since the start of her visit, or perhaps even *because* of it, Faunon had grown stronger and more coherent. Sharissa was pleased, but realized that it all meant nothing so long as they were prisoners of the Tezerenee.

"This Darkhorse," interrupted Faunon. "You mentioned him as a fellow prisoner. Is the dragonlord so powerful that he could bind this stallion to his will?"

Outside, something thumped against the side of the wagon. The sorceress listened for a moment, but when it was not repeated she decided it was nothing. "He wasn't before. They're growing stronger, Faunon. Soon, they'll rape this land as they did the last . . . and I can do nothing to stop them!"

"Nimth. That's what it was called, wasn't it? The world we fled from? The world the Vraad ravaged?"

She nodded.

His mouth was a grim line. "I doubt they will find this domain so pliable. It has faced others before your people. There were many who wanted to adapt the land to them instead of working with it. Whenever that happened, the land seemed to make *them* adapt."

"What do you mean?"

"Have you felt any different since coming to this world? Any change at all?"

"I felt more at home than I ever had on Nimth. It was a glorious change for me." For the first time, she recalled the wine and food in her hands. The young Vraad showed it to Faunon, who momentarily dropped his question and smiled at the sight. "Is that wine? Could I have a bit of that before I continue? Our friends have given me nothing but brackish water, albeit all I could drink."

"Let me help you." She brought the wine to his mouth and tilted it. Faunon, his eyes on her, swallowed twice and then indicated she should stop.

"Thank you . . . gods! What sweet honey!"

"The Tezerenee make it."

"Proving that they have at least one good quality, I suppose." While she broke apart some bread and cheese for him, he returned to his subject. "Having spent these few wonderful moments with you, I can see that you and the land would have no quarrel. The same cannot be said for the dragon men, however. The land will not tolerate them."

Sharissa thought to ask him if he knew of the founders and how their kas, their spirits, *were* a part of the land now, but the telling of that would take her much too long.

A heavy weight fell against the wagon, striking so hard that the entire structure shook.

"Are we under attack?" Faunon asked, frustration at being chained during a time of danger taking over. The sorceress had thought of trying to remove the chains, but, recalling that they were like her collar, knew it would be an exercise in futility.

She rose. "I'll see what it is."

"You could be killed!"

"I'll not wait for whatever it is to come to us!"

With great caution, she reached for the door handle. Sharissa raised her other hand, ready to cast a spell the moment she opened the door.

A hulking figure from without burst through the door as if it were dry kindling.

"Lllaaady Zzzzzerrreeeee," it hissed.

It wore what looked like the remnants of armor, not that it needed any, for it had a natural scale armor of its own that went from head to foot. The fiend was almost human in form, but bent awkwardly, as if it was trying to move as a man but not built for the purpose. The hands were more like the paws of the riding drakes and ended in equally sharp talons.

Worst of all was the visage. As the body could only mock that of a human, so too did the face, only more so. The eyes, though crystalline like a Vraad's, were long and narrow. The horror's nose was virtually nonexistent, two mere slits in the center. Its mouth was full of teeth that were pointed and made for tearing flesh from a kill.

It was coming for her.

"Lllaaady Sharisssssssa!" It reached out for her, but she jumped back just in time. The creature was like some legacy of mad Nimth. She tried to concentrate, knowing that only seconds separated her from death. Physically, the frightened sorceress was no match, but her powers might save her if she could only think.

If only it would stop flashing those teeth! she kept thinking.

"Sharissa!" Faunon called from behind her. That snapped her out of it. It would not only be she that perished if she failed to act, but also Faunon, who could not even defend himself.

"Lllaaady, I—"

Whatever it sought to say, Sharissa would never know. A spell formed in her mind and was completed accordingly. Brilliant, scarlet bands swarmed around the reptilian terror, who fought them with the savagery of an animal cornered. The bands began to tighten around its arms and legs. Sharissa breathed easier.

A yellow aura originating from the creature evaporated the bands just as it seemed the battle had been won.

"Yooou mussst—" the creature started to say, forked tongue lashing in and out of its mouth.

Before her eyes, it twitched once—and fell forward, already dead.

There was an arrow in the back of its neck. The shot had been so perfectly aimed that death had been instantaneous.

"Inside!" a voice shouted.

Two Tezerenee in full armor came rushing in. One of them bent down and inspected the sprawling figure while the other kept his sword ready should it turn out that, impossible as it was, the monster still lived.

"Well?" roared the same voice that had ordered the two inside. Lochivan peered in, his bow ready.

"Dead, milord."

"Roll it over."

The warrior who bent by the corpse removed the arrow and did as Lochivan commanded. Everyone stared at the horrible features.

"This is the armor of one of our own, milord."

"I can see *that*." Lochivan looked up at Sharissa. "Are you injured at all?"

"No." For the first time in weeks, she was actually happy to see him. "I held it back, but it had sorcery of its own."

"Yes, I know. It killed one of the sentries outside by sorcery. Quietly, too. The other sentry did not notice until the first fell to the ground. By that time, it was too late for him to save himself, much less the first man."

"Milord!" The Tezerenee who had studied the dead monstrosity stumbled back, unable to hide his shock. "This is one of us!"

"What? Impossible!" Handing his bow to the other man, Lochivan knelt and inspected his kill. His hand roved over what remained of the armor and then to the face. He stared hard and long, trying to make sense of what lay before him.

Sharissa, too, was staring long and hard. Unbidden came the memory of the warrior she and Lochivan had confronted in the corridor just before her public humiliation by Barakas.

"Lochivan," she started. "Do you recall the man we met in the hall? The one doubled over from illness?"

He looked up. "I recall him." Unlike his father, the sorceress was aware that he could name every Tezerenee in the clan, be they born by those of the founding blood or outsiders who had joined the ranks at one time or another. It was even a point of pride with him. "That would make this . . ." Lochivan turned to one of his men. "See if Ivor can be found! He was among the chosen for this expedition since he was a part of the first."

Hearing this, Sharissa's brow furrowed. Was it pure coincidence? "Is Ivor a relation?"

"A cousin. Obedient, little else. He was one of the earliest to cross over from Nimth."

As the one warrior departed to fulfill his desires, others arrived. One saluted Lochivan, who stood. "Well?"

"There are three dead. We found another man gutted a short distance from here."

"Nothing more?"

"Nothing."

"Dispose of this . . . this . . . dispose of him in a discreet manner. Is that understood?"

"Yes, milord."

While the others began dragging the body out, Lochivan noticed Faunon for the first time. Ignoring Sharissa, he marched over to the elf and knelt by him.

"What trick was that, elf? Are your fellows out there now?" He gripped Faunon's jaw in one hand. "Have I been too lenient with you?"

Sharissa's relief at seeing Lochivan faded. He had no right to treat Faunon so. "What could he know? What part could he have played, Lochivan? Look at him. You've reduced him to little more than a shell!"

"It . . . it . . . is all r-right, my l-lady." With the return of the Tezerenee, Faunon was exaggerating his condition. Sharissa tried not to react, understanding that Faunon wanted them to believe he was weaker than he was. To Lochivan, the captive replied, "I know . . . nothing, friend. That I swear t-to you. Do you think I w-would have invited such . . . such a menace into this p-place when I cannot even defend myself? I w-would rather you slit . . . slit my throat than for . . . for me t-to be torn apart by so grisly a beast."

"Do you claim that the elves did not do this?"

"Your man was ill before this, Lochivan," Sharissa reminded him again. It had not been proven that this was indeed the one called Ivor, but she suspected such evidence would be forthcoming. "It could have been something else."

He sighed. Standing, the Tezerenee removed his helm and scratched at his throat, where the dry patches of skin had spread. It had become so familiar a habit with him that he no longer even complained when it itched. "Perhaps you are correct. The Seekers have been conspicuously absent."

She did not understand. "I thought the aerie we travel to had been abandoned and the Seekers were dead."

"There are a few to weed out. Survivors, nothing more."

A change in the expression on the elf's visage made the young sorceress's eyes dart to Faunon and quickly back again. At mention of the caverns, he had become lost in thought, as if making some connection that she could not. Once Lochivan left, perhaps she could—

"I am afraid that I must terminate your conversation with the prisoner," the armored figure said at that moment. "You will be given another chance to speak with him, I think. For now, I would prefer that you be where I can guard you better."

"Me? It was one of your people that suffered—"

"And he came for you. It may be that you are seen as a risk to whoever is responsible. I want nothing to happen to you, Sharissa." Lochivan's tone softened toward the end.

She wanted to argue, but the outcome would be the same regardless. Behind the Tezerenee, Faunon indicated that she should agree. Too much protest and they might change their minds about allowing her to talk to him again.

"Very well." It was doubtful that sleep would be so easily forthcoming.

"Let me escort you back."

"That will not be necessary." She did not want him touching her.

"You will be safer. This may not be an isolated incident."

As before, there could be only one outcome. Conceding defeat, she nodded and gave him her hand.

"You have . . . have my gratitude as . . . as well," Faunon commented as the Tezerenee was about to lead her out. "How fortunate that you were so nearby."

Meaning that Lochivan had either been spying on them or had been waiting for Sharissa to leave the wagon. The Tezerenee glanced her way, but did not return the elf's comment. He did, however, lead the slim woman out of the wagon much more swiftly than necessary.

Outside, several Tezerenee were still moving about. Two moved to clean the debris that had once been the door. Sharissa looked for signs of the sentries' bodies, but they had already been cleared away. She felt some pity for them, but not quite as much as she would have for the elves their kind had slaughtered weeks ago. Much of what the Tezerenee suffered they had brought upon themselves.

Only two days from the citadel and this had occurred. As she and Lochivan walked away from the carnage in silence, Sharissa wondered what the coming days had planned.

Somehow, she felt it would only be worse.

XIII

"She sleeps, sire."

"Good." They stood in his tent, the three of them. He used the tent as his base of operations, which was why he felt justified in having it when the rest of his warriors slept outside. The patriarch was only partly clad in armor, it having taken him longer than normal to dress. He found it a bit disturbing, but laid aside that minor annoyance in the face of the outrageous incident with the abomination.

Reegan, fully clad and more than a little angry at the loss of sleep, asked, "What did you do with its carcass, Lochivan?"

His brother, still kneeling, replied, "It is being buried discreetly. Father, the monster is none other than one of our own. Reegan, you know of Ivor?"

"It was *Ivor*?"

One of our own, the Lord Tezerenee wondered. *They have struck down one of our own in the very midst of my camp and despite my precautions!* The entire area had been carefully laced with defensive spells. He had always eschewed such things in the past, preferring to rely on the readiness of him and his people, but of late he had not moved as swiftly as before and his clan appeared more hesitant than they had during their first days here.

"Three other men died. All adopted outsiders."

A small loss, but a loss nonetheless. Some of the other Vraad who had joined his clan would be growing nervous. The patriarch needed things to stay on course in order to assuage their fears. The expedition would have to be more alert than they had been.

"What happened to him? What sort of change?"

Lochivan bowed his head. "I do not know. It was suggested that the Seekers might have done this."

"Suggested by whom? The elf?" Reegan sneered. "Of course he'd blame them! He's covering for his—"

"Reegan, be silent!" The patriarch tugged at his beard and mulled over the possibilities. "If it was the elf or his friends, I imagine they could do just as well if he were rescued. They would not leave him to our mercy. Tell me, Lochivan, does he seem like the suicidal sort?"

"He's a warrior, father, and willing to risk himself, but I think this would be asking too much from him. His death would serve no purpose."

From out of the corner of his eye, Barakas saw his eldest building himself up for another tirade. The patriarch turned in time to stall the outburst. Reegan frowned, but remained silent.

"Ask those who knew Ivor better if he has acted differently of late." A thought occurred to the Lord Tezerenee. "He was a member of the first expedition?"

"Yes, sire."

Could it be that Ivor had discovered or touched something he should not have? Did some trap lie in wait for the Tezerenee? Barakas thought of the box and its unwilling occupant. He had been wise to bring along the dweller from that emptiness that Dru Zeree had called the Void. Taking the caverns might not be so simple after all.

"What do you intend, Father?" Reegan dared to ask.

"We will continue on at the same pace. Losses are always to be expected. More may fall before this is ended. Even one of you may succumb."

Reegan and Lochivan shared an expression of anxiety. It did not occur to the patriarch that he himself might succumb. He *was* the clan, after all.

"Let it be known tomorrow that Ivor and the others died honorably. Ivor especially. You are both dismissed."

His sons bowed and quickly departed, no doubt first intending to alert their siblings as to what had been discussed before obeying his other commands. Barakas, meanwhile, forewent removing his half-worn armor for a time, instead continuing to ponder the incident that had claimed the lives of the warriors and almost that of Sharissa Zeree, too. In a sense, he almost envied Ivor one thing. The hapless warrior had come closer than anyone to truly knowing the glory of the dragon that was the clan's totem. His only trouble was that he had not had the will to master whatever spell had affected him.

Had it been himself, the patriarch decided, he would have turned the transformation to his own desires. He had the will that Ivor had lacked. He, lord of the Tezerenee, would have become the living symbol of the clan.

Barakas started to scratch himself, but, realizing what he was doing, forced his hand down. In the past few days, the rash and dry skin had begun to recede. Soon, he would be rid of the irritation. The more it was fought, the less it became.

It was, as he had preached so often, merely a matter of will.

They talked and talked, yet what they struggled to say escaped his ears. Most were difficult to focus upon after a time, as if the more he tried to define their features the more murky they became.

Gerrod could only stare at them, caught up in some inexplicable spell of fascination that would not allow him to turn from them and search for the way out of this madhouse. Every move that the warlock succeeded in making toward that effort only brought him to new and equally disturbing visages.

"Dragon's blood!" he whispered for what was either the first or the hundredth time—Gerrod could no longer keep track. He barely knew himself anymore, much less what happened around him. A drake could have stalked him at its leisure, taking him as he stood there like a fool. Yet, it was impossible to pull away.

With a mixture of fear and childlike awe, Gerrod stretched a tentative hand forward and touched one that most resembled him.

A difference he could sense but not see spread throughout the room. Something began to tug on his cloak, but, caught up in his dreaming, the warlock barely even noted it. He heard a faint sound that might have been a summons or merely the wind, an insignificant noise that Gerrod quickly forgot.

The hood of his cloak was pulled down over his eyes.

Gerrod struggled, seeking to return to his gazing even though a part of him knew the danger of that. He could not remove the blinding hood, however, for powerful arms caught him as a pincer might have, preventing him from even raising a hand in his defense.

The siren whispering of the faces in the crystal was

overwhelmed by excited hooting in his ears. He was dragged backward by one or more powerful forms.

The whispering ceased. The compulsion to stare at his twisted reflections dwindled away to near nothing.

His captor released him. Gerrod fought for breath that had been denied him for some time, although he had not realized it until now. The warlock turned around and faced the one who had dragged him free.

It was the apparent leader of the Quel. The armadillolike creature looked at the Vraad with what seemed to be open concern.

"I . . . I will be fine in a moment," Gerrod told it, reacting to what he thought was a question. He hoped the crystal translated his words and thoughts properly.

The Quel hooted in an unintelligible manner and pointed at the human before it, ending the gesture with a shake of one clawed paw. Gerrod looked at himself and frowned in confusion until he recalled that he could no longer understand the Quel's hoots. What had happened to the crystal was beyond him; he could not recall dropping it in the chamber or, for that matter, leaving it anywhere.

Gerrod cursed, utilizing his father's name as part of the bitter epithet. Now of all times was a situation demanding explanation, and he had lost track of his only means of communication. He wanted to know what the purpose of the chamber was and who had built it. The warlock could hardly recall the events just prior to his reluctant entrance into the mad cavern. Had the Quel built it, or had they found it? From the way they acted, he thought the latter might be a better choice, but his mind was too fogged to be trusted.

Despite the ordeal he had suffered, Gerrod wanted to go back. Not in a haphazard fashion, as his first journey had entailed, but carefully, with full respect and preparation for the power within.

He was about to indicate with his hands that he desired to return to the crystal cavern when the world spun around him. Gerrod watched the ground rush toward his face, only to have the collision halted by the ready arms of his armored companion, who seemed to be expecting just such an incident. The warlock had no time to think why that might be so, for he passed out the next instant.

* * *

When he awoke, the Quel were huddled around him, passive in their interest in his condition until they saw that he was conscious. Then, like players donning masks, the earth dwellers grew excited at his recovery. Gerrod frowned, hoping they would take his expression for concern over his own condition—which it was in part—and not because he was suddenly suspicious of their interest in him.

They had brought him to another chamber, one that barely passed human standards for survival. He was on a mat of some sort that smelled too much of his hosts and cold earth. The warlock slowly rose, fending off assistance by the Quel with a shake of his head. The massive creatures backed away far enough to give him room. It was impossible to say whether they once more played at emotions, but Gerrod thought they seemed a bit surprised at the speed of his recovery. No doubt their own kind had entered the chamber of crystal before him, but what had happened to those unfortunates was something they had not revealed to the Vraad so far.

Far worse than me, he decided. *Far worse if their fear of that place is real.* He was certain it was; the Quel, whatever their purpose was, would have been better served if they had pretended confidence rather than fear, which added to Gerrod's supposition that they *were* frightened of what they had discovered.

What did they see in that place?

"I need—" The warlock stopped as the leader gave him a crystal, either the same one or one identical to it; Gerrod had no idea.

Mind intact . . . the fear not eaten . . . question?

So that was it. Those who had preceded him had lost their minds to some sort of fear. Whatever the Quel saw, it was too much for them. Yet, someone had pulled him free. How?

While he pondered that, the armadillolike being repeated its question.

"I'm fine." Not quite the truth, but good enough for them. Gerrod had no intention of telling them about the voices—his voice—that still whispered inside his head. The voices wanted him to return to the chamber, to come back and listen once more to what they had to say.

He would. Of that he was certain. Even if the Quel decided otherwise, the warlock would return to the chamber.

Food consumed . . . time passing . . . question?

The alteration in the course of the conversation took him by surprise, but it took him only a moment to puzzle out the meaning. He was being asked if he required food; how much time had passed since his fainting spell?

"How long have I been unconscious?"

The answer was nothing monumental; he had been unconscious for what was, if he had Quel time standards figured out, no more than two hours, maybe three. The blackout had actually done him more good than bad; Gerrod had not been given a chance to recover from the trek earlier in the day. He still coveted a full night's slumber, but crumbs were always better than nothing at all. For once, life as a Tezerenee paid off. Under his father's rule, each clan member had learned to work at his optimum with only the least bit of sleep.

His stomach argued that food was another commodity that he had, of late, dealt little with. Gerrod wondered whether the food here would be as unappetizing as the mash the patrols had carried. Perhaps, but he would eat it nonetheless. For the task lying before him, a task he was not even certain he understood, the Tezerenee would need his strength.

As if already sensing his acknowledgment, a newcomer, smaller than the rest but still almost the human's height, brought him a bowl of some soupy substance. Gerrod, his eyes on the tinier Quel, sniffed the contents . . . and shivered. He broke his gaze and looked down at the bowl.

The mash would seem a delicacy in comparison.

When he looked back up, the tiny Quel was gone. He wondered if he had finally met a female. None of the other Quel were inclined to respond to his casual thought, but Gerrod was certain he was correct in his assumption. If so, then those with him were almost certainly males—unless, of course, the newcomer had merely been a juvenile. The Vraad could not accept that, however, and reinforced his newfound belief by thinking of his present companions in male terms as much as possible, despite their otherwise identical appearance to the smaller Quel.

Under the unblinking observation of the inhuman assembly, Gerrod ate. The meal went down quickly, partly because they had given him no spoon, thus forcing him to tip the bowl and gulp down mouthfuls of the disgusting muck. He swallowed faster after the next wave of noxious scents fluttered up his nostrils during the first taste.

"No seconds, please," Gerrod muttered as he handed the

nearly empty bowl to one of the other creatures, who promptly threw it aside as if no one would ever wish to use it now that the human had. That reminded the warlock of his true situation. For all their act of friendliness, these Quel were no more companionable than the sentries who had brought him here. They had thrust him willingly into a situation that had broken the minds of one, possibly more, of their own kind. If not him, an elf or the representative of some other race would have done just as well. The Quel did not care; it was more important to find out about their discovery.

The leader chose that moment to hoot deep and long to his fellows. Without protest, the others began to shuffle out of the chamber. No one paid any more attention to the lone Vraad, not even the commanding Quel, who stood by in silence while the others departed. Only when the two of them were alone did the massive beastman turn to his guest.

The mask slipped then, revealing some of the true mind behind the inhuman visage. A savage yet calculating mind as deadly in its way as those of the Tezerenee's own folk. Had not Gerrod been able to remind himself that he was, as far as he could see, the Quel's only key to the crystal cavern, the warlock would have feared for himself right there and then. They needed him, else they would not have taken care of him while he recovered. Despite the physical danger that the Quel before him represented, the warlock was able to smile.

Perceptions of the chamber . . . statement!

The odd voice/images in his head jarred him, but he quickly recovered. "You want to know what I saw, is that it? You want to know why I still have my mind?"

Agreement . . . statement!

Would there be any harm in telling the truth? Gerrod doubted it and so he told the creature everything he had observed, heard, and felt. It seemed perfectly acceptable to do so, despite his present status. Throughout it all, the Quel leader remained motionless, as though hypnotized by his tale. Occasionally, he would project a question, mostly about some minor detail. The Vraad learned little from the questions save that there had to have been more than one victim of the chamber. How many Quel had tried to conquer the fear within and failed? More than once he sensed the very edges of what the Quel had discovered, but each time his captor buried the images and emotions before too much slipped by.

All too soon, the story ended. Gerrod was struck by sudden anxiety. Was he wrong? Had he given them what they needed? Was he no longer of use?

The sole remaining Quel leaned forward, his breath more fetid than the haunting aroma cast by Gerrod's recent repast. *Cooperation . . . continued existence . . . statement!*

The warlock nodded, trying to ignore the rapid beating of his heart. "I like living. I'll cooperate."

Purpose of crystals . . . weapon against enemy/foe bird folk . . . statement!/question?

"What? Oh." Gerrod nodded, yawning. "It might be a weapon you could use against the Seekers." He had no idea *how* it might be used as such, but Gerrod was certain it could be turned into a weapon. By that time, he hoped to turn it on his captors instead.

A neglected part of his mind summoned up the fate of Sharissa, recalling to him his original purpose. He fought it down, convincing himself that this crystal chamber would aid him in that respect, if only by giving him time to plot his escape. That he would have been drawn to the cavern regardless was a point he tried not to dwell upon. Forsaking Sharissa for his own interests, even for a time, was something he would have expected of his father.

Period of rest . . . statement!

"I . . ." Gerrod could not recall what it was he had wanted to say. He yawned—long and hard this time. A sleeping potion in his food. Why had he not thought of that? The warlock laid his head back and yawned again. Did it really matter? He could begin his escape plans when he woke. Yes, that sounded better. He would be well-rested after this, and any plan required his utmost strength and concentration.

Agreeable . . . passive be . . . statement! came the projection from the Quel beside him. Gerrod nodded. Whatever his host wanted, so long as it meant sleep. Come the morrow—or *whenever* he finally woke—the Tezerenee would begin his plotting.

As he began to drift off, Gerrod thought he heard someone chuckle. It was not a sound that Quel were capable of imitating properly, and he knew it was not his own voice he heard. For a time, the warlock struggled to stay awake, waiting for the sound to reoccur. He was still straining to hear it again when he finally lost the struggle with the god of sleep and faded away.

* * *

Escape, he found later, would not be so simple. Two days—estimated, since he could not see the sun—passed. It was not merely the efforts of his companions that kept him in the underground world, but his own overwhelming sense of discovery. There was too much that beckoned him in a way akin to the chamber of crystal, albeit not with such consistent attraction. Though they were by no means the masters of crystal sorcery that the builders of the chamber had been, the Quel were not without skill. Gerrod had yet to see, much less inspect, the thing that they called the "gatherer," but he imagined it to be a gem of astonishing proportions if what the lender conveyed to him was true. How it was able to absorb and distribute the magical forces for use by the Quel was a thing beyond him. It was, besides the ancient cavern, the only place they would not allow him to roam.

Walking with the leader, who *was* male after all, the warlock fingered some of the small gemstones in his belt pouch. They were akin to the one that allowed him to speak with the Quel and probably could be turned to that use, but he had other ideas concerning them. It was surprisingly easy to obtain them; they were mined in such vast quantities that he had been stunned when first shown. Each young Quel was brought here soon after birth. They were identical in almost every way to the parents, save for the soft almost unfurrowed shells that would change and harden over the years. The crystals of understanding, which was as close as Gerrod could comprehend the title, were among the first and foremost received by the young when the shells grew ridged. The hard skin would eventually grow to cover most of each crystal, forever making it a part of the creature and ensuring that, at least from the Quel side, communication of a sort would always be maintained.

Stealing three from a hill of thousands had been childishly easy. So easy, in fact, that Gerrod wondered from time to time whether his companion had *wanted* him to take the gems. No matter. They represented the first inklings of a plan of escape, a plan that would only take place once he had returned to the cavern and confronted the truth behind the faces—not to mention whatever other secrets lay within.

Let us not forget Sharissa! he chided himself. It was becoming too easy to lose track of his situation. Not just Dru Zeree's daughter, either. It was also too easy to forget what his true visage resembled—an aging, doddering fool of a Vraad. That was what Gerrod saw every time his reflection caught his eye.

A nervous Quel rushed up to the leader and the two began a series of rapid responses to one another. Even with the crystal, the warlock could make no sense of what they said. The images he received were murky, almost as if the Quel were making an effort to prevent him from understanding. It did not surprise him; he knew that his time with them was limited to his usefulness. He also knew what they would do when the secrets of the crystal cavern were theirs.

The leader whirled on him, dark eyes narrowed. He hooted low and quick, a sign of anger and worry as Gerrod read it. *The surface . . . spy in the sky . . . observation of intention . . . statement!*

The Tezerenee was dragged along while he was still attempting to decipher the message. Something was happening on the surface, a scout or someone . . . in the sky?

A Seeker?

The three of them entered yet another chamber that Gerrod had not come across before. How extensive was the domain of the Quel? He had been given to believe that they held only a remnant of their former power. If so, then their empire had rivaled that of the Seekers in scope.

A handful of Quel surrounded an image. The warlock, peering over tall, rounded shoulders, watched as a tiny figure fluttered over a miniature land no larger than Gerrod's forearm. The entire scene was being projected through a crystal that stood on a tripod in the middle of the room.

It was indeed a Seeker. Gerrod did not recognize the landscape, but from its rocky and nearly barren appearance, he felt safe in assuming it was part of the peninsula that was the Quel's home.

The Seeker paused in midflight, its wings beating rapidly to keep it in the air. The image was too small to identify it as male or female; as with the Quel, the two sexes were too similar to identify readily.

One of the watchers grunted and touched a side of the crystal. The scene magnified. It was a female, the Tezerenee saw, though the information made no difference. He still did not know why a lone Seeker would risk death to come to the land of its hereditary enemies.

Reaching to her neck, the avian tugged at a chain. Gerrod squinted and saw the medallion hanging by a chain around her throat. The medallion was almost the Seeker equivalent of the crystals the Quel utilized; it generally protected its wearer and contained some vicious spell. Not a few of his clan had died facing weapons such as this. The Tezerenee moved as close as he could to the image. Beside him, the Quel leader glanced his way, but ignored him further when he saw what the tiny human was about.

The Seeker removed her medallion—and promptly dropped it into the dirt far below her.

Among the Quel, there was a stirring of confusion.

The leader gave a command, again something that Gerrod could not make out. He knew by now that he was being purposely blocked out.

Some of the Quel turned to their superior with a sense of confusion evident in their movements. One bleated, the questioning note undeniable.

Shoving the hapless Vraad to one side—and almost against the far wall—the leader faced his questioner and repeated his command.

Dipping his head, the questioner returned to the crystal and, under the watchful gaze of all present, including the recovered Gerrod, touched another face of the crystal.

During the brief encounter, the Seeker had remained where she was, still hovering. Only as the one Quel touched the gemstone did the Vraad realize that the avian had been offering a truce. She would have to know that the Quel controlled this region. Her life had been offered in exchange for a meeting.

The Quel leader chose to decline that offer.

Blinding brilliance filled the image, forcing many of the huge, armadillolike creatures to shield their eyes and momentarily stunning the unprepared human. Gerrod blinked time and time again until at last some semblance of vision returned to him. He looked up, trying to see around the swimming spots that dotted everything in sight. The image, too, had cleared, and the warlock was able to make out glittering hills and the occasional tough plant. Of the Seeker, he saw no sign.

The same Quel who had controlled the crystal before now touched it again. Gerrod watched the scene shift, abandoning the sky view for one that observed more of the surface. The leader hooted, his tone and stance smug.

When he saw what remained of the ambassador of the Seekers, the Tezerenee was relieved that he could not smell it as well.

The Quel were well-defended. The lone avian never had hope. In what reminded Gerrod of a horrible parody of many a fine meal he had eaten, her charred corpse lay sprawled on the hard ground. The female's face, what was left of it, was buried in the soil, saving the warlock from seeing her accusing eyes. She had come in peace—unless his captors knew otherwise— and they had burned her to death.

Their weapon had been the land itself. Many of those gleaming fragments seemingly scattered about the countryside actually served another purpose. Like the array of gems that brought light to this world beneath the surface, these had been arranged just so. With their knowledge, the Quel merely manipulated a few at a time to create a beam of intense light. It was a horrific application of the childhood habit of burning bugs with a simple lens.

Our people are truly related, he thought in disgust. Such a trick would have appealed greatly to many of his fellow Vraad. His father would have found it a marvelous toy to add to his arsenal.

Around him, the various Quel began to lose interest now that the crisis was past. Only Gerrod seemed concerned over what the Seeker had wanted in the first place. It was not likely she would sacrifice herself. Something had concerned her and her kind enough for them to take this chance. He wished he had studied her closer. What condition had the avian been in before her death? Was it only his imagination or had she seemed worn, defeated in purpose?

Madness . . . bird people . . . death . . . statement!

The Quel who always accompanied him had returned to his side. The message was garbled, but at least they were communicating with their "guest" again. Gerrod understood enough; his host thought the Seeker had to have been insane to do what she had done. As for whose "death" the huge creature referred to, Gerrod could not say. There were too many interpretations that made sense considering the enmity between the two races.

Certain that he and his companions would be departing, Gerrod turned toward the chamber's mouth and took a step. A heavy hand belayed that thought by catching at the shoulder and twirling him about until he came to face the leader again.

The Quel leaned close—too close, as far as the warlock was concerned. He covered his nose.

Tomorrow . . . cavern of crystal . . . Gerrod/elf/Vraad searching . . . Seekers dying . . . statement!

The hooded figure could only nod wordlessly as his eyes met and broke away from those of the Quel master. Something had come of this after all. He would finally be returned to the cavern. At last, he could study the ancient wonder and find the reason for its existence, for those damnable faces. In the process, he would turn it to his own needs, not those of the armored monstrosities who held him.

Yessss . . .

The short, sibilant response was not Quel in origin, yet neither did it seem human. Gerrod hesitated, not certain whether he had imagined it or not. The Quel moved about as if nothing were amiss. Beside him, the leader indicated that it was *now* time to depart. Gerrod obeyed without question, but his mind still searched for a repeat of the brief yet chilling statement.

Nothing. A figment of his imagination, most likely. He could come up with no other satisfactory explanation, yet even that one felt weak. What else *could* it be, though?

Gerrod was quietly but soundly urged toward the corridor by the same massive paw that had halted his progress a moment before. Just as he reached the mouth of the cavern chamber, however, he paused again, unable to relieve his mind of this peculiar burden. If only a figment, why did it seem so real, so familiar? Why could he not dismiss it, a simple one-word phantasm of his mind? And why did he now, without warning, fear to enter the very cavern he had so desired to return to for the last two days?

The Quel urged him on again. As he walked, the warlock could not help wondering once more just what it was the Seeker had wanted and what possible threat ignorance of her message would bring down upon his captors . . . not to mention *himself?*

XIV

Barakas gazed up at the mountains towering before them and smiled. "Magnificent! Truly worthy!"

Even Sharissa, whose mind continued to dwell upon that terrifying yet sad incident of a few nights before, had to agree with him. The mountains *were* majestic, more so because they were natural formations, not something that had been conjured up, as in the old days of Nimth.

"No one can long look at the Tybers and not feel their power," Faunon whispered to her. He had, in the last day, been given leave to ride at the head of the expedition alongside Sharissa. The elf had finally agreed to guide them, mostly out of concern for the young sorceress. She found his interest in her both pleasant and embarrassing, and matters were not helped by his occasional glances and reassuring smiles.

Merely fellow prisoners, she told herself. *Our only common interest is escape from here.* That he was a welcome change from most of her kind she was not yet willing to admit to, not even to herself.

Escape was still out of the question so long as the patriarch controlled or contained Darkhorse. Sharissa tore her eyes from the grand scenery and studied the box that was slung near the Lord Tezerenee's leg, ready for quick use, if necessary. It was never far from his side, and she already knew that the spells were specifically tied to him, making the chance of someone else opening it slim—at least without injuring or even killing the occupant within the box. Darkhorse could be destroyed; that was something she knew to be very true by now. He was not the invincible, godlike being from beyond that her father's tales had once indicated to her. Rather, he was very, very vulnerable to many things. *Too* many things.

"This would be a good place to strike," Faunon whispered to her, meaning the Seekers, who had yet to make an appearance during this entire journey. Even though they had at last reached the mountains, which still meant another day's journey to the base of the one they sought, the Tezerenee were not acting overconfident. Many of those born to the clan were undoubtedly replaying their near massacre by the avians some fifteen years before over and over again in their thoughts. Everyone talked of the incident with the unfortunate Ivor, a victim, it was decided, of some twisted avian spell.

Faunon had tried to convince them otherwise, but his voice went unheard in this matter. He was convinced that Ivor had been transformed into that monstrosity by another power he claimed lay deep beneath the caverns the Seekers had used as an aerie. Only Sharissa believed him, and she had to admit that part of her belief was based on growing emotions for Faunon.

Up ahead of the column, scouts on airdrakes were flying back to the column. Lochivan rode the lead beast, his own request. The expedition halted at the patriarch's command and waited for the scouts to land.

"Father." Sharissa noted that his voice had grown hoarse. Lochivan leaped off his mount and knelt before Barakas. He gave his elder brother a cursory nod and said, "We ride amidst a region soaking in untapped power."

"I told you that," Faunon could not help pointing out. So much of what he said went through the ears of his captors and out into the heavens. The elf turned to Sharissa and, with a wry smile, asked, "Why did they bother to bring me along if they won't believe anything I say?"

Reegan twisted around in his saddle. "Be silent!"

The sorceress knew that Faunon was taking risks every time he spoke out, especially when he was near Reegan. Perhaps because he desired her so much, the heir apparent was the first one to take note of the link between Sharissa and the prisoner. The huge Tezerenee was jealous.

Lochivan continued. "We saw little sign of recent avian activity, but we found several Seekers who had died at one point or another. It appears that they were *fighting* among themselves."

"Indeed?" Barakas stroked his beard and sank into deep thought. Lochivan, waiting for the sign to continue, absently scratched at his throat.

"We can ride right in and take over," Reegan suggested with his usual lack of timing and thought. Sharissa almost felt sympathy for him.

The patriarch only shook his head. "Do not be absurd again. There *have* to be Seekers about. Not all of them would be so obliging as to flee or die for our sakes. If we had charged in, swords ready and magic flying, we would probably be dead now. This is still *their* domain for a time. They will defend it to their utmost."

"We cannot stay here until we've rooted them all out of the rocks," the heir protested. "That might take years."

"*That* I agree with." The Lord Tezerenee tapped the side of the shadow steed's horrible prison as he pondered a decision.

He ceased the tapping and eyed the box with new interest. "Perhaps there is a more efficient way."

Sharissa urged her mount closer to the patriarch, her heart sinking as what Barakas might be plotting occurred to her. "Haven't you put him through enough? Isn't that box pain enough for him to endure?"

"This should be relatively painless, I think."

"You know what I mean!"

"More lives will be saved by this in the long run, my dear Sharissa," Barakas replied, his smile as false as his words. "At least . . . *Tezerenee* lives."

He lifted the box so that it rested in one arm and ran his hand over it, repeating the same pattern he had earlier, albeit in such a manner that it could be performed with a single hand, not two. Sharissa could sense the bond that tied the Tezerenee lord to the spell and thus Darkhorse to him. She still had no idea how to free the ebony stallion from it, and that was what held her back from escape. Barakas was by no means an opponent she could hope to overcome by direct action. Only by biding her time would she have a chance—but when would that be? The sorceress had no intention of waiting until she was married and bearing the children of Reegan. The very thought stirred her to renewed determination. Perhaps at some point on this very expedition Sharissa would find a means of solving her troubles.

She could only hope.

Barakas lifted the lid.

A wave of darkness rushed forth, almost as if the patriarch had unleashed night upon day. Yet, this darkness screamed its pleasure and fear, screamed wordlessly as it slowly coalesced into the familiar form of Sharissa's tormented friend.

"Movement! Sound! Sight! By the ungodly Void, I am free of it again! Free!"

A few of the Tezerenee shifted in nervousness, fully aware of what the overwhelming creature before them could do if allowed full will. Barakas and those of his sons who rode with the column sat in relaxed silence, fully confident in the patriarch's hold on the eternal.

His initial thrill at being released from the torturous container abating, Darkhorse glared at his armored keeper. Even Lochivan, who now stood beside the drake his father rode, and Reegan found other things to contemplate rather than meet those cold eyes. Barakas, on the other hand, met them with the same commanding indifference that he met most other things with. He knew very well who held sway here, and all of the eternal's staring would not lessen the truth of that.

"*What* do you *want* of me?" the shadow steed bellowed. His front hooves tore at the earth below. Sharissa did not doubt that he wished it was the clan master beneath those heavy hooves.

"I have a task for you, one that should prove simple considering your abilities."

"Barakas, please don't *do* this to him!" the sorceress called, her pride a forgotten thing in the importance of the moment.

The patriarch turned and studied her briefly. Although the dragonhelm hid most of his features, she could hear the disdain in his words. "Do not demean yourself, Lady Sharissa. A good warrior makes use of all weapons available to him, and I would be remiss if I did not use one of my greatest. He will ensure that no harm comes to you."

"To her?" Darkhorse paused in his kicking. He looked from the patriarch to Sharissa. "What threatens her?"

"Nothing, Darkhorse! He—"

A gauntleted hand touched the lid of the box, causing the demon steed to freeze and Sharissa to quiet almost instantly. "*She* rides with us into the interior of this mountainous region. I cannot guarantee her safety should we be attacked. You know the strength of the creatures who control this domain. Terrible it is, wouldn't you say?"

Darkhorse laughed, but there was little defiance left in him. He had been nearly broken by the periods of imprisonment in the box. "I served you in such a way earlier, monstrous one! I . . . I told you of those creatures, the elves"—he indicated an alert Faunon—"and where they could be found. Your sorcery, then, was not sufficient for the task! I *gave* you lives I had no right to give!"

A nod was the only acknowledgment he received from the lord of the Tezerenee. "This should prove much easier and more fulfilling, then. These are Seekers, creatures of the kind who attacked and captured your old companion, Dru Zeree. These are the creatures who would do harm to his daughter. They make no exceptions; her life means as little to them as my own does. If we were attacked, it will be difficult to keep an eye on her."

"I have my *own* power with which to battle them," she

reminded the two. "If it comes to a struggle, I will fight them. I do *not* want needless deaths."

Despite her assurances, the ebony stallion wavered more. "You have not seen them as I have. They mean little to my power, but you . . . you lack my resilience."

"So she does," Lochivan agreed, aiding his parent in the Tezerenee effort. Barakas gave a slight shake of his head that Sharissa noticed. He needed no aid in this matter, she knew. The patriarch held all the trumps.

"I gave you the elves because I feared for her . . . and I feared that cursed creation of yours! Do not ask me to add to my sins! If they come for you, *then* I will take them!"

"There was a time when you would have taken Dru Zeree. Do you remember that?" The Lord Tezerenee's hand toyed with the lid.

"I did not know better then!" Darkhorse's head was bowed. Sharissa knew what he was recalling. A simple yet powerful being existing in the regions of the Void, the eternal had no concept of life and death. Absorbing the few outsiders he came across in the endless limbo had meant nothing. Only after his time with her father did Darkhorse begin to comprehend the value of one's existence. If he or those he cared for were attacked, the stallion would fight. To kill those who did not even know of him, however . . .

"You have your choice, of course. I would be minded to let you remain out if you perform well, but if I cannot trust you to even protect one you profess to care for, I see no reason to leave you free. Who knows what havoc you might cause. Yes, perhaps returning you to the box until the day comes when I might find a task worth the trouble of summoning you again—"

Barakas began to tilt the open box in the direction of Darkhorse. To Sharissa's shock and dismay, she saw that her father's old companion was quivering with fear. He had even grown a bit distorted, as if his fright were so great it even interfered with his ability to hold shape.

"There is no need for that."

His voice, for all its deep rumble, was meek and abashed. Darkhorse stared at the ground beneath him, unwilling to look at those before—especially her. Sharissa shook her head, and tears ran down her cheeks.

"I will find these Seekers for you . . . and eliminate their threat."

A beatific smile crossed the patriarch's half-hidden visage. "Thank you. I see no reason why you cannot begin now. Do you?" He pointed at the mountains far ahead. "I want you to search there, near our destination. Search the northern region until I summon you back."

Darkhorse shook his head, sending his mane flying. He seemed taken aback by something. "But that leaves—"

"I have *given* you your task. I want it performed as I said. No rebellion. Nothing will happen to *anyone* here if you obey me to the letter. I *promise* you that."

The demon steed snorted. "You are more foul than anything spawned among the endless realms I crossed during my now-regretted search for this accursed world."

"Yes, we must talk of those places when *this* realm is secured. Now, *go*!"

Darkhorse dipped his head in a mocking salute. "I am your servant, dragonlord."

Rearing, the ebony stallion turned and raced off. Sharissa watched the receding figure, then turned to Faunon for support. The elf wore a dour look. He did not seem that sympathetic to Darkhorse's plight.

"Faunon, I—"

"They died because of him. That is what he said."

"It was *his* doing!" She pointed an accusing finger at Barakas, who was turning to watch their antics with mild amusement. Many of the other Tezerenee were watching, too, but Sharissa did not care. She would say what she had to say. If Faunon abandoned her because he could not accept Darkhorse's earlier actions, then the sorceress would be alone in her efforts. That might be an obstacle she could overcome, but his absence would create an even worse problem for her.

You are too romantic to be a Vraad, her father had once told her. Perhaps so, but she felt no reason to change, even if it meant hurt.

"There will be time for discussion later," Barakas interrupted, evidently deciding there were better things to do.

Sharissa quieted, hoping that Faunon would see things clearer if he had time to let his emotions cool. He might then see what fear could do to even the bravest of creatures. The elf did not know Darkhorse; he could not see the child that the eternal was. Recalling her own youth, not that distant in the past,

Sharissa knew the limits of a child, even as strong a one as the dweller from the Void.

Ahead of them and high in the sky, the dark form soared out of sight.

Securing the box, Barakas told Reegan, "We move out now. The confusion will be to our advantage."

"Yes, Father." The heir turned and signaled to the column.

The Tezerenee readied their weapons and spells. Lochivan rejoined the scouts, who, once he was settled on his steed, urged their mounts into the air. Lochivan's band circled the column twice and then spread out ahead of it.

"We are in the company of madness," Faunon whispered.

Tilting her head just enough to see him, Sharissa once more tried to explain Darkhorse's apparent weakness of spirit to the elf. He cut her off with a look and whispered, "The anger was more for their benefit. I understand all too well the limits one faces. If not for your suggestion, I would have likely broken soon, anyway. These dragon men are very skilled at what they do, especially the pleasant one."

She glanced up at the tiny figures of Lochivan and his airdrake. "I once thought I knew the true man."

Faunon grimaced. "You probably do. His pleasant attitude is no game, so far as I saw. He would probably smile while he cut your throat if something amused him."

"That's—" The Vraad was about to say that the elf's words were cruel, but then she recalled her most recent encounters with Lochivan. If it benefited the clan and his father, Lochivan would have indeed cut her throat, all the while explaining that he hated to do it but there was no choice in the matter. His lord and master had ordered him to do it, and thus there was no room for argument.

An invisible wave struck Sharissa. She moaned and nearly lost her grip on the reins. Her mind was on fire, and she had a great urge to unleash her power at random if only because it was what burned her.

To her side, Faunon shouted, but she could not understand his words. Several Tezerenee were also shouting, one of them the patriarch himself. The pain-riddled enchantress put a hand to her head, but the pressure within was too much. She started to slide to her right. Part of her knew that if she fell from her drake she would be trampled by one of the others, for the reptilian mounts had grown skittish, but Sharissa lacked the concentration to maintain her grip.

An arm caught her before the sorceress could slip very far. At first she thought it was Faunon, and so she smiled. Only when things came into focus did she see that it was *Reegan* who had saved her. He had backed up his mount and put himself between the two captives. Over his shoulder Sharissa could see Faunon burning a hole with his eyes through the Tezerenee's wide back.

"Are you well?" he asked, genuine concern tempering his otherwise gruff voice.

"Yes . . . I am." She disengaged herself from his grip as quickly as she was able, but not before his hand slid down her side a bit. Her smoldering expression made him release her that much quicker, and he immediately urged his drake forward. Reegan did not look back even when he was once more near his father.

"I tried to get to you," Faunon informed her, their mounts once more side by side. Bound to his animal by the magical chains, his mobility was limited. "But he was over here as soon as it hit us. I was lucky he did not *push* me off my animal! His eyes carried that intention!"

"What . . . what happened to us?"

"The demon has met the enemy," Barakas declared. He gazed back at the young Zeree with excitement radiating in his every movement, every breath. "The first blow has been struck, I think."

A second later, a blue light flashed in the distance. It was bright but brief.

The patriarch turned back to see what startled his people so, but missed the light. Reegan informed him of what had happened. Barakas nodded.

"We can expect more such waves and probably worse before this is over."

"They might *kill* him!" Sharissa raged. "You were able to capture him! What happens if they kill or capture him?"

A shrug. "Then it will amount to the same thing. If he's captured, I can hardly let him be turned on us, especially you. I think your black friend would agree with me on that."

She pulled back in shock at his response. "You'll kill him?"

"Eliminate the threat to our security, yes. Darkhorse would

never want to bring harm to you. He would prefer my way, rest assured.''

From another point nearer to the column but to the left of the previous location, a rumble and minor explosion brought renewed silence to the Tezerenee. Sharissa was both relieved and dismayed by the second blast; it meant that Darkhorse still survived, but it also meant that he had probably killed for her. If the Seekers lived in such a weakened state as the sorceress had been led to believe from the evidence, then it was possible that they might have left the expedition alone. Not so now. Now, there would most definitely be an attack. The avians would know that Darkhorse was controlled by the Tezerenee, and if they could not destroy the weapon, they might be able to destroy the one who unleashed it instead.

It was apparent that Barakas thought the same. He ordered his men to even greater caution, if that was possible. As swift and accurate as the shadow steed was, he would not find all of the Seekers. They were too skilled, too crafty for that, even if they were mere reflections of their former might.

The column renewed its steady crawl toward the caverns. According to Lochivan, the late Rendel's notes had indicated that his brother had titled the mountain Kivan Grath. That had brought a harsh laugh from Faunon, who understood the meaning of the name.

''*Kivan Grath*,'' he had announced in grandiose tones. '' 'The Seeker of Gods'! How very, terribly true!''

Asked to explain, the captive elf returned to his tale of ancient sorcery and some dark thing now lurking in the depths of the underground caverns perforating the mountain.

The selfsame mountain had been in sight for the past few days, looming over even its taller neighbors by quite some height, but now it was nearly the only thing they could see before them. Regardless of whatever else lay in sight, Kivan Grath overwhelmed the scene. It was still hours away, but a casual glance might lead one to believe that no more than a single hour would be needed to reach it. The leviathan's size wreaked havoc on perspective. Everyone had trouble believing it could be so tall; they were more willing to believe that it *must* be closer than the patriarch had estimated.

A second wave of random magical force washed over the riders, but this time they were at least prepared for its coming if not its intensity. It was terrible enough that the land here radiated a power of its own; the forces unleashed by both the Seekers and Darkhorse added a new dimension of fear. So far, the only effect was a twisting, churning sensation that touched every spellcaster—and that included most of those assembled for the expedition. The longer they were forced to endure it, the more chance it might affect them in other, more horrifying ways. No one had forgotten Ivor.

"We should turn back!" Sharissa argued as the second wave passed.

No one but Faunon paid heed to her words, and he was not in any condition to follow through on her suggestion. The Lord Tezerenee acknowledged her comments, but replied, "It will be over soon. The first expedition found only a few scattered flocks."

She was not satisfied with his response. "What if they hid the bulk of their strength for when you returned with greater numbers? How much better to snare many rather than a few! We could be attacked from all sides at any time!"

To her surprise, the patriarch nodded. "I *expect* to be attacked—and at any moment!"

"But . . . you can't be serious . . . Darkhorse is . . ."

"He *is*," Faunon said, the elf shocked nearly as much as Sharissa was. "Look at him. He has ridden us into the tearing beak of the bird folk . . . and performed the deed willingly!"

Turning away from the two stunned captives, Barakas laughed. The sorceress scanned the high ground on either side of them. Some of the Tezerenee had airdrakes, but most had only the swift but ground-locked variety. Granted the Vraad had massive sorceries at their beck and call, much of it the vile but deadly Nimthian sort, but that might end up bringing death to them just as readily as the medallions of the Seekers. As with their former home, this world did not deal well with the old sorcery. The greater the spell, the worse the backlash.

It was interesting—and worrisome, Sharissa had to admit—to see many of the armored figures around her turning to one another with apprehension. Had the patriarch neglected to inform his people that he *knew* they would be riding into a trap? Had they been led to believe that Darkhorse would clear much of the danger away?

Beside his father, Reegan suddenly straightened and pointed at something in the distance. It was Lochivan and the scouts . . . but were there fewer of them than there had been before?

"It's about to start," Barakas commented needlessly. He looked around in expectation.

The sky darkened as manlike forms filled the air above them.

"To your duties!" Reegan shouted. Tezerenee were already raising their bows or some other weapon. If it came to a physical assault, those with swords and lances would defend against any attackers who tried to kill the archers while they reloaded. Several Tezerenee were grouping together in what was obviously the beginnings of a major spell. Others were attempting personal conjurations. Barakas sat on his drake and waited. Sharissa wondered at his sanity, but forgot him when she realized Faunon was completely defenseless. A well-placed rock would put an end to him.

The avians had the advantage. They controlled the sky and the high ground around the column. They knew the land. While there was room for the drakes to maneuver, it was all open to the Seekers.

She wondered why the Seekers did not just bury the entire Tezerenee expedition under tons of rock. Perhaps they no longer had that ability, considering the numbers who had perished because of some prior spell.

"Why does he not summon the demon back?" Faunon wanted to know. "We would stand a better chance!"

"I don't know!"

A warrior behind them reached for his throat and gasped. That was all. He fell from his steed and was lost under the milling forms of the drakes.

Archers were already firing. Two Seekers plummeted to the ground, already dead, but most of the others had moved out of range.

Sharissa's mind was tugged in all directions as the two sides warred on the sorcerous plane. Men screamed around her, but she could not afford to aid them. Instead, she pulled Faunon to her and cast her best defensive spells.

"You should be fighting them," Faunon counseled. "The avians will not ignore us for long merely because we behave. They will save us for when the true threats have been eliminated."

A huge form fell in front of them, sending the drakes into a fearful rage. The sorceress was forced to contend with both beasts, but she still managed to bring them under control. The missile proved to be the corpse of one of the bird folk. It had hit the ground with such intensity that much of it was no longer recognizable. Whether sorcery or arrow had killed the Seeker was a moot point, but it raised another danger. With the avians directly above the column, it was possible that even in death a Seeker might take a foe with him. Sharissa craned her neck and gazed into the heavens. It seemed to her that the greatest concentration of Seekers was over their present location.

Lowering her head, the exasperated sorceress again saw Barakas sitting calm amidst chaos. He was doing little more than surveying the scene and shouting out the occasional order. He *was* waiting for something.

His eyes met hers and she was certain that he smiled, although the helm, of course, made it difficult to be certain. As if responding to her anger and confusion, the patriarch pointed into the sky behind her. Sharissa spun around on her saddle, fearing that even more Seekers were winging their way toward the doomed column, cutting them off from any retreat.

There was indeed a mass of winged terrors racing toward the battle, but they were not Seekers.

They were Tezerenee. Not one band, but two. They converged from the east and west, coming together just as they reached the mountains. While their numbers were not as great as those of the avian attackers, they had height and mass to their advantage. They also had the confusion of battle to count upon. Several of the Seekers noted them, but that knowledge did them little good. Engaged in combat, both magical and physical, with the column, they could not break away without opening themselves up to a rain of death from below.

Many tried just that, regardless of the risk. Seeker magic was evidently more limited, at least as far as this particular group was concerned. Those who turned to flee proved inviting targets for the archers, who brought down many before the spellcasters could take their own turn. A few Tezerenee still fell; not all of the avians were abandoning the struggle. The bird people seemed to radiate a quiet desperation as they fought the humans, as if they knew that they were fighting to preserve what was already lost to them. Yet as their arrogance and miscalculations had evidently unleashed some horrifying spell back upon their own—as Faunon and the petrified corpses had suggested to her—so now did those same faults thrust the Seekers into a trap from which there was little hope of escape.

Barakas had expected a trap and laid one of his own. This was why the expedition had moved as slowly as it had. The patriarch had sent out two smaller forces composed of airdrake riders and hidden them somewhere in the wooded lands southwest and southeast of here. Somehow, they had come just in time, though Sharissa could not recall any signal. She had certainly sensed nothing.

The patriarch, she knew, would be more than pleased to explain later. What mattered now was surviving until the newcomers were able to finish the task at hand.

"Beware!" Faunon shouted. "One has his sights upon us, Sharissa!"

That much was true, but the young Zeree felt no assault. Instead, faint images swirled about her imagination, images she vaguely recognized as Seekers.

"Sharissa?" The elf bounced against her, the only thing he could do to stir her since he was bound.

"No! Stop that!" she warned. "It's trying to tell me something!"

Above, the Seeker dodged two arrows. It increased its mental assault, strengthening the images Sharissa perceived.

Seekers in a cavern . . . the cavern the Tezerenee sought.

Her father had told her of the fashion by which the avians communicated with outsiders, but he had indicated touch was necessary for the best understanding. That was not possible, but there *were* barriers that *could* be brought down.

"Sharissa! You are dropping your defensive spells!"

"I know! Trust me!" She hoped he would not press her, for her own resolve in this was wavering. What if she were playing into the talons of the Seeker?

The last barrier fell . . . and the Vraad sorceress was deluged with vivid images of what had been and what might be. The vision of Seekers hard at work on a master spell through which they hoped to rid themselves of the last of the Quel, the massive armadillolike race that had preceded them as masters of this continent. Sharissa gasped at the sight of the horrifying beast, although deep down she knew she was absorbing some of the avian's fear and hatred of the elder race.

The spell was not totally of their own fabrication. Another had influenced them in its making. Something made the image blur, and she found herself now seeing the effects of that spell. It had not been a sorcerous backlash that had killed so many of the avians, but a successful but costly full reversal of the very spell. They had realized that what they unleashed would not stop with merely the Quel, and if they allowed it to go unchecked until their old enemies were no more, then it would be too strong to ever stop.

It had taken the greater part of their population to force the—Sharissa saw a vision of fur, teeth, and huge claws digging through earth, but received no name for the monstrosities—into the lands north, where they could be made to sleep until it was possible to destroy them all.

The image blurred again and she was back in the cavern, but her view kept shifting, as if she were traveling through the system of passages leading deep into the earth. The Seeker's fear touched her; he did not want to have to show her what lay below, but it was necessary for her understanding.

Faunon was shouting in her ear, trying to stir her, she supposed, but his words were so long and drawn out that they sounded like moans. Everything around her had slowed. Her mind had become attuned to the swift thoughts of the avian, who was desperately trying to communicate as much as possible before—

Pain and then total emptiness rocked her. The baffled sorceress screamed, knowing that what she had felt was *death*. With great effort, she forced the chilling sensation down and opened her eyes.

The patriarch's second force had engaged the avians, who were trying to both retreat and fight. Lochivan's mount flew by, though she only got a glimpse of the Tezerenee himself. Of the Seeker who had been trying to communicate with her, she could see nothing.

"He fell among the drakes yonder," Faunon informed her, knowing who she sought. "There probably is not too much of him left."

His cold tone received a vicious glare from her. He stared back at her in defiance. "I saw that he was about to die. I have seen what has happened to those caught up in a linking of minds when one dies. Sometimes the survivor goes mad . . . or simply drops dead. That was why I was shouting at you!"

"He was telling me . . . telling me . . ." Sharissa's head swam.

"Were you injured?" another voice asked, disturbing her recollection of what the avian had tried to warn her about.

"*No*, Reegan, I was *not*."

"They're trying to retreat," the heir apparent informed her. Even though there was still combat going on, he no longer seemed to care. Sharissa was more important. Had it been Faunon or Gerrod, she would have been pleased by the attention. Not from this one, though. Never from Reegan.

"They're being slaughtered," she corrected him with grimness.

The attack had been, in the long run, a pathetic last gasp by the bird folk, and now they were paying dearly for it. Darkhorse was still out there, either killing them or—and she felt guilty for hoping it was the former and not the latter—dead from one of their spells. She did not care for what the Seekers were, but her brief contact with them had at least made them worthy of some respect. Knowing they could not hold back the invaders, one of them had tried to at least warn them of some threat.

But *what* threat?

Mountainsides were no longer safe for the avians. The airdrakes ferreted them out and, in many cases, tore them apart without any command issued by the rider. Some Seekers proved more fatalistic; Sharissa saw one female throw herself upon the nearest warrior, even though it meant exposing her undefended back to the other. She died from a drake's slash, but not before her own talons took out the throat of her opponent.

Barakas was coordinating the reorganization of the column, leaving the bulk of the fighting to those in the air.

"They must have been desperate to pull such a stupid stunt as this," Reegan added. "I expected more from them." He laughed for no reason that Sharissa found humorous.

Faunon shook his head. "They were desperate, yes, but never stupid. Not the bird folk. If they did this for any reason,"—he looked at Sharissa—"we will know about it before long."

"What's that?" The patriarch was riding over to them. There was blood on his armor from some encounter. He was in a jovial mood, as if something he had feared lost had been found again. Sharissa noted he was breathing heavier than she would have thought. The battle, as short as it had been, had taken more out of Lord Barakas than she suspected he thought.

This was her chance. As much as she yearned to study the treasures left behind by the founders and those who had followed them, the desire was far outweighed by the knowledge that the caverns also held an apparent evil that frightened even the once-mighty Seekers. It had, if she understood the images thrust upon her by the dead avian, brought about the downfall of their empire.

"Barakas, this is our last chance to turn back. If you would just listen—"

"Turn *back*?" The clan master was flush with enthusiasm now, which possibly meant that he had not been as confident as he had pretended to be prior to the attack. "I should say not! We've eliminated what little threat remained to us! There will be no more Ivors now, no more hidden threats!"

"But there's something in the caverns that—"

"The *elf's* tale again? I thought better of you, believing nonsense like that . . . or perhaps you don't. Perhaps you're just trying to spread fear, as he tried."

"I saw one of the damned birds try to attack her, Father," Reegan offered. "It's likely shock or some nightmare cast by the beast before it was skewered."

Barakas found that acceptable, stilling any further argument from Sharissa with a wave of his hand. "I'll hear no more of it, then."

The two captives looked at one another. Faunon gave her a brief, bittersweet smile. The sorceress bit her lip, but knew the cause was lost for now, if not forever.

The Lord Tezerenee had already forgotten her. He turned his eyes skyward, where two drakes were descending upon the group. One was the creature Lochivan utilized, a mottled monster larger than any of the rest by almost half. The other likely belonged to whoever had been placed in charge of the secondary force.

"Ahh, here they are!"

Remaining seated, Lochivan saluted his sire. "Was it satisfactory, Father?"

"Most." Barakas scanned the region once more, as if afraid he had missed something important the previous times he had looked around. "And still plenty of daylight with which to work."

The newcomer to the expedition scratched at his neck until a glare from his lord made him pause. "As you predicted, Father, the demon made a perfect signal. We could hear and see his battles from where we waited."

"Did you doubt it, Wensel?" One hand touched the box. "It might be a good time to call him back, I think."

Lochivan was squirming in his saddle. Sharissa was certain that he, like Wensel, wanted desperately to scratch, but knew better than to do so in the presence of Barakas. Possibly because he sought to keep his mind off the itching, Lochivan asked, "What are your orders, sire?"

The box was forgotten for the moment. "I want the entire force ready in a quarter hour, save for those needed to flush out the few surviving birds. I want us moving on immediately after that time limit has expired! Do you understand me?"

Once more Sharissa would have liked to attempt to convince Barakas of the danger awaiting them, but once more she knew that he would not listen, that her warnings would only *fuel* his desire to be there sooner.

Faunon whispered, "Courage. This is something we *must* go through now. If they are going, it is better that we do, too."

"Separate those two," the patriarch commanded, pointing at Sharissa and the elf. "His words have been twisting her resolve. Until I say otherwise, they will *remain* separated. Lochivan, I give you charge of the elf. Reegan, you protect the Lady Sharissa."

"Yes, Father!" The heir smiled at Sharissa, who turned away only to find her eyes resting on Kivan Grath.

Barakas followed her gaze. "Yes, there it is. So very near now." He turned his mount toward the north and the mountain, but not before adding, "With any luck, my lady, we will be camping at the foot of that mountain this very evening! Maybe even the outermost caverns, if the sun holds true!"

"Why not fly there now?" Reegan asked. "There's nothing to fear."

"And no more reason to hurry. This is *our* world now, Reegan. We have all the time we could ask for in which to explore its treasures and shape it to our tastes." Barakas studied the sun. "Which does not mean we shall dawdle here any longer. You have your tasks; be about them. Reegan, you and the Lady Sharissa will come with me."

"My lady?" As the heir apparent urged his mount next to hers, Sharissa could not help thinking of the Seekers, who had once ruled this domain and were, in so many ways Barakas could not see, similar to the Tezerenee. They, like the patriarch, had probably once thought that time was their servant, not their enemy.

The avians' empire had lasted centuries, perhaps even millennia. Now, riding again toward the towering Kivan Grath, the place of the Seekers' folly, Sharissa wondered if Barakas's empire would even last out tomorrow.

XV

Like the toothy maw of some great petrified beast, Sharissa thought as she stood near the base of Kivan Grath and stared up into the cavern mouth that was their goal. To some, like Reegan, it still seemed foolish to camp at the foot of the mountain when they could be exploring the cavern. To the captive sorceress, it was foolish to be anywhere near here in the first place. That she had even for a time looked forward to exploring this ancient place and the artifacts within, shamed her. If nothing else, it had detracted from the goal she *should* have been striving for—namely, escape for herself and her companions.

They had returned Faunon to his wagon prison. As for Darkhorse, he was still free of the box—a promise Sharissa had been surprised to see Barakas keep—but he was carefully monitored by the Tezerenee. The patriarch had allowed her to speak with the shadow steed for a few minutes after their arrival here, but no more. Darkhorse, usually vocal, had become more and more reticent. He did not like being used, especially for the tasks set for him by Lord Barakas.

The eternal's assault in the northern mountains had been the signal by which the other Tezerenee force had known when to attack. Barakas had not said so, but it was clear that, while he could have used Darkhorse in the battle—something that might have saved some of the lives of his own followers—he did not completely trust his hold on the ebony stallion. That in itself encouraged the young sorceress, for where there were uncertainties, there was the potential for exploitation.

But what? She had to be careful. Barakas was, in many ways, an unpredictable quantity. Much of what he did, as he had admitted, was for effect, not merely for success. If a plan of his own design meant a few more lives but misdirected the efforts of his adversaries, the Lord Tezerenee was willing to live with those extra costs.

And, for some horrible, inexplicable reason, so were his people, the very ones he was willing to sacrifice.

To her right, the warrior whose task it was to watch her this evening straightened to attention. Sharissa did not even have to turn to know who it was. Barakas would have summoned her to him, not come to speak to her. Reegan had already been to see her, evidently in a pitiful attempt to renew his bid for her hand—as if they needed her approval for that. Of the remaining Tezerenee, only one other bothered with her.

"Is there a specific reason you wanted to see me, Lochivan?"

He chuckled, and his voice rasped as he spoke. "You always amuse me, Sharissa."

She did not look at him, preferring now the haunting image of the darkened caverns above. They were little more than dark patches in areas not quite as dark, but it was enough. Anything, so long as it and not Lochivan occupied her eyes. "Did you want something?"

"Only a few moments of your time." The tall Tezerenee was directly behind her now. For some reason, she found his nearby presence even more chilling than of late. It was not merely because of his betrayal, but some growing change in the patriarch's son himself. "First, your elf is well. I saw no reason to press him on any questions tonight. Thanks to you, he has been very cooperative."

"I'm glad . . . for *his* sake . . . but I wish you'd stop referring to him as *my* elf."

Lochivan shifted so that he now stood near her right shoulder. She could hear his breathing, a slow, scratchy sound that made her wonder if he was suffering from the altitude a little. Even ignoring the mountains, the land itself was well above sea level. One or two Tezerenee were already suffering some altitude sickness. Overall, however, it was not proving to be a problem; most of the dragon clan had grown accustomed to altitude from countless time spent riding airdrakes.

"He *is* your elf. I see it, and I know Reegan sees it. In fact, he wanted to speak to the elf a short time ago. Did he speak to you, by any chance?"

"Reegan was here."

"And by your tone, he was rejected again. Tread carefully, Sharissa. Each day of life for your friend is a bonus at this point. My brother would be willing to risk father's ire if it meant disposing of a rival . . . even if it's one who has no hope, anyway."

She did not know which part of his comment troubled her more, the threat to Faunon's life or the fact that Lochivan saw how close the two captives were growing to one another. Perhaps it was even the personal interest he had in the situation. His tone was not that of an outsider looking in but rather someone who had a personal stake in the results and not merely because Reegan was his brother. Sharissa recalled his earlier words.

"And would you be willing to risk the patriarch's ire, too? Does Faunon have something to fear from you?"

His hand briefly stroked her arm, causing her to tremble. The guard, of course, would be blind to all this, or else Lochivan would have never dared touch someone his father had chosen for the heir. "I am his—*your*—only hope."

"What do you *mean?*"

His breathing had been gradually growing worse, more harsh and rasping. "It isss...is growing late. Good night, Sharissssa."

"Lochivan?" She turned, but he was already walking away. Any thought that his departure was due to what he had hinted to her vanished as the sorceress saw him clutch his sides. His breathing had worsened even more in the few seconds since. Sharissa took a step toward him, wanting to help the Tezerenee lord despite her personal feelings.

The guard blocked her path. "Lord Lochivan desires privacy, my lady."

"He's ill!"

"A passing fever, Lady Sharissa." The guard, a woman, stared through the young Zeree.

"Did he tell you that? I don't recall him having the chance to do so."

"No, my lady. I make my own judgments. I've seen similar of late. Besides, if the Lord Lochivan wanted aid, he would have requested it." The Tezerenee sentry's voice was mechanical; she had been trained well by her masters. If they chose not to speak of their ills, she would defend that decision to her utmost.

Lochivan was already lost in the darkness. Sharissa sighed at yet another example of clan obstinance and infuriation. If she lived among them for the rest of her days—a horrid thought *that!*—she would never understand them.

"It's getting late, my lady. You should be rested for tomorrow," the guard suggested pointedly.

She nodded, knowing that sleep would be something long in coming under the watchful eyes of Kivan Grath. Taking one last look at the leviathan that both invited and repelled her, Sharissa gave the warrior woman leave to lead her back to the rest of the camp.

The wind was picking up. To her ears, it began to sound like a mournful wail—possibly a lament for those foolish enough to believe they were going to be able to make the mountain's secrets their own without a greater cost.

The morning came both too soon and yet not soon enough. The light of day lessened some of the uneasiness that Sharissa felt, but, as she had expected, her night had been one of tossing and turning. From the looks of the Tezerenee, who had already preceded her in rising, she was not the only one who had slept troubled. A surliness had spread throughout the camp. Many of the Tezerenee were also scratching at their throats, chests, and limbs, a sign that the rash was still running rampant. The sorceress was thankful that what with her close involvement with the dragon clan she had not contracted whatever it was that affected them. How long would her luck last, however?

Her latest guard, yet another woman, brought her some food. Simple fare even by Tezerenee standards. Food was the least of the expedition's interests this morning; most of the Tezerenee were visibly impatient to be about the task of invading the ancients' lair and seeing just what it was they had been fighting for. By the time she was finished, the Tezerenee were already organizing themselves for the short climb and what they hoped would be a treasure trove of power and riches.

Riches. For all he sought greater and greater power, Barakas was not one to turn down any jewels and such that might have accumulated over the millennia.

A warrior arrived shortly after her meal. He knelt as if her rank actually meant anything to his masters and said, "Mistress, your presence is requested by our lord ruler. Now, if possible."

If possible? she thought wryly. If Barakas was requesting her presence, he expected her to comply, not dawdle, and everyone knew that. Still, Sharissa decided she would set her own pace this time. Rising slowly, she asked the kneeling warrior, "Does he say what it is he wants me for? Is it urgent?"

"He indicated that you would be among those beside him when he entered the caverns in glorious triumph."

Of course. It would be a gesture of his so-called respect for her and a strictly symbolic gesture. The sorceress smoothed her clothing, taking special care to draw out the simple action for twice as long as necessary. By the time she was finished, the warrior had dared to look up, wondering, no doubt, what was taking this outsider so long to obey the patriarch. Sharissa gave him a regal smile and indicated he had permission to rise. He did so, but with jerking movements that revealed some of his annoyance. Like so many Tezerenee, he and her guards were never certain how she was supposed to be treated. A prisoner this one might be, but she was also a respected guest of the clan master.

It was a predicament that probably required more thought than they were used to. Sharissa kept her amusement hidden as she followed the newcomer and her own guard to the patriarch.

From a distance, she located both Darkhorse and Faunon. The latter, spellbound, sat atop a winged drake. His visage was that of one who is resigned to death and merely wishes to know the time it will occur. When he turned and saw Sharissa, however, he was able to give her a brief, tired smile. She smiled back, but her heart grew heavy.

Darkhorse was more of a distant blot, but she sensed as well as saw the eternal. The huge, ebony stallion paced back and forth as if confined to a corral, although the eagle-eyed sorceress could perceive nothing. Sharissa tried to contact him through subtle manipulation of her power, but a wall of blankness stopped her efforts each time. *She* might be free from her magical bonds, but the other two were not. As long as they were slaves to the clan's power, she would be unable to contact much less help them through sorcerous means. The patriarch had planned well, completely separating the three most troublesome elements of his band from one another.

Barakas and a small group, likely his sons judging by their stances, awaited her near the northern edge of the camp. From that location, they had an excellent view of the cavern mouth.

Reegan noticed her first and whispered to his father, who had been in the midst of explaining something involving a parchment he held in one hand. The sinister box lay at his feet, a tantalizing treasure the woman knew she would never get near if she tried to take it. The patriarch turned and greeted her as if she were a prized daughter. "Aaah! Lady Sharissa! Good! Ready for this momentous day?" To one of the helmed figures, he suddenly said, "We may begin now! Ready the expedition! Those remaining behind here are to be alert and not to fear! They will share equally in what we find within! Assure them of that!"

The Tezerenee he had spoken to saluted and vanished to obey.

Walking to meet her, Reegan offered his hand. Sharissa reluctantly took it, but only because Faunon's visage formed in her mind. If she allowed the heir small victories, he might not be so inclined to murder. Reegan smiled as if she had just granted him her love and tightened his grip on her hand. The warrior who had brought her and her personal guard both departed in silence, no longer needed. Besides so many of the ruling family of the Tezerenee, there were a number of ready sentries within sight. Only a madman would attempt something among so many deadly, skilled fighters.

Her attention drifted as she watched Barakas turn away from her, pick up the devilish box that bound Darkhorse to the Tezerenee clan master, and hand it to an expectant Lochivan. Though her eyes were on the box, she also noted how the latter stood as if pain still taunted him. He was too far away for her to tell if his breathing was still impaired.

"The demon goes first," the Lord Tezerenee said. Lochivan nodded, glanced her way, and walked off, the artifact tucked under one arm. His pace was much quicker than she would have thought necessary, as if he wanted to be away from his father before Barakas noticed something was amiss.

"Your airdrake awaits, my lady," Reegan whispered. Sharissa followed the wave of his other hand and saw the beasts. The sorceress had not given much thought as to how they would reach the cavern mouth, assuming that the clan had at least a dozen different methods. Riding yet another drake was not among those she would have chosen, but it was probably safer, relatively speaking. Materializing at the entrance of the cave system would, as Barakas had once pointed out, be an act of folly. The Seekers might be gone, but it was almost a certainty that they had left gifts of an unpleasant nature behind. There might even be more of them hidden in the caverns, although Lochivan's surprisingly easy entrance during the first expedition seemed to indicate otherwise. Still, Sharissa could not help thinking that so much good luck *must* be a trap. It could hardly be *this* easy to take the aerie.

She found herself thinking that last statement again when the drakes began to land and nothing had touched them. Several warriors had landed before them and set up a line of defense, but they had nothing to show for their efforts. Not so much as one trap had been found—and the Tezerenee were nothing if not thorough when it came to their search. Ahead of them and pacing back and forth like an officer inspecting his troops, was Darkhorse. He glared at the coming Tezerenee, but would not even blink in Sharissa's direction. Whether he was still ashamed to be in her presence or whether he was merely bitter about the offhand way his hated master was utilizing him was impossible to say at this point. Knowing Darkhorse as she did, it could have been both.

"I like this not," Reegan muttered, but no one paid him heed save for the captives.

They dismounted and stood before their goal. Several guards rushed over to take their mounts. Only the initial party would fly up here. Other Tezerenee were already making their way up the winding, treacherous paths that had been cut into the rock long ago by some forgotten race but had fallen into disuse with time.

"Do we take the elf?" one of the figures nearest to Barakas asked, his every word and movement showing deference. Sharissa could not recall which of his offspring had come on the journey, but this *had* to be one of them.

"Of course, fool! Why bring his carcass along if not to make use of it!" Reegan growled.

The patriarch nodded, allowing his eldest's outburst to go by without reprimand—this time. "Undo his feet, but see that his arms remain bound behind him." Barakas smiled as he admired the height of the cavern maw. "I see no reason why we cannot proceed."

He marched forward without any other preamble, catching many of his people by surprise. Lochivan snapped his fingers in Darkhorse's direction, and the shadow steed, evidently knowing what was required of him, trotted close but not too close to the patriarch's left side, matching his pace. Reegan and Lochivan followed and were in turn succeeded by the rest. The heir apparent paused only to signal two guards to lead Sharissa up to where he was. Faunon was also steered toward the front of the party, but closer to Barakas, which prevented the sorceress and the elf from even looking one another in the eye.

"Light," Barakas requested with the tone of one who knows he will receive whatever he desires.

One of his faceless sons raised a hand palm upward. From his palm, tiny spheres of flame leaped to life. One after the other, they departed their birthplace and took up residence in the air above the party.

When a full dozen of the dancing elementals floated around their heads, the patriarch ordered a halt to their creation. The light bearer closed his hand, smothering a tiny sphere just bursting into being. Sharissa knew the balls were not alive, but could not help thinking of the act as akin to a nasty child crushing a butterfly in his hands. Tezerenee, like many Vraad, cared little for the tiny things in life. Such deaths were inconsequential.

"Dragon's blood!" The stunned oath, considering what lay before them, would have seemed insufficient save that it came from the patriarch, the one among them least inclined to such shock. As for the rest of them, Sharissa herself included, they could only marvel at what the light revealed.

The cavern radiated history. It was not so much something to be seen as felt. The incredible age of the place could not be denied. Perhaps the ruined city and pocket-universe citadel of the founders held more specific knowledge, but those places dealt more with the original race itself. This citadel within a cavern, on the other hand, was a tapestry of sorts outlining the successive yet failing races of the lands now called the Dragonrealm.

While there were traces of those who had preceded them, it was the handiwork of the last inhabitants, the avian Seekers, that was most dominant. Other than a few broken medallions, she had never seen any products of their civilization. The paintings covering one smoothed wall, however, could only be Seeker in creation. Each spoke of freedom of the sky and conquests, many of them against the creatures called the Quel. There *were* scenes of aerie life, such as the raising of young and what appeared to be a festival. Some of the paintings were life-size, and all of them were oddly colored, as if the bird folk perceived colors differently. Angles were also askew, and Sharissa recalled how truly birdlike the avians' eyes were.

They were, she had to admit, beautiful. Beautiful and sad, in retrospect of what had happened.

Sculptures and reliefs, mostly of Seekers in flight, also dotted the chamber. One was simply that of a head more than twenty feet in height. The subtle differences in each figure made her wonder if they represented specific folk in the avians' history. She would probably never know. If the Tezerenee worked true to form, most of this would be replaced. The

Seekers had likely acted the same centuries ago when they had taken this cavern over from the previous tenants.

So many other things drew the eyes, but what demanded the most attention in the end were the rows of towering effigies made to resemble creatures both true and fanciful. It was possible, Sharissa thought, that they even represented some of the races that had preceded the Seekers. Like a swarm of ants, the Tezerenee began to spread out as they approached the huge figures. Reegan and Sharissa followed the patriarch. Lochivan was one of the few who seemed little interested in what he saw. He seemed satisfied to stand back while the others wandered over to the massive, lifelike statues. Sharissa, noticing his reluctance, saw him touch the box. Darkhorse, still pacing Barakas, suddenly froze in midstep. She was certain that the ebony stallion was still conscious, but the spells of the patriarch prevented her from discovering whether or not that was true. The young Zeree lost her interest in the marvels around her and tried to go to him. Reegan, seeing the object of her change of heart, refused to release his grip, however.

"Nothing'll happen to the demon," he muttered, trying not to disturb his father, who was lost in study of the statues. "Lochivan will just keep him out of the way."

There was a crash from behind them. Sharissa, the patriarch, and the rest whirled around, fully expecting that a trap had been sprung at last. Instead, a fearful warrior stood beside a platform that he had bumped into. A crystal and parts of the platform itself had shattered. The fragments glowed briefly with escaping power.

Barakas stared the man down, then turned to the rest of those in the cavern. "The next man who breaks something will find *himself* in as many pieces! Explore, but do so with care!"

He turned his attention back to the statues. Some of them were damaged, and a few had been tipped in what had nearly been a domino effect. Barakas touched one of those standing, a figure that was tall, gaunt, and resembled one of the walking dead.

"Gods!" he shouted, pulling his hand free almost the instant after he had touched the effigy.

"What is it, Father?" Reegan asked, not so much concerned as fascinated by his father's surprise.

"It . . . there's . . . forget it! No one touches these until I say so! Do you all *understand* me?" His eyes focused on Sharissa. "Not until more is known about them."

"We should be away from this place," Faunon suggested, both unnerved and frustrated at being here.

"Nonsense." Almost in defiance of the elf's words, Barakas pointed to a series of tunnels to the left of the cavern entrance. "I want those traced for a good thousand paces. If they go further, mark your place and return here. The same with those behind this,"—the patriarch surveyed what stood behind the effigies. It was a ruined set of steps that rose for some distance and ended nowhere in particular—"this dais. Yessss, a throne must have stood here once."

Soldiers rushed to obey, their places instantly filled by newcomers. Barakas removed his helm and watched them for a moment. The dragonlord then smiled at Faunon as if he had proved to the elf that there was nothing to fear, that he, the patriarch, had the situation under his complete control.

The Tezerenee were everywhere now, each warrior trying his or her best to please their lord and master. They skirted around artifacts and broken relics as they scoured the tall cavern chamber for anything of interest. Now and then, one of them would find something of sufficient importance that the patriarch would deign to investigate himself. Several times he vanished from sight, even daring short excursions into various subchambers.

Like a plague of thieves! Sharissa gritted her teeth. How much would be lost despite Barakas's warning to be careful? This was a search that should have required months of careful work, not a few hours of haphazard running around.

While the Tezerenee searched, the three captives waited. Darkhorse was still frozen in place, and Lochivan, who still made no move to aid in the search, appeared to be disinclined to release him. Two guards watched over the anxious elf. Faunon flinched every time a warrior touched something or passed within arm's length of the massive statues. As for Sharissa . . . she was forced to endure Reegan's nearness and the fact that she was not being allowed to even participate, despite Barakas's offer back in the citadel.

The latter problem became less significant as Reegan held her closer. With no one paying attention, the heir apparent was growing more and more familiar with her. He leaned near and whispered, "This will be the throne room of *my* kingdom, Sharissa. Did you know that?"

Rather than turn her face to his—and risk his suddenly desiring a kiss or some such foolishness—she stared at the statues. They were so very lifelike, Sharissa almost thought they *breathed*. . . .

"The elf gave us a rough idea of what this continent is like. One of his fellows had a map, although we didn't tell your friend that until we could see if he was lying—which he wasn't, lucky for him. Father's got the land divided between my brothers and me. Thirteen kingdoms now that Rendel's dead and Gerrod's as good as the same. We lost Zorain in the fight yesterday, or else there'd be fourteen."

She had no idea who Zorain was save that he had obviously been yet another offspring of the patriarch. More to keep him babbling about something other than their would-be relationship than because she was interested, the sorceress asked, "What about your sisters and your cousins?"

He shrugged. "There'll be dukedoms and such, not that it matters. Father has it all worked out."

Were the eyes of the catman figure she now stared at staring *back* at her? Impossible . . . *wasn't* it? "Where does he plan to rule? What kingdom will your father rule?"

His stiffening body made her glance at him despite her resolve. "He never says."

The statues called her eyes to them once more. They had an almost hypnotic way about them, one that *demanded* her attention. "That doesn't sound like the Lord Barakas Tezerenee."

Reegan said nothing more, but another short glance showed his brow furrowed in thought. He was also scratching at his throat where the dry skin caused by the rash had spread all over his neck and probably down his chest. His unsightly appearance only made the effigies that much more inviting to gaze at.

"Lochivan! Reegan!" The patriarch's voice echoed again and again throughout the cavern passages. Small, hideous creatures, disturbed by the loud noise, fluttered from their darkened places, realized they were in light of some sort, and scurried back to the sanctuary of the cool shadows.

"You'll have to come with me," the bearlike Tezerenee needlessly informed his prize. Sharissa did not argue; it would have been useless and, besides, standing around only frustrated her more. At least now she might learn something of value to her own goals.

The two of them passed close to Darkhorse. Though his cold blue eyes had no pupils, Sharissa knew that he watched her. Thinking of his predicament, she looked over to where Lochivan still stood, apparently trying to decide what to do about the eternal. In the end, he left the hapless creature the way he was, something that infuriated the sorceress further. It seemed that Darkhorse was to spend the rest of his existence trapped in one infernal torture or another and only because the Tezerenee found it useful.

Before this day was over, she would have another talk with Barakas. If it meant sacrificing some of her own liberty—small as that was—then so be it.

Lochivan joined the two, his eyes never veering from the path before him. He walked as if he wanted little to do with his brother or the woman to whom he had hinted deep affection for. This close, Sharissa could hear his rasping breath again. His gait was off as well, though not in any one way she could fix upon. It was almost as if he had broken some bones and had them reset by someone with no knowledge of what they were doing.

She noted the present location of the box, for all the good it did her. Lochivan kept it away from her, one arm cradling it much the way an infant would have been—not that she could imagine any of the Tezerenee holding a child.

"Where are you, Father?" Reegan called. The voice had come from somewhere behind the crumbling dais, but the back wall seemed pockmarked with passages, any one of which might be the tunnel the patriarch had chosen.

A warrior stumbled out of a passage and, realizing who stood before her, quickly saluted. "You were seeking clan master?"

"Yes, is he in there?"

She nodded, stepping aside as quickly as possible. "He is several hundred paces below. The tunnel dips and finally ends in another chamber. You will find him there."

Reegan nodded his satisfaction with her report. "Be about your duties, then."

When the soldier was gone, Lochivan turned to his brother. He sounded no better than the last time. "Take the Lady Sharissa and go on ahead. I . . . I will be along in a moment."

The other Tezerenee studied his younger brother for a moment, then nodded. "May it pass quickly."

"It will. It is only a matter of *will*. As he has always said."

It took no great thinking to understand that they spoke of the rash or disease that had afflicted so many of them. Lochivan seemed to be suffering more than the others, although she had hardly been among the Tezerenee long enough to know that for certain. Sharissa tried to take one last peek at Lochivan, but Reegan purposely steered her so that she would have to look through him to see what was happening to his brother.

Someone had lit the dry, ancient torches that stuck out from the sides of the passage. The Seekers, she recalled, were also creatures of the light, which made the torches no great surprise. What she still marveled at was why they had lived in such a place as this when they so obviously reveled in flight.

They were near the end of their trek when a figure came walking up the passage from the opposite direction, virtually blocking their path. The patriarch and his eldest blinked at one another. Sharissa, studying the clan master, was puzzled by the equally puzzled look dominating his features.

"Lochivan is following us, Father. He should be here in a few moments."

Sharissa tried to make herself as small as possible in the hopes that Barakas would pay her no mind. A suspicion was dawning that she was uncertain as to whether to reveal or not to the Tezerenee.

"And what has he discovered?" the patriarch asked. Behind him, two warriors appeared. They seemed a bit confused about why the passage was blocked by their masters.

The question left Reegan at a loss for a moment. He finally sputtered, "N-nothing! It was *you* who summoned *us*! You called to Lochivan and me. I brought the Lady Sharissa because—"

"Never mind." A grim expression settled onto the Lord Tezerenee's face. "Turn around this instant. We are heading back to the main cavern."

"But why—"

"I did *not* summon you at all!" the patriarch growled in exasperation.

Swallowing hard, Reegan fairly spun Sharissa around. She allowed herself to be led ungently back up the way they had just come, her mind racing. Her suspicions had been correct, but was she in error for not saying anything? If this were some avian trap, would not she suffer as well?

They burst out of the side passage, almost catching Lochivan by surprise. His back to them, he slammed his helm down over his head and turned to see what the trouble was. The sorceress glimpsed the box lying to one side, so close but impossible to touch with so many dragon men nearby. Besides, there was still the danger of trying to destroy it without affecting Darkhorse.

"You!" Barakas shouted at his other son. "You heard me, too, then?"

"Yesss, Fath—"

"Damnable birds! What are they up to?"

Was there a hint of fear, Sharissa wondered, amidst the patriarch's blustery anger?

They followed Barakas around the ancient dais and out into the center of the cavern. Tezerenee were filling the chamber, weapons drawn from sheer habit even though many now were more able with sorcery. The patriarch paused and searched for the enemy. Sharissa tried to join him, fearing for her companions, but Reegan pulled her back. She found his concern commendable, albeit unwanted.

Barakas turned in a complete circle, searching for some attack, some reason for the trickery played on his sons. It was clear he noticed nothing out of the ordinary, however, for the sorceress heard him swear.

She tried again to see her companions. Her view of Faunon was completely blocked by the milling, armored bodies of dozens of Tezerenee soldiers. Darkhorse, however, was another matter. Tall as he was, the top of his head was still visible despite the waves of high-helmed warriors still pouring into the cavern chamber.

As if drawn to the eternal by Sharissa's own interest, Lord Barakas strode toward the petrified steed, his followers parting like a living sea before his wrathful form. "You!"

The shifting of the crowd bettered her view. Darkhorse, of course, did not respond to the patriarch's angry and accusative call. He could not as long as Lochivan held him that way.

"This is *your* doing somehow!" he shouted. Without turning around, the clan master added, "Lochivan! Release him so he can answer my questions!"

"What nonsense are you bellowing, dragonlord?" the ebony stallion roared without preamble. His hooves scarred the floor as he vented his own frustration and anger in the only way allowed him.

Barakas faced him without fear. "What trickery do you play here, demon? Should I return you to the box?"

The physical change in Darkhorse's manner shook Sharissa to the bone. He cringed and shook his head in an almost human manner. "I do not *know* what you mean! I have done nothing! I *saw* nothing!"

"Do you deny the summons in my name that brought my sons to me?"

Darkhorse eyed the human as if he were mad. "I do not deny it! I heard it, but it was none of *my* doing! You of all people should know how thoroughly tied I am to you!" He shook his head again, this time in what the sorceress recognized as disgust in himself and his captor. "I heard the call and watched them as they passed my field of vision! Ask any others here if they heard the call and then ask yourself if I could have even performed that little magic?"

"I've no need of asking my own what they heard!" the patriarch's tone was as intense as Sharissa had ever heard it. He almost seemed close to a fit. She could not recall his ever acting thus in the fifteen years since the crossover from Nimth.

Barakas was losing control of himself.

He clamped his mouth shut and stared at Darkhorse for a moment longer before turning and facing his people. "None of you heard or saw anything other than my voice? No one is missing who should not be?" There were murmurs among the throng that indicated negative responses to both questions.

They'll be turning to Faunon next, she thought. He should be safe, she knew, considering that the chains and bonds kept him from performing any sorcery as much as the box and spell did the same for Darkhorse. Still, being one more familiar with this land, the elf might be in for some very deadly questioning.

The crowd shifted again, partially revealing the area where the Tezerenee had kept the elf. Sharissa tried to find him, to at least make eye contact with him.

Where *was* he?

She tried to squirm around, but Reegan, his mind on what his father was about, held her tighter without even realizing it. In frustration, she leaned by his ear and whispered harshly, "You can let me be! I won't run anywhere, you know!"

It proved to be the wrong thing to do. His attention on her now, the heir realized that she was trying to locate the elf. His jealousy apparent even through the helm, he turned to glare at his supposed rival.

He, too, failed to see any sign of Faunon.

"The elf!" Reegan roared, pulling all eyes to him. Sharissa grew numb, understanding now why she could not find Faunon.

Lochivan, one of the first to follow his brother's gaze, completed what Reegan had been trying to relate to the others. He spoke in sibilant but clear words, his breathing growing heavier with each syllable. "The elf isss gone! He hasss essscaped!"

Her silver-blue hair cascading down into her face, Sharissa shook her head at their misunderstanding. She doubted very much that it was by choice the elf had vanished. He had been in no condition to make any escape. That meant that either someone or something had helped him to flee ... or taken both Faunon and the guards for much darker, deadlier reasons.

——— XVI ———

The Quel did not always think in terms of night and day, a fact that turned Gerrod about more than once. His companionable captors kept track of the passage of days for many general purposes, but sleep evidently was something one did when one was tired and not because the sun had set. Even at night, the caverns were generally lit, some of the energy of the sun having been stored away in crystals whose function mimicked that of the gatherer crystal. This excess energy allowed the earth dwellers to work at their project on a full-day basis, newcomers spelling those whose period of work was at an end.

Now Gerrod stood before the pitch-black entranceway to the cavern of crystals—or cavern of *faces*, as he had come to think of it. This was his third time at this place, the second having occurred approximately yesterday by his calculations. He felt as if he had hardly recovered from *that* farce. Five minutes trying to combat the whispering visages, to conquer them, had left him drained, helpless. Only the fact that he had prearranged with the Quel leader a time limit had saved him. It had also, unfortunately, proved to him that he could not succeed in there without performing one particular spell first.

The Gerrod Tezerenee who stood before the fearsome chamber was a different Gerrod than the one the Quel had first captured. Sharissa would have known him. She would have seen the face she was so very used to, the one that, until now, had been a mask only for the last year or more.

He was young again, full of a great vitality that was more than what rest and food alone could bring. Utilizing the chamber demanded physical strength and endurance of the supplicant. Gerrod, loathing every moment required of the spell, had summoned the old Vraad sorcery again, uncertain as to what damage it might cause but knowing he had to be at his physical best for the chamber. Those who had designed the chamber had been more, so *much* more than the lone Tezerenee. Even now, temporarily young again, he risked overtaxing his mind and heart.

A Quel beside him hooted in impatience. The creature's call did not translate, which meant that it was merely a hint, not some statement berating his hesitation. Nonetheless, Gerrod knew he had to begin. The longer he waited, the less patient his inhuman companions would grow.

He stepped inside . . . and back into the world of madness.

The faces began their urgent whispering again. He still had no idea what they were trying to tell him, and this time the warlock did not care. Only one task was of any importance now.

His head started to swim. "Not *this* time!"

Long, forced strides took him across the chamber. His last two visits were jumbled memories, but he thought he recalled a set of crystals in the wall that differed from the others. At the very least, faces had not stared back at him from there.

Might they be the key to controlling this place?

He was already tiring. Even his renewed youth was not sufficient. A new, wild fear arose within him, that his spell was wearing away. He had wanted to save the rejuvenation spell until death was nearly calling for him; there was no telling how many times he could extend his life span this way. Binding himself to the magic of this world held no promise, either. Extend his life he might, but as what sort of creature? A part of him whispered that his fears were all panic and nothing more, but the warlock paid as little heed to that whispering as he did the rest.

A little further. His goal lay before him, almost within arm's reach. The whispering grew more intense and he almost paused, hearing for the first time a snatch or two of coherent speech.

"—not bow to me! If they will not, I will raze the city and all its—"

"—and that I should have started all this! Would that I could have turned time back, warned my—"

No! He would *not* listen! With a deep breath, Gerrod lunged at the wall where the faceless crystals were fixed.

The chamber was flooded with intense light.

The hood protected his eyes for the most part, although annoying sprites danced about for several seconds before his constant blinking dispersed them. Gerrod blinked one last time and turned to see what changes he had wrought. He knew without having to look that the whisperers had vanished. Certainly they had at least stopped their infernal murmur.

For a short time, he could only stand there, wondering if perhaps he had transported himself somehow to another chamber.

There was a world beyond the walls. No matter which direction he looked, save for where the controlling crystals were, Gerrod gained the impression that he was now inside a glass room of sorts. The many facets of the crystalline walls distorted the images, but the warlock could easily make out hills to one side and a smattering of trees near them. If he turned halfway around, he saw more hills and a grassy field in which a small herd of what appeared to be wild horses grazed.

"Where is this place?" he muttered. "Where *am* I?"

As if in response, the world vanished, to be replaced by a view that—he narrowed his eyes and studied the landscape before him—that could only be his father's Dragonrealm as seen from one of the *moons!*

"Serkadion Manee's bones!" he whispered in awe. The ancient Vraad would have relished this sight. Gerrod had read some of the elder Zeree's tomes, including one by the long-lost Manee himself. A vain soul, he had shared one thing with the sorcerer and Gerrod. A love of discovery, especially when it concerned knowledge.

"Sharissa!" he whispered to himself, so used to talking out loud for the mere sake of hearing another human voice. "I can use this to find her!"

And small good that will do you! the warlock thought in the next instant. *How will knowing where she is help when you yourself are a prisoner here!*

Where *was* here? He studied the vast display, taking into account the slight deviations due to the multitude of crystal faces that made up the image, and finally found what he sought. A tiny mark much like a dragon glowed near the outermost tip of the continent. It was a peninsula, as he had thought.

"And Sharissa Zeree?" It was a wild hope, but that was the only kind Gerrod knew of late.

As he feared, nothing happened.

"Perhaps if I picture her." He thought it would be an impossible task, so rarely had he seen her in the past few years, but her face and form proved quite distinct from the moment Gerrod concentrated. Her flowing silver-blue hair, the perpetual smile that was caused by the peculiar yet haunting curve at each end of her mouth, the bright, inquisitive eyes that glittered so much more than those of other Vraad...

"Dragon's blood!" The poetic touches to his thoughts were ousted before the truth of them became too much. He succeeded in keeping his imagination to the more mundane, picturing her as best he could and thinking *location...location...* in so adamant a way that the other, more private thoughts could not gain a foothold again.

The panoramic display before him clouded... and became a dark cavern so overwhelming that Gerrod forgot for a moment that he was *not* standing within it, but only viewing it from afar.

Better...

The cavern scene vanished as Gerrod's sudden panic at the ghostly whisper in his mind made him think of escape. No new image replaced the old; the crystalline walls remained cloud-filled.

"Who is that?" he shouted.

There was no response; he had hardly expected one, but had tried nonetheless. He shook his head, thinking of the whisperers and how they still intruded in his thoughts even though they had vanished. His imagination was plaguing him, nothing more. Gerrod kept expecting to hear their voices, so it was not surprising that he should conjure one up now and then.

Satisfied that the voice was no more than his own musings, the warlock returned to the task at hand. Soon, the Quel would work themselves up enough to send one of their own in to retrieve him. He wanted progress before that time, either something to give to them to prove he was aiding their cause or enough knowledge that he could utilize this massive artifact to find and flee to Sharissa.

He returned to the controlling crystals and, with great respect, touched them. His thoughts on the young Zeree, Gerrod was not surprised when the clouds dwindled away and he found himself staring at the mouth of a cavern.

"Better," Gerrod whispered, unconsciously mimicking the fanciful voice. The basic manipulations were surprisingly easy to understand once you knew about the controls, the hooded Vraad noted. *Why should they make it too complicated? It would only make using it frustrating. And here I was a moment ago fearing I might never learn anything!*

Gerrod was not overwhelmed by his success. Anyone with even a basic knowledge of the workings of crystal sorcery would have been able to accomplish what he had. Still, better that *he* had found it rather than his father or one of his brethren . . . or just about any other Vraad other than the Zerees, for that matter.

"This is a cavern, yes, but show me where . . ." He smiled as the map returned, indicating that the place in question was . . . was *far* to the northeast! "Only two-thirds of a continent away! A good thing I didn't end up in the sea with such accuracy as that!"

Mountains. A vast northerly chain of mountains. His brother, Rendel, had made some notes about these mountains, especially one in particular. Rendel, as secretive as any Vraad, had never written why the one mountain, Kivan Grath it had been named, was so important to him. Anyone who knew him, however, such as Gerrod or his father, understood that even the slight references indicated something of great import. That there were also mentions of Seekers and history in that same passage, albeit in seemingly unconnected paragraphs, was enough for the warlock.

"Your *treasure trove*," he muttered. "The place you abandoned your clan for!" It had to be . . . but if Sharissa was there, then that meant that the Tezerenee were there also. That, of course, meant his father.

Now, more than ever, he had to find a way to reach Sharissa. The secrets of the founders were not something to be left to the imaginative if single-purposed mind of his progenitor.

Another, simple touch of the controls . . .

Where had *that* thought come from? His hands moving as if directed by another, Gerrod slowly reached for the master crystals. *Was* there a way to travel from one location to the other? Nothing in the chamber seemed affected by the devices of the Quel, but he had been afraid to attempt any sorcery of his own, for fear it would touch him more than he desired. He still distrusted utilizing the magic of either torn Nimth or this world, but using the crystal chamber's power would not, the warlock believed, affect him since it did not require any part of him save simple thought.

There were other considerations that might have contradicted his suppositions, but desperation made him ignore them as he touched the first of the gemstones.

The familiar hooting of a Quel made him pull his hands back.

At the mouth of the chamber, the Quel leader, the only one willing to risk himself, stood staring at the sight before him. His animal features were partly covered by a metal helm that covered both ears completely and left only narrow slits for the eyes. A thick coil of rope was bound about the waist of the behemoth and stretched beyond the entranceway, enabling those without to pull their ruler to safety once he had his prize—Gerrod himself.

"Not yet," he called, trying to act calm, even disgusted. If the Quel could be convinced to leave him be for a bit longer.

With great effort, the massive beastman turned and peered at him. Gerrod still did not know what it was that affected the Quel so, but the lead helm was the only way they could even tolerate the cavern for more than a few moments. Unfortunately for them, even the helm had only limited protection.

From what he had learned to read in the posture of his underground acquaintances, the Quel was in shock. What the newcomer saw was hardly what he had expected to see. There was no sending by the Quel ruler; he might have seemed literally dead on his feet if Gerrod had not been able to make out his breathing.

Act!

The thought was overwhelming, not that the frantic Tezerenee needed much urging. He was already thinking that the chamber itself was a certain sign of the progress he had made—progress that should have been immediately brought to the attention of his hosts. Turning back to the controlling crystals, Gerrod fumbled with them.

He heard the Quel stir behind him, hooting a warning that the Vraad paid no attention to. Gerrod fought desperately for domination of his hands; they strived to move in unfamiliar patterns, as if they, not he, knew what was best.

The Quel was not armed, which gave Gerrod a few more precious seconds, but the moment the huge, armadillolike beast was within arm's reach, the warlock was dead and both of them were quite aware of that notion.

Hearing the heavy footfalls, the snarling Vraad relinquished his claim on his own hands and let them play across the pulsating gems.

The chamber grew blindingly brilliant again. Gerrod, prepared for either this or death from the neck-shattering blow caused by a Quel arm, closed his eyes.

A shrill, jagged shriek tore at his eardrums.

When the light faded and he still found himself among the living, the Vraad cautiously opened his eyes.

He was in a cavern, but not the crystalline one.

Stunned, he spun in a circle and scanned his surroundings with fish eyes. This was no image conveyed by a fantastic magical array of crystals; this was a very real and very familiar cavern. The one, in fact, where Sharissa awaited rescue.

Where is she, then? he asked himself, knowing better than to speak out or make any other sort of noise that would attract his former clan. *And what do I do when I find her? Fight the combined talents of my father, brothers, sisters, cousins, and every gifted outsider they've dragged along?*

It had, Gerrod discovered in horror, never *truly* occurred to him that he might actually arrive at this point. To be certain, he had *assumed* he would, but other than materializing, grabbing Sharissa Zeree from those who guarded her, and whisking the slim, beautiful sorceress away, the warlock had never given any consideration to a workable plan. Now, this close, he needed one desperately.

A dim light from a crack in the cavern ceiling kept him from standing in total darkness, but Gerrod decided to risk things further by supplying himself with illumination of his own. A spell of such insignificance, even though it was of Vraad sorcery in origin, could hardly affect him, could it?

He refused to consider the matter and flicked his fingers. A tiny blue flame burst into life in his palm. Despite its size, its light spread far enough to let him see more clearly what might lurk nearby. Gerrod took in his surroundings again, grateful that there appeared to be no horrific change. The cavern walls were still filled with shadows, but nothing capable of hiding some monstrous subterranean creature. The satisfied Vraad began walking around searching for a direction in which to travel.

What he found first was the Quel leader—what remained of him.

A rise had hidden him from view, but, now revealed, he was a ghastly reminder to Gerrod of what sorcery could do to those careless or accidentally caught at the fringe.

Even in the tiny blue light, the back of the Quel glittered, a tiny celestial map of twinkling stars. The shell was the only part of the earth dweller that had not been brutally ravaged by the ruler's unexpected passage. Gerrod turned away briefly at the sight of the head, a spreading wreckage of metal and flesh. One of the Quel's arms had been torn off and scattered somewhere out of sight. The legs were twisted over the shell as those of a rag doll might have been but not any way in which a creature with bones would have liked to experience.

Bits of rope still remained, causing the warlock to wonder what the other Quel might be thinking.

"I'd like to say I'm sorry about the sudden departure and its cost to you," he muttered at the tattered corpse. "But the truth is that I'm *not*." The pale Vraad contemplated the remains before him and added, "It could have been quicker and less disgusting, I suppose."

Seeing the Quel had altered something within Gerrod. He had been reminded of his own mortality once too often in the past fifteen years. Not only did he face death from his present course of action, but every use of Vraad power tore at both him and the land within which he was forced to abide. Why exactly the Quel had suffered such a fate and he had not only added to his fears. How could he hope to save Sharissa when he did not even know how to save himself?

The hooded Tezerenee tried to convince himself it was only nervousness that played on his emotions, but the attempt to calm himself failed.

I can show you the way to safety . . . for yourself and those you care for . . . I can give you . . . life . . . forever . . .

"But—"

I brought you forth from the underworld of the Quel and guided your hands when the critical moment came. I urged you forward when you might have slipped back and failed. Yessss . . . I am your savior more than thrice over.

The voice in his mind, with its impelling, hypnotic tone, could not be denied this time. It was not a remnant from the legions of the whisperers, whose tale he still did not understand, nor was it his overtaxed imagination. No, this was someone who spoke to his innermost self, who sought to offer guidance that he only now realized he needed in order to preserve himself.

If you would have these things I offer you, then follow my path downward.

"Path?" he asked, though it was a certainty that his newfound companion hardly needed to hear him to know his mind.

My path . . . the invisible being said.

A cavern passage that Gerrod could not recall seeing earlier stood before him—no more than fifty feet from him, in fact. The tunnel was illuminated, but not by gemstones in the wall or ceiling, as the Quel had designed them, but from a narrow path in the very center of the passage floor. The warlock peered down the cavern tunnel and saw that it continued on out of sight . . . but not before the passage itself sank downward.

"What about Sharissa? What about the one I came for?"

All will be yours . . . if you follow my path. . . .

Was there a hint of childlike eagerness in the voice's tone? Gerrod found he did not care. The offer was too inviting, too perfect in its timing, for him to resist very much. He stepped toward the tunnel.

Extinguish the light.

"The light?" He glanced at the blue flame floating before him. "My light?"

Your light . . . yesss . . . only then . . . yesss, that is the way of things . . . only then can you follow my path.

It seemed such a small, insignificant thing to ask that Gerrod merely shrugged acquiescence and closed his hand into a fist. The blue light winked away.

Now . . . follow.

He did, not noticing the time as he moved deeper and deeper into the depths of the cavern system. The path was always there before him, glowing with willingness to guide him. Sharissa always remained in his mind, but as something he more and more came to believe he could only achieve with the aid of that which awaited him at the end of his journey. That the notion grew the more he listened to the smooth words of the voice did not occur to him.

Time at last seemed to pull at him, slow him down. Gerrod had lost track of how many turns he had made and whether they had been to the left or the right. That he was ever descending was the only certainty he knew.

A little more . . . just a little more.

He came at last to the mouth of a cavern. The glimmering path faded to nothing just beyond. From where Gerrod paused, no more than five paces from that maw, he could see nothing but darkness. Pure darkness, as if light had no place being here.

You came across such darkness before, the voice, so very confident now, reminded him. *Beyond that darkness was the light of the chamber that brought your release from your captors. You recall that, don't you?*

The parallels between this cavern and the crystal one were not lost upon Gerrod. Steeling himself, he walked the last few steps and passed through into the cavern.

It was still as black as Darkhorse's body—and almost as unnerving.

"Where are you?"

Here.

Ahead of him, the warlock caught a glimmer of something moving, something that glowed in flashes, as if not all there. It had a vague shape, somewhat animalistic in nature, but which animal Gerrod found it impossible to say. More than one, perhaps.

"Who . . . what are you?"

I am . . . your guidance.

Not quite the answer that the Tezerenee was looking for, but he certainly could not argue with his peculiar benefactor, especially whenever the comforting tones of the creature washed away his uncertainties.

As they were now. *Your kin will not find you here. Their senses will not reach. You are safe.*

"Shar—"

She is well. They are confused. I have played a game with them. Your friend has been very useful in that, for the ideas come from her memories.

Again, there was shifting in the darkness. Two burning coals that might have been eyes flared at the cloaked and hooded human, then vanished again.

"This would be the time to strike, to—"

Soon. Things have not yet been played to their completion. Very soon, now, however.

Gerrod hoped so. As much as he appreciated the assistance of this fantastic being, something kept nagging at him, pushing him toward flight. Why? Here, he was safe from his father.

Yesss . . . safe here from everyone.

The warlock shifted. He disliked having his thoughts so easily taken. It reminded him too much of the Quel.

No! roared the voice. *Let your mind stay open! Do not shield it!* The sheer force that struck the Vraad nearly toppled him. He stumbled back, wrapping his protective cloak tighter around his body.

Possibly realizing that it had overstepped itself, the creature in the dark returned to the smoother, calming tones with which Gerrod was more comfortable. *It is essential for your protection that you do not block me from your thoughts. I will not be able to aid you should you be assaulted unless I can be with you at all times. You understand that, don't you?*

It should not have made that much sense, but, for some reason, it did. Nodding, the warlock relaxed a bit. He was still concerned over many things, however.

"What will we do? How do you plan to rescue Sharissa?"

When the time comes, she herself will aid us. There will be confusion and fear among the armored ones. Trust that they will have too many other things to consider to keep their full attention on your female.

Sharissa Zeree was not his woman, but he could not bring himself to argue the fact, not when there were so many more immediate considerations with which to deal. "The Tezerenee are not weak; their combined might allowed them to cross a vast sea by magic alone. The dragon totem might be only a symbol, but it very well represents my father. He *is* the dragon, in many respects."

His words only brought low, mocking laughter from the darksome dweller. Once more, there was a flash of burning eyes and the barely visible outline of some great beast. Each time, the being looked different, as if it experimented with its appearance, seeking the most fearful and imposing.

He is *the dragon, as you say . . . and more so than either you or he or any of his people think!* The laughter rose briefly again. *Much more so!*

Standing alone in the pitch-black chamber, his spectral companion still chuckling, a spark of reason pushed Gerrod to wondering if perhaps he had been better off with the Quel after all.

____ XVII ____

"Watch her!" Barakas roared to Reegan, his temper, for the moment, completely out of control. The patriarch turned on his own people. "Why do you stand around? Find the elf! Tezerenee blood is on his hands!" Nothing was mentioned concerning the elven blood on the clan's hands, which might have given Faunon a good reason for anything he did to the dragon men.

"Do you want him alive?" Lochivan, his head turned away from his father, asked in his peculiar voice. To Sharissa, it seemed he was finding great interest in the stalactites or anything else other than the Lord Tezerenee.

The patriarch, too, did not even look at his son. The two of them might have been talking to other people. "Not necessarily."

Sharissa leaned forward, her anger held back only by Reegan's strong hands and the ever-present box that Lochivan presently carried. "Barakas! Don't do—"

"Take this." Lord Barakas pulled out a small object from a belt pouch. It looked like a small crystal to the struggling sorceress, but one that had been *constructed*, not formed by natural means. "Use it if you trap him in a chamber with no exit other than where you stand. Make certain that there is *nothing* of value in there first."

Bowing his head, Lochivan took the sinister artifact. Barakas retrieved the box at the same time, securing it in one arm. He looked thoughtfully at the still form of Darkhorse, who met the gaze of the patriarch with his own baleful eyes. Sharissa still could not see how anyone, even the patriarch, could meet those ice-blue orbs and not turn away.

"And do you want me to deal with yet another irritation to you, dragonlord?" Darkhorse dared to bellow. "It appears I must do all the work here! Of what use, then, are all these toy soldiers of yours?"

The barb struck as true as if a mortal blow from a sword.

Barakas jerked back and quickly glared away any rebellious thoughts by his people. He was perspiring, something that Sharissa had rarely noticed him doing. Each time an event went awry, a little part of him seemed to vanish. The gray that she had noticed in his hair seemed to be spreading, too, now that she took a closer look.

The others are suffering from some rash, but he suffers from aging! the Vraad sorceress marveled. *He fears he's losing control!*

Many of the Tezerenee had already departed, and the patriarch's last look had sent most of the rest running. Lochivan had been one of the quickest to depart. Only a handful of warriors, Reegan included, remained.

"You must be taught respect again, I see," the clan master whispered, his voice cold. He reached for the box.

Darkhorse shivered at first, then his eyes narrowed as he steeled himself for the patriarch's worst. "The one who truly needs to learn respect is *you,* lord drake!"

"You've not tasted all that this can do, demon. I think the time has come to truly reprimand you!"

"No, you won't!" Sharissa focused on the patriarch and willed her power to the forefront.

The skin and armor of Lord Barakas crackled and wrinkled, but only a moment. He looked down at what she was doing to his form and took a deep breath. As he exhaled, the devastation to his body dwindled. The cracked skin healed itself and the armor resealed. His eyes were death as he looked up at her.

"Dragon's oath, Sharissa!" Reegan muttered in her ear. He attached something cold and numbing to her throat. Sharissa felt as if a part of her had been torn away and knew that she had wasted her one chance to utilize her abilities. The Tezerenee had again nullified her. "You shouldn't have done that, not at all! He let you wander loose only because he had other spells handy to keep you under control! Didn't you ever wonder?"

She had not, and that might be proving fatal now.

"*After* I have punished this errant monstrosity, Lady Sharissa, I fear I will have to teach you your manners, also! I will regret that, but it will be necessary."

He touched the box and turned expectantly to Darkhorse.

The shadow steed quivered, awaiting the pain. When he realized that nothing had happened, that he was apparently free of the box, he laughed loud. "Ohh, I have *waited* for *this,* dragonlord!"

He leaped at the startled patriarch.

For all his speed, the eternal could not reach the patriarch in time. Sharissa, struggling anew with a distraught Reegan, watched as Darkhorse slowed more and more the nearer he tried to get to his adversary. Barakas continued to draw swift patterns over the box, trying to regain some sort of control. At that moment, the best either could do was a stalemate.

A voice that sounded like Lochivan's shouted, "Reegan, you half-wit! Forget her and help Father!"

The heir apparent obeyed instantly, the Tezerenee code of serving the clan master—set down by Barakas himself, of course—enough impetus to sway him. He shoved Sharissa back toward a pair of guards standing near the ancient effigies and started forward. The sorceress doubted he even had any idea what he could do.

One of her new watchdogs reached out to take hold of her, but another armored figure caught her arm first. Both Sharissa and the warrior looked up into the helmed countenance of Lochivan.

"I'll take the Lady Sharissa. Help get aid. We may need my brothers and sisters."

The two guards obeyed without question, as they had been trained to do, but the young woman eyed her companion with growing suspicion. Lochivan was moving without the pain of a few minutes before and his voice was smooth, much the way it had always been before recent events. It was almost like standing next to a ghost image from the past.

"This way," he urged.

"What are you—"

"Do not argue."

They were walking into the midst of the towering statues, Lochivan looking as if he wanted no one to follow them. Sharissa wanted to ask where they were going, but then she lost all interest in that as something new demanded her attention.

The statues were pulsating. Not randomly, but like a massive heartbeat. The sorceress glanced at the human and inhuman visages, fully expecting to see the mouths open and the eyes blink. They did nothing of the kind, yet she knew that life did indeed reside within those forms and that it had been stirred to action by someone.

"This will be good enough." Lochivan came to a halt in a region that Sharissa saw was approximately the center of the area surrounded by the effigies. He seemed to be waiting anxiously for something to happen.

Something *was* happening, but not what he wanted. The magics of the two combatants were illuminating the cavern chamber like flashing lights at a festival. Darkhorse and Barakas were still trapped in their stalemate, both powers aglow. Tezerenee surrounded them, all afraid that anything they did might accidentally throw the balance against their lord. Reegan wandered at the outer edge of the circle that had formed out of tense, armored bodies, and Lochivan, standing opposite him, was—

Lochivan?

"It happens! Hold tight!" her companion warned her just as she looked up, realizing now that he was not the son of the patriarch but . . . but *what?*

Her question vanished as instantly as the cavern itself did. One moment they were standing in the center of a growing field of power, the next they were standing in darkness.

Doppleganger or not, she held tight to him. There was a coldness about the dark that she cared little for. It reminded her of a tomb or some other place where death was dominant. Even noting that her ability to utilize her powers had returned did not ease her mind.

Come to me, my children. Enter my court and be safe from those above.

They did, Sharissa almost without choice. Her body moved forward before she had even come to a decision. The false Lochivan was beside her, matching her pace. She could not see him clearly enough, but the sorceress was certain he was almost as confused and frightened as she was, a peculiar thing since it was he who had brought her to this place.

There is no need to fear. I will protect you. I have given my oath on that.

She could, of course, question the fact that she did not know how trustworthy their unseen protector was; if Sharissa was correct in her assumptions, then this *was* the evil that Faunon had spoken about so often in the past.

Evil is . . . evil is sometimes power misunderstood. Yesss, that is the way of it.

It was reading her mind too well. Sharissa strengthened her mental shields.

It chuckled. *Allow me to relieve your fears. Elf, your lady is here.*

"Sharissa?" Faunon's voice cut through the darkness. A dim glow, reddish in color, formed an aura around a figure moving toward her. When it was nearly within arm's reach, she could see that it *was* Faunon. Sharissa almost leaped into his arms when she recalled that the Lochivan beside her was a copy. How did she know that this one was not?

Tell her who you are, elf. Prove to her that she is among friends.

From the expression on Faunon's face—if it *was* Faunon—he did not completely share the unseen speaker's opinion. Nonetheless, he tried to convince her. "Touch my hand, Vraad. Carefully if you like."

Separating from the false Tezerenee, she reached out a tentative hand. Her fingertips grazed the top of his left hand. As she started to pull away, he grabbed hold of her wrist. His grip was gentle but firm. The sorceress felt a tingle run through her.

"Faunon!" She started to reach for him, then recalled her other companion. "But who is this, if not Lochivan? I know you! I could tell that much the way I could tell this was Faunon."

"You do know me, Sharissa." The armored figure also wore a dim, red aura, something she had not noticed before. Sharissa gazed down at her hands and saw no such thing surrounding her, yet it should have been impossible to see her fingers in this darkness.

What magic was afoot in this place . . . wherever it was?

Lochivan's treacherous form faded into a cloaked figure whose face was half-buried in the confines of a deep hood.

"Gerrod?" She was more ready to believe it was just another trick. Gerrod was across the seas to the east.

"It is me, Sharissa. Master Zeree came to me, suspecting that I could follow you where he could not." The warlock spread his hands in a gesture of embarrassment. "I went astray for a time, but I've found you at last."

"Gerrod!" She hugged him tight, so pleased to see *someone* with a link to home. The hooded Tezerenee stood with his arms open, uncertain as to whether to return the hug or not.

All is well now. Friends are together at last, came the voice.

Her initial euphoria died as Sharissa recalled the present. She stepped back and looked up into Gerrod's countenance. "Where are we? What is this place?"

"As near as I can tell, we are deep below the mountain my late and unlamented brother Rendel called Kivan Grath."

"Then the dragonlord and his people are *above* us!" Faunon blurted out.

They will not come here. I have seen to that.

"Who is this, Sharissa?" the warlock asked, indicating the elf. She could sense a growing tension between the two and feared that it was she who was the root of it. Never before had she suspected Gerrod of such jealousy, but it was evident in his words and his stance. How long had he loved her? She cared for him, yes, but . . . did she care for Faunon more?

"This is Faunon. An elf. A prisoner of your father."

"*This* is a Tezerenee?" Faunon searched himself fruitlessly for a weapon. Someone, likely their unseen savior, had released him from his bonds. Seeming to recall this, the elf steadied himself in a manner of someone summoning up the will to cast a major spell.

She quickly intervened, for it appeared Gerrod was about to counter Faunon's attack with one of his own. "No! Stop it, you two! Faunon! Gerrod despises his clan almost as much as you do!"

"Almost?" the warlock snorted.

"How does he come to be here?"

"Simple enough to tell." Only meeting Sharissa's eyes, Gerrod related his experiences, including his confrontation with Darkhorse's counterpart, the Quel city, and the crystal cavern. Faunon took much of it in with skepticism, but the unseen entity, who remained silent during the actual telling, finally acknowledged the truth of it.

Even as I took you and your guards, elf, so too did I bring this one . . . and your lady. There was no mistaking the pride it carried.

"And what *are* you?" the elf demanded, turning to face where he believed the unseen being must be.

The laughter that assailed their minds was a bit too uncontrolled for Sharissa's tastes. Yet, there was something familiar about the creature . . . something . . .

She recalled what it was. "I know you! I know what you are!"

Do you?

"I do!" She looked at Gerrod, who would understand what she was about to say. "He—it—is one of the servants of the founders, one of the *guardians!*"

Gerrod was skeptical. "They abandoned this plane. There was argument over whether they should obey the dictates of the Faceless Ones or even if the founders' experiment should be continued. There was apparently one that—"

"That broke from their ranks!" Sharissa peered into the

darkness, searching for something to focus on. She thought she saw two glittering specks, eyes, perhaps, but could not be certain. "You're the outcast, the renegade!"

Faunon was about to ask what she spoke of, but her last words had struck a nerve—if it had nerves—of the being.

I am outcast and renegade because I see the future as it must be! I will not be servant to dusty memories! I will be the future!

"And lo, a god was born . . ." muttered the elf.

Yesss, I like that! I will be a god as they were!

It was time, Sharissa decided, to turn the conversation to another direction. The guardian was building itself up to a megalomaniacal outburst of truly godlike proportions and had to be brought down. "And what about us? Why are the three of us here? Why bother rescuing us?"

Hesitation. Then, *I remember Dru Zeree. I remember his knowledge. You are his offspring. You possess the same traits. When I sensed you among the Tezerenee, I knew that I must take you. Use you.*

"He told me something of the same sort," whispered Gerrod.

"And me?" asked Faunon, not at all sounding as if he really wanted to know.

You are here because of her, but I'm certain you will make yourself useful.

Sharissa was drawing conclusions from what had been said, but she needed more. The sorceress hoped her thoughts were sufficiently obscured, else she was playing directly into the mad guardian's hands—not that it had any. "What about Darkhorse? Why not bring him here?"

This time she was positive she felt the entity stir in growing anxiety. *He has no place here.*

"But he, like Faunon, is a friend. A *good* friend!"

Twin coals, fully ablaze, burst forth from the darkness. They glared at the trio, the eyes of a would-be god, but Sharissa, at least, felt more like a child was trying to make a scary face at her than that she was being menaced by a fearsome being with the power to do anything it wished. How godlike *was* the guardian? Was it bluffing?

He has no place here. Not in my world.

"What are you going to do with us?" Gerrod wanted to know. He looked weary and disgusted with himself.

Do? Nothing! I am your friend. I am friend to you all. You will witness my experiment and the culmination of my vision. I have succeeded where the founders failed! I will bring to this world the successors they failed to create! There will be so much to do—

"And you want us to *guide* you!" At last Sharissa understood their place in the outcast's vision. It had broken away from the others after countless millennia of absolute loyalty. "The Vraad manipulated their world for generations, but you, for all the time you've existed, have little or no experience at this! All your existence you have served the founders' wishes!"

Faunon found this incredible. "He *wants* us to help him control the lands!"

You will help me . . . or I will let you leave.

The trio stood there for several seconds, waiting for some clarification, but the guardian was silent. Finally, her patience already thin, Sharissa took it upon herself to ask the fatal question. "What sort of threat is that? What waits for us out there?"

The eyes were joined by the vague outline of a tremendous beast—possibly a wolf. From the way it winked in and out of existence, it was obvious that the outcast was testing forms, trying to find one that pleased it. *While we have talked—for longer than you think—the new kings of the land are being born.*

Her eyes widened. She had thought that their conversation had been delaying the work of the guardian.

Your thoughts, Sharissa Zeree, and those of your companions, are mine as well. It chuckled again, taking amusement in their confusion and realization.

"What's happening above?" Gerrod demanded. "What's happening to my people?"

Concern? For them? I am merely bringing out their true nature—both here and in the splendid citadel they have built. They were worthy of rule before, but now their success is guaranteed!

While Gerrod stared without seeing, his mind on his brethren and the fate the renegade had cast for them, Sharissa sought some way to turn back what had been set in motion. "Your own kind will not permit this, guardian! The land itself, the legacy of your masters, will stir at this affront! You've broken the most sacred of laws set down by the founders!"

She had hoped to stir uneasiness, but the entity was *gloating*, not fearful. *The land sleeps for as long as I will it and those others like me have left this plane. They will not know what occurs until after it is done and I have proved myself!*

The warlock, meanwhile, had stirred himself to life once more. He took a step toward the barely seen outline in the dark and shouted, "Damn you! I'm asking again! What have you done to them?"

The laughter again. *We will see how well they truly follow the totem of the drake.*

Gerrod turned around, seeking the entrance to this cavern. "I've got to go to them! Warn them!"

"You hate them!" Faunon quickly reminded him. Nonetheless, the elf, too, looked as if he wanted to find any path leading away.

The hooded Tezerenee did not deign to reply, but Sharissa understood. Gerrod cared for his clan, for individuals within it. His hatred was for those who ruled it—his father, Reegan, Lochivan—and he was not even willing to consign those three to whatever fate the guardian had in mind.

There is no way out of here, came the triumphant voice in their heads. *And you would only suffer the same fate as they.*

"It's *true*," Faunon whispered to Sharissa. "I cannot find a passage anywhere!"

A living fury came among them. Gerrod, looking all too much like the drake that his people looked to as their symbol, confronted the elemental. There was a stirring of power like none that the sorceress had felt in fifteen years. In fact, it reminded her of only one thing, but the intensity of it was beyond what should have been available to the warlock.

Vraad sorcery. *Oh, Gerrod!* She shook her head in disbelief and reached out with her senses to verify the horror before her. *You've broken the barrier between worlds! You've let the foulness that we created seep into our midst!*

She understood some of why he had performed the unthinkable, but that did not forgive him—even if this proved to be enough to aid them in escaping.

A quake rocked the cavern as the warlock unleashed a tangle of glowing, scarlet tendrils at where the guardian supposedly was.

"The curse of the Vraad!" Faunon snarled, emotions in turmoil. He had told her that his legends spoke of the way of the Vraad race, yet she knew that while he loathed what Gerrod represented, he, like her, hoped it would at least do some good.

Gerrod's spell did not stop. He continued to feed the life-force of Nimth into it, twisting that world a little further and doing untold damage to the Dragonrealm at the same time. Even with all of that, there was still no reaction from the target of his wrath save that the dim image had vanished. It was still there, however. All three of them could feel its overwhelming presence.

By now, the tendrils filled the space before the threesome, illuminating the chamber as it had never been illuminated since their arrival. Sharissa silently verified that there was, indeed, no passage out. This cavern was a bubble in the mountain rock.

Gerrod screamed as his body finally gave in to the rigors of his sorcery. He collapsed to the floor.

The tendrils pulsated with such intensity that the sorceress and the elf had to cover their eyes.

Silence lingered for more than a minute, by Sharissa's reckoning.

Slowly and so quietly that they at first thought that they had imagined it, the laughter of the mad guardian rose and reverberated around them.

The tendrils winked out of existence.

Gerrod looked up, his face drawn and far older than his father's. The toll of unleashing so much destructive sorcery had drained more than his strength; it had drained a part of his life from him, too.

A fitting position to be in, it said, and they all knew it referred to Gerrod's sprawled form. He had only risen to his knees by the time it added, *Fitting for one who faces his new deity!*

Faunon was shaking his head in dismay, but Sharissa was not satisfied with the outcome. Was it her imagination, or did the presence of the outcast seem just a little bit less oppressing than it had been before the attack?

It did not reprimand her for the traitorous thought, another interesting note.

Still, the guardian was enjoying its latest victory. The two fiery eyes returned, focusing on the trio as a whole. *I think perhaps I would like you two to join your poor companion!* Sharissa felt an unstoppable urge to kneel. Despite the uselessness of doing so, she fought it all the way to the ground. *I think it is time to give your god the dues deserved!*

Her head was just being forced downward—mortals were not *supposed* to look up in the presence of gods, of course—when another voice entered her head and commented, *Rest assured, outcast, you will receive* all *that is due to you.*

The cavern exploded into turmoil. The two humans and the

elf fell flat in the hopes of avoiding what seemed like the world itself at war. Even the tremors caused by Gerrod's spell had not rocked the cavern like this. Sharissa glanced up and saw that the ceiling was cracking in places. She hoped that none of the pieces that chose to fall would be above them. With no passage out, they were trapped. Trying to teleport out during such madness would have a greater chance of making them part of the mountain than sending them to safety. That their best odds lay in lying still and hoping for the best was not something the younger Zeree cared to contemplate.

A bolt of purple lightning flashed across the cavern. Something roared in the dark. The floor cracked next to Faunon, who quickly rolled over to Sharissa when it became apparent the fault would continue right underneath his original position. Large chunks of rock and earth broke free of the ceiling and plummeted downward, one landing within a few yards of the frozen sorceress. She muttered ancient Serkadion Manee's name and tried not to think about where the next fall would land.

As quickly and violently as it had begun, the tempest died. The three were plunged into darkness, not even their auras remaining to give them some sense of light.

"Sharissa?" Faunon's voice was like a beacon. "Are you hurt?"

She coughed, clearing some of the floating dust from her lungs, and, in the same quiet tones, replied, "I think so. I won't trust that until I can see myself. Gerrod?"

There was no answer. His last image burned into her thoughts, Sharissa stirred herself to movement.

"Where are you going?" the elf asked.

"I need to find out what happened to Gerrod."

Would light aid you in this?

She froze at the return of a voice to her mind. "I don't need your mockery now. If he's dead, it's your doing! What happened?"

The voice was almost indifferent, a great contrast to earlier conversations. *I think you mistake me for the other. Is that so?*

"What do you mean?"

I am not the outcast, the one who would be a god. I have been called such by others of your kind, but I have never yearned for that which was not my calling.

"You're another guardian?" She wished there was light, even though she still would have seen nothing. Unless they willed it, the guardians were always invisible.

The chamber lit up so bright that Sharissa was blinded. An

angry curse from behind her told the Vraad that Faunon, too, had not been prepared.

Gerrod was not affected by the light; he lay on his stomach, his cloak and hood obscuring most of his body. She quickly moved to his side.

I am.

"What?" Her question came back to her. "Oh. I see. Are you . . . you must be . . ." She could not think, being busy in checking the Tezerenee's condition. Sharissa gasped when she pulled back the hood. Gerrod was an old man, wrinkled and dying. "No!"

It is his own doing. He should have never sought what we had barred from this world.

"I don't *care* about that! Can you help him?"

I could. Guardians, it seemed, shared many of the same faults.

She looked up at the ceiling, ignoring the loose rocks as she shouted, "Please!"

For the daughter of Dru Zeree.

Gerrod groaned. His eyes opened. Sharissa, looking down, saw that he was as she had always known him. His strength had been returned to him with as much effort as she would have used in taking a single breath. "Thank you."

"For what?" the warlock asked, thinking she talked to him.

I have spared you where I should have punished your impudence, Gerrod of the Tezerenee.

"You!" The warlock rolled to his feet, ready to take on what he imagined was his opponent of before.

Your link to the dead world is no more. I have reconstructed the barriers, made them far stronger than you could ever be. Also, as I told Sharissa Zeree, I am not the renegade. If you prefer, your own people gave me a name, however irrelevant it is. Let me appear to you as I did to them.

The cavern was tested by yet another tremor, albeit a much more subdued one than those prior. Where the ground had split open, gas drifted skyward. The cavern grew warmer and, to their dismay, molten earth began to spew forth.

Have no fear for your lives.

Rock, loosened by the series of quakes, broke from the ceiling. Sharissa looked up, saw one above Faunon's head slip free, and started to shout a warning. Before she could do so, however, the fragment, as if moving of its own accord, ceased its downward motion and *flew* toward the growing eruption, where it was joined by more of its kind.

More rock and molten earth gathered. A shape formed, only a vague parody at first, but more and more distinct with each passing second. Sharissa was thankful the cavern was so huge; the thing before them nearly touched the ceiling itself. Fragments kept breaking off as it expanded, but nothing came within even a few feet of the trio, much less the ground itself. The fragments would return to the leviathan and merely help strengthen some other portion of its body.

When the great wings stretched, impossible wings of stone and magma that refused to obey gravity's dictates, Sharissa was almost certain that she knew who and what stood before them.

They were all on their feet now, worn but unharmed. The sorceress frowned at the massive unliving creature, trying to keep in mind that this was merely a shell the guardian had made and nothing more. "The Dragon of the Depths?"

That is it.

Faunon was beside her. It felt good to have him near, especially after facing such chaos. He leaned close, as if whispering would not be heard by a thing that could read their minds at will, and asked, "You know *this* one, too?"

"He—it—can be trusted." *I hope so,* she added to herself. To the new guardian, she asked, "How did you come to be here? The other one was certain it had protected itself from the danger of discovery."

The mock dragon dipped its head. The indifference gave way to a touch of embarrassment. Most of the guardians, the great familiars of the ancients, had little in the way of separate personalities. Only a few, such as the two they had met this day, could be called individuals. *It was not the outcast we sought. What drew us here was the warlock here.*

"Me?" Gerrod withdrew to the confines of his cloak, giving him the appearance of a living shroud.

Somehow, the guardian made the eyes narrow, though they were only bits of stone surrounding glowing balls of fiery earth. *We did not sense the renegade, for it had shielded itself well, but, with so much of its power already in demand, it could not sufficiently shield the presence of so much Nimthian sorcery.*

"Then Gerrod actually did you a service," Sharissa interjected, fearing that the warlock might still face some punishment.

The dragon head withdrew. *Not by choice . . . but because of the magnitude of the outcast's crime, the warlock is forgiven . . . for now.*

Glancing at Gerrod, the sorceress's relief gave way to renewed worry. From what she could read in his stance and his shadowed features, the patriarch's son was not defeated. He would attempt, someday, to reestablish his link.

My time grows short, and there is much to do. I will take you from here and place you where you must be.

She was not certain she understood what the guardian meant, but decided to trust its judgment. It had befriended her father, after all. Instead, she asked, "What became of the outcast?"

That one has evaded us for the moment . . . but it will eventually be taught the folly of its ways.

Knowing how time meant little to these virtually immortal creatures, Sharissa wondered what damage the renegade would cause before that. She decided not to ask.

"And my clan? What about them?" The warlock walked closer, defying the entity who had stripped him of so much power. "What about the insanity your counterpart plotted for them?"

The long hesitation stirred the curiosity of all three. The Dragon of the Depths seemed to be considering its response carefully, as if even it was uncertain it cared for the answer. Sharissa walked over to where Gerrod stood and put a comforting hand on his shoulder. He shrugged it off, not even looking her way. More hurt than she cared to consider, the young woman returned to Faunon, who tried to smile in sympathy but failed.

The land will do what it chooses to do, and I will abide by that decision.

"That is no answer!" the angry Tezerenee shouted.

It is the only answer. It is the sum of my existence. If the land finds some use in the renegade's actions, which will still not excuse that one, then the experiment will follow that new path. If not, the land, not I, will choose to reverse what was done.

"But the renegade interfered with the experiment! If what it said was true, it even dared to subdue the mind of the land!"

All true and all irrelevant now. Before their eyes, the mock dragon began to crumble. A wing collapsed and the lower jaw dropped to the cavern floor and shattered. Despite the din, the voice was still very clear in their minds. *The land will decide . . . but you have a choice in the matter. I tell this to you, Sharissa Zeree, because of the respect with which I hold your progenitor. Whatever changes are wrought upon your kind, those who fight them will only succumb that much more harshly. You have a choice in how you are adapted to this world. The elf is proof of that. His kind have remained more or less untouched.*

The three stumbled back as the body collapsed and the magma receded down the hole it had spewed forth from.

And now, I will take you to where you must be.

"What do you mean 'must be'?" Faunon, who had stayed silent most of the time, shouted at the last moment. Understanding his sudden worry, Sharissa would have lent her voice to his—but the cavern and the guardian had vanished and they were now *elsewhere*.

"Well," came a familiar voice, one that hinted at no sleep for days and terrible stress suffered during those waking hours. Any arrogance was little more than mockery now. "Welcome back . . . and you, too, my son."

Elsewhere was the main cavern that Sharissa and Faunon had been plucked away from by the mad guardian. The voice belonged to the patriarch, who sat upon a high-backed throne now standing atop the dais and looked down at the three stunned gifts that had been placed before him.

——— XVIII ———

"I must admit that I had not thought to see you—any of you—again since your escape, what is it, five days ago?"

"Five days?" Faunon leaned his head toward Sharissa's. "We were not down there more than an hour!"

"So we thought, but the first guardian hinted that we might have been talking longer than it appeared. Who can say what they're capable of? That means the damage could only be worse if—"

"I would *appreciate* it," the patriarch interrupted. He straightened. His armor was covered in dust and—she squinted—

blood? "Yes, I would appreciate it if you would recall who it is you face. I am, after all, lord of this domain."

"This sounds very familiar," Gerrod muttered. His father, possibly understanding what he said, focused on him. The warlock retreated into his cloak.

"You. For all that you have disappointed me, I am pleased to see you. I suspect, however, that you have not come here because you seek admittance into the clan again."

Gerrod shook his head. Some of the Tezerenee present stirred at that. Sharissa, scanning the cavern, thought that there were less of them than she recalled from last time. Many of them were wounded, too. *What had happened since her untimely departure?*

"Reegan." At Lord Barakas's summons, the heir separated from the others and hurried up the steps. The patriarch gave him a hand. Reegan took hold and aided his father in rising. "Nonetheless, I am still pleased to see you, if only because I might require your intuitive skills."

"What happened here, Father? Is everyone... is everyone the same?"

"An interesting way to put it. I might find it even more interesting to find out where you have been that you would ask such a thing." With Reegan's aid, he traversed the steps, stopping when he was at the bottom. "For now, however, I think it would be best if I told you what has happened. We've been busy of late."

As the patriarch began, Sharissa looked around for Lochivan. There was no sign of him, and she wondered whether it was his blood that stained the Lord Tezerenee. Also missing was the infernal box prison. "Where's—"

Barakas snapped his fingers. Guards belatedly surrounded the trio. Gauntleted hands stumbled to attach small collars to the necks of each. There was a bit of a struggle as Gerrod fought to keep his hood on. When it was at last down, he looked at the others as if expecting horror. Sharissa realized he did not know what the Dragon of the Depths had done for him. Knowing that despite his status he was still one of their lord's offspring, the guards replaced the hood when they were finished.

The patriarch shook his head at the warrior's obvious inefficiency. "Things are falling apart... and if you speak before I allow it, I will have them silence you. You don't want that, Lady Sharissa. None of us is in a very pleasant mood." To his clan in general, he commanded, "Bring forth one of the changelings!"

There was some scurrying, and a pause in which Barakas took time to steady himself. He became aware of Sharissa's questing eyes and quietly said, "All in good time, my lady. All in good time."

At that moment, the ranks of disheveled warriors gave way to four others carrying a bundle the size of a body. Gerrod took a step forward, but the patriarch shook his head. The newcomers waited, fascinated to be sure, but also prepared for the worst.

They were not disappointed. Sharissa had been waiting for this and was not surprised at what rolled out of the blanket that the Tezerenee lowered to the floor before them. Faunon nodded his head; he had also expected this. Only Gerrod was truly taken aback.

"What sort of abomination is that?"

"It was a cousin of yours once," the clan master informed him. "There were seven others besides this one. It took us all this time to hunt them down, and more than twice as many warriors to kill them."

The corpse was of a creature resembling the unfortunate Ivor as he had been those few moments Sharissa had confronted him, only this one was even more reptilian than that hapless soul. The shape was not even quite humanoid anymore, but almost truly like that of a drake.

"It looks like a Draka," Faunon commented.

"Draka?" Reegan asked.

"They have many names, many of which sound similar. Some think they ruled here long before the avians and the Quel. They serve—*served*—the bird folk. Of late, they've grown far more savage than they should be."

"I've seen them. Unimportant." Pulling himself free, the patriarch limped over to the disconcerting body. "*This* was one of my people, not some monster! I want to know what happened and who was responsible!" He gave the elf a long, appraising look. "Perhaps I should have had Lochivan question you more thoroughly."

Sharissa could not hold back. "Where is Lochivan now?"

"He is ill . . . and it is he who watches the demon's prison." That was all he would say on the subject, although she was certain there was more he was not telling.

Gerrod pulled free of his guards and, despite his father's

warning, moved closer to examine his former cousin. He touched the leathery skin and removed some of the tattered bits of armor that still hung to the corpse. From what Sharissa could see from her vantage point, the shapeshifting Tezerenee had torn part of his armor off and literally burst through the rest. How much pain had that entailed? How much pain did the transformation itself entail?

The guards moved to bring the warlock under control, but Lord Barakas suddenly waved them back. To his estranged son, he said, "I will want to know how you come to be on this continent later, but for now I would appreciate whatever you can read from this . . . this horror."

He received no response, but that was Gerrod's way. The hooded Tezerenee probed for a moment or two longer and then looked up in the direction of, but not exactly at, his progenitor. "I'd like Sharissa to see this."

Reegan whispered something to his father, but Barakas shook his head. He looked at the waiting Zeree. "Go to him, but be careful about what you say or do. There will be no second escape. Especially for your elf."

In response to an unspoken command, one of Faunon's guards put a knife to the elf's throat. Sharissa gritted her teeth in order to keep from saying something that her captor would hardly appreciate. Escape was hardly one of her concerns at this time; she lacked the strength for anything so strenuous as that.

Joining Gerrod, she inspected the corpse. As she expected, he wanted to do the talking.

"This is what I've feared all these years—this and the fact that we are aging far more quickly than we were prone to back in Nimth."

"What are you mumbling?" Reegan asked, suspicious of anyone, it seemed, who was on better terms with Sharissa than he was. That included a vast number of people, as far as she was concerned.

Gerrod stared at his elder sibling with disdain. "I was wondering when the first of these appeared."

"There was one during the journey here," Sharissa offered. That first one had likely been one of the more magically sensitive Tezerenee. Or perhaps he had been a test for the outcast guardian, a way of assuring that what it sought to do was possible without killing the victim.

"There wasss another," announced a hissing voice. From

one of the passages, an armored figure that could only be Lochivan stumbled forward. Despite the patriarch's claim that his son was ill, Lochivan wore full armor, even a full helm. He also carried the box, which was evidently making it difficult for him to maintain his balance, but he refused the aid of two warriors who came to his side.

"You are not supposed to be here," Barakas told him. Nonetheless, he was visibly proud of the fact that Lochivan would not give in to whatever was affecting him. "You should be resting."

"In thissss place? I heard the voicessss and came to sssee. Gerrod's question, however, desservess asss complete an answer as possible if we are to deal with thisss matter."

"When was the first one?" Gerrod acted as if he had never left the clan.

"During the first expedition. He killed another man before we could ssstop him. That wasss why I wasss ready for Ivor. I recognized the sssigns."

Barakas looked a bit troubled. "You told me they died when one of the drakes went wild."

Lochivan laughed, harsh and almost inhuman in his manner. He was now at the edge of the circle of nervous bodies surrounding the prisoners, the patriarch, and the poor, twisted form on the floor. "I thought the sssituation under control, even with Ivor'sss appearance. I thought I had made a pact that would sssave usss!"

"What are you talking about? You must be feverish!"

"He's not." Sharissa understood. Lochivan had known what was going to happen to her. That was what he had meant that one evening. He had made a pact that included her safety . . . so he supposed. In a sense he had been correct. Unfortunately, Lochivan had also been dealing with a being that chose to interpret the pact in whatever way suited it.

The patriarch turned on her. "What's that you say?"

"Tell him, Sharissa!" Gerrod urged. "Tell him, or by the claws of the drake I'll do so!"

She nodded. It would be best for them if the Tezerenee knew. It might even make them abandon this place as the Seekers had chosen to do. "We've met the one you made the pact with, Lochivan." She paused to let that sink in. "I think what you've seen is its way of fulfilling that pact."

"Impossible! I worked for the ssssurvival of the clan! These horrorsss are not what I desssired!"

"Ivor and the others were how the guardian thought your clan would best survive this land."

"Stop right there!" Barakas roared. He pointed an accusing finger at the unsteady figure. "You will tell your tale later, and the truth had best be spoken!" The patriarch kicked at the rubble as he strode toward Sharissa and Gerrod, both of whom rose at his coming. "First, we will hear *your* story!"

Sharissa willingly related it. Gerrod and even Faunon also contributed, recalling as much as they could. All three were in unspoken agreement that if the Dragon of the Depths had dropped them here, it was to their interest to convince their captors of the urgency of their plight.

The Lord Tezerenee listened in silence, his only reaction to glance on occasion from one of his prisoners to another. The time difference interested him enough to provoke a question or two, but the rest was heard unhindered.

When Sharissa concluded with the second guardian's decision to send the three here, Lochivan spoke up despite the threat of punishment from his father. "Their tale tells most of it . . . but I thought the scourge was the land's doing, not this outcast abomination."

"I am still not certain on that," the patriarch said. "But that is neither here nor there."

"We've told you the truth about everything, Father!" Gerrod insisted.

To the surprise of all, Lord Barakas smiled. "And I am certain that you have! If so, then the danger is past! You said yourself that the renegade fled from the Dragon of the Depths! He has saved us again!"

Sharissa grimaced. This was not going the way it should. "Have you forgotten what the Dragon of the Depths said? There is no guarantee that this is over or that something worse is not yet to come!"

He indicated the corpse. "The first of those appeared the day you vanished; the last, three days later. There have been none since, and I would say there will *be* none again!" Looking down at the remains of what had once been one of his subjects, the patriarch added, "Someone drag that away and bury it. Let him and the others be remembered with honor, victims of a foe now fled!"

"Typical!"

"What was that, Gerrod?"

"Nothing, Father! Only that you've not changed! I prayed that, at least for mother's sake, you might have!"

"Alcia!" All triumph faded from the clan master's rough-hewn visage. "The citadel!"

"Citadel?" Gerrod looked at Sharissa for clarification.

"Your father forced Darkhorse to help him build a glorious citadel to the south of here." She pointed at the box that Lochivan carried. The bitterness could not be held back. "That is Darkhorse's reward for his efforts, his prison!"

"My mother and the others are not here?"

"Alcia." Barakas raised his hands above his head. "I sent a message announcing our imminent entrance into the caverns, but . . . nothing since then! They won't have known! I must go to her and see!"

He stood there for several seconds, his eyes closed. The room was filled with a sense of expectation. Sharissa was the first to wonder why the patriarch still stood where he was when it was obvious he had intended to teleport to his lady.

That thought had also occurred to Barakas, for he lowered his hands and stared at her in wonder. "The power! I had it! Now . . . there is still some, but I cannot summon sufficient for the task!"

"You won't find that power at your beck and call anymore!" It was Faunon who spoke, to the surprise of Sharissa. At a nod from Barakas, the guards released their hold. He purposely joined Sharissa and put an arm around her waist. She was a bit shocked at first, but found almost immediately afterward that she wanted him there.

"We are the only spellcasters here now, and our strength is not sufficient at this time to be of any aid."

"Step away from her!" Reegan bellowed. He drew his sword and started toward the couple.

"Reegan!" The voice born to command froze the heir in place. Barakas then added, "Continue, elf! What great revelation have you to make?"

"Sharissa probably knows," Faunon said, "but I spoke up without thinking, so it's my duty to tell you."

"Then be on with it, before I decide to let my eldest further denigrate himself!"

"Father—"

"Silence!"

Sharissa caught the barest hint of a smile on the elf's lips before he spoke. "The tales of our ancestors speak enough about the way of Vraad sorcery for me to recognize it. The sorcerous stench is enough to make me wish I had no ability to sense its presence. She also spoke of it during our time together—how it had suddenly returned to you."

"My link!" Gerrod looked at Faunon with a mixture of surprise and respect.

"When one makes a hole, things tend to leak out."

"The Dragon of the Depths resealed the barrier, made it stronger," Sharissa finished. "You're back to the way it was before."

Crystalline eyes narrowed. "You will take me there! One or both of you!"

Faunon snorted. "Even if I desired to, Vraad, neither of us has the strength, not after what we've been through. I am not even certain if it is safe to do so. My folk have lived here for far longer than you, and we have stories—"

"More blasted tales!"

"We have *stories*," he continued, relishing his role even though Sharissa could see that he understood the risks of pushing the patriarch too far, "about the times when the land is woken . . . as it has been by the renegade guardian."

"And what do thossse ssstoriesss sssay?" Lochivan asked. He had the box in both hands now, as if he intended to present it to Sharissa. Had Darkhorse known the Tezerenee was manipulating him? Had the eternal nearly sacrificed himself in order that Sharissa might be free? She hoped there would come time for the answers. She hoped there would come time for Darkhorse.

"That those who bring notice to themselves in such turbulent times may find they will soon not know themselves. That is what they say."

"Reegan," Barakas began, a fierce anger spreading across his features. "If the elf will not speak plainly on his next attempt, you have my permission to put him to the sword."

"Faunon," Sharissa warned.

He took her hand with his free one. "You remember what the second guardian said, that we could control the change. It's been so in the past. When the land is awake, there is wild sorcery. Those who make too much use of their power become more malleable, more sensitive to . . . change."

Barakas studied the ancient cavern. In a quieter voice he said, "I had decided to make this the citadel from where I would coordinate the rule of this land, a fitting choice since it would have been within the domain of my heir." Sharissa was interested to see that Reegan did not seem too pleased with that decision. He had hoped for a kingdom of his own, not one in which he would have little more status than before. The patriarch did not seem to care. "It seems it will have to wait a while, but it *will* be mine! Reegan! Attend me!"

Erasing the bitter cast, the heir apparent came to his father's side. "Sire?"

"You will remain here and continue efforts to ready this place. Be alert."

"Yes, Father."

"I also want the swiftest drakes readied for travel. Two dozen—no, one dozen! No more than necessary!" The patriarch turned to the trio. "*You* three will accompany me!" He waved off all protests, including one from Reegan, who hardly cared for the thought of Sharissa being taken away from him. Focusing on the sorceress, Barakas continued, "If I thought I could trust you, I would have those bands removed. As it is, they will remain around your throats. Do not think to remove them without my permission; you will find that they can bite!"

Sharissa started to speak, to say that this was something they all had to be concerned about, but she knew that the clan master would never believe she would ride willingly with him.

Lord Barakas Tezerenee looked around at his people. "Well? What are you standing around here for? There is much to do!"

The dragon warriors scattered, save for those few whose task it was to either protect their master or await further commands that might arise. Reegan remained, although Lochivan and the box, much to Sharissa's distress, had vanished. The hurried expedition to the Tezerenee citadel would only take her farther from the eternal.

"We will leave within the hour," the lord of the Tezerenee announced to his prisoners, "and ride until the drakes can run no more. We will sleep until they are sufficiently rested and then ride until exhaustion takes them again."

"And what of us?" Gerrod asked. "We are already worn out . . . as you must be."

"We are Tezerenee, Gerrod. The name Tezerenee *is* power, in case you have forgotten. We will endure what we must for the sake of the others! These two"—he indicated Sharissa and Faunon—"will just have to struggle along."

The warlock snorted, muttering something about speeches and beliefs, but his father had already turned away.

Although they were not given much opportunity for rest, the patriarch true to his word when he had said that they would be leaving within the hour, the three did receive some food. Their lost days had wreaked havoc with their inner clocks, though, so the meal was first eaten in hesitation. Only when food began to warm her did Sharissa feel the pangs of hunger. From then on, she ate in eagerness, noting that her companions did the same.

Sentries watched them to make certain no one fiddled with the collars. Barakas had warned them of the danger of doing so, but evidently knew that here were three who could most definitely be trusted to try escape at some point. They would need their full abilities to do so.

They sat where they had been standing earlier, no one apparently having thought seats a necessity in this place. Only the patriarch's throne—where they had gotten that monstrosity, she could not guess—resembled anything designed for sitting, and that looked much too uncomfortable for most people. It was the type of throne she would expect from Barakas, a thing that required patience and stubbornness to endure.

For the brief time remaining, the sorceress concentrated on the stone leviathans mere yards away. Even with her powers muted again, something that seemed to be a habit of late, she could sense the life stirring within them. Why no one else did was beyond her. Faunon did look up now and then as he ate, almost as if he noticed something from time to time but could not place it. Was she that much more in tune with this world than they were? Sharissa had accepted her new home without question, marveling in the natural beauty that she, too young, had never known in Nimth. Perhaps that was one reason that she had learned to manipulate the binding forces of the world as none of the others had yet.

That did not explain why the powers within the effigies were growing greater in intensity with each passing minute.

What would happen when the land truly awoke? Was this the first sign?

Her thoughts died as Barakas returned to the central chamber. He still limped, but concern for his bride and his fledgling empire was making him ignore all but the worst pain. Reegan trailed behind him, looking like a hatchling drake that had been reprimanded by its mother. No doubt he had been trying, without success, to convince his father to either leave her here or let *him* journey with them.

The patriarch nodded to her. "You have been properly fed, Lady Sharissa?"

He seemed to use a title only when he wanted something, she realized. Steadying herself, she replied, "Fair enough for now. We could still use some rest."

"When you are with us long enough you will learn to sleep while your steed keeps going."

"I hope not to be with you long enough for that."

Barakas gave her a thin-lipped smile. "Honesty. It is a commendable trait, albeit a useless one right now."

"Father—"

"Silence, Reegan. You have duties, if I recall. Perform them as is fit for the future clan master . . . the future emperor."

The hulking Tezerenee glanced longingly at Sharissa, who made a point of *not* looking his way. Dejected, Reegan saluted his father and departed.

For one of the few times in her recent memory, the patriarch removed his helm. Sharissa was shocked to see that the gray in his hair was spreading. There were grooves in his face that only time and weariness could have carved. It reminded her somewhat of Gerrod's visage after his near catastrophe with Vraad sorcery down in the mad guardian's cavern.

Lord Barakas Tezerenee was not getting old; he *was* old.

"He *will* be emperor before long," the patriarch assured them. He met his estranged son's gaze and saw the emotion in there. "Yes, I am growing old at last. The dragonlord is nearing his end. Probably a few more decades and nothing else."

"At least you have lived all those millennia," the warlock returned. He indicated his own face. "There will be lines on this face soon enough. This world likes to kill those who will not bow to it."

The armored monarch cocked his head to one side as he studied Gerrod. Then, smiling a mocking smile, he shook his head and turned his attention back to Sharissa. "I have something I want of you."

"I'm hardly surprised."

"Hear me out. If you aid me, I will no longer pressure for a marriage between you and my eldest. You and the elf can go off wherever you please.''

''Everyone always wants to throw us together,'' Faunon commented. Food, even this food, had done much to restore his humor, even if he and the others were still prisoners.

He was ignored by the clan elder. ''Well?''

''You haven't told me what you want of me.''

Gerrod leaned forward before his father could speak and warned, ''Be careful of any promise made! Even oaths can be broken!''

''There will be no breaking of oaths!'' Barakas seemed ready to kick his son back in place, but possibly knew how it would make him look to the sorceress. ''This concerns your family, especially your mother and siblings!''

The warlock tried to pretend he did not care, but Sharissa already knew that, despite his abandoning the ways of his father, Gerrod had no desire to see his former folk come to harm.

''What is it you want?'' she asked, in part trying to turn the patriarch's focus away from his son. Each time it turned there, the chamber grew noticeably colder.

He scratched his throat, but, unlike so many of the other Tezerenee, Barakas no longer suffered from the rash. ''I want your cooperation—and theirs—for the time needed to ascertain what may or may not have befallen those at the citadel—and especially the Lady Alcia.''

It was a bit of a rambling answer, but the thrust of it moved her as she thought not possible. Barakas might be her adversary, but his concern for his bride outweighed even his drive for power.

''I will swear by the spirit of the drake that you will gain your releases when I am satisfied that we face no threat. Well?''

''All of us?''

''All of you.''

She studied him for several seconds, organizing her thoughts. There was one more thing Sharissa wanted of him, and now was the only moment she had a chance of getting it. If she let this pass . . . ''Darkhorse must be included.''

His altering expression almost made her regret her demand, but she could not leave the shadow steed under his control.

''You want the demon?'' He struggled to regain composure and succeeded—in part. ''Take him! Even with our sorcery reduced, we will prevail!''

"Then you have my cooperation." Her words were said in a simple and straightforward fashion.

Her quiet response made him halt his tirade. Barakas took a deep breath before saying, "My gratitude, Lady Sharissa. You will find I will keep my word in this, despite my sons and their opinions otherwise."

Meaning Gerrod and Reegan, she thought.

"Now that it is settled," the patriarch continued, "I may tell you that the drakes are ready for us. Guards!"

In quick order, they were brought to their feet and marched through the cavern until they came to the entrance that Sharissa and the Tezerenee had entered by almost a week ago. To her surprise, the patriarch bypassed several powerful flying drakes and started down the side of the mountain to where the wingless riding drakes awaited.

"We're not going by air?"

Gerrod, who understood the workings of his clan better than did his companions, explained. "It is Father's evident opinion that we would be too conspicuous from the sky. Besides, for the speed of this journey, travel by land will be swifter. An airdrake must rest more often, especially if it is carrying someone."

"That explains our relatively slow pace coming here," Faunon suggested. "He wanted time for his second force to reach here and be rested."

Aside from their guards, a handful of other Tezerenee were supposed to accompany them. Sharissa was surprised but relieved to see that Lochivan was one of them and that he still carried the box with him.

Barakas noticed his ill offspring. "Who told you to be here?"

"I mussst redeem myssself."

The patriarch looked uncomfortable, as if he wanted all the eyes around him to be looking anywhere else but at him and Lochivan. "Your *illness . . .*"

"I will keep it under control," the tall figure said in his strange voice. He did his best to allow no one else to see his face, possibly because he was so ravaged it would have disgusted some of his folk.

"I wonder . . ." Gerrod muttered.

"You wonder what?" she asked.

He turned, not having realized that he had spoken out loud. "Nothing. Just a thought."

The conversation between the patriarch and Lochivan grew

muted. After a short exchange, Barakas finally nodded. It was difficult to read Lochivan by his movements, but he seemed very relieved.

"We've lost much of the day already," Barakas said to the others. "Please mount up."

They obeyed. When everyone was ready, the patriarch turned in his saddle and faced those of his people who would remain here. One of the Tezerenee held high a staff upon which the banner of the clan waved in the wind. Under the fluttering flag, the rest of the warriors, Reegan included, knelt.

"I shall return shortly. We have defeated threats both physical and magical, and this cavern, this natural citadel, will be the base from which an empire spanning this entire continent will be ruled. I have designated kingdoms for each of my most loyal sons,"—Barakas did not even glance in Lochivan's direction—"and my eldest, Reegan, will co-rule here until my death, when he becomes emperor. Thirteen kingdoms and, within those, twenty-five dukedoms for those deserving!"

"Another grand and glorious speech," Gerrod whispered in sour humor to Sharissa.

The patriarch did not hear him—or chose not to. "We have been separated from our people, and there is concern for their safety! In my mind, there is little to fear, but it behooves me to ride there in person! Once I have satisfied myself that things are in order, I shall return with more of our brethren and we shall began the *true* process of making this land ours!" He stared at Kivan Grath, as if it represented the entire continent. "We *will* shape this domain to *our* will!"

Barakas folded his arms, the signal that his speech was at an end. The Tezerenee rose and cheered as they were supposed to. Reegan unsheathed his sword and raised it in salute.

"Pomp and circumstance," Gerrod muttered.

"We *ride* now," the patriarch informed them, glaring at his unrepentant son.

Not completely willing to trust the outsiders, the patriarch left the managing of their drakes to the guards who rode beside them. One of those sentries took the guiding rope of Sharissa's mount and began to lead it, but slowly so as to allow the clan master's animal to move ahead. It was mandatory that the Lord Tezerenee lead, if only as a symbolic gesture.

The remnants of the expeditionary force continued to sound their approval and allegiance as the party moved out. Had she not been so exhausted already—and thinking about how tired she would be when they finally *stopped*—the sorceress would have admired their enthusiasm much more. As it was, she only hoped that they would still have such enthusiasm a month from now.

One of the Tezerenee standing nearest to where she was removed her helmet and began to scratch at an ugly patch of dry, red skin covering most of her throat and part of her chin. Sharissa stared at it briefly, but then the warrior guiding her drake pulled on the rope and the animal turned, putting the warrior woman and the others behind the young Zeree. Exhausted as she was, she did not bother turning around to get a second glance.

Besides, there were too many more important matters to consider. Far too many to worry about an annoying but evidently insignificant rash.

XIX

It was well after the midnight hour when the patriarch gave in to the urgings of his people to rest the drakes before they collapsed in midrun. By that time, Sharissa was nearly asleep in the saddle. Despite the clan master's assurance that she would come to learn how to truly rest while riding, the sorceress was more than happy to crawl off the unruly beast and drag herself to a safe and secure spot where she could try to regain at least a tiny portion of her strength. Gerrod and Faunon were not much better, nor were the Tezerenee themselves, even though they had actually had some rest at one point or another.

Only the patriarch seemed energetic, but it was the energy of the anxious, the worried. If he kept it up too long, it would drain him.

Sharissa's sleep proved little more relaxing. She dreamed as she never had before, but there was little in those dreams to give her comfort. In one, a hand rose from the earth and seized her, twisting her like clay and reshaping her in a hundred myriad forms, all horrific. In another, Faunon and she were embracing. It was a pleasant scene, and she knew that she was about to be kissed. Then his face had become some reptilian parody, but he had still tried to kiss her. That one had woken her up and kept her awake for more than half an hour, so real had that close visage been.

There were others, but they by and by were only shadowy memories, too vague to bother her much. Only one thing about them remained with her, and that one thing was enough to make her shiver.

Throughout several of the nightmares, she could hear the sound of the insane guardian's mocking laughter. It seemed to cross from one dream to the next. It was still ringing in her ears when a tap on her shoulder woke her again.

Sunlight burned her eyes. Faunon smiled down at her. He seemed fresher, but there were still marks of exhaustion on him. Sharissa did not care to think what she must look like. It amazed her that anyone could still find her attractive. At present, it would not have surprised her to look into a mirror and see a visage that would make a drake beautiful in comparison.

The elf extended a hand, which she took. As he pulled her to her feet, Faunon said, "It was a choice of one of them waking you or me taking on that task. I knew you were still exhausted, but I thought you might like to see my pale face a bit more than you would their metal masks."

"Very much so." She enjoyed the contact between them and let it linger a bit before releasing his hand. "Is there food?"

"I would not have disturbed you if there had not been." He waved a hand at two bowls by their feet. A stew, much like the one that the Lady Alcia had once fed to her so long ago and smelling almost as good. She recalled that incident because it had seemed so out of place when dealing with one of the Tezerenee. Sometimes it was troublesome to remember that the clan's mistress had been born an outsider, that there had been no clan until Barakas had pulled together his disjointed group of relations and welded them into the only true family among the Vraad. Not known for being familial, the concept of a clan was something known only from the early days of the race. Barakas, however, had assured that it would never be dismissed lightly—and his bride had been his other half in the struggle. She, almost as much as the patriarch, had helped to make the Tezerenee the force they were.

Sharissa found herself hoping that nothing had happened to her.

"Where's Gerrod?" she asked, trying to put the Lady Alcia from her thoughts.

Faunon handed her one of the bowls. He hesitated, then answered, "I saw him last with his brother. They journeyed away from the camp."

Trying to do something for Lochivan's illness? It was the only reason she could think of. Not all of their past differences had been ironed out, but a common concern for their own people had, at least, brought them temporarily together. Had it been any other family, the young woman would have been happy for Gerrod. As it was, she hoped he was not becoming one of them again.

A shadow fell upon them. The two looked up into the dragonhelm of a Tezerenee. "My lord bids tell you that we leave shortly. Prepare yourselves."

Her companion groaned as the warrior marched off. "I have seldom ridden so much. To think I once thought a horse a terrible animal to cope with. Merely sitting astride one of these monstrosities is worse."

"What are you expecting to find?" she asked abruptly. Sharissa felt a need to know as much as she could, and Faunon was her only source of information. Of all of them, only he had been born to this land.

The humor of a moment before slipped away, revealing the serious soul beneath. "I do not know, my beauteous Vraad. The only thing predictable about the land's ways is its unpredictability. I regret to say that the two of us have just as likely a chance of being correct." He took her hand. "I am sorry I cannot help you."

She squeezed the hand and, on impulse, leaned forward and kissed him. While he was still staring at her in open shock, the sorceress smiled and said, "But you do."

For the second time, they rode as if the renegade guardian itself was snapping at the tails of their mounts. Gerrod and Lochivan, who had come back just before preparations for the day's mad journey were complete, separated as if things had not changed between them. Sharissa had looked at the warlock for some sort of explanation, but Gerrod had merely pulled his hood over his head and buried himself in the all-encompassing cloak. The only thing she could tell was that he was even more worried than yesterday.

The sun was high in the sky when they departed. Again it was a mad race, everyone seeking to maintain the pace that the patriarch had set. This day's was worse than the first, and Sharissa had a suspicion why. She was certain he had tried again to teleport to the citadel and, of course, failed. That only made it more essential that they cover as much ground as possible each day.

It was impossible to speak, but she did glance at Faunon whenever possible. He returned her looks with a tight-lipped smile. Until the coming of the Tezerenee, he would have never thought riding a drake possible. He probably still did not.

On her other side, beyond the Tezerenee guard who paced her, Gerrod stared straight ahead. Only once did he turn his eyes to Sharissa, but the hood shadowed them so well that it was as if she stared into the sightless face of a dead man. She turned away and regretted it a moment later, but, when she sought to apologize, his attention had already returned to the path ahead.

To find Lochivan, she had to crane her neck and look back, a dangerous trick to attempt for very long, which meant that she was forced to do it more than once just to get a good glimpse of him. He was riding at the back end of the column, his head down so that even if he had not been wearing a helm, she would have been unable to see his face. At the side of his saddle bounced Darkhorse's insidious prison, apparently in Lochivan's permanent keeping despite his betrayal. Angry at herself for not demanding the eternal's release from the box, Sharissa swore she would bring that up with Barakas the moment they stopped. If she could convince him that Darkhorse would listen to her and not seek vengeance, then he might prove willing to allow the ebony stallion freedom. Perhaps if she mentioned the aid that Darkhorse could give them . . . though that depended on how strong the eternal was. He had, she recalled with bitterness, been punished hard for his attack upon the lord of the Tezerenee.

It was night again when they finally halted. Drakes were good for long bursts of speed, but then they had to rest much longer than horses. They also had to be fed, and that meant meat. For this journey, the Tezerenee had packed as much as they could carry of the special feed that they added to the beasts' meals. Mixed in with the meat, it would greatly supplement their needs and prevent any chance, however slim, that the drakes might snap at their masters in their search for fresh food.

As she had sworn, Sharissa sought out the patriarch as soon as she had dismounted. Behind her trailed her latest silent shadow. Barakas she found speaking to one of the other guards, evidently setting the watch for the night. Barakas could delegate everything if he chose, but that was not his way. A leader, she had heard him say long ago, did not sit back and grow fat and lazy. He worked with his subjects, reminding them of *why* he was their lord.

Barakas dismissed the warrior just as she walked up to him. In the background, she caught the vague image of Lochivan spending an overlong period of time busying himself with his steed. He seemed to be watching his father closely, as if wanting something.

"What is it you wish, Lady Sharissa?" the patriarch asked. He sounded as worn out as she felt.

"I have a request of you, my Lord Barakas."

"Formal, is it? Tell me something first, my lady. Are you rested enough to make good use of your abilities?"

Somehow this encounter had been turned around and he was now asking a favor of her. She kept her peace, thinking it would be best to hear him out. It might help her own cause. "I'm hardly rested, if that is what you mean. If you want to know if I can teleport to the citadel, I doubt it. All I remember with any confidence is the interior; you wouldn't let me journey outside the walls very much, if you recall."

"Something I think I am about to regret, yes?"

"I'm sorry." The sorceress was. It seemed there was never anything she could do, but, in this case, it was the patriarch's fault. "And if it is all the same to you, I would prefer not to materialize inside . . . just in case."

"I understand. I was attempting to appear outside the gates myself." Barakas tugged at his graying beard. "And sorcery might not be safe yet. When I tried just before the day's ride, I sensed something—immense, is the only way I can describe it—spreading throughout the region of the citadel."

She thought of the land awakening and the outcast laughing, all still fresh in her mind from the dreams. "Do you think that—"

"I do not know what to think." He dismissed the subject. "You had a request you wished to make of me."

"It concerns Darkhorse."

"Does it now?" In the deepening dark, she could not see his eyes now, but she knew they were narrowed, suspicious. "And *how* does it concern him?"

She took a deep breath. "I've given you my word that I will help you, and you've given your word that you will release all of us. Until the latter happens, however, I was hoping that you would let Darkhorse out—"

"He is my assurance that you will abide by your side, Lady Sharissa."

The young Zeree nodded. "I understand how you feel after the attack, but he will listen to me. If I ask him to abide by my decision, he will do so, I'm certain. If not . . ." She hesitated, wondering what the eternal would think of this offer. "If not, you can trap him inside once more and I won't make a protest."

There was silence for a time, then; "I will consider it over my meal."

"You've bound him to the box again. He can't do you any harm now!"

"Never underestimate an opponent, especially a wounded one. They are often the deadliest." The patriarch nodded to her. "You will hear from me. I promise."

He walked off without another word. Sharissa frowned and looked for Lochivan again, but the patriarch's son had vanished.

She wondered why the lord of the Tezerenee had left his other children behind. Even Lochivan would have remained at the caverns had he not defied his father. Was it that Barakas worried about what they might face? Was Lochivan only here because he had confronted his father with the Tezerenee need for honor and redemption? Gerrod did not count; he was almost an outsider as far as his sire was concerned.

"My lady," her shadow suddenly said, jarring her back to the here and now. "You should get food and rest. My Lord Barakas will be demanding us to be ready when he is."

"Very well." She wondered when she would receive her answer. Tonight? Tomorrow?

Whenever he chooses to give it, Sharissa finally decided with a frown. She turned and wandered back to where Faunon would already be waiting with food for the two of them.

"Whenever" actually proved to be just before she lay down to sleep. Most of the others were already resting, but she had located a stream and, despite the protest of the bodyguard, washed her clothing and cleaned herself. The warrior, to her surprise, respected her privacy and kept his eyes as much as possible on the nearby foliage. As tired as she was, Sharissa would have hardly cared if he *had* looked. She was only happy to be clean. Amongst the items packed for her were traveling gowns much like the one she wore. Where they had come from she could only guess, but they fit her perfectly and prevented her from having to put on the wet outfit once she was finished. They accented her form quite well, and she wondered if perhaps they had been brought along on the journey from the citadel, where Lady Alcia might have had them made for her.

Heavy footfalls warned her of the approach of a Tezerenee unconcerned with silence. Faunon and Gerrod, both sleeping within a few yards of her, either did not hear the newcomer or thought best not to interfere in what they knew nothing about.

"Lady Sharissa."

As was the way of the Tezerenee, only the patriarch had a tent. The sorceress and her companions slept in travel blankets provided by the clan, their heads resting on small mats provided with the blankets. To Sharissa, long used to expeditions exploring the ruins of founder settlements, this was heaven compared to riding a drake for hour upon hour. She was almost sorry she had to talk to Barakas now, but reminded herself it was for Darkhorse's sake.

"I was hoping you would make use of the creek. Refreshing, was it?"

"I would have appreciated your telling my watchdog that. I had to argue with him."

"My apologies."

"Have you made a decision about Darkhorse?"

"I have. I will not release him. You I may trust, but not the demon."

She felt anger stirring. "He won't—"

He silenced her. "That is my decision. I am, however, willing to do something for you and your elf."

"What?"

"Tomorrow, his weapons, and any you and Gerrod had, will be returned to you. Though I do not trust enough to remove your collars, I allow that you need some defense. We may need you three. You'll also be allowed to ride with your hands unhindered."

It was not what she had wanted, but it was better than having her request rejected and receiving nothing else. Still, she could not help comment. "You have me confused, Lord Barakas. I'm not certain whether we are prisoners or partners."

He laughed, but it was forced. "I find many things confusing of late, my lady. Good night."

Sharissa watched him walk off, still limping a bit. At times like this, she could feel pity for the aging dragonlord. Unfortunately, all that Sharissa had to do to wipe away the pity was recall what he did to those who failed or defied him.

Like Darkhorse or Gerrod.

True to his word, Barakas returned their weapons. Faunon took his sword back with no argument, but the look on his face made Sharissa smile for a brief time. Gerrod was far more cynical about things. As he pointed out, the odds were greatly against them if they attempted to escape. Either Barakas or Lochivan alone could take the three of them on and probably win.

Thinking of Lochivan, Sharissa searched for him in the hopes of speaking to him before the patriarch called for them to mount up. She found him already in the saddle, dragonhelm on, but bent over a bit as if his stomach pained him. The box was no longer attached to the saddle, which meant that Barakas had likely retrieved it. That did not concern her so much now as what might be wrong with her former friend.

"Lochivan? Are you all right?"

"My sssstomach turnsss, nothing more!" He refused to look at her.

"Lochivan—"

Her daily shadow rushed to her. "My lady, the patriarch bids you to mount your beast! We leave now!"

"You heard him," growled Lochivan. "It isss time to ride!"

She allowed herself to be led away, but the sorceress kept her eyes on the ill Tezerenee for as long as possible. Lochivan was worse than he had ever been. He should have never joined them. The trek was proving too harsh for his system to endure, even despite his admirable willpower.

Gerrod and Faunon, seated on their drakes, were waiting for her. The warlock glanced back at his brother and down at her, his expression a mixture of many conflicting thoughts. When she tried to ask him what he was concerned about, the hooded

Tezerenee shook his head and found other things with which to busy himself.

"Follow!" Lord Barakas called, urging his mount forward. At the rate he was pushing them, they would see the citadel late tomorrow and reach it the following morning. Not as fast as he wanted, but swift enough for the rest of the band.

Hour upon hour they rode, pausing only to move around obstacles and break for a short meal. Sharissa still found herself unable to get used to the awkward, reptilian gait of the drakes and began to wish for more padding for her saddle. Faunon, she noticed, rode almost as tight-lipped as she did. Gerrod, on the other hand, being a Tezerenee, rode with the skill and ease only one trained early on could show. He seemed lost in thought, something not uncommon with him.

With the control of her mount mostly in the hands of her Tezerenee escort, the young Zeree spent much of her time looking around, seeking anything out of the ordinary that might spell peril for their party. She also took an occasional glance back at Lochivan, who was having more and more trouble controlling his own beast. That by itself was disturbing; it might mean that Lochivan was far more ill than he was pretending to be to the others.

It was no more than an hour before sunset when she noticed him lagging behind.

Her first glimpse showed him more than a dozen lengths behind the others. The second glimpse revealed a bent-over Lochivan trying to maintain control of his drake, who was starting to run off to the side.

She signaled to the Tezerenee next to her that he should look back. Sharissa watched him stiffen when he saw the trouble the patriarch's son was having with a simple task. The Tezerenee turned back to his charge and handed the guide rope to her. Then, urging his monstrous steed forward, he pulled up to the front of the party.

A handful of seconds later, Barakas was calling the party to a halt. By this time, Lochivan was probably at least a hundred lengths behind. His drake, in fact, had turned around and started back the way they had come.

"Lochivan!" the patriarch roared.

His son did not respond. Lochivan might have been unconscious for all he moved. Still, the patriarch tried again.

Sharissa had no patience for this. She turned her reluctant

mount toward the distant figure. "If he does not come when you call, it might be because he has not the power to do so! He might be too ill to do anything for himself!"

With that, she urged her drake on, breaking through the unsuspecting Tezerenee and racing for Lochivan.

"No, Sharissa! Wait!" Gerrod cried.

Taking advantage of the confusion of the moment, Faunon ripped the guide rope from the hands of his own escort and rode off after the fearful sorceress. She gave him a look of thanks as he broke through after her, then concerned herself with trying to catch the other drake before it decided to take its helpless rider on a mad run into the wilderness.

"Lochivan!"

She saw him stir. He was still hunched over in a way that to her looked excruciating, but now he was at least acting. More than half the distance separating the party and the straggler were now behind her. She no longer had any idea if anyone was following her save Faunon. For all she knew, it went against the ways of the clan to aid someone who could not control his own illness. It would be just the draconian type of thought that the clan would choose to follow.

When only a third of the distance still remained, Lochivan suddenly straightened and glanced back. He kept most of his back to her, craning his neck just enough to see her. Even had he not worn the helm, it would have been impossible to see his features, to read the pain that was likely near to crippling him.

She had no idea what to expect from him, but his reaction, when it finally came, so startled her that she almost reined the riding drake to a halt.

Keeping his back turned to her, Lochivan waved her away. Sharissa blinked, wondering why he would turn back the aid he so obviously needed. She had no intention of turning back anyway. Even if the Tezerenee thought he did not need help, the sorceress *knew* he did.

From behind her, Sharissa heard Gerrod's straining voice. He, like his brother, wanted her to turn *away*.

"Lochivan!" she called. "You need help! You're ill, Lochivan!"

"Turn away and *flee*!" he shouted. His voice sent shivers through her, for it was far, far worse than anytime prior. He sounded more like an animal struggling to free itself from a trap than a man.

The Tezerenee's drake began to buck, completely confused as to what its rider wanted of it. Lochivan kept waving the reins as he sought to discourage Sharissa from coming any closer. "Leave me be! Ssssave yourssssself, you little fool! Lissssten to my brother!"

He was hunched up again, as if straining against his armor, of all things. Sharissa tried to get close enough to reach him, but her mount suddenly balked. She kicked its sides and swore at it as she had seen so many Tezerenee do, but the creature refused to go any closer, instead skittering back and forth where it was, much to her growing annoyance.

Lochivan was practically folded in two, and his pain was now so terrible that he did not even try to hold back. His shriek only made the situation that much worse, for it renewed the frenzied back-and-forth movements of the drakes. Sharissa had to hang on for dear life—and then wondered why she was bothering with the drake. It would be easier at this point to abandon the mount and run to Lochivan.

Trying not to think about what a confused creature such as the ill Tezerenee's drake might do when she moved too close, Sharissa leaped off her own mount. From the edge of her field of vision, she saw Faunon pull up nearby and immediately abandon his own animal. To her horror, he ran directly toward the menacing jaws of the frightened drake.

"Deal with him!" the elf shouted. "I will bring the monster under control!"

She nodded, saving her gratitude for when this task was done, and cautiously made her way to Lochivan's side.

He was shivering, his visage still turned away from her, and his armor seemed not to match the shape of his body. The leg that she could see from where she stood looked to be broken, judging by the angle at which it was bent. How that had happened on the back of a riding drake was a question Sharissa could find no answer for. When she finally pulled him to safety, she could concern herself with questions.

"Lochivan! Dismount! That monster could throw you off!" In his condition, that might prove fatal. She moved a few steps closer. Now he was only just out of arm's reach. To her right, the sorceress saw that Faunon had caught hold of the reins, which Lochivan, in his pain, had finally lost. So far, he was keeping the drake from running amok, and that was all Sharissa could hope for.

"Get away from me!" He growled, waving one gauntleted hand at her while still trying to look away. Had the disease ravaged him so, or . . . could it be?

She lost hold of the frightening thought as his hand came within reach. Lunging, Sharissa took hold.

"Nooo!" With a turn of his wrist, Lochivan's gauntlet came loose—revealing a *twisted, clawed hand covered in dark, grayish scales!*

He turned toward her then, his other hand reaching for the helm that seemed to no longer fit him and was, in fact, straining to *burst*. "I warned you, Sharissa! I wanted you to not sssssee thisss! I wanted no one to sssssee this!"

The rest of the party had arrived. Barakas was already off his mount and running toward his son when Lochivan reached up with his clawed hand and, voicing his agony again, pulled the helm back so that his visage was no longer obscured.

"Serkadion Manee! Oh, Lochivan, no!"

"Yessss, Sharissa!"

A scaled monstrosity stared back at her, toothy smile mocking the wearer himself. It was small wonder the helm had seemed tight. The nose and mouth had molded into one and were expanding even as she watched. Despite its strength, she could see that the armor was tearing apart in many places as every part of the body went through the transformation at the same time.

Lochivan had not only become what poor Ivor or those at the cavern had become, but he was already progressing beyond them.

Their true nature . . . The mad guardian had said something like that when speaking of what the Tezerenee would become. She could hear the elemental laughing even now. The Tezerenee had not crossed from Nimth to the Dragonrealm by physical means; their spirits had entered flesh-and-blood golems that magic had created in this world. Those bodies, however, had not been formed from flesh taken from anything human. No, in his infinite wisdom and a desire to make the drake even more a symbol of his clan, Barakas had dictated that the source of those new bodies would be the dragons discovered on this world.

And now those bodies were becoming what they should have been in the first place.

"Lochivan!" The patriarch came up beside Sharissa and reached out a hand toward his son. The other Tezerenee, save Gerrod, who kept as far away as possible, were circling drake and rider.

"I wassssn't ssstrong enough, Father! I failed! I could not redeem mysssself!"

"Forget that! I can help you!"

"No one can! I . . . I have trouble even thinking of myssself assss ever being human! It . . . it issss . . . almost as if my mind changessss assss my body doessss!"

Barakas, ignoring the wild look in the reptilian eyes of his son, moved within arm's reach. His tone was smooth but commanding. "You are Tezerenee, Lochivan! Our very name is power! There is nothing that can withstand our will! You have only to let me help you fight it! You have only to let me—"

He broke off as a hissing Lochivan sprang from the back of the drake and launched himself at the patriarch.

"Lochivan!" Sharissa started to reach for him, to pull him from his father, but Faunon, abandoning the riding drake, reached her first and pulled her away.

"Are you mad?"

"Let me go!" She struggled unsuccessfully in his grip.

"They will help their master!" He indicated the Tezerenee.

The warriors scurried toward the two struggling figures. Afraid of accidentally wounding their master, they sheathed their swords. Three pulled knives out.

Lochivan, still hissing, looked up as the closest man tried to grab his left arm. With astonishing speed and savageness, the patriarch's son slashed out, ripping through armor and taking with it several layers of flesh. The warrior screamed and stumbled back, wounded but not out of it. Two more took hold of the abomination that had once been one of their lords and dragged him off of his father. Barakas quickly scrambled back. There was blood on him, but it was that of the unfortunate warrior.

"Secure him!" Gerrod, still maintaining his distance, called out. "He's growing stronger by the—"

Lochivan tore one arm free and, before anyone could react, reached over and took hold of the man gripping his other arm. He swung the warrior around, knocking one of his other attackers to the ground, and then *threw* his victim to the ground headfirst. Sharissa turned away as she saw the Tezerenee's neck snap backward as he struck the earth.

Two of the warriors tried to drag the unconscious one away, but Lochivan, never hesitating, turned and leaped at them. One who had his knife ready lunged and caught the misshapen figure on the shoulder where the armor had ripped apart. The blade dug into flesh, then snapped as it struck bone. Hissing, the bleeding Lochivan reached out and caught the man by the neck. When he pulled his taloned hand away a breath later, Lochivan carried part of the man's throat. The Tezerenee was dead before his mutilated corpse even fell atop his unconscious fellow.

"We should leave!" Faunon whispered. "That thing is liable to kill us all at this rate! At the very least, you should leave! I can help fend it off for a time!"

Sharissa shook her head. She knew that Faunon meant well, that he was worried for her, not for him. "I have a better idea. Let me go."

"So you can try to reason with him again? He is beyond listening now!"

"But Barakas isn't!"

He frowned, but, seeing the look in her eyes, nodded. As soon as his grip lessened, Sharissa made her way to the patriarch, Faunon close at her heels. The elf, likely very thankful now that Barakas had given him a sword, kept himself between his Vraad and the beast in the circle.

"Barakas!" Sharissa reached the patriarch, who stood staring at his lost son and not moving at all. "Barakas! I can help you!"

That brought him back to the present. "What can *you* do, Lady Sharissa?"

She pointed at the collar. "There are only three here who have power enough to stop Lochivan! I know him! Let it be me!"

"Release you? You have no care for Lochivan, Sharissa! He betrayed you, remember?"

"That doesn't mean I want him ending up like this! He may even kill all of us if you don't!"

Barakas glanced at his son, who was trying to catch one of the four remaining adversaries unwary. The circle had moved so that the unconscious warrior was now safe, but not for long if even one more man fell.

"Very well."

To her surprise, he simply reached over and gently removed the tiny band. "As simple as that?"

"Of course, but only I can do it."

She whirled and faced Lochivan. In her mind's sight, she saw the rainbow and the lines as only she of all the Vraad could see them. They were one and the same, only a matter of perceptions, but they represented the lifeforce, the power of this world. A force only she could, so far, manipulate to the necessary intensity.

Let my spell work! Let him not be too strong!

The battle had kicked up clouds of dust, and that was what she chose to use as the base of her containment spell. Faunon might think she would choose to kill the monster, but Sharissa could not do that. She was not a Tezerenee; she would imprison Lochivan if she could.

Lochivan, bloodlust evidently blocking all thought, did not notice how the dust settled thicker and thicker on his body. The Tezerenee did, however, and sought to take advantage. They were using their swords now that the clan master was safe. One of them thrust and caught Lochivan on the arm. He tried to grab the blade but missed.

"Stop! Kill only if you have to!" Barakas called. The decision was not likely to be popular, but the warriors would obey.

By now, Lochivan realized that something was wrong. The draconian visage curled up in animalistic anger, and he shot a deadly glance at the only one his mind recalled could be the source.

"Sharisssssa!"

She almost lost concentration at his call. Had she not been so worn from riding, the spell would have been completed by now. As it was, the sorceress had to struggle the nearer she came to the finish, and each second meant Lochivan was still a threat.

"Sharissssa!" He struggled toward her, moving almost in slow motion. At first she thought her eyes were playing tricks, but then she realized that he *was* glowing. Lochivan was fighting the spell.

"No!" She threw all that she had left into it.

The misshapen form froze, an earthy statue of a beast enraged because it could not claim at least one last victim.

"The Dragon of the Depths be praised!" Barakas whispered.

"You might thank Sharissa, too!" Faunon muttered.

Sharissa smiled in relief and nearly fell into the elf's arms. "That was too close!"

One warrior went to check his unconscious comrade. The others waited by the encrusted figure, their swords raised and their helmed visages turned toward their liege.

"What do we do, Father?" Gerrod, still atop his beast, asked.

Barakas glanced at his remaining son, at Lochivan, and then

at Sharissa. His voice shook at first, but he quickly corrected the shameful error. "Mount up. Everyone. Now."

"The dead, my lord?" one of the warriors asked.

"There is no time for them. Remember their names and that will be sufficient for their immortality."

Sharissa separated from Faunon and moved close enough so that she could whisper privately to the patriarch. "The spell won't hold him forever. He's growing stronger and stronger...and his body's growing, too."

"Will it hold long enough for us to be far from here?"

"It should, but—"

The lord of the Tezerenee turned from her, walking slowly toward his own beast. "Then that is all I need to know."

Gerrod rode over to Sharissa and Faunon, two riderless drakes sandwiching his own. He handed the reins to the elf and smiled grimly at Sharissa. "Do not ask me to explain his decision. I think I am just as surprised as you."

The wounded Tezerenee was helped atop his drake. He would see to his arm as they traveled. The other warrior, now conscious, needed help in the guidance of his mount from one of his brethren, but seemed all right otherwise. By the time Sharissa had mounted, the remnants of the party were ready to ride. Barakas took one last lingering look back at the still figure, then signaled the advance.

Beyond the horizon, the citadel and its own mysteries awaited them.

XX

It seemed much too soon and far too late when they arrived at the outskirts of the walled citadel of the Tezerenee.

"The gates are open," Faunon informed them while they were still a distance away. His eyes were much better than theirs. Once it would have been next to nothing for the Vraad to alter their eyes to their needs, but none of those with the elf even voiced the thought, not with the unpredictability of sorcery.

"I hear nothing but the birds in the trees," Gerrod added. "The citadel is silent."

Sharissa glanced at the patriarch and saw that his hands gripped so tightly around the reins that it was a wonder the reins did not snap. She could see that he wanted desperately to ride as swiftly as he could through the gates and see what had befallen his empire, but the training that he himself had imparted upon the clan held him back. No warrior went riding madly into danger unless he had something in mind.

The sun of a new day was barely over the horizon. No one spoke of Lochivan's tragic struggle, for fear of the look that crossed the patriarch's countenance when that event was even hinted at. Besides, now was the time to worry about what lay before them—and whether or not it might be better to turn and ride away.

"Stay together," Barakas finally muttered. He started to urge his mount forward, but Sharissa reached over and put a hand on his arm. He looked at her with nearly dead eyes.

"A suggestion . . . and a request."

"What?"

"Darkhorse. He'll help us here, especially when he knows I mean to enter regardless of his protests. It would be the best for all our sakes."

"Very well."

She blinked in surprise, watching as he lifted the box so that it rested on his lap. The ease with which she had convinced him worried her at the same time that it cheered her. Much of the patriarch's indomitable spirit had died over the past days. There was no predicting what he might do in his present state, and the sorceress had no desire to become part of some death wish. Still, she had sworn to help him for the time being, and she would not break that promise.

To herself Sharissa admitted again that she *wanted* to know what had happened—provided she survived that knowledge, too.

The Darkhorse who fled from the box this time was a greatly subdued creature. He did not shout, nor did he stamp and gouge the earth to show his fury. Instead . . . he wavered.

"What . . . what is it now, dragonlord?"

"Darkhorse!" Sharissa was stunned by the tentative tone of his voice. He had almost as little spirit as the patriarch. Her sympathy for the clan master dwindled to a shadow of itself as she wondered what sort of punishments he had meted out to the eternal.

"Sharissa." Darkhorse bowed his head low and would not look her in the eye. The ice-blue orbs seemed dimmer than she recalled.

"Will he be all right?" Faunon quietly asked her. "It almost seems that we might have to protect *him*."

"Even if he cannot, he will be better off free of that horrible device!"

The patriarch stirred himself. "Demon, your friend has requested we seek your assistance. The citadel of my people may now be a deadly trap to all those who enter. We might have need of your considerable power."

"My power is not so considerable now," the shadow steed muttered. "I have trouble keeping my form even. Why ask, anyway? You have my life in your hands. Merely command me as you have before."

Barakas looked down at the box in his hands. He looked at Sharissa. A spark of life still remained in his eyes. To the ebony stallion, he replied, "I made a pact with the Lady Sharissa. A pact of freedom if she will do this thing for me. That pact includes you."

He threw the box to the ground with as much strength as he could muster.

Darkhorse's horrific prison shattered with such ease that Sharissa and the others could only stare at it for several seconds.

"Hurrah," murmured a sardonic Gerrod in the background.

Life, or something akin to it, returned to the Void dweller. Darkhorse laughed, relief and the strain of so agonizing a captivity vying for dominance. He was still very weak, but now he at least had spirit. Sharissa smiled.

"I owe you much, patriarch, for what you did to me, but I will abide by my friend's pact. When this is done, however, we depart and, should your path and mine cross again, there will be a reckoning."

The warriors reached for their weapons, but Barakas waved them off. "I expected no less."

The shadow steed, still wavering in form, turned to face the party's objective. "Then let us be on with this task. I yearn for an end to this."

Grimacing, the young sorceress urged her mount forward.

She, too, yearned for an end, but wished he had phrased things differently.

Gerrod rode up to where she and Faunon were and pressed his animal between theirs. The elf frowned in his direction, but kept silent because of the warlock's friendship with her.

"I have something for the two of you . . . small tokens of luck, nothing more." He reached out and handed each of them a small crystal. "Humor me and keep them with you." Before they could ask what he intended, the warlock was behind them again. No one else had paid particular attention to the exchange, so concerned was the rest of the party with their kin who had remained in the citadel.

Darkhorse trotted several paces ahead of them as they neared the Tezerenee settlement, he being the one least likely to face injury if surprised. Sharissa's eyes narrowed as she studied the open gate. It was not merely open, but almost off its hinge and very battered, as if something had sought to break through— but from the *inside*.

The riding drakes stirred and began sniffing the air.

"They smell blood," Faunon said, his eyes not leaving the battered gate.

"How do you know?" she asked. She could see no sign of blood, but that did not mean there was none.

"I can smell it, too. An acrid, coppery smell it is."

"Silence!" hissed the patriarch.

Maintaining careful hold of the reins of their animals, the party reached the open entranceway. The broken gate left more than enough room for a massive drake to pass through. Darkhorse paused and turned to the humans.

"Do I enter?"

"What do you sense?" Sharissa asked in a quiet voice.

"Everything and nothing!" He glared at Barakas. "I can no longer trust my senses."

"Enter, then," muttered the lord of the Tezerenee. "Enter, scan the area, and return to us."

"I live to *serve* you," mocked the unsteady stallion. He turned back to the huge arch and trotted inside.

Sharissa nearly held her breath the entire length of his absence. She recalled how it had felt to combat Lochivan and Ivor, both of whom had displayed astonishing potential in sorcery. In being transformed into these abominations, it seemed that the Tezerenee were also being adapted to the powers of the land itself. Why not, if the renegade had wanted them to be the new masters? Certainly with foes like the Seekers and the Quel still living, the new kings would need all the skills they could acquire.

Darkhorse returned. He was puzzled. "There is nothing that I can see or sense in any other way. This place is a chaotic maelstrom of force. If there is anyone here, I cannot tell you."

"No bodies?" Gerrod asked, much to the shock and anger of his former clansmen.

"There is blood, but no bodies, not even bits." The ebony stallion smiled humorlessly at the patriarch.

"We enter, then," was all Barakas had to say in turn.

The citadel was in ruins. Many of the smaller buildings had been completely leveled; others missed walls or parts of the ceiling. Rubble was strewn everywhere. One of the towers had collapsed, crushing the building below it. Even part of the surrounding wall had been battered.

"Random violence," the elf commented. "There seems no purpose in any of the destruction. Some of it looks as if the attacker ceased in midstream and departed."

"There is one consistency," Sharissa remarked. Lord Barakas turned at the sound of her voice. She pointed at one of the battered walls of a building that still at least partly stood. "Most of the rubble, save for the damage to the protective wall, lies in the courtyards and open areas."

"Meaning?" the clan master asked, not caring for her delay in stating the point.

"Meaning that the destruction came from within the buildings for the most part, then spread out here." She defied him to counter her claim with any of his own.

His only reply was "We will move on and see how the rest of the place fares. Only then will we investigate inside."

He was stalling and everyone knew it, but no one wanted to be the first inside the buildings—where the true carnage might be awaiting them.

A short time later, they noticed the prints in the earth. They had come across drake prints throughout their search, even before they had entered the citadel, but not so many as this. There were prints *everywhere*, many of them bloodstained. Sharissa was intrigued despite herself by the thoroughness with which the drakes appeared to have scoured this area.

At the clan master's command, two of the remaining warriors rode forward for a piece and vanished around some buildings.

"Where did you send them?" Sharissa asked, not liking anything that lessened the strength of their party.

"To verify something for me. They will be in no danger. The other gateway is not far from here."

"And us, Father?" Gerrod asked, his eyes darting here and there as if he expected a hundred Lochivans to leap out at them.

"We dismount. I need see no more of the yard. It is time to investigate the buildings."

Knowing the futility of arguing, Sharissa and her companions dismounted in silence. Two Tezerenee took charge of the steeds. As the sorceress smoothed her clothing, she happened to glance up at Darkhorse.

She could see *through* him!

"Darkhorse!" All thought of the ghostly citadel pushed aside for the time being, Sharissa ran over to the eternal and tried to touch him. His eyes were closed, and his form seemed wracked with pain.

"I . . . I am weaker than I supposed, Sharissa! I fear that I will be very ineffective for quite some time!"

"But you *will* be all right?"

"I . . . believe so." Darkhorse opened wide his eyes and glared at his former captor. "My apologies . . . for . . . any inconvenience, dragonlord! I do not know what could be the matter . . . with me!"

What remark the patriarch was to make would remain lost, for the two Tezerenee given the unenviable task appeared around the corner. They seemed anxious but not frightened, a good sign as far as the sorceress was concerned. Anything that frightened the Tezerenee was not something she had any desire to face.

The two dismounted the instant they reached the party. Both knelt before their lord.

"Speak."

One warrior, taller and thinner than his companion, said, "It is as you supposed, Lord Barakas. There is a great trail formed by the gathering of many drakes and leading out of the other gateway. The gateway itself is far more battered than the one we entered by. I would have to say a great exodus occurred here."

Barakas looked around to make certain the others had heard. His gaze fell for an extended time upon Sharissa.

"How long ago was this exodus?" Gerrod asked.

The second Tezerenee looked at his master, who nodded permission to him to reply to Gerrod's question. "A week, we decided. A few traces are older, a few younger."

"It started so soon..." Barakas studied the two scouts. "You saw no life."

"More blood and the remains of a riding drake, my lord," the first one responded. "It still wore part of a bridle. One of its own had killed it."

One of its own or something just as savage? Sharissa wondered if the same thought was going through the mind of Barakas. Why would two riding drakes struggle? They were trained to work beside one another. It would take fear or bloodlust of unbelievable proportions to make them turn on each other.

"We have our answer, then," the patriarch announced, turning so that he looked at everyone. "There was danger and people died, but the many trails indicate that the bulk of the clan has abandoned the citadel, choosing to go south, I suppose."

"Why would they abandon this place?" Gerrod asked, ever, it seemed, seeking to estrange himself further from his progenitor. "Something must have made them. Where is it, Father? Where did it go? Not after them, I think. There is still something here. Can you not feel it?"

"I feel nothing."

"So I have noticed."

Barakas reached for his son, but the warlock was too swift. Sharissa came between them.

"Stop it! Lord Barakas, if the others rode off, we should follow them, not remain here and risk encountering trouble that might prove too great for us to handle!"

The patriarch cooled down. "Perhaps you are correct. Perhaps we should—" He broke off. "Alcia!"

"What about her?"

He looked at the sorceress as if perplexed she would ask such a thing. "She's in the great hall!"

The rest of the party stirred, wondering how the lord of the Tezerenee could know that. Sharissa hesitated, then asked, "What makes you say that?"

"I heard her voice, of course!" Barakas looked at his companions as if they had all turned deaf. "She just called to us! She needs our assistance!"

Sharissa and the others stared at him.

"Bah! My ears are still good even if yours aren't!" He turned away and started toward the building in which the great hall lay. Though they had not heard anything, three of his warriors followed close behind. The other two remained with the riding drakes. Sharissa's companions looked to her, knowing that her oath bound them here.

"We could leave now," suggested the elf. "There seems nothing to accomplish here, and I do not like the thought of following someone who imagines voices."

Gerrod turned and stared after his father. "I *thought* I heard a sound like a voice . . ."

Sharissa frowned. "Why didn't you say anything?"

"Because I made out nothing distinct. Certainly not my mother calling us! I think I'd recognize that!"

"I wish I could *feel* anything that made sense!" she muttered. Sighing, the spellcaster started after the vanished Tezerenee. "I think we'd better follow him."

Something large hissed. Sharissa ignored it, thinking it merely one of their mounts, when Faunon put a hand on her shoulder and hurriedly whispered, "Sharissa! To your left!"

Staring out from the broken doorway of one of the nearby buildings, a savage-looking drake blinked at them. It was more than twice the size of the steeds, a true dragon. From the way it moved, it had just woken up. Reptilian eyes glared at the tiny figures and then at the suddenly apprehensive mounts. The two Tezerenee struggled to maintain control over the simple beasts.

"We rode right by that thing!" whispered Gerrod. "My father seems to have grown lax in his abilities as a warrior and a leader. He should have never—"

"Never mind that now!" Faunon touched the hilt of his sword, but then thought better of it. He glanced at the riding drakes, and Sharissa realized he was looking for a bow and quiver. There were at least three, but reaching them meant attracting the further attention of the waking horror.

With a hopeful smile on his face, the elf winked at her and took a step toward the mounts.

The dragon focused on him, growing more alert with each second.

"Go, elf!" urged Gerrod. "It will come for us soon enough! If the bow increases our odds, it will be worth it!"

As if the hooded Tezerenee's words were its signal, the dragon broke through the wall, hissing as it struggled to drag its entire body through the gap it had made. Faunon rushed to the nearest bow and started removing it and the quiver from the shifting drake.

Sharissa knew that he would get only one shot off. She also knew that Faunon could have used his sorcerous abilities but feared that the repercussions, as he had hinted, might be worse than the attack. The sorceress, on the other hand, had no such qualms.

She raised her hand and repeated the spell she had cast on Lochivan.

Dust rose around the dragon. It roared, snapped at the particles flying about, and then shook its head.

A wild force struck Sharissa and sent her falling back. Gerrod only partly succeeded in stopping her fall. The hard earth jarred her and made it impossible to focus.

"It's moving faster!" Gerrod roared. Through blurred eyes, she noticed his face strain with concentration, as if he sought to unleash a spell of his own despite his acknowledged aversion to the magic of this world. Behind them, the two sentries were shouting loudly, but she could not turn her head enough to see either them or Faunon.

A large, dark shape burst into her field of vision and raced to meet the charging leviathan head-on. Even with her vision watery, Sharissa recognized Darkhorse. "No!"

Weak from the teachings of Lord Barakas, the shadow steed was nearly little more than a true shadow. Yet, his presence could not be denied by the dragon, who moved to deal with this sudden rival.

"He will hold it, but for how long?" the warlock asked as he pulled Sharissa to her feet. "That thing struck back at you with power far greater than Lochivan's, did it not?"

"Yes . . . that's right."

"As I feared." She felt him stiffen and looked to see what bothered him so.

Another dragon, identical to the first, was climbing out of the ruins of another building behind the party.

"It is as if they were waiting for us to come!" Faunon, the quiver looped over him and the arrow already nocked, drew a bead on Darkhorse's adversary. He let loose instantly, but the dragon, as if sensing the new assault, somehow twisted enough so that the arrow, destined for one of its eyes, bounced off thick scale. "Rheena!"

The riding drakes were beyond control. Several hissed at the coming monstrosities, making Sharissa wonder if it might not be better to let them loose. Surely a dozen of them could easily dispatch these two.

A third hiss told them that things might not be so simple after all.

They're coming from everywhere! she realized.

There was a scream from where the Tezerenee had been struggling with their steeds. Gerrod suddenly pulled her to the side, toward the steps where Barakas had gone. Faunon followed almost instantly, nearly falling on her. A huge brown-green form dashed past her.

"The riding drakes have broken free!" she warned her companions needlessly.

"Much to the regret of all, especially the two poor fools my father left to hold them!" Gerrod rose, pulling the other two up with him. "One was trampled. I don't know what happened to the other, but I know that was his scream!"

Around them, chaos was coming to full bloom. The freed drakes scattered, some running and some turning to fight the intruders.

More dragons were creeping out of the ruins.

"This is mad!" Gerrod coughed as the dust raised by one of the drakes floated about the trio. "How could we not even sense so many? Where did they come from?"

"Don't you realize, Vraad?" Faunon snarled, waving an arm in the general direction of the creatures. "These are your loving relations!"

"Impossible!"

A familiar laugh echoed in their heads.

A new race of kings . . . it said, the voice dwindling in intensity with each word, as if the renegade guardian were fleeing now that its work was done.

"So much for the vaunted power of the other guardians and their masters!" the warlock muttered. "That thing has been waiting for us! It probably kept them silent so it could teach us a fatal lesson for not obeying it before!"

So it seemed, although Sharissa could not see how the outcast could have known they would come when they did. Still, that was a worry for another time. Right now their lives were all at stake. The rampaging monsters were all around them, cutting off any hope of escape through the gateways. It was doubtful that they could have outrun the horrors anyway.

"This way!" Faunon called, pointing in the direction the patriarch and the others had gone. There was still the question of what was happening to them. If the outcast guardian was responsible for the voice the patriarch had thought was his bride's, then it could be nothing good.

They started up the steps and were halfway when she recalled Darkhorse. He was still engaged with the one dragon, dancing about and entrancing it much the way a snake might entrance its victim. The eternal, however, had little strength now, and against a creature that had already proven its natural magical abilities, the shadow steed stood a good chance of being defeated. Whether he could die or not was something Sharissa had no desire to discover.

"Darkhorse! This way!"

He seemed not to hear her. She began retracing her steps, but Faunon and Gerrod pulled her back up.

"Look before you run!" Faunon reprimanded her. He turned her head so that she could see the dragon making its way toward them. Unlike the others, who seemed more a mix of browns and greens like the riding drakes, it had a silverish cast to it and eyes that gleamed with more intelligence. It avoided the battling drakes and stalked the tiny figures with true purpose.

"But *Darkhorse* . . ."

"You know he only stays because you do! He'll leave when you are safe! Take her, Tezerenee!"

Gerrod did, securing a hold while the elf readied his bow. With the elf backing them up, they continued to climb the steps. Faunon released an arrow once he was at the top, but it hit just before the dragon's forepaws. The shot brought them a few seconds, but little more.

"And I used to pride myself on my shooting!"

"I think the dragon might have had something to do with it!" Gerrod suggested as he pushed Sharissa on. "I felt a tug, as if it made use of sorcery in its defense!"

"Rheena pray for us if it did!"

The doors of the building were open and, to their surprise, undamaged. Once through, Sharissa and Gerrod closed them while Faunon stood back and kept watch just in case. When the doors were finally bolted, they took a moment to catch their breaths.

"Where . . . where can my father be with all this commotion?" the young Tezerenee asked between gulps of air.

"The great . . . the great hall is where he said he would be," Sharissa suggested. "It's our best bet!"

"And then what? Sharissa, do you think your sorcery can teleport us out of here?"

She had already wondered about that and suspected that the answer was no. Even if the guardian was truly gone, the wild magic inherent in the dragons outside was wreaking havoc upon her own abilities. There was also Faunon's warning about utilizing their powers during this time.

If it came to life or death, however, she would do what she could and damn the consequences.

They jumped away from the door as a massive weight pushed against it, causing the hinges to creak dangerously.

"Gerrrrod!" a voice without called.

"Dragon's blood!" the warlock nearly choked as he stepped farther and farther back from the doors. His pale visage was the color of bone. "I know that voice, but which one? Esad? Logan?"

"It hardly matters! I think the time has come to retreat from the doors!" Faunon suggested. "Sharissa! Do you know the way we have to take?"

He had only had limited access to this building. Gerrod had never even been inside here. Sharissa was the only one familiar with the building's design, not that the path was that difficult. Time was, however, of the essence.

She nodded. "Just follow me!"

Ignoring the severity of their predicament, the elf asked, "Do you think we'd rather wait around here?"

They could hear the dragon trying to break its way in as they ran, and it was obvious that the doors would not hold too long. Sharissa hoped to find the patriarch and then lead the party to the upper floors, where it would be impossible for the dragons to reach them. So far, they had seen none with wings, but that might not remain so. If these dragons were what she thought they were, then wings might be merely the next step in their evolution.

Together we can do something, she kept telling herself. *With my power, Faunon's, and what the rest can contribute, we should be able to teleport us all to safety.*

Should was the optimum word.

So engrossed was she in the planning of their escape that she nearly fell across the body lying across the closed doors of their destination.

"Careful!" Faunon caught her. It seemed that someone was always catching her. Sharissa felt brief pangs of frustration, but forgot her aggravation with herself when she saw who—or rather, *what*—she had nearly tripped over.

It was one of the Tezerenee. His head had been nearly severed from his body, but with good reason. With his helm off to one side, the trio could see that he, like Lochivan, had progressed through a part of the transformation.

"He was perfectly normal when we last saw him!" Gerrod objected.

"But he isn't now!" Sharissa forgot about the body and rushed to the doors. "Help me get these open . . . and pray we don't find another like him waiting for us!"

They heard yet another hiss down one of the corridors. Heavy thuds warned them in advance that this part of the citadel was not empty.

The doors proved not to be bolted, but something had been placed behind them that made it difficult at first to push them open. The combined efforts of the three, not to mention the knowledge that another dragon was only minutes from discovering them, proved superior to whatever held back the doors.

Sharissa peeked in as the doors spread apart and barely held back a gasp.

Lord Barakas stood with his sword out before him, as still as a marble statue. The great hall was in ruins, and she saw part of the mangled corpse of one of the patriarch's remaining two men. The other was nowhere to be seen, although it was almost a certainty that he, like the first, was dead.

Facing the clan master from where the thrones had once stood was the largest of the dragons that any of them had yet seen in the citadel.

"Now what do we do?" Gerrod asked.

The hissing in the corridors had multiplied. Sharissa did not think they had any choice, especially since it sounded as if the outer doors were beginning to give. She gritted her teeth and replied, "One dragon is always better than two or three!"

They stepped inside, and Faunon and the warlock quickly closed and bolted the doors behind them.

Barakas and the dragon before him had still not moved. It was as if they were waiting to see who would look away first.

The dragon, a huge, emerald and black beast, bled from a number of cuts around its eyes and throat. Part of the patriarch's armor was in tatters, and he looked to be bleeding, although it was hard to say since his back was turned to them. Sharissa wondered why the dragon looked so familiar and then realized the monster resembled the ancient dragonlord in the ruins of the founders' settlements. Was this what the renegade had wanted the Tezerenee to become?

Reptilian eyes glanced the trio's way, but Barakas, oddly enough, did not choose to strike. The dragon, turning its attention back to the patriarch, almost appeared *disappointed* in his lack of effort.

Barakas, never taking his eyes from the dragon, called back, "Get out of here! I command you! Go on without me!"

"We would like to, Father," Gerrod responded with a touch of sarcasm in his tone, "but the family insists we stay for dinner!"

Outside the great hall, they could hear the hissing of more than one drake.

"Gerrrrod?" The dragon leaned forward, completely ignoring the armed Tezerenee, yet Barakas still made no move. "Gerrrod."

"Gods!" The warlock stumbled back as the jaws opened, and they stared into the beast's huge maw.

The behemoth suddenly recoiled. Sharissa thought it looked *ashamed* and horrified by Gerrod's reaction. The mighty head turned and reptilian eyes stared down at the patriarch. "Let it be donnne!"

Before their eyes, the dragon struck at Lord Barakas, but in so clumsy a manner that its lower jaw missed the top of the clan master's helm by several inches. The attack also left the dragon's throat completely open, but even then, Barakas hesitated before striking. When he finally attacked, it was as if his draconian adversary had purposely left itself open, for it delayed in withdrawing its head.

The patriarch's sword, propelled by his tremendous strength, went up through the throat, the back of the jaws, and directly into the brain of the beast.

The silence of the tableau lent an eerie feel to it. Making no sound despite the horrible pain it felt, the dragon pulled back. Barakas remained where he had been since the threesome had entered, defying almost certain death if the thrashings of the dying creature proved very violent.

Yet, the dragon did not thrash. It twitched as it moved, and the blood, a trail that began on the chest and hands of the clan master and continued back to the dais, continued to pour from the wound like some hideous river. With so much pain evident, it was surprising to all of them that the dragon seemed almost at peace.

Heavy thuds against the doors reminded Sharissa and her companions of their own danger. They moved closer to the center of the great hall. Barakas still had no eyes for them; he only seemed interested in the death of the leviathan. As it began to settle into the final moments of life, the patriarch walked slowly toward the dragon's head. The eyes, already glazing, watched him with what interest the dying beast could muster. It made no attempt to snap at him. Barakas knelt beside it and, removing his gauntlets, began *caressing* his adversary on the neck.

"Lord Barakas," Sharissa dared call out. "We need to leave this place! The others will be through those doors before long!"

He looked up at them. There was no life in his voice as he said, "I killed her."

"You cannot kill them all, though, Father!" the warlock argued, evidently thinking that the patriarch was intending to take on each and every beast as it came.

Sharissa understood what Gerrod did not and tried to keep him from saying anything more. "Lord Barakas! Is there another way out of here that might lead us to a safer place?"

"I killed her because she asked me," he replied, rising and staring at his son. "It was a struggle for her to keep her own mind, but she was always the strongest besides myself. I almost thought she might have fought back the foul magic as I had done."

Gerrod's eyes jerked from his father to the dead beast. "Dragon's blood, Father! that . . . that *cannot* be—"

"Yes, Gerrod. That is my Alcia."

"That *thing* is—was mother?" The younger Tezerenee, Sharissa realized, had never taken the transformations and followed them to their logical conclusions. If one Tezerenee was affected, they all were, even the lord and lady who ruled. Barakas had survived through his incredible will. The Tezerenee still back at the caverns had probably survived in part because of his very presence. Of course, there was also the possibility that the renegade guardian had acted more cautiously in the caverns, considering that the region was a former stronghold of its creators.

A downpour of heavy thuds left cracks in the walls and ceiling of the chamber. Sharissa stood directly in front of Barakas and forced him to look at her. "Barakas! *Is* there a place we can go from here where the dragons won't be able to reach us?"

Behind the helm, his face screwed up in thought. He almost looked pained by the effort. She pitied him for what he had been forced to do, but there was no helping Lady Alcia anymore. Now was the time to worry about those still living.

He finally shook his head. "No. Nothing. The other entrances lead out into the main corridors."

"Which we know to be filled with our friends," Faunon remarked. He had the bow ready. The first drake through would have little room to navigate, making it a perfect target for one of his skill.

"We're trapped, then," she said. "Unless we teleport from here."

"Very risky!"

She indicated the buckling doors. "Compared to that?"

"A communal effort will be needed. I doubt I have the power to either teleport us or open a gate long enough for us to go through. Do you think you could do it?"

"No." That had been one of her first considerations. A communal effort was the only choice she had discovered. Sharissa had hoped the elf might suggest another. "We'd best get to it, then! Gerrod! Are you up to it?"

The warlock slowly nodded. "Yes. Anything to be away from this damnation! What about my erstwhile father?"

The clan master had retreated into his other world again. His dreams had been shattered, and one of the strongest driving forces behind that dream, the Lady Alcia, was dead at his own hands. If anything could have broken the powerful Vraad's will, these could . . . and *had*.

"Hold on to him. We'll take him along. I can't leave him in here like this."

Hinges creaked as the dragons pounded away. Sharissa felt weak probes searching for them. The drakes were going through a change that entailed more than physical transformation. They were being adapted, as the guardians had said, and part of that adaptation was an affinity for the sorcery of this world. Sharissa hoped that the remnants of her party would be gone before the dragons became too skilled.

They stood in a small circle, holding each other's hands. Sharissa acted as the focus, drawing strength from her companions, even the somnambulant lord of the Tezerenee. Faunon suggested drawing an image from his mind and sending them there, but she lacked the concentration to do so. That left only a blind teleport, risky but their only hope.

"Wait!" Gerrod released her hand and dug into his clothing. He removed a crystal identical to the ones he had given to his companions earlier. "Take this and concentrate on the elf's thoughts!"

"What will happen?"

"I gave you the other ones because the Quel use them for reading and translating thoughts! They work from a distance, and I thought it would be a good way for me to find you if we got separated. I should have told you, but that's not important now! If you concentrate on your elf, what he thinks will be transmitted to you!"

She took the crystal and did as he described, finding with joy that Faunon's thought image was so clear that it was almost as if they were already there. She focused on the location.

The dragons' probes grew stronger. Inhuman emotions began to seep through, biting at her concentration.

The chamber faded.

The chamber reappeared.

"No!" They fell in a heap, shaken by the reversal. Sharissa felt a mind that she knew to be draconian laugh at them. *Do not leave ussss, Sharisssssa Zereeee! Do not take our lordssss from ussss!*

From the way Gerrod jerked, she knew he had heard the dragon, also. It was the same one that he had identified as one of his brothers.

The doors burst open, swinging back so hard they crashed into the walls and sent bits of rock flying.

The dragons swarmed toward them, the silver one in the front.

XXI

A dark, fleet phantom burst forth from the ground before the silver dragon.

"Back, lizard! Back or I shall stamp your pretty face into the rock!"

Out of surprise more than anything else, the huge monsters stopped. The silver dragon hissed at Darkhorse and roared, "Awaaaay from ourrr frrriendsss, demon! Awaaay from our tenderrr little frrriends!"

"I think not!" The eternal struck the floor with his front hooves, sending lightning sparks at the foremost drakes. The silver one hissed again and backed away.

"Sharissa! Come to me! You and your companions! Hurry now!"

Their eyes on the leader of the horde, Sharissa and the others rushed to Darkhorse's side. Gerrod had to lead his father, who simply stared at the dragons and muttered something that sounded like "Tezree" to Sharissa's ears.

"Be ready!" the shadow steed whispered when they were by him. "If I cannot—"

He never finished. The silver dragon, eyes on the party, caught sight of the great form lying limp across the farmost part of the hall.

"Motherrr!" The outraged roar echoed throughout the citadel.

The silver dragon charged.

"Too late, my friend!" Darkhorse bellowed.

The great hall and its foul inhabitants winked out of existence—to be replaced by a lightly wooded land.

"Praise Dru!" The eternal sank to his knees in the high grass. Sharissa quickly looked around and saw that everyone else was accounted for. She exhaled and hugged Faunon, so relieved was she to find they were safe.

With some reluctance, the two of them finally separated.

Gerrod, still guiding his oblivious father around, curtly asked, "And where are we now?"

The area they stood in the midst of was part of a fairly flat region. Far, far to the north, the sorceress thought she could make out a mountain chain, although whether it was the same mountains in which lay the caverns was impossible to tell from this distance. At the moment, she only cared to know if they were safe or not.

"I think I recognize this," Faunon said, scanning the area again. "I think we may be south of the citadel."

"Far south?" she asked.

"Far enough."

"Unless they have the ability to track our magical trail," the warlock interjected, eyeing the elf in a way that Sharissa did not like. "It was how I ended up in all this madness, tracking the trail he left behind."

Looking at Darkhorse, Sharissa was horrified to see that he was becoming *transparent*. "Darkhorse! What's happening to you?"

"I . . . fear that I have almost exhausted my . . . myself. My being. The dragonlord . . . was . . . not lacking in his . . . his enthusiasm when he punished me!" He eyed Barakas, who stared at the trees without seeing them. "I cannot say I regret his present circumstances! I would wish him worse, but I know you would not care for such hate!"

"I can understand your bitterness, Darkhorse. Don't think I can't."

"Perhaps. That does not matter now. Give me but a moment and I will send you on the final leg of your journey." The ebony stallion slowly rose, and his form solidified a bit.

She was not certain she understood. "Where are you sending us?"

He snorted. "Where else? Home to your father and his mate!"

"But . . ." Her eyes met Faunon's. "But what about you?"

"What about me?" the elf asked, moving closer. In the background, she saw Gerrod turn in open disgust.

"Can you make it back to your people?"

"If I was going there." He gave her a weary smile. "I thought I was going with you."

It was what she wanted to hear, but she still could not accept his decision. "You probably won't be able to return here! The ocean voyage is deadly!"

"I have no reason to return, Sharissa. The elders were hardly even interested in my expedition. As far as they were concerned, this was the latest in a series of new masters of the land, nothing unusual. They agreed to our going more because they knew we would go anyway than because they really cared." He cut off any further objections with a long kiss.

Sharissa reluctantly broke away. "Then there's nothing holding us back. Darkhorse can—"

Gerrod, buried so deep in his cloak that his features were almost indistinguishable, interrupted. "I have a boon to ask of you, Sharissa."

"What?" Now that it had been decided that they were all leaving, she wanted to be done with the spell. To see her father and stepmother... to live a peaceful existence, at least for a time...

"Take care of my father. In his present state, he is useless to all, even himself. Someone needs to watch over him."

"And what about you, Vraad?" Faunon asked, turning a critical eye on the warlock. "Where will *you* be that you cannot care for him?"

"Here. I am not going with you."

Even the elf was stunned by the answer. Sharissa took a step toward Gerrod, but he retreated a like distance. Finally, she was able to ask, "But *why*? Why would you want to stay here?"

The sorceress had no way of knowing if he looked her in the eye or not, so dark were the shadows summoned up by the deep hood. "My interests lie here. My studies and such. Besides, my presence will only be a further strain on the powers of the demon horse." He shrugged, trying to be nonchalant where Sharissa could see by his very posture he was the opposite. "I have nothing I need return to."

Knowing Gerrod as she did, however, Sharissa knew the futility of trying to argue him out of his decision. Yet, she tried to come to him again, wanting to at least bid him a proper farewell and thank him for all he had suffered for her sake. The warlock would have none of her thanks, though. When she took another step, he shook his head.

"No time! He grows weaker and weaker, and all of us should be gone before the dragons or something else finds us."

At mention of him, Darkhorse steadied himself. He did not look at the hooded Tezerenee, but rather at those who *were* going.

"Where will you go, Gerrod?" Sharissa asked, wanting, at the very least, that much from him.

He would not give her that satisfaction, only saying to her, "I have an idea." The warlock raised a hand in farewell. "Good luck to you, Sharissa. I shall always remember you and your father."

"The time has come!" the eternal announced. "This will be our only chance, so prepare yourselves!"

Sharissa slipped her hand into Faunon's and drew the silent Barakas to them with her other. She met the elf's smile with one of her own, but then turned to stare at Gerrod one last time.

The warlock was already gone.

"Ger—" she started.

The world winked out of existence—and winked back in the next moment.

"We are here," announced a very weary voice. "I'm sorry. This is the best I can do."

"Where are we?" Sharissa did not recognize the region, but there were many parts of the other continent, too many parts, that she had no knowledge of.

Faunon looked up. "The sun has shifted greatly. More than a third of a day." His tone spoke of his admiration for the eternal's efforts. "We have traveled quite a distance!"

"This . . . this is the continent on which . . . on which your folk make their colony, Sharissa. I regret that I . . . I could not bring you there, but it is probably for the best. I have no desire to see them again." He rose, his very form wavering in the light wind. "Now it is time for *me* to take my leave."

"Not you too!" Was she to lose everyone now that she was almost home?

"I am sorry to leave you in these straits, but I am at my end. I *must* go, Sharissa." The shadow steed dipped his head in his equivalent of a bow. "I must replenish myself, and that cannot be done in your world."

"When will you be back?"

He almost did not answer, but, seeing her face, the eternal gave in. "Not, I think, in your lifetime. Not even in the lifetimes of your grandchildren, I suspect."

Suddenly, the woods seemed a very dismal and dark place. "Father will be upset with you. You only came back into his life."

A stentorian sigh. "I will miss both of you. Give him my gratitude for his teaching and his friendship. I will treasure them both as I mend myself."

"*Will* you return?"

"Someday. Good-bye."

Sharissa blinked. Darkhorse was no longer there. She felt a sudden urgency and quickly reached for Faunon. "You won't leave me now, will you?"

"Hardly. They would have to drag me away fighting."

The Vraad sorceress restudied the lands around them, frowning. "I still don't know where we are." The wind blew her hair in her face. She pushed it aside and added, "We could be on the far side of the continent."

Faunon squinted to the west. "There is a hill that stands out among the others in that direction. If we climb it, we should be able to see for mile upon mile."

"Climb it?" Sharissa did not feel up to breathing, much less climbing.

"Walk to it and climb it. Both a must, I regret to say, my Vraad, unless *you* have the will and strength to teleport us there. I think my own reserves a little doubtful at the moment."

Her heart was willing, but that was hardly sufficient. Sharissa shielded her eyes and studied the descending sun. As much as she wanted to be home, there were other things to consider—their helpless companion, for one. Barakas was even now simply standing and staring at his gauntleted hands—which were still *covered* in the blood of the transformed Lady Alcia.

That settled it for her. "I have a better idea. I think it best if perhaps we stayed here, rested the night, and proceeded in the morning. We can't be very close to the colony or else I would have sensed something. Tomorrow, we'll both be better. Besides," —she indicated the patriarch. As he stared at his bloody fists, he continued to mumble his nearly incomprehensible litany. The sorceress wondered how long he would remain that way—"I've got to help him wash away that blood, if only for *my* sanity!"

Faunon accepted her judgment and volunteered to find wood for a fire and food for their much-abused stomachs. He pulled out the crystal that Gerrod had given to him. "Do you still have yours?"

"I do. I cupped it when the spell failed. I couldn't bear facing Gerrod if I lost a second one." Now she would never have to worry about that. The somber warlock was far, far away and would likely never return. She considered their present location. "There must be water around somewhere. That's what we should look for first."

They were in luck. A small stream lay only a short distance

from where Darkhorse had brought them. It was little more than a thin trickle, but even that seemed overwhelming to the suddenly thirsty duo. Even Barakas found interest in drinking. Sharissa had hoped that the cool water would snap the patriarch back to his senses, but he merely wiped his mouth and sat down by the stream. The former clan master had not even removed his gloves, so detached was he from everything.

Some sun still remained. Faunon disappeared into the forest, moving with the speed and quiet Sharissa had always imagined his kind capable of. She, meanwhile, started the task of helping Lord Barakas clean his armor. Had anyone told her that she would someday be doing this, the tall woman would have laughed. Now, it seemed like the correct thing to do. The patriarch was little more than a baby at present.

Her efforts were more or less wasted. The blood had already stained and dried on his clothing. She was, at best, able to lessen the horrifying effect of his appearance, but anyone taking a closer look would see the telltale stain on the armor. Tomorrow, when her will was stronger, she would use sorcery to eliminate what remained.

Barakas noted her efforts in an almost casual manner, occasionally breaking from his mutterings, which now sounded like "Prrr..." and "Tze...," and telling her, "They won't come out. The blood's seeped to my skin. It will never come out."

After she had given up, he returned to his same somnambulant state. Sharissa finally brought him over to a tree and let him sit there with his back against the trunk. She then turned to attending to her own needs.

Darkness was now fast approaching, and Faunon was still not back. Sharissa understood how difficult his task might be, but she still began to worry. Even knowing she was here on the other continent, the sorceress feared that the night would somehow separate her from her last and most important companion. Barakas, in his present state, did not even count. She was alone, for all it mattered. Trying not to think of that, the Vraad began picking up fallen branches with which she could start a fire. Sharissa thought of creating one without wood, but even that effort seemed too much. Besides, she had always prided herself on not depending on her abilities when simple physical work was sufficient. To be any other way went against what her father had taught her.

At sundown, Faunon returned. He had wood to add to that

which Sharissa had gathered from the nearby area and, most important, berries and a rabbit. She was thankful that he knew how to prepare it; the thought of having to cope with that after trying to wash the blood from Barakas almost made her ill.

The meal was sparse, but sufficient for their present needs. Sharissa gave the patriarch an equal share, which disappeared into his mouth in quick time. She had removed his helm, and so during the meal it proved impossible not to keep searching his face for some response, but the only thing he did when not muttering was screw his face up in thought again. She wondered what it was he was thinking about. There was a desperation in his eyes, that much she could see.

After the meal, they chose to retire. Faunon volunteered the first watch, assuring her that, as an elf, he could rest while still remaining conscious of what was around them. When she gave him a threatening look, he promised that he *would* wake her when her time came. Sharissa did not want him trying to take on the entire task by himself. Faunon was as worn as she was.

Sharissa fell asleep almost before her head even touched the ground. The dream began in that same instant. It was a chaotic chase of sorts, with the weary sorceress trying to keep ahead of a dark, loathsome thing of mist that stared at her with a thousand eyes. She escaped her horrific pursuer only to walk into the open maw of a great dragon with Gerrod's head upon it. Sharissa turned and fled from this monstrosity, only to hear the vicious laughter of the renegade guardian.

The chase went on and on, monsters and memories mixing in haphazard fashion.

When she jerked away, her first thoughts were of the relief of being freed of the endless cycle. Then she realized what had woken her and wondered whether or not the dreams might have been preferable.

"Nooooo! I am Tezerenee! Tezerenee is power!"

Faunon was already up and running toward the patriarch, who knelt against the tree and held himself so tight that Sharissa wondered if he thought he was going to come apart. His shouts became less and less coherent, reducing to the clan name and "power."

Sharissa moved to his side and tried to get through to him. "Barakas! Listen to me! There's nothing wrong! You're safe here!" It occurred to her that he might be physically injured, but in the chaos no one had looked beyond his outward appearance. "Lord Barakas! What ails you? Tell me and I might be able to help!"

"Tezerenee . . . Powerrr . . ."

"I think he might be calming," suggested Faunon. Barakas seemed to be slipping back into his catatonic state. She hated to see that, but it was better than his wild manner. The patriarch was strong enough to injure both of them.

The worried sorceress leaned closer. "Barakas?"

His movements were lightning, even against those of Faunon. Barakas shoved the two of them aside and, with an animalistic roar, ran for the deepest part of the forest.

"Stop him!" Sharissa cried.

"Too late," her companion muttered, but he tried regardless. The two of them followed the dragonlord's trail, trying to listen for the heavy footfalls that should have been so evident in the silence of night. Yet, the patriarch was as silent as a specter and faster, it seemed, than even the elf.

They gave up the chase only a few minutes later, forced to admit they could not even find his trail. For the elf, a creature of the woods, this was especially exasperating.

"It's as if he floated off or simply vanished! I should be able find *some* trace!"

"Could he . . . could he have become like Lochivan?"

"Could we have missed a dragon?" he responded. "Better yet, could a dragon have missed us?"

She tried to scan the area, but the trees blocked what little light the moons were willing to give them. "He seemed frightened of something!"

"Likely he was reliving his disasters. That would be enough to shake anyone. He might even have been dreaming of the death of his mate."

Tzee . . .

"Did you hear something?" she asked.

"Nothing. I am too worn to even listen. I am sorry, Sharissa, I truly am. If I could find his trail, I would keep going. The only thing I can say is that we could come back here in the morning and see if the trail reveals its secrets to us."

Where might Barakas be by then? Faunon was correct, though. They stood no chance of finding the patriarch. She doubted the light would change things. Barakas was gone. Gone forever, the final victim, Sharissa hoped, of his ambition to create an empire.

The irony was, his legacy *was* an empire—and of the very creature he had raised up as the symbol of his clan.

They returned to their encampment and settled down again. Sleep was not so soon in coming this time, but when it did, Sharissa was thankful to find it deep and dreamless.

Tzee . . .

It was difficult to breathe. Sharissa rolled over, trying to ease the constriction in her lungs.

Tzee . . .

She thought it was a dream at first, but then it occurred to her that if it was, she should not have been thinking so. She should have been enmeshed in it.

Tzee . . .

Rolling onto her back, Sharissa opened her eyes.

Her nightmare stared back at her.

She screamed, and was not ashamed that she did. Anyone would have screamed at the dark, cloudy mass atop her, a mass from which countless eyes peered at her. A sound kept echoing in her head, a sound that originated, the terrified sorceress was certain, from the horror above her.

It was the scream that sent it fleeing. She heard Faunon's voice as he shouted to her and watched in fear and amazement as the unnerving mass rose swiftly and fled into the deep woods. The elf chased after it, but it moved with the grace and daring of the fastest hawks and was gone even before he took a dozen steps.

All the while, Sharissa heard the same nonsensical sound in her head. *Tzee . . . Tzee . . .* The sound did not die away until long after the nightmare was over.

"Sharissa! Rheena, I will never forgive myself for being so stubborn! I broke my vow and tried to take the entire night's watch! It . . . that thing . . . must have come just after I dozed off!"

The sun was just rising, but the Vraad barely noticed it. Though the creature, whatever it was, had fled, she could not help feeling that they were still not alone, that someone else was still watching them.

"I have never seen anything like that!" the elf exclaimed, holding her as much for his comfort as he was for hers. "It made a sound in my head—"

"'Tzee,'" she said. "It kept repeating 'Tzee.'"

"That was it!"

"Tezerenee?" Sharissa whispered to herself.

"What?"

"Nothing." She cared not to think about it any longer. The possibility unnerved her more than the dragons had. She rose from the ground, allowing Faunon to aid her. There was still something not right. "Faunon, do you sense anything?"

His eyes narrowed, and he glanced about the area. "I had not given it much thought, not with that thing around, but...could it be it has not left after all?"

That might be the answer, but Sharissa could not accept it. This was something she had felt before, a familiar presence or presences. Not the guardians, but...

Stepping away from Faunon, the sorceress faced the seemingly empty woods. "Very well! You've been polite! You've not shocked me! I know you're there now, so you might as well come out!"

"Who are you—" The elf forgot his question as several figures slowly emerged from the trees. There was no place they could have been hiding. One moment they had not been there, the next they were. A dozen at least, all wearing the same long, cowled robes and moving with the symmetry that only they could accomplish. One might have thought they were all of one single mind.

The not-people, the Faceless Ones as others had called them, circled the Vraad and her companion.

"Sharissa! Do they mean us any harm?"

"One never knows," she answered truthfully. "I hope not."

A wan smile touched his face. "Since I have met you, my Vraad, I have been in one constant state of disarray. I never know what to expect!"

"I've fared no better," she admitted. One of the blank-visaged beings separated from the rest and stopped before her. "You're here." The sorceress tried to act as brave as she sounded. "What now? Why have you come?"

In answer, the long figure raised its left hand and pointed. They looked.

Like the Faceless Ones, it was standing where it could not have been standing a breath or two earlier. It was wide enough to admit both of them, though that was not what first drew their attention. As ever, it was the artifact itself that commanded the viewers' gazes. Standing there was an ancient stone archway upon which scurried a multitude of tiny, black, reptilian creatures in one seemingly endless race. The gray, stone archway covered with ivy was only one of many shapes this thing had, but each one radiated a feeling of incredible age and the notion that this structure was more than the portal it appeared to be. This was a thing *alive*.

"My father calls it the Gate," she informed Faunon. "A capital on the noun. He always felt it was more of a name, not a description."

"Is it truly alive?"

A shrug. "Was that thing that attacked us alive? I'm beginning to think that this is a world as insane as Nimth."

The leader pointed again.

"It wants us to enter, I think, Sharissa. What do you suggest?"

She did not trust the Faceless Ones completely anymore. They had an agenda of their own, and she was certain it did not always match that of her folk. Still, she could think of no reason to refuse—and wondered then if the cowled beings would even let her. "I think we should go through. I think it might be for the best."

He squeezed her hand. "We go through together. I have no desire to be left behind."

That thought frightened her. Would the not-people do that to her? Did Faunon have no place in their plans? Sharissa tightened her grip and nodded to the one before them. "Together, then."

Acting as if it wanted to assuage their fears, the leader led the way to the living portal. The featureless figure did not even pause. As it walked through the arch, they saw a flash and then the image of a building that the sorceress had no trouble recognizing.

Her face lit up. "Follow it! Now!"

They fairly leaped through.

On the other side, she paused and took a deep breath. Faunon caught the smile on her face and relaxed. "Are we there?"

She indicated the magnificent citadel on the top of the hill. Between the two and the grand structure was a well-groomed field of high grass and blossoming flowers. Sharissa could not recall a sight that had ever filled her with such relief and happiness. She started to run, pulling Faunon along and shouting to him, "This is home!"

So thrilled was Sharissa that she would later have trouble recalling the trek from where they had materialized to the gates where her father and stepmother had been waiting.

* * *

"They wanted us outside," Ariela told her stepdaughter. "We wondered why. I often wish they would at least create mouths with which to talk."

"They might have to explain too much, then," Sharissa returned. "I don't think they would like that."

The foursome stood in the courtyard of the citadel that was the main point of Dru Zeree's pocket universe. They had spent the last two hours sitting and talking, learning what they could from one another about events here and overseas. Her father had offered them food and drink immediately, recognizing their need for both. Sharissa cast the simple spell herself, wanting to taste the pleasure of having her concentration and strength at more reasonable levels. She noted that it also seemed easier in general to complete a spell here than it had on the other continent. She pondered the theory that the land or the guardians might have had something to do with that, but decided not to mention it to her father for now.

Dru Zeree gave his daughter another long hug. "I thought I'd never see you again! When Gerrod vanished, I wasn't certain whether he would find you! He was my only hope." The master mage looked a bit uncomfortable as he added, "I'm sorry he didn't come back."

Ariela saved Sharissa the trouble of responding by turning attention to Faunon. "I thought I had seen the last of my own kind. I hope that Sharissa will allow you a minute now and then that I can usurp! It would be pleasant to discuss elfin life once in a while."

"To be sure. You can tell me what it will be like living among the legendary, cursed Vraad. So far, the experience has been mixed." Faunon smiled quickly so that no one would think he was having regrets.

"Perhaps you can start that now," Dru suggested, putting an arm around Sharissa. "I would like to talk to my daughter for a few moments. Not long, I promise you. Both of you still need rest."

"I'd like to sleep for a month or so," the younger Zeree admitted.

"Only a short conversation, then."

Faunon gave his thanks to the sorcerer for all the latter had done for him and allowed himself to be led away by the Lady Zeree, who knew that her husband would relate to her the essentials of the conversation when they were alone later.

Dru turned and admired some of the fantastic, sculptured bushes in the courtyard. So skillfully shaped, the animals they represented seemed ready to frolic. Such frivolity, however, was far from the spellcaster's mind.

"So the clan of the dragon is no more."

She walked beside him. "In a sense, the clan of the dragon now lives up to its name."

His smile held little humor. "I suppose so. I don't know whether to feel sorry for them or fear for us. We will have to make some changes, and I don't think everyone will agree to them. Since the departure of Barakas, Silesti's been talking of taking his followers and establishing a second colony."

"That would be foolish!"

Dru shrugged. "It would be their choice. The triumvirate no longer has a purpose in his eyes."

"But, if there does one day come trouble from the dragons . . ."

"By that time, Sharissa, we will hopefully be prepared. Let us not also forget that trouble might come from unseen directions, too. The children of the drake might prove our allies some day."

She looked at him in disbelief. "Those things? Never! Father, if you had been there, seen Lochivan change and heard the voice of the silver dragon . . . you'd never say what you just did!"

He steered the two of them toward the direction that the Lady Zeree and Faunon had gone. "The Dragon of the Depths was here for a brief time. It left a simple message, but until you arrived and told us of events, I had no idea what the guardian was talking about."

Sharissa waited, knowing her father would continue.

"The guardian said that I should take heart, that each race of kings began as tyrants and monsters but only this one can be taught to go beyond that. I asked what that meant and where you, Sharissa, were. The guardian ignored my pleas, though, and simply finished by saying that change *never* ends and we, more than anyone else, can shape our own future."

Her father frowned, still mulling over the possible meanings of the statements. Sharissa, knowing that the colonists also faced the founders' adaptations, understood better, but decided that explaining could wait until things had calmed again.

"That was all?" she asked.

"No, before that the sentinel warned that I should watch the Faceless Ones. Nothing more. I'd almost forgotten that."

"And where are they?" She had not seen one since crossing. Even the one who had preceded them had not been in the field when they crossed.

"Around. They appear totally uninterested in your arrival."

"They hide their true feelings well." She paused and, while he waited with fatherly patience, admired the peace and serenity of the moment. So much had happened and so much was still to happen. The changes wrought upon the Tezerenee might look minor in comparison. Her own experiences had changed her forever, giving her an even wider realization of the importance of the colony's survival and the place she might make for herself and her family. Burying herself in her work was fine, but it meant she missed some of the more subtle alterations. That would change. It *had* to change.

The children of the drake have their future, the determined woman thought. *Now it's time to ensure that we do, too*.

Tomorrow would be soon enough, Sharissa decided. At the very least, she deserved *one* day of relaxation, one day to rebuild her strength for the coming onslaughts of change. She hoped Faunon would not regret coming with her.

Sharissa hoped *she* would not regret coming back.

"Shall we find the others?" her father asked, perhaps thinking that she was so tired that she was beginning to drift off in his arms.

"Let us do that," the sorceress said, stirring herself and smiling at the elder Zeree. "And promise me that today we will all do nothing! Absolutely nothing!"

"If that's what you wish. Now that you're home, however, you will have all the time you want to relax and recover."

Her response was to kiss her father on the cheek. As they departed the courtyard in search of the two elves, Sharissa thought that between family and the future, she would hardly have time to relax and do nothing after this day was over.

For some reason, it did not bother her that much.

XXII

In the great Tyber Mountains, the golden dragon roared. Frustrated and angry at himself, he again took out his anger upon the tattered remnants of a banner and other bits abandoned weeks ago by the few frightened little creatures who had escaped him and his kind. They had fled to the south, but he had chosen not to follow them once they departed the mountains. The Tybers, his struggling memory recalled, had been given to him. *He* was lord here.

So many things strained to burst forth from the fog in his mind. He knew of the sorcery that was his to control, but actually doing so was still beyond him. It was beyond all of his clan. Each day, however, the dragon king knew he grew a little closer to understanding the magic. It was the same with the wings. They had only started growing out of his back in the last few days. Pathetic little things, they would someday aid him in claiming the heavens.

Wings and magic were things he desired; many of the other bits straining to be recognized only confused him. A name, something he, as monarch of this drake clan, did not need. All knew who he was. He had killed two others to establish that claim.

Reegan. Why did it seem so familiar? What were *Tezerenee?* And who was the tiny two-leg that dared be where no other of his kind did? The little creature wrapped itself in a cocoon of sorts and stared at the dragon king as if they knew one another. For reasons his mind could not cope with, the dragon found himself unwilling to chase this little morsel. Since it kept a respectable distance, he let it be. It was a sign of his greatness that he allowed it to live, of course.

The dragon tore at the banner again. There was not much left of it, but he was always careful to leave something. He found he enjoyed mauling the tiny piece of cloth, though why was beyond him. Being what he was, it did not seem important.

Sharp, reptilian eyes noted the shadows that suddenly covered the ground before him. The dragon that had been Reegan looked up and, seeing the winged ones he knew to be mortal enemies, he roared his challenge. Within the vast confines of the mountains, other drakes responded to his summons. The winged ones had taken some of their brethren for slaves, and that was something he could not tolerate even though the bird folk's days were numbered. They might hold a thin advantage now, but the more time that passed, the sooner it would be to the day when the *drakes* ruled all.

The avians were descending around him. They meant to take *him* this time, it seemed. He roared yet again, calling his people and challenging the birds at the same time. When they were close enough for his tastes, the huge dragon charged.

As with the future itself, he would not be denied his place in this land.